THE GOLDEN SHORE

THE GOLDEN SHORE

GREAT SHORT STORIES

SELECTED FOR YOUNG READERS

WITH AN INTRODUCTION BY

William Peden

ILLUSTRATED BY

KARL STÜCKLEN

PLATT & MUNK, PUBLISHERS

NEW YORK

Library of Congress Catalog Card Number: 67–17176

ACKNOWLEDGMENTS

The editor is grateful to the authors, agents, and publishers listed below for permission to reprint selections in this volume.

"THE SAILOR-BOY'S TALE" by Isak Dinesen. Copyright 1942 by Random House, Inc. Reprinted from *Winter's Tales* by Isak Dinesen by permission of the publisher, and by permission of Putnam & Company, Ltd., London, for Canada.

"TEN INDIANS" (Copyright 1927 Charles Scribner's Sons; renewal copyright © 1955 Ernest Hemingway) is reprinted with the permission of Charles Scribner's Sons from *Men Without Women* by Ernest Hemingway.

"LEVIN'S PROPOSAL" is from *Anna Karenina* by Leo Tolstoy, newly translated and with a Foreword by David Magarshack. Copyright © 1961 by David Magarshack. Reprinted by permission of The New American Library, Inc., New York.

"DINNER" (Copyright 1928 International Magazine Company, Inc.; renewal copyright © 1956 Ellis A. Lardner) is reprinted with the permission of Charles Scribner's Sons from *Round Up* by Ring Lardner.

"THE JELLY-BEAN" (Copyright 1920 Metropolitan Newspaper Syndicate; renewal copyright 1948 Frances Scott Fitzgerald Lanahan) is reprinted with the permission of Charles Scribner's Sons from *Tales of the Jazz Age* by F. Scott Fitzgerald.

"AWAKENING" is reprinted by permission of S. G. Phillips, Inc., from *Collected Stories* by Isaac Babel. Copyright © 1955 by S. G. Phillips, Inc.

"TWO SOLDIERS" by William Faulkner. Copyright 1942 by Curtis Publishing Company. Reprinted from *Collected Stories of William Faulkner* by permission of Random House, Inc.

"COUSIN TERESA" from *The Complete Short Stories of Saki* by H. H. Munro. All rights reserved. Reprinted by permission of The Viking Press, Inc.; and by permission of The Bodley Head, Ltd., London, who publish *The Bodley Head Saki.*

"RUFUS," copyright © 1957 by the James Agee Trust, is reprinted from *A Death in the Family* by permission of Ivan Obolensky, Inc., New York, New York.

"CHARLES'S HOLIDAY" (Copyright 1944, 1945 by Evelyn Waugh) is reprinted from *Brideshead Revisited* by Evelyn Waugh, by permission of Little, Brown and Co., New York, and A. D. Peters, London.

"A LITTLE CLOUD" from *Dubliners* by James Joyce. Originally published by B. W. Huebsch, Inc., in 1916. All rights reserved. Reprinted by permission of The Viking Press, Inc.

"DEFENDER OF THE FAITH" from *Goodbye Columbus* by Philip Roth. Copyright © 1959 by Philip Roth. Reprinted by permission of Houghton Mifflin Company, publishers. This story originally appeared in *The New Yorker.*

"THE DARING YOUNG MAN ON THE FLYING TRAPEZE" by William Saroyan, copyright 1934, © 1962 by William Saroyan. Reprinted by permission of the author.

"OF THIS TIME, OF THAT PLACE" by Lionel Trilling. Copyright 1943 by Lionel Trilling. Reprinted by permission of The Viking Press, Inc. This story first appeared in *Partisan Review.*

CONTENTS

INTRODUCTION

This anthology is, to my knowledge, unique. There have been collections of short fiction built around a basic theme or subject before, many of them. And there have been numerous anthologies designed, as is this one, primarily for youthful readers. But as far as I know there has never been a collection of short stories by major authors concerned primarily *with* young people and designed primarily *for* young people.

This is the unifying idea of *The Golden Shore*. Here are thirteen short stories and four chapters from novels, all of which in one way or another depict incidents or problems in the lives of young people, young people from several lands and many backgrounds and various periods of time. The authors include three of the giants of nineteenth-century fiction (Tolstoy, Thomas Hardy, and Henry James), several of the major writers of our own century (James Joyce, Ernest Hemingway, and William Faulkner), and some relatively recent writers like the late James Agee. The characters you will meet in these stories are as varied as the authors who created them; among them are a fourteen-year-old Odessan Jew who abandons his violin lessons to learn about life and art, a talented American college student whose classmates consider him a freak, an unhappy young Irish father trapped in a web of frustration and despair, and a Scandinavian youth who rescues a falcon from the rigging of his ship and sets in motion a bizarre sequence of events.

Most of these stories are as fresh and meaningful today as when they first appeared in print. It has been some years, for example, since I had reread Samuel Butler's *The Way of All Flesh,* the novel which shocked and outraged many tradition-bound readers when it was first published in England in 1903. Yet Butler's account ("The Watch") of Ernest Pontifex's love for an erring servant girl and his rebellion against his parents is striking in its contemporaneity and in the similarity between Ernest and that more recent adolescent rebel against conformity to stultifying adult values, Holden Caulfield of *The Catcher in the Rye.* They are blood brothers, these two.

Similarly the other stories are impressive in their modernity and universality. The dilemma of the Halborough brothers in Hardy's "A Tragedy of Two Ambitions," written approximately three-quarters of a century ago, is as timely and timeless as that involving Sergeant Marx and Sheldon Grossbart in Philip Roth's "Defender of the Faith," published within the last decade. The pangs suffered by Hemingway's Nick Adams ("Ten Indians") and F. Scott Fitzgerald's Jim Powell ("The Jelly-bean") are not limited to any one epoch or generation; they are as much a part of the life process as the forces which destroy the central character of William Saroyan's "The Daring Young Man on the Flying Trapeze" or produce the destructive daughter-father relationship of Henry James's "The Marriages."

Human nature, these stories suggest, has tended to remain essentially the same, at least within the framework of the tradition of Western civilization, regardless of time and place, birth and fortune. Customs, habits, and attitudes vary. Our world and its problems simultaneously shrink and expand under the impact of social, scientific, ideological, and moral change. Yet man's struggles, problems, and dilemmas are continuously recurrent; birth and death, joy and sorrow, love and hate, victory and defeat mean pretty much the same to most of us today as they did to the characters in these stories.

Central to most of the stories anthologized here is the conflict between the individual and authority—or the Establishment, the status quo, tradition-as-such, or whatever the individual reader wishes to label it. This conflict takes many forms, but particularly dominant is that between child and parent which is subject and theme of such diverse stories as James Agee's "Rufus," Butler's "The Watch," James's "The Marriages,"

Evelyn Waugh's "Charles's Holiday," and Isaac Babel's "Awakening."

"In heaven's name," cries Smolich, the wise adult in "Awakening," "what have your parents been thinking of for fourteen years?" In one form or other, these words echo and re-echo throughout most of the child-parent stories in this collection. Few of the adults depicted in these pages are as maliciously self-centered as Waugh's Mr. Ryder or are as blind to the problems of youth as Butler's Mr. and Mrs. Pontifex; indeed, there are few if any traditional "villains" in this gallery of grownups. For the most part, like Rufus' aunt in Agee's *A Death in the Family,* they simply fail to understand their children or their problems. Parents and their offspring, such stories suggest, unfortunately tend to dwell in two different worlds, and they live their lives according to diametrically opposing attitudes and values. Only an occasionally perceptive and compassionate human being, like Nick's father in Hemingway's "Ten Indians," can help his son without attempting to solve his problems for him or punish him because of the youth's inability to do so.

In other stories the conflict may be between the individual and the uncompromisingly stubborn or destructive nature of "things as they are," as is the case with Saroyan's "Daring Young Man on the Flying Trapeze" in which the protagonist is destroyed by economic forces—in this case the American Depression—over which he can exert no control whatever. Distinctions of class and caste can precipitate the personal misfortunes of the characters, as they do in Hardy's "A Tragedy of Two Ambitions" or Fitzgerald's "The Jelly-bean," where the characters are thwarted by societal conditions or suffer what Hardy once called "the ache of modernism." Or the battle may involve an individual who is unable or unwilling to conform to the norms of "standard" or "acceptable" social and intellectual behavior, as is the case in Lionel Trilling's "Of This Time, Of That Place," or the story may center around the absurdity of current "in" or "camp" notions, as it does in Saki's "Cousin Teresa."

Whatever the nature of the conflict, these stories collectively suggest that life is a struggle, one in which the individual must fight with whatever weapons he possesses, and for very high stakes—his individual survival, physical, intellectual, emotional, or creative as the case may be. It may come as a surprise to some readers of this collection that so few of the selections—Ring Lardner's "Dinner," Saki's "Cousin Teresa," and Waugh's "Charles's Holiday"—are more humorous than otherwise. There are no old-fashioned "happy ending" stories here, the reader will soon discover, no romantic tales in which Prince Charming rescues the Beautiful Maiden from the Horrible Dragon. Since its beginnings more than a century ago, the so-called "modern" short story has tended to be a serious literary form, and the fiction in *The Golden Shore* is no exception. If frustration and defeat are conspicuous in these pages, so are their opposites. And there is continuing significance in these narratives of young people who, tested by often bitter experience, are depicted in the process of becoming that rarest, most precious of all created things, a human being.

Columbia, Missouri, 1967

William Peden

THE GOLDEN SHORE

ISAK DINESEN

The Sailor-Boy's Tale

The barque *Charlotte* was on her way from Marseille to Athens, in gray weather, on a high sea, after three days' heavy gale. A small sailor-boy, named Simon, stood on the wet, swinging deck, held onto a shroud, and looked up toward the drifting clouds, and to the upper top-gallant yard of the main-mast.

A bird, that had sought refuge upon the mast, had got her feet entangled in some loose tackle-yarn of the halliard, and, high up there, struggled to get free. The boy on the deck could see her wings flapping and her head turning from side to side.

Through his own experience of life he had come to the conviction that in this world everyone must look after himself, and expect no help from others. But the mute, deadly fight kept him fascinated for more than an hour. He wondered what kind of bird it would be. These last days a number of birds had come to settle in the barque's rigging: swallows, quails, and a pair of peregrine falcons; he believed that this bird was a peregrine falcon. He remembered how, many years ago, in his own country and near his home, he had once seen a peregrine falcon quite close, sitting on a stone and flying straight up from it. Perhaps this was the same bird. He thought: "That bird is like me. Then she was there, and now she is here."

At that a fellow-feeling rose in him, a sense of common tragedy; he stood looking at the bird with his heart in his mouth. There were none of the sailors about to make fun of him; he began to think out how he might go up by the shrouds to help the falcon out. He brushed his hair back and pulled up his sleeves, gave the deck round him a great glance, and climbed up. He had to stop a couple of times in the swaying rigging.

It was indeed, he found when he got to the top of the mast, a peregrine falcon. As his head was on a level with hers, she gave up her struggle, and looked at him with a pair of angry, desperate yellow eyes. He had to take hold of her with one hand while he got his knife out, and cut off the tackle-yarn. He was scared as he looked down, but at the same time he felt that he had been ordered up by nobody, but that this was his own venture, and this gave him a proud, steadying sensation, as if the sea and the sky, the ship, the bird and himself were all one. Just as he had freed the falcon, she hacked him in the thumb, so that the blood ran, and he nearly let her go. He grew angry with her, and gave her a clout on the head, then he put her inside his jacket, and climbed down again.

When he reached the deck the mate and the cook were

standing there, looking up; they roared to him to ask what he had had to do in the mast. He was so tired that the tears were in his eyes. He took the falcon out and showed her to them, and she kept still within his hands. They laughed and walked off. Simon set the falcon down, stood back and watched her. After a while he reflected that she might not be able to get up from the slippery deck, so he caught her once more, walked away with her and placed her upon a bolt of canvas. A little after she began to trim her feathers, made two or three sharp jerks forward, and then suddenly flew off. The boy could follow her flight above the troughs of the gray sea. He thought: "There flies my falcon."

When the *Charlotte* came home, Simon signed aboard another ship, and two years later he was a light hand on the schooner *Hebe* lying at Bodo, high up on the coast of Norway, to buy herrings.

To the great herring-markets of Bodo ships came together from all corners of the world; here were Swedish, Finnish and Russian boats, a forest of masts, and on shore a turbulent, irregular display of life, with many languages spoken, and mighty fights. On the shore booths had been set up, and the Lapps, small yellow people, noiseless in their movements, with watchful eyes, whom Simon had never seen before, came down to sell bead-embroidered leather-goods. It was April, the sky and the sea were so clear that it was difficult to hold one's eyes up against them—salt, infinitely wide, and filled with bird-shrieks—as if someone were incessantly whetting invisible knives, on all sides, high up in Heaven.

Simon was amazed at the lightness of these April evenings. He knew no geography, and did not assign it to the latitude, but he took it as a sign of an unwonted good-will in the Universe, a favor. Simon had been small for his age all his life, but this last winter he had grown, and had become strong of limb. That good luck, he felt, must spring from the very same source as the sweetness of the weather, from a new benevolence in the world. He had been in need of such encouragement, for he was timid by nature; now he asked for no more. The rest he felt to be his own affair. He went about slowly, and proudly.

One evening he was ashore with land-leave, and walked up to the booth of a small Russian trader, a Jew who sold gold watches. All the sailors knew that his watches were made from bad metal, and would not go, still they bought them, and paraded them about. Simon looked at these watches for a long time, but did not buy. The old Jew had divers goods in his shop, and amongst others a case of oranges. Simon had tasted oranges on his journeys; he bought one and took it with him. He meant to go up on a hill, from where he could see the sea, and suck it there.

As he walked on, and had got to the outskirts of the place, he saw a little girl in a blue frock, standing at the other side of a fence and looking at him. She was thirteen or fourteen years old, as slim as an eel, but with a round, clear, freckled face, and a pair of long plaits. The two looked at one another.

"Who are you looking out for?" Simon asked, to say something. The girl's face broke into an ecstatic, presumptuous smile. "For the man I am going to marry, of course," she said. Something in her countenance made the boy confident and happy; he grinned a little at her. "That will perhaps be me," he said. "Ha, ha," said the girl, "he is a few years older than you, I can tell you." "Why," said Simon, "you are not grown up yourself." The little girl shook her head solemnly. "Nay," she said, "but when I grow up I will be exceedingly beautiful, and wear brown shoes with heels, and a hat." "Will you have an orange?" asked Simon, who could give her none of the things she had named. She looked at the orange and at him. "They are very good to eat," said he. "Why do you not eat it yourself then?" she asked. "I have eaten so many already," said he, "when I was in Athens. Here I had to pay a mark for it." "What is your name?" asked she. "My name is Simon," said he. "What is yours?" "Nora," said the girl. "What do you want for your orange now, Simon?"

When he heard his name in her mouth Simon grew bold. "Will you give me a kiss for the orange?" he asked. Nora looked at him gravely for a moment. "Yes," she said, "I should not mind giving you a kiss." He grew as warm as if he had been running quickly. When she stretched out her hand for the orange he took hold of it. At that moment somebody in the house called out for her. "That is my father," said she, and tried to give him back the orange, but he would not take it. "Then come again tomorrow," she said quickly, "then I will give you a kiss." At that she slipped off. He stood and looked after her, and a little later went back to his ship.

Simon was not in the habit of making plans for the future, and now he did not know whether he would be going back to her or not.

The following evening he had to stay aboard, as the other sailors were going ashore, and he did not mind that either. He meant to sit on the deck with the ship's dog, Balthasar, and to practice upon a concertina that he had purchased some time ago. The pale evening was all round him, the sky was faintly roseate, the sea was quite calm, like milk-and-water, only in the wake of the boats going inshore it broke into streaks of vivid indigo. Simon sat and played; after a while his own music began to speak to him so strongly that he stopped, got up and looked upward. Then he saw that the full moon was sitting high on the sky.

The sky was so light that she hardly seemed needed there; it was as if she had turned up by a caprice of her own. She was round, demure and presumptuous. At that he knew that he must go ashore, whatever it was to cost him. But he did not know how to get away, since the others had taken the yawl with them. He stood on the deck for a long time, a small lonely figure of a sailor-boy on a boat, when he caught sight of a yawl coming in from a ship farther out, and hailed her. He found that it was the Russian crew from a boat named *Anna,* going ashore. When he could make himself understood to them, they took him with them; they first asked him for money for his fare, then, laughing, gave it back to him. He thought: "These people will be believing that I am going into town, wenching." And then he felt, with some pride, that they were right, although at the same time they were infinitely wrong, and knew nothing about anything.

When they came ashore they invited him to come in and drink in their company, and he would not refuse, because they had helped him. One of the Russians was a giant, as big as a bear; he told Simon that his name was Ivan. He got drunk at once, and then fell upon the boy with a bear-like affection, pawed him, smiled and laughed into his face, made him a present of a gold watch-chain, and kissed him on both cheeks. At that Simon reflected that he also ought to give Nora a present when they met again, and as soon as he could get away from the Russians he walked up to a booth that he knew of, and bought a small blue silk handkerchief, the same color as her eyes.

It was Saturday evening, and there were many people amongst the houses; they came in long rows, some of them singing, all keen to have some fun that night. Simon, in the midst of this rich, bawling life under the clear moon, felt his head light with the flight from the ship and the strong drinks. He crammed the handkerchief in his pocket; it was silk, which he had never touched before, a present for his girl.

He could not remember the path up to Nora's house, lost his way, and came back to where he had started. Then he grew deadly afraid that he should be too late, and began to run. In a small passage between two wooden huts he ran straight into a big man, and found that it was Ivan once more. The Russian folded his arms round him and held him. "Good! Good!" he cried in high glee, "I have found you, my little chicken. I have looked for you everywhere, and poor Ivan has wept because he lost his friend." "Let me go, Ivan," cried Simon. "Oho," said Ivan, "I shall go with you and get you what you want. My heart and my money are all yours, all yours; I have been seventeen years old myself, a little lamb of God, and I want to be so again tonight." "Let me go," cried Simon, "I am in a hurry." Ivan held him so that it hurt, and patted him with his other hand. "I feel it, I feel it," he said. "Now trust to me, my little friend. Nothing shall part you and me. I hear the others coming; we will have such a night together as you will remember when you are an old grandpapa."

Suddenly he crushed the boy to him, like a bear that carries off a sheep. The odious sensation of male bodily warmth and the bulk of a man close to him made the lean boy mad. He thought of Nora waiting, like a slender ship in the dim air, and of himself, here, in the hot embrace of a hairy animal. He struck Ivan with all his might. "I shall kill you, Ivan," he cried out, "if you do not let me go." "Oh, you will be thankful to me later on," said Ivan, and began to sing. Simon fumbled in his pocket for his knife, and got it opened. He could not lift his hand, but he drove the knife, furiously, in under the big man's arm. Almost immediately he felt the blood spouting out, and running down in his sleeve. Ivan stopped short in the song, let go his hold of the boy and gave two long deep grunts. The next second he tumbled down to his knees. "Poor Ivan, poor Ivan," he groaned. He fell straight on his face. At that moment Simon heard the other sailors coming along, singing, in the by-street.

He stood still for a minute, wiped his knife, and watched the blood spread into a dark pool underneath the big body. Then he ran. As he stopped for a second to choose his way, he heard the sailors behind him scream out over their dead comrade. He thought: "I must get down to the sea, where I can wash my hand." But at the same time he ran the other way. After a little while he found himself on the path that he had walked on the day before, and it seemed as familiar to him as if he had walked it many hundred times in his life.

He slackened his pace to look round, and suddenly saw Nora standing on the other side of the fence; she was quite close to him when he caught sight of her in the moonlight. Wavering and out of breath he sank down on his knees. For a moment he could not speak. The little girl looked down at him. "Good evening, Simon," she said in her small coy voice. "I have waited for a long time," and after a moment she added: "I have eaten your orange."

"Oh, Nora," cried the boy. "I have killed a man." She stared at him, but did not move. "Why did you kill a man?" she asked after a moment. "To get here," said Simon. "Because he tried to stop me. But he was my friend." Slowly he got onto his feet. "He loved me!" the boy cried out, and at that burst into tears. "Yes," said she slowly and thoughtfully. "Yes, because you must be here in time." "Can you hide me?" he asked. "For they are after me." "Nay," said Nora, "I cannot hide you. For my father is the parson here at Bodo, and he would be sure to hand you over to them, if he knew that you had killed a man." "Then," said Simon, "give me something to wipe my hands on." "What is the matter with your hands?" she asked, and took a little step forward. He stretched out his hands to her. "Is that your own blood?" she asked. "No," said he, "it is his." She took the step back again. "Do you hate me now?" he asked. "No, I do not hate you," said she. "But do put your hands at your back."

As he did so she came up close to him, at the other side of the fence, and clasped her arms round his neck. She pressed her young body to his, and kissed him tenderly. He felt her face, cool as the moonlight, upon his own, and when she released him, his head swam, and he did not know if the kiss had lasted a second or an hour. Nora stood up straight, her eyes wide open. "Now," she said slowly and proudly, "I promise you that I will never marry anybody, as long as I live." The boy kept standing with his hands on his back, as if she had tied them there. "And now," she said, "you must run, for they are coming." They looked at one another. "Do not forget Nora," said she. He turned and ran.

He leapt over a fence, and when he was down amongst the houses he walked. He did not know at all where to go. As he came to a house, from where music and noise streamed out, he slowly went through the door. The room was full of people;

they were dancing in here. A lamp hung from the ceiling, and shone down on them; the air was thick and brown with the dust rising from the floor. A moment after Simon had come in the crowd withdrew to the walls to clear the floor for two sailors, who were showing a dance from their own country.

Simon thought: "Now, very soon, the men from the boat will come round to look for their comrade's murderer, and from my hands they will know that I have done it." These five minutes during which he stood by the wall of the dancing-room, in the midst of the gay, sweating dancers, were of great significance to the boy. He himself felt it, as if during this time he grew up, and became like other people. He did not entreat his destiny, nor complain. Here he was, he had killed a man, and had kissed a girl. He did not demand any more from life, nor did life now demand more from him. He was Simon, a man like the men round him, and going to die, as all men are going to die.

He only became aware of what was going on outside him, when he saw that a woman had come in, and was standing in the midst of the cleared floor, looking round her. She was a short, broad old woman, in the clothes of the Lapps, and she took her stand with such majesty and fierceness as if she owned the whole place. It was obvious that most of the people knew her, and were a little afraid of her, although a few laughed; the din of the dancing-room stopped when she spoke.

"Where is my son?" she asked in a high shrill voice, like a bird's. The next moment her eyes fell on Simon himself, and she steered through the crowd, which opened up for her, stretched out her old skinny, dark hand, and took him by the elbow. "Come home with me now," she said. "You need not dance here tonight. You may be dancing a high enough dance soon."

Simon drew back, for he thought that she was drunk. But as she looked him straight in the face with her yellow eyes, it seemed to him that he had met her before, and that he might do well in listening to her. The old woman pulled him with her across the floor, and he followed her without a word. "Do not birch your boy too badly, Sunniva," one of the men in the room cried to her. "He has done no harm, he only wanted to look at the dance."

At the same moment as they came out through the door, there was an alarm in the street, a flock of people came running down it, and one of them, as he turned into the house, knocked against Simon, looked at him and the old woman, and ran on.

While the two walked along the street, the old woman lifted up her skirt, and put the hem of it in the boy's hand. "Wipe your hand on my skirt," she said. They had not gone far before they came to a small wooden house, and stopped; the door to it was so low that they must bend to get through it. As the Lapp-woman went in before Simon, still holding onto his arm, the boy looked up for a moment. The night had grown misty; there was a wide ring round the moon.

The old woman's room was narrow and dark, with but one small window to it; a lantern stood on the floor and lighted it up dimly. It was all filled with reindeer skins and wolf skins, and with reindeer horn, such as the Lapps use to make their carved buttons and knife-handles, and the air in here was rank and stifling. As soon as they were in, the woman turned to Simon, took hold of his head, and with her crooked fingers parted his hair and combed it down in Lapp fashion. She clapped a Lapp cap on him and stood back to glance at him. "Sit down on my stool, now," she said. "But first take out your knife." She was so commanding in voice and manner that the boy could not but choose to do as she told him; he sat down on the stool, and he could not take his eyes off her face, which was flat and brown, and as if smeared with dirt in its net of fine wrinkles. As he sat there he heard many people come along outside, and stop by the house; then someone knocked at the door, waited a moment and knocked again. The old woman stood and listened, as still as a mouse.

"Nay," said the boy and got up. "This is no good, for it is me that they are after. It will be better for you to let me go out to them." "Give me your knife," said she. When he handed it to her, she stuck it straight into her thumb, so that blood spouted out, and she let it drip all over her skirt. "Come in, then," she cried.

The door opened, and two of the Russian sailors came and stood in the opening; there were more people outside. "Has anybody come in here?" they asked. "We are after a man who has killed our mate, but he has run away from us. Have you seen or heard anybody this way?" The old Lapp-woman turned upon them, and her eyes shone like gold in the lamplight. "Have I seen or heard anyone?" she cried, "I have heard you shriek murder all over the town. You frightened me, and my poor silly boy there, so that I cut my thumb as I was ripping the skin-rug that I sew. The boy is too scared to help me, and the rug is all ruined. I shall make you pay me for that. If you are looking for a murderer, come in and search my house for me, and I shall know you when we meet again." She was so furious that she danced where she stood, and jerked her head like an angry bird of prey.

The Russian came in, looked round the room, and at her and her blood-stained hand and skirt. "Do not put a curse on us now, Sunniva," he said timidly. "We know that you can do many things when you like. Here is a mark to pay you for the blood you have spilled." She stretched out her hand, and he placed a piece of money in it. She spat on it. "Then go, and there shall be no bad blood between us," said Sunniva, and shut the door after them. She stuck her thumb in her mouth, and chuckled a little.

The boy got up from his stool, stood straight up before her and stared into her face. He felt as if he were swaying high up in the air, with but a small hold. "Why have you helped me?" he asked her. "Do you not know?" she answered. "Have you not recognized me yet? But you will remember the peregrine falcon which was caught in the tackle-yarn of your boat, the *Charlotte,* as she sailed in the Mediterranean. That day you climbed up by the shrouds of the top-gallant mast to help her out, in a stiff wind, and with a high sea. The falcon was me. We Lapps often fly in such a manner, to see the world. When I first met you I was on my way to Africa, to see my younger sister and her children. She is a falcon too, when she chooses. By that time she was living at Takaunga, within an old ruined tower, which down there they call a minaret." She swathed a corner of her skirt round her thumb, and bit at it. "We do not forget," she said. "I hacked your thumb, when you took hold of me; it is only fair that I should cut my thumb for you tonight."

She came close to him, and gently rubbed her two brown, claw-like fingers against his forehead. "So you are a boy," she said, "who will kill a man rather than be late to meet your sweetheart? We hold together, the females of this earth. I shall mark your forehead now, so that the girls will know of that, when they look at you, and they will like you for it." She played with the boy's hair, and twisted it round her finger.

"Listen now, my little bird," said she. "My great grandson's brother-in-law is lying with his boat by the landing-place at this moment; he is to take a consignment of skins out to a Danish boat. He will bring you back to your boat, in time, before your mate comes. The *Hebe* is sailing tomorrow morning, is it not so? But when you are aboard, give him back my cap for me." She took up his knife, wiped it in her skirt and handed it to him. "Here is your knife," she said. "You will stick it into no more men; you will not need to, for from now you will sail the seas like a faithful seaman. We have enough trouble with our sons as it is."

The bewildered boy began to stammer his thanks to her. "Wait," said she, "I shall make you a cup of coffee, to bring back your wits, while I wash your jacket." She went and rattled an old copper kettle upon the fireplace. After a while she handed him a hot, strong, black drink in a cup without a handle to it. "You have drunk with Sunniva now," she said; "you have drunk down a little wisdom, so that in the future all your thoughts shall not fall like raindrops into the salt sea."

When he had finished and set down the cup, she led him to the door and opened it for him. He was surprised to see that it was almost clear morning. The house was so high up that the boy could see the sea from it, and a milky mist about it. He gave her his hand to say good-by.

She stared into his face. "We do not forget," she said. "And you, you knocked me on the head there, high up in the mast. I shall give you that blow back." With that she smacked him on the ear as hard as she could, so that his head swam. "Now we are quits," she said, gave him a great, mischievous, shining glance, and a little push down the doorstep, and nodded to him.

In this way the sailor-boy got back to his ship, which was to sail the next morning, and lived to tell the story.

ISAK DINESEN (Baroness Karen Blixen-Finecke) was born near Elsinore in 1885, the daughter of a Danish officer who wrote books about hunting. In 1914 she married Baron Blixen and moved with him to British East Africa, where they managed a coffee plantation. Her book *Out of Africa* was written from her experiences there. Isak Dinesen wrote fluently in both English and Danish, and her books usually appeared simultaneously in both languages. She died in 1962.

Among her best-known works are *Seven Gothic Tales* and *Winter's Tales,* from which "The Sailor-Boy's Tale" is taken. The story's restrained emotion and mythical quality elude the easy term "Gothic" that is often applied to Isak Dinesen's work.

ERNEST HEMINGWAY

Ten Indians

After one Fourth of July, Nick, driving home late from town in the big wagon with Joe Garner and his family, passed nine drunken Indians along the road. He remembered there were nine because Joe Garner, driving along in the dusk, pulled up the horses, jumped down into the road and dragged an Indian out of the wheel rut. The Indian had been asleep, face down in the sand. Joe dragged him into the bushes and got back up on the wagon-box.

"That makes nine of them," Joe said, "just between here and the edge of town."

"Them Indians," said Mrs. Garner.

Nick was on the back seat with the two Garner boys. He was looking out from the back seat to see the Indian where Joe had dragged him alongside of the road.

"Was it Billy Tabeshaw?" Carl asked.

"No."

"His pants looked mighty like Billy.'

"All Indians wear the same kind of pants."

"I didn't see him at all," Frank said. "Pa was down into the road and back up again before I seen a thing. I thought he was killing a snake."

"Plenty of Indians'll kill snakes tonight, I guess," Joe Garner said.

"Them Indians," said Mrs. Garner.

They drove along. The road turned off from the main highway and went up into the hills. It was hard pulling for the horses and the boys got down and walked. The road was sandy. Nick looked back from the top of the hill by the schoolhouse. He saw the lights of Petoskey and, off across Little Traverse Bay, the lights of Harbour Springs. They climbed back in the wagon again.

"They ought to put some gravel on that stretch," Joe Garner said. The wagon went along the road through the woods. Joe and Mrs. Garner sat close together on the front seat. Nick sat between the two boys. The road came out into a clearing.

"Right here was where Pa ran over the skunk."

"It was further on."

"It don't make no difference where it was," Joe said without turning his head. "One place is just as good as another to run over a skunk."

"I saw two skunks last night," Nick said.

"Where?"

"Down by the lake. They were looking for dead fish along the beach."

"They were coons probably," Carl said.

"They were skunks. I guess I know skunks."

"You ought to," Carl said. "You got an Indian girl."

"Stop talking that way, Carl," said Mrs. Garner.

"Well, they smell about the same."

Joe Garner laughed.

"You stop laughing, Joe," Mrs. Garner said. "I won't have Carl talk that way."

"Have you got an Indian girl, Nickie?" Joe asked.

"No."

"He has too, Pa," Frank said. "Prudence Mitchell's his girl."

"She's not."

"He goes to see her every day."

"I don't." Nick, sitting between the two boys in the dark, felt hollow and happy inside himself to be teased about Prudence Mitchell. "She ain't my girl," he said.

"Listen to him," said Carl. "I see them together every day."

"Carl can't get a girl," his mother said, "not even a squaw."

Carl was quiet.

"Carl ain't no good with girls," Frank said.

"You shut up."

"You're all right, Carl," Joe Garner said. "Girls never got a man anywhere. Look at your pa."

"Yes, that's what you would say," Mrs. Garner moved close to Joe as the wagon jolted. "Well, you had plenty of girls in your time."

"I'll bet Pa wouldn't ever have had a squaw for a girl."

"Don't you think it," Joe said. "You better watch out to keep Prudie, Nick."

His wife whispered to him and Joe laughed.

"What you laughing at?" asked Frank.

"Don't you say it, Garner," his wife warned. Joe laughed again.

"Nickie can have Prudence," Joe Garner said. "I got a good girl."

"That's the way to talk," Mrs. Garner said.

The horses were pulling heavily in the sand. Joe reached out in the dark with the whip.

"Come on, pull into it. You'll have to pull harder than this tomorrow."

They trotted down the long hill, the wagon jolting, At the farmhouse everybody got down. Mrs. Garner unlocked the door, went inside, and came out with a lamp in her hand. Carl and Nick unloaded the things from the back of the wagon. Frank sat on the front seat to drive to the barn and put up the horses. Nick went up the steps and opened the kitchen door. Mrs. Garner was building a fire in the stove. She turned from pouring kerosene on the wood.

"Good-by, Mrs. Garner," Nick said. "Thanks for taking me."

"Oh shucks, Nickie."

"I had a wonderful time."

"We like to have you. Won't you stay and eat some supper?"

"I better go. I think Dad probably waited for me."

"Well, get along then. Send Carl up to the house, will you?"

"All right."

"Good night, Nickie."

"Good night, Mrs. Garner."

Nick went out the farmyard and down to the barn. Joe and Frank were milking.

"Good night," Nick said. "I had a swell time."

"Good night, Nick," Joe Garner called. "Aren't you going to stay and eat?"

"No, I can't. Will you tell Carl his mother wants him?"

"All right. Good night, Nickie."

Nick walked barefoot along the path through the meadow below the barn. The path was smooth and the dew was cool on his bare feet. He climbed a fence at the end of the meadow, went down through a ravine, his feet wet in the swamp mud, and then climbed up through the dry beech woods until he saw the lights of the cottage. He climbed over the fence and walked around to the front porch. Through the window he saw his father sitting by the table, reading in the light from the big lamp. Nick opened the door and went in.

"Well, Nickie," his father said, "was it a good day?"

"I had a swell time, Dad. It was a swell Fourth of July."

"Are you hungry?"

"You bet."

"What did you do with your shoes?"

"I left them in the wagon at Garner's."

"Come on out to the kitchen."

Nick's father went ahead with the lamp. He stopped and lifted the lid of the ice box. Nick went on into the kitchen. His father brought in a piece of cold chicken on a plate and a pitcher of milk and put them on the table before Nick. He put down the lamp.

"There's some pie too," he said. "Will that hold you?"

"It's grand."

His father sat down in a chair beside the oilcloth-covered table. He made a big shadow on the kitchen wall.

"Who won the ball game?"

"Petoskey. Five to three."

His father sat watching him eat and filled his glass from the milk-pitcher. Nick drank and wiped his mouth on his napkin. His father reached over to the shelf for the pie. He cut Nick a big piece. It was huckleberry pie.

"What did you do, Dad?"

"I went out fishing in the morning."

"What did you get?"

"Only perch."

His father sat watching Nick eat the pie.

"What did you do this afternoon?" Nick asked.

"I went for a walk up by the Indian camp."

"Did you see anybody?"

"The Indians were all in town getting drunk."

"Didn't you see anybody at all?"

"I saw your friend, Prudie."

"Where was she?"

"She was in the woods with Frank Washburn. I ran onto them. They were having quite a time."

His father was not looking at him.

"What were they doing?"

"I didn't stay to find out."

"Tell me what they were doing."

"I don't know," his father said. "I just heard them threshing around."

"How did you know it was them?"

"I saw them."

"I thought you said you didn't see them."

"Oh, yes, I saw them."

"Who was it with her?" Nick asked.

"Frank Washburn."

"Were they—were they—"

"Were they what?"

"Were they happy?"

"I guess so."

His father got up from the table and went out the kitchen screen door. When he came back Nick was looking at his plate. He had been crying.

"Have some more?" His father picked up the knife to cut the pie.

"No," said Nick.

"You better have another piece."

"No, I don't want any."

His father cleared off the table.

"Where were they in the woods?" Nick asked.

"Up back of the camp." Nick looked at his plate. His father said, "You better go to bed, Nick."

"All right."

Nick went into his room, undressed, and got into bed. He heard his father moving around in the living room. Nick lay in the bed with his face in the pillow.

"My heart's broken," he thought. "If I feel this way my heart must be broken."

After a while he heard his father blow out the lamp and go into his own room. He heard a wind come up in the trees outside and felt it come in cool through the screen. He lay for a long time with his face in the pillow, and after a while he forgot to think about Prudence and finally he went to sleep. When he awoke in the night he heard the wind in the hemlock trees outside the cottage and the waves of the lake coming in on the shore, and he went back to sleep. In the morning there was a big wind blowing and the waves were running high up on the beach and he was awake a long time before he remembered that his heart was broken.

ERNEST HEMINGWAY was born in Oak Park, Illinois, in 1898 and died in 1961 at his home in Ketchum, Idaho. His books set a tone and style that amounted to a revolution in modern writing and have been widely imitated. Hemingway got his start as a reporter on the Kansas City *Star*. As a war correspondent, infantryman, bullfighting and boxing *aficionado,* and big-game hunter, he plunged first-hand into experiences he would write about.

Paris in the twenties brought encounters with Fitzgerald, Gertrude Stein, Ford Madox Ford and James Joyce, and here Hemingway developed as a brilliant craftsman. He wrote *The Sun Also Rises* during this time, and in 1929 *A Farewell to Arms* brought financial success. The Spanish Civil War, which he covered as a newspaper correspondent, provided the material for *For Whom the Bell Tolls* (1940). In 1953, after the publication of *The Old Man and the Sea,* he was awarded the Nobel Prize and the Pulitzer Prize.

Hemingway was a master of the short story, and in "Ten Indians" his clean, stripped-down style and dialogue carry a powerful emotional impact.

LEO TOLSTOY

Levin's Proposal

Princess Kitty Shcherbatsky was eighteen. She had come out that winter, and her success in society was much greater than that of her two elder sisters and greater even than her mother had expected. Not only were nearly all the young men who danced at the Moscow balls in love with Kitty, but two serious suitors had presented themselves that very first winter: Levin and, immediately after his departure, Count Vronsky.

Levin's appearance at the beginning of the winter, his frequent visits and quite manifest love for Kitty, had led to the first serious discussion between Kitty's parents about her future and to differences of opinion between the prince and the princess. The prince was on the side of Levin and kept saying that he could wish nothing better for Kitty. The princess, with the way women have of going around a question, kept saying that Kitty was too young, that Levin had done nothing to show that his intentions were serious, that Kitty was not in love with him, and she brought all sorts of other objections; but she said nothing about her chief objection, namely that she hoped for a better match for her daughter and that she did not like Levin and did not understand him. When Levin suddenly departed, the princess was delighted and said to her husband triumphantly, "Well, you see, I was right!" When Vronsky appeared on the scene she was still more delighted, confirmed in her opinion that Kitty ought to make not only a good but a brilliant match.

For the mother there could be no possible comparison between Vronsky and Levin. The mother did not like Levin's strange and uncompromising opinions, his awkwardness in society, which she was convinced was due to his pride, and, as she saw it, his uncivilized life in the country with his constant preoccupation with cattle and peasants; nor did she like the fact that, while in love with her daughter, he kept visiting the house for six weeks, waiting for something, looking around, as though he could not make up his mind whether he was doing them too great an honor by proposing to her daughter, and he did not seem to realize that by visiting a house where there was a marriageable girl, he ought to have made his intentions clear. And then suddenly he left without doing so. "What a good thing he is so unattractive and that Kitty did not fall in love with him," thought her mother.

Vronsky satisfied all the mother's desires. He was very rich, intelligent, of noble birth, had a brilliant career before him in the army and at court, and was altogether a most charming person. Nothing better could be wished for.

Vronsky was paying marked attention to Kitty at balls, danced with her, and came to the house, so that there could be no doubt whatever about the seriousness of his intentions. But in spite of that, the mother had been terribly worried and anxious all that winter.

The princess herself had been married thirty years before, and her marriage had been arranged by an aunt. Her future husband, about whom everything was known beforehand, came, looked at his future wife, and was looked at in turn himself; her aunt, the matchmaker, ascertained and reported to each party the impression made on each other; the impression was favorable then on the appointed day the expected proposal was made to her parents and accepted. Everything had happened very easily and simply. At least so it seemed to the princess. But with her two elder girls she had realized that the seemingly ordinary matter of marrying off one's daughters was not so easy or so simple. The apprehensions she had suffered, the thoughts she had been worried by, the money that had been spent, the clashes with her husband she had to go through when her two elder daughters, Dolly and Natalie, were married! Now, since the youngest daughter had come out, she was going through the same apprehensions and doubts, and having even worse disputes with her husband than she had had over the two elder. Like all fathers, the old prince was particularly punctilious where his daughters' unsullied reputation and honor were concerned; he was unreasonably jealous, especially about Kitty, his favorite, and at every step he would make scenes with the princess for compromising her daughter. The princess had grown used to this at a time when her elder daughters were getting married, but now she felt that the punctiliousness of the prince was more justified. She could see that lately a great deal had changed in the customs of her social circle and that a mother's responsibilities had become still more difficult. She saw that girls of Kitty's age formed themselves into sets, were attending university courses, were more free in their relations with men, drove out alone, that many of them no longer curtsied, and worst of all, that all of them were firmly convinced that the choice of a husband was their and not their parents' business. "Today marriages are no longer arranged as before," these young girls thought and said, and even some of their elders said the same thing. But how marriages were arranged now, the princess could not find out from anyone. The French custom, according to which the parents decided the daughter's future, was not accepted and was condemned. The English custom of allowing the girl complete freedom of choice was not accepted, either, and indeed was quite impossible in Russian society. The Russian custom of employing a matchmaker was considered disgraceful, and people, including the princess herself, laughed at it. But no one knew how to marry or give in marriage. Everyone with whom the princess discussed this question said the same thing: "Really, in our day it's high time to put an end to all those antiquated customs. After all, it's the young people who get married and not their parents, so the young people must be allowed to manage this business as they think best." But it was all very well for people who had no daughters to talk like that; the princess knew perfectly well that if her daughter were allowed to make friends with any man she liked, she might fall in love with someone who had no intention of marrying or who would not make her a good husband. And however much people tried to persuade her that in our time young people must be allowed to arrange their own lives, she refused to believe it any more than she would believe that loaded pistols could be the best toys for five-year-old children. That was why the princess was more worried about Kitty than she had been about her elder daughters.

Now she was afraid that Vronsky might content himself with paying his addresses to her daughter. She saw that her daughter was already in love with him, but she comforted herself with the thought that he was an honest man and would not take advantage of it. But at the same time she knew that the freedom now in vogue among young people made it easy to turn a girl's head and that in general men thought very little of seducing a girl. The week before, Kitty had told her mother about a conversation she had had with Vronsky while dancing the mazurka with him. This conversation had partly reassured the princess; but she could not be completely reassured. Vronsky had told Kitty that they, that is to say, he and his brother, were so used to obeying their mother in everything that they never made up their minds to do anything of importance without first consulting her. "And now too," he said, "I'm expecting my mother's arrival from Petersburg as something that will make me especially happy."

Kitty had repeated this without attaching any particular significance to his words. But her mother interpreted them differently. She knew that the old woman was expected any day and that she would approve of her son's choice, and she thought it strange that he did not propose to Kitty for fear of hurting his mother's feelings; nevertheless, she was so eager for the marriage itself and above all for the relief from her anxieties, that she believed it. However distressed the princess now was to see the unhappiness of Dolly, her eldest daughter, who was thinking of leaving her husband, the anxiety about her youngest daughter's fate, which was now about to be decided, completely absorbed her. With the appearance of Levin that afternoon, a new anxiety was now added to her worries. She was afraid that her daughter, who at one time had seemed to have been attracted to Levin, might refuse Vronsky out of a feeling of exaggerated loyalty and that, in general, Levin's arrival might complicate and delay matters which were now so near conclusion.

"What is he doing? Has he been here long?" the princess asked, referring to Levin, as they returned home.

"He arrived today, Mother."

"There's one thing I'd like to say . . ." began the princess, and from the serious and animated look on her face Kitty guessed what she was going to say.

"Mother," she said, blushing and turning quickly to her, "please, please don't talk about it. I know, I know all about it."

She wanted what her mother wanted, but the motives underlying her mother's desire offended her.

"All I want to say is that having raised the hopes of one person . . ."

"Mother, darling, for goodness sake, don't speak. It's so awful to talk about it."

"Very well, I won't," said the mother, seeing the tears in her daughter's eyes, "but one thing I must say, my dear. You've promised to have no secrets from me. You won't have any, will you?"

"Never, Mother, none whatever," replied Kitty, blushing and looking her mother straight in the face. "But I've nothing to tell you at the moment. I—I—if I wanted to, I should not know what to say or how. . . . I don't know. . . ."

"No, with those eyes she could never tell an untruth," thought the mother, smiling at her agitation and happiness. The princess smiled to think how tremendously important what was going on in Kitty's heart must appear to her, poor child.

After dinner and the beginning of the party, Kitty felt like a young man before a battle. Her heart pounded violently and she could not keep her thoughts fixed on anything.

She felt that this evening, when the two men would meet for the first time, must be the most decisive day of her life. And she kept picturing them to herself, either singly or both together. When she thought of the past, she dwelt with pleasure and tenderness on the memories of her relations with Levin. Memories of childhood and Levin's friendship with her dead brother lent a peculiar poetic charm to her relations with him. His love for her, of which she was quite certain, was flattering and made her feel happy. And she could recall Levin with a light heart. In her memories of Vronsky, on the other hand, there was a kind of strained feeling, though he was a thoroughly well-bred man of the world, a man of even temper; but there seemed to be a sort of insincerity, not in him, for he was very simple and charming, but in herself, while with Levin she felt quite natural and untroubled. On the other hand, as soon as she thought of her future with Vronsky, a dazzling perspective of happiness rose before her; with Levin her future seemed rather misty.

Going upstairs to dress for the evening and glancing into the looking glass, she was pleased to see that this was one of her best days. She was in full possession of all her powers, which was so necessary for what was going to happen; she had a feeling of outward serenity; she felt that her movements were free and graceful.

At half past seven, as soon as she had gone down into the drawing room, the footman announced: "Konstantin Dimitreyvich Levin." The princess was still in her room and the prince had not yet come down.

"This is it," thought Kitty, and the blood rushed to her heart. She was horrified at her pallor as she glanced into the looking glass.

Now she felt certain that he had come so early for the sole purpose of finding her alone and proposing to her. And now for the first time the whole thing appeared to her in quite a different and new light. It was only now that she realized that the question—with whom would she be happy and who was the man she loved—did not concern her alone, but that in a moment she would have to humiliate a man she was fond of. And humiliate him cruelly. . . . Why? Because he, poor darling, loved her, because he was in love with her. But it could not be helped. It had to be done. It must be done.

"Oh God, must I tell him so myself?" she thought. "But what shall I tell him? Must I really tell him that I do not love him? Shall I tell him that I love another? No, that's impossible! I'd better go away. Yes, go away."

She was walking up to the door when she heard his footsteps. "No, it's not fair! What have I to be afraid of! I've done nothing wrong. What will be, will be. I'll tell the truth. Besides, it's impossible to feel embarrassed in his presence. Here he is," she said to herself as she caught sight of his powerful and diffident figure and his shining eyes fixed on her. She looked straight into his face, as though imploring him to spare her, and gave him her hand.

"I'm afraid I have come too soon!" he said, glancing round the empty drawing room. When he saw that his expectations were realized and that there was nothing to prevent him from speaking his mind, his face clouded over.

"Oh no," said Kitty, and sat down at the table.

"You see," he began without sitting down or looking at her, so as not to lose courage, "all I wanted was to find you alone."

"Mother will be down in a minute. She was very tired yesterday. Yesterday . . ."

She spoke without knowing herself what her lips were saying, and she did not take her beseeching tender eyes off him.

He looked at her; she blushed and fell silent.

"I told you I did not know whether I should be here long, that—that—it depended on you."

She dropped her head lower and lower, not knowing herself what she would say to what was coming.

"That it depended on you," he repeated. "What I wanted to say was . . . What I wanted to say . . . You see, what I have come for is to ask you to be my wife!" he said, hardly knowing what he was saying; but, feeling that the worst had been said, he stopped short and looked at her.

She was breathing heavily and not looking at him. She was overwhelmed with rapture. Her heart was full to the brim with happiness. She had never expected that his declaration of love would have made so strong an impression on her. But that lasted only for a moment. She remembered Vronsky. She raised her clear, truthful eyes to Levin and, seeing his desperate face, replied quickly:

"I'm afraid it cannot be. I'm sorry . . ."

How near she had been to him a moment ago and how important she had been in his life! And how distant and what a complete stranger she had become to him now.

"It couldn't have been otherwise," he said without looking at her.

He bowed and was about to leave.

But just at that moment the princess came in. She looked horrified at finding them alone together and at seeing their distressed faces. Levin bowed to her and said nothing. Kitty was silent. She did not raise her eyes. "Thank God, she has refused him," thought the mother and her face brightened with the usual smile with which she greeted her visitors on Thursdays. She sat down and began asking Levin about his life in the country. He too sat down, awaiting the arrival of other guests which should enable him to slip away unnoticed.

Five minutes later Kitty's friend the Countess Nordston, married the previous winter, came in.

She was a thin, sallow-faced, ailing, and nervous woman with brilliant black eyes. She was fond of Kitty and her affection for her, like that of every married woman for young girls, expressed itself in a desire to see Kitty married in accordance with her own ideal of happiness, and for that reason she wanted her to marry Vronsky. She never liked Levin, whom she had often met at Kitty's house at the beginning of winter. Her constant and favorite diversion when she met him was to make fun of him.

"I love it when he looks down at me from his great height; he either breaks off his clever conversation with me because I am too stupid or condescends to stoop to my level. It amuses me very much. I mean, the fact that he talks down to me. I'm very glad he can't stand me," she used to say about him.

She was right because Levin really could not stand her and despised her for the things she was so proud of and considered to be one of her greatest merits—her highly strung temperament, her ultra-refined contempt and indifference for everything that was coarse and middle-class.

The relations between Nordston and Levin were such as are often met with in high society when two people, outwardly remaining on friendly terms, despise each other so much that they are incapable of treating each other seriously, or even taking offense at one another.

The Countess Nordston at once pounced on Levin. "Ah, my dear Mr. Levin, so here you are again in our depraved Babylon!" she said, offering him her tiny yellowish hand and reminding him of what he had said at the beginning of winter about Moscow being a second Babylon. "Well, has Babylon been reformed or have you been corrupted?" she added, glancing round at Kitty with an ironic smile.

"I'm greatly flattered that you remember my words so well, Countess," replied Levin, who had had time to recover himself, and immediately assuming his usually banteringly hostile attitude towards her. "They must have made a very strong impression on you."

"Why, of course, I write them all down. Well, Kitty, have you been skating again?"

And she began talking to Kitty. Awkward as it would have been for Levin to leave just then, he would have preferred it to staying for the rest of the evening and watching Kitty, who kept glancing at him from time to time but avoided catching his eye. He was about to get up, but the princess, noticing that he was silent, turned to him.

"Will you be long in Moscow? I believe you're very busy with your rural council and you can't be away long."

"No, Princess, I am no longer busy with the rural council," he said. "I've come up for a few days."

"There's something peculiar about him," thought the

Countess Nordston, scrutinizing his stern, serious face. "He doesn't seem to be very keen on expounding his views. But I'll draw him out. I do love to make a fool of him when Kitty's about, and I will."

"My dear Mr. Levin, explain to me, please—you know all about these things—why at our Kaluga estate all our peasants and their womenfolk spend all they possess on drink and never pay us anything now. What's the meaning of that? You always praise the peasants so much."

At that moment another lady entered the room and Levin rose.

"I'm sorry, Countess, but I really don't know anything about it and I'm afraid I can't tell you anything," he said and glanced at the army officer who had come in behind the lady.

"That must be Vronsky," he thought and glanced at Kitty to make sure. She had already had time to have a look at Vronsky and she, in turn, glanced at Levin. From the look of her involuntarily beaming eyes, Levin understood that she was in love with that man, and he understood it as clearly as if she had said so in so many words. But what kind of man was he?

Now, right or wrong, Levin could not but stay; he had to find out what kind of man it was that she loved.

There are people who when they meet a successful rival, no matter in what, are ready to shut their eyes to whatever is good in him and see only what is bad; others, on the contrary, are anxious to find those qualities in their successful rival with which he has prevailed over them, and with aching hearts seek only the good in him. Levin belonged to the second category. But he had no difficulty in finding what was good and attractive in Vronsky. He was immediately aware of it. Vronsky was a dark, thick-set man of medium height with a good-natured, handsome, and extremely calm and determined face. Everything about his face and figure, from his black, closely cropped hair and freshly shaven chin to his wide, brand-new uniform, was simple and at the same time elegant. Having let the lady pass ahead of him, Vronsky went up to the princess and then to Kitty.

As he approached her, his fine eyes began to shine with a special tenderness, and bending carefully and respectfully over her with a barely perceptible happy and (so it seemed to Levin) modestly triumphant smile, he held out his small, broad hand to her.

Having greeted and spoken a few words to everyone, he sat down without once glancing at Levin, who had not taken his eyes off him.

"Let me introduce you," said the princess, pointing to Levin. "Konstantin Dimitreyvich Levin, Count Alexey Kyrillovich Vronsky."

Vronsky got up and, looking amiably into Levin's eyes, shook hands with him.

"I believe I was to have dined with you earlier this winter," he said, with his frank, unaffected smile, "but you had unexpectedly left for the country."

"Mr. Levin despises and hates the town and us townspeople," said Countess Nordston.

"I can see my words must have made a strong impression on you that you remember them so well," said Levin and, remembering that he had made the same remark earlier, he blushed.

Vronsky looked at Levin and the countess and smiled.

"Do you always live in the country?" he asked. "Don't you find it dull in winter?"

"No, not if one has something to do and, besides, I'm never bored in my own company," Levin replied sharply.

"I like the country," said Vronsky, noticing but pretending not to notice Levin's tone.

"But I hope, Count, that you will never agree to live in the country always," said the Countess Nordston.

"I don't know, I've never given it a fair trial," he said. "I had a curious feeling once," he went on. "I've never missed the country, our Russian country, with bast shoes and peasants, so much as when I spent a winter with my mother in Nice. Nice, as you know, is dull in itself, and even Naples and Sorrento are all right only for a short time. But it is there that one has a vivid recollection of Russia and particularly of the Russian countryside. They seem to . . ."

He was addressing both Kitty and Levin, turning his calm and friendly gaze from the one to the other. He was evidently saying whatever happened to come into his head.

Noticing that the Countess Nordston wanted to say something, he stopped without finishing what he had begun and listened attentively to her.

The conversation did not cease for a moment, so that the old princess, who always kept two heavy guns in reserve, namely classical and technological education and universal military service, in case the conversation suddenly flagged, had no need to move them into action; neither had the Countess Nordston any opportunity to tease Levin.

Levin wanted to join in the general conversation, but couldn't bring himself to do so because he kept saying to himself, "Now I'll go," but he did not go, as though waiting for something.

The conversation turned on table rapping and spiritualism, and Countess Nordston, who believed in spiritualism, began to describe the miracles she had witnessed.

"Oh, Countess," Vronsky said with a smile, "you must really take me to a séance next time. I've never seen anything supernatural, though I've been constantly looking for it."

"Very well, next Saturday," replied the Countess Nordston. "But what about you, Mr. Levin? Do you believe in it?"

"Why do you ask me? You know very well what I'm going to say."

"But I'd like to hear your opinion."

"My opinion," replied Levin, "is that this table rapping merely proves that our so-called educated class is no better than the peasants. They believe in the evil eye and spells and witchcraft, while we—"

"Well, then, you don't believe?"

"I cannot believe, Countess."

"But what if I have seen it myself?"

"Peasant women, too, say they have seen house goblins."

"So you think that I'm not telling the truth?"

And she laughed mirthlessly.

"Why no, Mary, Mr. Levin only said he could not believe," said Kitty, blushing for Levin; and realizing it and feeling still more exasperated, Levin was about to reply, but Vronsky, with his frank, cheerful smile, hurried to the rescue of the conversation, which was threatening to become disagreeable.

"So you don't admit that there can be something in it?" he asked. "But why not? We admit the existence of electricity, which we do not know anything about. Why then should there not be some new force as yet unknown to us which—"

"When electricity was discovered," Levin interrupted quickly, "only the phenomenon was discovered; its cause and its effects were unknown. Centuries passed before people thought of applying it. The spiritualists, however, started with tables writing for them and spirits appearing to them and only afterward began to say that it was an unknown force."

Vronsky listened attentively to Levin as he always listened to people, evidently interested in what he was saying.

"Yes, but the spiritualists say at present we don't know what this force is, but there is such a force and it functions under certain conditions. Let the scientists find out what the force is. No, I don't see why there should not be a new force, if it—"

"Because," Levin interrupted, "with electricity every time you rub a piece of resin against wool you produce a certain phenomenon, while here it isn't every time, so that it cannot be regarded as a natural phenomenon."

Probably feeling that the conversation was assuming too

serious a character for a drawing room, Vronsky made no reply, but trying to change the subject, he smiled and turned to the ladies.

"Let's try now, Countess," he began, but Levin wanted to finish saying what he had in mind.

"I think," he went on, "that this attempt of the spiritualists to explain their miracles by some sort of new force is most unsuccessful. They speak openly about a spiritual force and yet want to subject it to a material test."

They were all waiting for him to finish and he was conscious of it.

"And I think you'd make a first-class medium," said the Countess Nordston. "There's something so very ecstatic about you."

Levin opened his mouth and was about to say something, but blushed and said nothing.

"Come, Princess," Vronsky said to Kitty, "let's try table rapping at once, please. You don't mind, do you, Princess?" he asked Kitty's mother.

And Vronsky got up to look for a round table.

Kitty got up to fetch a table, and as she passed Levin, their eyes met. She was deeply sorry for him, particularly since she was herself responsible for his unhappiness. "If you can forgive me," her look pleaded, "then please forgive me. I'm so happy."

"I hate everybody, and you and myself," his eyes replied, and he picked up his hat. But he was not to go yet. As soon as the others were arranging themselves round the little table and Levin was about to go, the old prince entered and, after greeting the ladies, turned to Levin.

"Ah!" he began delightedly. "Been here long? I didn't even know you were here, my boy. Very glad to see you."

The old prince sometimes addressed Levin in familiar terms and at other times more formally. He embraced Levin and, while talking to him, did not notice Vronsky, who had risen and was quietly waiting for the prince to turn to him.

Kitty felt that after what had happened her father's cordiality was painful to Levin. She also noticed how coldly her father responded at last to Vronsky's bow and that Vronsky looked at her father with good-natured bewilderment, trying to understand how and why anyone could be so unfriendly to him and failing to understand it, and she flushed.

"Prince, let us have Mr. Levin," said Countess Nordston. "We want to try an experiment."

"What sort of experiment? Table rapping? I'm sorry, ladies and gentlemen, but in my opinion playing quoits is much more amusing," said the old prince, looking at Vronsky and guessing that it was his idea. "There is some sense in a game of quoits, anyway."

Vronsky looked steadily and with astonishment at the old prince and with a faint smile at once began talking to the Countess Nordston about the big ball that was to take place the following week.

"You will be there, I hope?" he said to Kitty.

As soon as the old prince had turned away from him, Levin went quietly away, and the last impression he carried with him that evening was Kitty's smiling, happy face as she answered Vronsky's question about the ball.

After the visitors had gone Kitty told her mother of her conversation with Levin, and in spite of the pity she felt for Levin, the thought that she had received a proposal of marriage made her happy. She had no doubt that she had acted rightly, but she lay in bed a long time unable to sleep. She was haunted by one impression. She kept seeing Levin's face with knitted brows, his kind eyes looking gloomily and dejectedly from under them as he stood listening to her father and now and again glancing at her and at Vronsky, and she felt so sorry for him that tears started to her eyes. But she at once began to think of the man for whom she had exchanged him. She recalled vividly his strong, manly face, his great calm, and his goodness that came out in everything he did; she remembered the love which the man she loved bore her, and she felt happy again and laid her head on the pillow with a happy smile. "I'm sorry for him, I'm sorry, but what can I do about it? It's not my fault!" she kept saying to herself; but an inner voice said something different to her. Was she sorry for having made Levin fall in love with her or for having refused him? She did not know. But her happiness was poisoned by her doubts. "Lord have mercy on me, Lord have mercy on me, Lord have mercy on me!" she repeated to herself till she fell asleep.

At that very moment below, in the old prince's little study, her parents were having one of their frequent scenes about their favorite daughter.

"What? I'll tell you what!" shouted the prince, waving his arms about and immediately wrapping his squirrel-lined dressing gown round him again. "You have no pride, no dignity; you're disgracing, ruining your daughter by this stupid, infamous matchmaking!"

"But for goodness sake, Prince, what in heaven's name have I done?" the old princess was saying, almost in tears.

She had come to say good night to her husband as usual, feeling happy and contented after her talk with her daughter, and though she had not intended to tell him about Levin's proposal and Kitty's refusal, she did hint to him that she believed the matter with Vronsky was quite settled and that he would propose to her daughter as soon as his mother arrived. And it was then, in reply to her, that the prince suddenly flared up and started shouting at her.

"What have you done? I'll tell you what. To begin with, you entice an eligible young man into your drawing room, which of course will become the talk of all Moscow and rightly so. If you give a party, invite everybody and not a selected number of eligible fools. Invite all the brainless puppies" (so the prince called the young men of Moscow), "engage a pianist and let them dance. But don't let us have the sort of thing we had tonight—don't throw them at her head. It makes me sick to look at it. I tell you it makes me sick! And you've got what you wanted, you've turned the poor girl's head. Levin is a thousand times the better man. As for that Petersburg coxcomb, they turn them out by machine. They're all the same, they're all trash. Even if he were a prince of the blood, my daughter has no need to run after him!"

"But what have I done?"

"Why . . . " the prince cried angrily.

"I know that if I were to listen to you," the princess interrupted him, "we'd never see our daughter married. If that's what you want, we might as well go and live in the country."

"I wish we did."

"But be fair! Am I currying favor with them? Not a bit of it! A young man, and a very nice young man, has fallen in love with her and she, too, I believe . . . "

"Yes, you believe. And what if she really falls in love with him and he has no more intention of marrying than I have? Oh, I wish I hadn't seen it! 'Oh, spiritualism! Oh, Nice! Oh, the ball!' . . ." And imagining himself imitating his wife, he curtsied at each word. "And when we have really made Kate unhappy, when she really takes it into her head to—"

"And what makes you think so?"

"I don't think, I know. We have eyes for these things and women haven't. I can see a man who has serious intentions—that's Levin. And I can see a popinjay like that conceited coxcomb who only wants to have a good time."

"Oh well, once you get an idea into your head . . . "

"You'll remember my words, but it'll be too late, just as with poor Dolly."

"All right, all right, we won't talk about it," the princess stopped him, remembering the unhappy Dolly.

"By all means, good night!"

And having made the sign of the cross over each other, husband and wife kissed and went to their separate bedrooms, feeling that each of them remained of the same opinion.

The princess had been at first firmly convinced that this evening had settled Kitty's future and that there could be no doubt as to Vronsky's intentions; but her husband's words disturbed her. And returning to her room, she, like Kitty, repeated a few times to herself, terrified of what the future might hold in store for her: "Lord have mercy on us, Lord have mercy on us, Lord have mercy on us!"

—*Translated by David Magarshack*

LEO TOLSTOY, the world's most prominent literary figure of his time, was born in 1828 into a family of aristocratic Russian landowners. Like his character Levin (who appears in this selection from *Anna Karenina*), Tolstoy was attracted to the Russian countryside and the peasants who worked his land. He fought to improve their living conditions, established a school for them (in which he taught for a while), and based his great novel *Anna Karenina* on the contrast between the country and the corrupt cities.

At 23 he joined the army and later served in the Crimea. Several of his early writings describe the Cossacks and the war, and these stories made his reputation. He traveled abroad but was always drawn back to the simplicity of country life. In 1862 Tolstoy married, and seven years later *War and Peace* was published. This masterpiece was based on the family histories of Tolstoy's father and mother, and his own family is one of the several chronicled and intertwined in *Anna Karenina*.

Tolstoy's continuous quest for moral values, reflected in his work, led to a religious conversion which profoundly affected his life and his later books. He died of pneumonia at a railway station, Astapovo, in 1910.

RING LARDNER

Dinner

Harry Barton was thirty-three years old, unmarried and good-looking. Young matrons liked him as a filler-in at dinner parties, but he hated dinner parties unless they promised an evening of contract. So it was with a heavy heart that he heard Grace Halpern's voice on the telephone.

"You've just got to do this for me! I know you'll hate it.

There won't be any bridge. But Frank backed out at the last minute and I can't get anybody else. I honestly tried. I tried Bill; I even tried Lester Graham, but neither of them can come. And I must have two bachelors because there are going to be two girls from out of town, girls who were in my class in boarding school. They really are peaches and I can't disappoint them. Please say—"

Harry was a bad liar and, besides, he liked Grace. He had had lots of good times at her house. He said yes and wished all the rest of the day that he hadn't.

He arrived late at the Halperns', too late to get half enough cocktails. He knew everybody there excepting the two peaches, a Miss Coakley and a Miss Rell. They were strikingly pretty, Miss Coakley a pony brunette and Miss Rell a rather tall, slender blonde. Harry thought maybe it wouldn't be so bad after all.

His hostess drew him aside before dinner was announced.

"I'm going to reward you for this. I'm going to let you sit between them at dinner. And remember, they're both free."

"What do you mean, free?"

"Not engaged or anything. And I think it's about time you were settling down."

The other bachelor, Dave Wallace, sat on Miss Coakley's left, with Harry, as Grace had promised, between Miss Coakley and Miss Rell.

"Grace tells me you're a great bridge player," Miss Rell said.

"No, but I like—"

"Which do you consider the greatest authority, Lenz or Works or Whitehall? I don't know anything about it myself, but I hear people arguing about it at home, I mean I live in Chicago. I belong to a bridge club there and I was just getting so the others didn't laugh at me when somebody introduced this horrible contract and I simply gave up. That's the game, you know, where you don't bid anything but slams and I just haven't the nerve, I mean in bridge. I don't want you to think I'm a coward in everything."

"I—"

"Because I'm not, I made a flight with Lindbergh in Washington. It was arranged through Congressman Burleigh. He's a great friend of my father's. You know, Burleigh the paint people in South Chicago. Oh, it was too thrilling for words! But I felt just as safe as if I'd been in a car, safer because once I was in a terrible smash-up out in Lake Forest and the doctor said I was lucky to escape without at least a few broken ribs.

"I was a little bit scared when we first started, but then I thought to myself this is the man who flew from Detroit to Paris and why should anybody be frightened just flying twenty minutes over Washington with him at the wheel. Have you ever been up?"

"Yes, I—"

"Then you don't know what a real thrill is. Honestly, it just makes you gasp, like the first time you dive in Lake Michigan. I really dive and I swim awfully well and some of the men say I swim awfully well for a girl. There's one man in Chicago, Lee Roberts—he and his wife are our best friends, I mean my brother's and mine—Lee calls me Gertrude Ederle; you know she's the girl who swam across the English Channel and back.

"Of course he says it just joking because naturally I'm not in her class. She's quite fat, isn't she? Or haven't you ever seen her? She looks fat in her pictures. But then you can't always tell from pictures. There was a picture of me in the rotogravure section that made me look simply hideous."

Mr. Halpern, on Miss Rell's right, spoke to her and Harry found himself attacked by Miss Coakley.

"Mr. Burton, I was just telling Mr. Walters about—I don't know whether you'd be interested or not—maybe you don't—but still everybody I've told, they think—it's probably—"

"I'm sure I'd like to hear it," said Harry.

"I hate to bore people with—you know how it is—you'd be too polite to—and this is so awfully—well, it isn't a thing that—it's just interesting if you happen—people in Baltimore—though we've only lived here a few—"

"If," said Harry to himself, "she doesn't complete a sentence in the next two minutes, I'm going to ask Grace for a highball."

"—it was some people who lived—well, our apartment was just two buildings—they were people you wouldn't want—but it was in a kind of secluded—not many apartments—it's a neighborhood that's just—and my sister's little boy goes to the same school as—"

"Grace," said Harry, "am I an old enough customer here to ask for a drink?"

"Whatever you like," said his hostess.

"I'd like a highball. I had a pretty tough day."

Miss Rell turned on him.

"Oh, are you in the Street? That's what they call Wall Street, isn't it? I should think it would be just thrilling! But I suppose it is hard work, too. You stand there all day and shout at other men, don't you, and they shout back at you? It must ruin your voice. Why, I know we went to the Illinois-Chicago game last fall and I got excited and yelled so for Illinois that I couldn't talk for a week."

"That must have—"

"Do you have football here in the East? Oh, certainly you do! I'd forgotten—Yale and Harvard. And which are the Giants? I never can keep them straight. My father and Lou—that's my brother; we're great pals—he and Father read the sporting page religiously every day. I tease them about it and they tease me about reading the society news and the movies. We have great tiffs over it, all in fun of course.

"Father is a great golfer, I mean really. He's fifty-four years old and he plays the Onwentsia course in sixty, or maybe it's a hundred and sixty. Which would be right? He wanted me to take it up and begged and begged till finally one day I went out and played nine holes with him.

"I made some wonderful shots, I mean I really did, and he said I had a perfect natural swing and if I would take lessons from the professor it wouldn't be long before I could be playing in tournaments, just for women I mean. Wouldn't that be exciting! But I just couldn't do it; I'd die!

"And besides, it seems to me that girls who win things in sports are always queer looking, at least most of them, and what chance would—I mean it would be almost unheard of if— Well, I just don't believe I could ever be a champion of anything. Do you play golf?"

"Yes."

"You ought to try it. It's lots of fun, especially for a man. I mean men seem to have such good times playing together, the nineteenth hole and all that. And I should think it would be such wonderful relaxation for you over the weekend after that Wall Street grind."

"I'm not in Wall Street."

"Oh, now I've got an expert here, I wish you'd tell me what are bulls and what are bears? Father's tried to explain it to me, but I can't get it straight."

"Well, a bull is—"

"Have you ever been to bull-fights, I mean in Spain or Mexico? They say they are terribly thrilling, but terribly cruel. I mean about the horses. You know what they do, don't you?"

"No. I never heard of them."

"Well, they bring out three or four old horses into the ring and men with spears spear the bull and get him mad at the horses and he goes after them and kills them and the blood makes him mad at everybody and then the man comes out and kills him. They call them toreadors."

"Who?"

"The man that fights the bull. Haven't you ever heard 'Carmen,' I mean the opera? There's a toreador in that. He sings a song; it goes, '*Toreador, en garde.*' That's the French. It's a French opera. Carmen is the girl; she works in a cigarette factory. First she falls in love with a soldier and then this toreador wins her away from him, but the soldier kills himself and her.

"I haven't heard it for years; I like to go to ones I haven't heard so much. We've got a simply gorgeous opera company in Chicago. Everybody says it's better than the Metropolitan. And Rosa Raisa is the greatest dramatic soprano I ever heard. She's Ruffo's wife. No, I guess she's Rimini's. Anyway, they're both baritones."

Again Mr. Halpern intervened and Harry took on Miss Coakley for another round.

"Mr. Walters and I were just— Don't you like Nassau better than—I mean for climate—and the different colors of the water—and it's ideal bathing, hardly any surf—of course lots of people prefer heavy surf—but for people like me who can't—and I think the crowd that goes there—and the tennis. Then there's that lovely garden, with the orchestra.

"Three of us girls—I think it was four winters—it was three winters ago. One night we went—it's the Holy Rollers—honestly they do the craziest—a man told us they were just—but I couldn't believe it, they were so—I think— Have you ever been there, Mr. Burton?"

"No."

"We went by land to—and then from Miami—when you wake up—it's the most beautiful—with the sun just rising over the islands—it's simply heavenly—it's just— Well, you have no idea!"

"Yes, I have," said Harry to himself, and aloud: "Grace, I'd like a highball. I had a tough day."

"The days are getting shorter," said his hostess.

"I imagine every day must be pretty hard for you men in the Street," said Miss Rell.

"I'm not in any street," said Harry. "Not even a path."

"I know how secretive you Wall Street men are," said Miss

Rell, "but I wonder if you would do me a favor. Just before I left home, I heard Father talking about some stock that I think he said he had a tip on—he's got a lot of influential friends that tell him things like that, but of course nobody like you who is right in Wall Street. Now it would be perfectly wonderful if you would tell me whether this stock is any good or not and then when I go home, I can tell Father what you said and who you are and he'll think his child isn't so dumb after all. Will you?"

"What's the stock?"

"Isn't it marvelous that I remember the name of it? It's General Motors."

"General Motors! Well, listen, if you'll keep this under your hat—"

"Oh, that reminds me, I saw your Mayor Jimmy Walker in the parade today and I told Grace I thought he was the only man in the world who could wear a high hat without looking silly. Do you know him? I'll bet he's fascinating to know. He's cute! I wish we had a cute mayor. I suppose you New Yorkers must think our town is a regular wild West show. It really isn't as bad as all that.

"Lou—that's my brother—he said the funniest thing the night before I came away. No, it was Wednesday night he said it and I didn't leave till Friday noon on the Century. What was I saying? Oh, yes, Father and Lou and I were waiting for dinner—you know we live on the North Side, just a block south of the park—and anyway there were some noises out on the street that sounded just like pistol-shots and Father hurried to the window and looked out and announced that it was just back-fire from a truck.

"Then Lou said, 'Well, I'm glad they're beginning to defend themselves.' He meant the trucks were firing back at whoever was shooting at them. Or would it be whomever? I never can get who and whom straight. But Lou is awfully witty; I mean he really is. He has had two or three things in 'College Humor.' What was your college?"

"The Electoral College."

"Oh, you're an engineer! And what are you doing on Wall Street? I suppose you gave up your profession 'for gold.' You ought to be ashamed of yourself! You might be accomplishing big things like building bridges. Which reminds me, do you play bridge?"

"Yes."

"You ought to, honestly. I'm not very good, but it's lots of fun. I belong to a club and we just have a circus. The other girls used to laugh at me, I was so dumb, but this last winter I got good; I mean really not bad at all. And then, just when I was doing so well, they decided to play this contract and I can't get it at all. You don't bid anything but slams and I just can't do that. I simply haven't the nerve."

"Have you ever been up with Lindbergh?" asked Harry.

"Yes. I'm not joking. I really mean it. It was while he was in Washington. My father arranged it through Congressman Burleigh. That's the Burleigh Paint Company in South Chicago. Mr. Burleigh is a congressman and one of Father's closest friends. It was the most thrilling experience I ever had in my life. And I wasn't frightened at all, only a little bit, like when you go in swimming and dive for the first time."

"Can you dive?"

"You ought to see me! Honestly, not boasting, I'm a regular Gertrude Ederle; you know, the girl that swam across the English Channel so many times. I wouldn't want to swim that Channel, though. It's bad enough in a boat. I'm a pretty good sailor, but the last time my brother and I crossed from Calais to Dover, well, 'it happens in the best of families,' as Briggs says, or is it Mutt and Jeff?

"Do you read the funny pages? I suppose I oughtn't to confess it, but I read them religiously. Father often jokes me about it and pretends the money he spent sending me to college was all wasted because all I got out of it was a taste for 'the funnies.' I answer him back by saying he went to college, too, and all he cares anything about now is golf. It's all joking of course. Father and I are the best friends and chums! What was your college?"

"The War College."

"Oh, West Point! I'd just love to go up there and watch them drill sometime! I've seen it across the river going by on the train and it looks lovely. And fall before last, Father and Lou and I went to the big football game between West Point and the Annapolis Navy. You know they had it in Chicago, at Soldiers' Field, in Grant Park. It's an enormous place and lots of people couldn't see the game at all, but our seats were grand. Father got them through Congressman Burleigh."

"Is that," asked Harry, "the Burleigh who's in the paint business in South Chicago?"

"Do you know him?"

"I bought a can of paint from him once when I was redecorating my garage."

"Why, he's one of Father's best friends. He's in Congress. How funny that you should really know him!"

"You can meet congressmen if you go at it the right way."

Miss Coakley was talking.

"Oh, Mr. Buckley, will you—? Mr. Walsh and I— Just what was it you said, Mr.—?"

"I don't remember saying anything," replied Dave Wallace on her left.

"Why, you— He did, too, Mr.— He said the Mauretania was the— And I said the Paris or the Majestic, or the Berengaria— Now we want you to give us your honest—"

"I never crossed on anything but the Santa Maria," said Harry.

"Oh, Italy, how I love it! I could simply— There's no other country—it just seems as if— If it weren't for my sister in Baltimore—maybe some day— But a girl is foolish—"

"Grace," said Harry, "how's the Scotch holding out?"

"The whole week must have been tough," said Grace.

"I don't see how you men live through it," said Miss Rell,

"standing there on the floor of the Exchange all day, shouting at each other. Why, it simply kills me just to stand and wait five minutes in a shop! To have to do it all day, I'd perish! How do you endure it?"

"Well, you know those little stools that golf fans carry around with them. I never go on the floor without one," said Harry.

"My father is the greatest golf fan in the world; I mean I really believe he is, without exception. He never plays less than four times a week and he's a fine player, I mean for a man his age. He's fifty-four years old and he goes around Onwentsia in a hundred and twenty. Can that be right?"

"Easily."

Dinner was over and they went into the living-room. Harry and Dave Wallace were together a moment.

"I notice you didn't talk much," remarked Dave.

"But what I said made a big impression."

"I'd have traded you Coakley for your dame. Your gal just goes along as if she were speaking into a mike, but Miss Coakley is a perpetual missing-word contest and it's impossible to keep out of it—every little while you feel as if you just had to guess what's left out."

"She called me Burton and Buckley."

"She called me everything from Welling to Wolheim."

Harry tried to hide behind the piano, but Miss Rell soon found him.

"If we could get two more, don't you think Grace would let us play bridge?"

"I don't know the game," said Harry.

"But I'd just love to teach you. I can teach you regular auction, but not this new contract, where you just bid and bid till you're dizzy."

"I haven't any card sense and besides, I think that liquor Grace gave me was bad."

"Oh, truly?"

"I'm going to ask her where she got it."

"I know a man, or at least my father does, who gets the real thing straight from Canada. Only he's out in Chicago."

Harry peremptorily summoned Grace into the hall.

"Grace, that's terrible Scotch you've got. It's given me the first headache I've had in years."

"I understand, and I'll tell them you were sick and had to go home. You were a darling to come and I'll never forget it."

"Neither will I."

At the door he said:

"Remember, old girl, I've left your schoolmates just as I found them. They're still free."

RING LARDNER, born Ringgold Wilmer Lardner in Niles, Michigan, in 1885, was one of the most brilliant, bitter satirists America has ever produced, and the most famous and popular funnyman of the twenties. He started as a sportswriter. With *You Know Me, Al,* a series of "letters" written by a ballplayer, Lardner became an American institution. His acid, wildly funny stories, parodies, and essays appeared in a syndicated newspaper column, in magazines, and in two volumes: *How to Write Short Stories* and *The Love Nest.* In his peak years Lardner was rich, famous, and beloved by a set of friends that included the Fitzgeralds, Franklin P. Adams, George Cohan, George Kaufman, and the Algonquin "Round Table" group.

In later years financial troubles, a dissatisfaction with "journalism," and the strain of having to be funny in print all the time began to wear him down. Ill and unhappy, he died of a heart attack at 48.

The social criticism implicit in Lardner's stories is never at war with their humor, and no writer has ever caught more hilariously the way people talk. "Dinner" might well be read as a cautionary tale for young ladies.

F. SCOTT FITZGERALD

The Jelly-bean

Jim Powell was a Jelly-bean. Much as I desire to make him an appealing character, I feel that it would be unscrupulous to deceive you on that point. He was a bred-in-the-bone, dyed-in-the-wool, ninety-nine three-quarters per cent Jelly-bean and he grew lazily all during Jelly-bean season, which is every season, down in the land of the Jelly-beans well below the Mason-Dixon line.

Now if you call a Memphis man a Jelly-bean he will quite possibly pull a long sinewy rope from his hip pocket and hang you to a convenient telegraph-pole. If you call a New Orleans man a Jelly-bean he will probably grin and ask you who is taking your girl to the Mardi Gras ball. The particular Jelly-bean patch which produced the protagonist of this history lies somewhere between the two—a little city of forty thousand that has dozed sleepily for forty thousand years in southern Georgia, occasionally stirring in its slumbers and muttering something about a war that took place sometime, somewhere, and that everyone else has forgotten long ago.

Jim was a Jelly-bean. I write that again because it has such a pleasant sound—rather like the beginning of a fairy story—as if Jim were nice. It somehow gives me a picture of him with a round, appetizing face and all sorts of leaves and vegetables growing out of his cap. But Jim was long and thin and bent at the waist from stooping over pool-tables, and he was what might have been known in the indiscriminating North as a corner loafer. "Jelly-bean" is the name throughout the undissolved Confederacy for one who spends his life conjugating the verb to idle in the first person singular—I am idling, I have idled, I will idle.

Jim was born in a white house on a green corner. It had four weather-beaten pillars in front and a great amount of lattice-work in the rear that made a cheerful criss-cross background for a flowery sun-drenched lawn. Originally the dwellers in the white house had owned the ground next door and next door to that and next door to that, but this had been so long ago that even Jim's father scarcely remembered it. He had, in fact, thought it a matter of so little moment that when he was dying from a pistol wound got in a brawl he neglected even to tell little Jim, who was five years old and miserably frightened. The white house became a boarding-house run by a tight-lipped lady from Macon, whom Jim called Aunt Mamie and detested with all his soul.

He became fifteen, went to high school, wore his hair in black snarls, and was afraid of girls. He hated his home where four women and one old man prolonged an interminable chatter from summer to summer about what lots the Powell place had originally included and what sort of flowers would be out next. Sometimes the parents of little girls in town, remembering Jim's mother and fancying a resemblance in the dark eyes and hair, invited him to parties, but parties made him shy and he much preferred sitting on a disconnected axle in Tilly's Garage, rolling the bones or exploring his mouth endlessly with a long straw. For pocket money, he picked up odd jobs, and it was due to this that he stopped going to parties. At his third party little Marjorie Haight had whispered indiscreetly and within hearing distance that he was a boy who brought the groceries sometimes. So instead of the two-step and polka, Jim had learned to throw any number he desired on the dice and had listened to spicy tales of all the shootings that had occurred in the surrounding country during the past fifty years.

He became eighteen. The war broke out and he enlisted as a gob and polished brass in the Charleston Navy-yard for a year. Then, by way of variety, he went North and polished brass in the Brooklyn Navy-yard for a year.

When the war was over he came home. He was twenty-one, his trousers were too short and too tight. His buttoned shoes were long and narrow. His tie was an alarming conspiracy of purple and pink marvelously scrolled, and over it were two blue eyes faded like a piece of very good old cloth long exposed to the sun.

In the twilight of one April evening when a soft gray had drifted down along the cottonfields and over the sultry town, he was a vague figure leaning against a board fence, whistling and gazing at the moon's rim above the lights of Jackson Street. His mind was working persistently on a problem that had held his attention for an hour. The Jelly-bean had been invited to a party.

Back in the days when all the boys had detested all the girls, Clark Darrow and Jim had sat side by side in school. But, while Jim's social aspirations had died in the oily air of the garage, Clark had alternately fallen in and out of love, gone to college, taken to drink, given it up, and, in short, become one of the best beaux of the town. Nevertheless Clark and Jim had retained a friendship that, though casual, was perfectly definite. That afternoon Clark's ancient Ford had slowed up beside Jim, who was on the sidewalk and, out of a clear sky, Clark had invited him to a party at the country club. The impulse that made him do this was no stranger than the impulse which made Jim accept. The latter was probably an unconscious ennui, a half-frightened sense of adventure. And now Jim was soberly thinking it over.

He began to sing, drumming his long foot idly on a stone block in the sidewalk till it wobbled up and down in time to the low throaty tune:

"One mile from Home in Jelly-bean town,
Lives Jeanne, the Jelly-bean Queen.
She loves her dice and treats 'em nice;
No dice would treat her mean."

He broke off and agitated the sidewalk to a bumpy gallop.

"Daggone!" he muttered, half aloud.

They would all be there—the old crowd, the crowd to which, by right of the white house, sold long since, and the portrait of the officer in gray over the mantel, Jim should have belonged. But that crowd had grown up together into a tight little set as gradually as the girls' dresses had lengthened inch by inch, as definitely as the boys' trousers had dropped suddenly to their ankles. And to that society of first names and dead puppy-loves Jim was an outsider—a running mate of poor whites. Most of the men knew him, condescendingly; he tipped his hat to three or four girls. That was all.

When the dusk had thickened into a blue setting for the

moon, he walked through the hot, pleasantly pungent town to Jackson Street. The stores were closing and the last shoppers were drifting homeward, as if borne on the dreamy revolution of a slow merry-go-round. A street-fair further down made a brilliant alley of varicolored booths and contributed a blend of music to the night—an oriental dance on a calliope, a melancholy bugle in front of a freak show, a cheerful rendition of "Back Home in Tennessee" on a hand-organ.

The Jelly-bean stopped in a store and bought a collar. Then he sauntered along toward Soda Sam's where he found the usual three or four cars of a summer evening parked in front and the little darkies running back and forth with sundaes and lemonades.

"Hello, Jim."

It was a voice at his elbow—Joe Ewing sitting in an automobile with Marylyn Wade. Nancy Lamar and a strange man were in the back seat.

The Jelly-bean tipped his hat quickly.

"Hi, Ben—" then, after an almost imperceptible pause—"How y' all?"

Passing, he ambled on toward the garage where he had a room upstairs. His "How y' all" had been said to Nancy Lamar, to whom he had not spoken in fifteen years.

Nancy had a mouth like a remembered kiss and shadowy eyes and blue-black hair inherited from her mother who had been born in Budapest. Jim passed her often in the street, walking small-boy fashion with her hands in her pockets and he knew that with her inseparable Sally Carrol Hopper she had left a trail of broken hearts from Atlanta to New Orleans.

For a few fleeting moments Jim wished he could dance. Then he laughed and as he reached his door began to sing softly to himself:

"Her Jelly Roll can twist your soul,
Her eyes are big and brown,

She's the Queen of the Queens of the Jelly-beans—
My Jeanne of Jelly-bean Town."

2

At nine-thirty Jim and Clark met in front of Soda Sam's and started for the Country Club in Clark's Ford.

"Jim," asked Clark casually, as they rattled through the jasmine-scented night, "how do you keep alive?"

The Jelly-bean paused, considered.

"Well," he said finally, "I got a room over Tilly's garage. I help him some with the cars in the afternoon an' he gives it to me free. Sometimes I drive one of his taxis and pick up a little thataway. I get fed up doin' that regular though."

"That all?"

"Well, when there's a lot of work I help him by the day—Saturdays usually—and then there's one main source of revenue I don't generally mention. Maybe you don't recollect I'm about the champion crap-shooter of this town. They make me shoot from a cup now because once I get the feel of a pair of dice they just roll for me."

Clark grinned appreciatively.

"I never could learn to set 'em so's they'd do what I wanted. Wish you'd shoot with Nancy Lamar some day and take all her money away from her. She will roll 'em with the boys and she loses more than her daddy can afford to give her. I happen to know she sold a good ring last month to pay a debt."

The Jelly-bean was non-committal.

"The white house on Elm Street still belong to you?"

Jim shook his head.

"Sold. Got a pretty good price, seein' it wasn't in a good part of town no more. Lawyer told me to put it into Liberty bonds. But Aunt Mamie got so she didn't have no sense, so it takes all the interest to keep her up at Great Farms Sanitarium."

"Hm."

"I got an old uncle up-state an' I reckon I kin go up there if ever I get sure enough pore. Nice farm, but not enough niggers around to work it. He's asked me to come up and help him, but I don't guess I'd take much to it. Too doggone lonesome—" He broke off suddenly. "Clark, I want to tell you I'm much obliged to you for askin' me out, but I'd be a lot happier if you'd just stop the car right here an' let me walk back into town."

"Shucks!" Clark grunted. "Do you good to step out. You don't have to dance—just get out there on the floor and shake."

"Hold on," exclaimed Jim uneasily, "Don't you go leadin' me up to any girls and leavin' me there so I'll have to dance with 'em."

Clark laughed.

" 'Cause," continued Jim desperately, "without you swear you won't do that I'm agoin' to get out right here an' my good legs goin' carry me back to Jackson Street."

They agreed after some argument that Jim, unmolested by females, was to view the spectacle from a secluded settee in the corner where Clark would join him whenever he wasn't dancing.

So ten o'clock found the Jelly-bean with his legs crossed and his arms conservatively folded, trying to look casually at home and politely uninterested in the dancers. At heart he was torn between overwhelming self-consciousness and an intense curiosity as to all that went on around him. He saw the girls emerge one by one from the dressing-room, stretching and pluming themselves like bright birds, smiling over their powdered shoulders at the chaperones, casting a quick glance around to take in the room and, simultaneously, the room's reaction to their entrance—and then, again like birds, alighting and nestling in the sober arms of their waiting escorts. Sally Carrol Hopper, blonde and lazy-eyed, appeared clad in her favorite pink and blinking like an awakened rose. Marjorie Haight, Marylyn Wade, Harriet Cary, all the girls he had seen loitering down Jackson Street by noon, now, curled and brilliantined and delicately tinted for the overhead lights, were miraculously strange Dresden figures of pink and blue and red and gold, fresh from the shop and not yet fully dried.

He had been there half an hour, totally uncheered by Clark's jovial visits which were each one accompanied by a "Hello, old boy, how you making out?" and a slap at his knee. A dozen males had spoken to him or stopped for a moment beside him, but he knew that they were each one surprised at finding him there and fancied that one or two were even slightly resentful. But at half past ten his embarrassment suddenly left him and a pull of breathless interest took him completely out of himself—Nancy Lamar had come out of the dressing-room.

She was dressed in yellow organdie, a costume of a hundred cool corners, with three tiers of ruffles and a big bow in back until she shed black and yellow around her in a sort of phosphorescent luster. The Jelly-bean's eyes opened wide and a lump arose in his throat. For a minute she stood beside the door until her partner hurried up. Jim recognized him as the stranger who had been with her in Joe Ewing's car that afternoon. He saw her set her arms akimbo and say something in a low voice, and laugh. The man laughed too and Jim experienced the quick pang of a weird new kind of pain. Some ray had passed between the pair, a shaft of beauty from that sun that had warmed him a moment since. The Jelly-bean felt suddenly like a weed in a shadow.

A minute later Clark approached him, bright-eyed and glowing.

"Hi, old man," he cried with some lack of originality. "How you making out?"

Jim replied that he was making out as well as could be expected.

"You come along with me," commanded Clark. "I've got something that'll put an edge on the evening."

Jim followed him awkwardly across the floor and up the

stairs to the locker-room where Clark produced a flask of nameless yellow liquid.

"Good old corn."

Ginger ale arrived on a tray. Such potent nectar as "good old corn" needed some disguise beyond seltzer.

"Say, boy," exclaimed Clark breathlessly, "doesn't Nancy Lamar look beautiful?"

Jim nodded.

"Mighty beautiful," he agreed.

"She's all dolled up to a fare-you-well tonight," continued Clark. "Notice that fellow she's with?"

"Big fella? White pants?"

"Yeah. Well, that's Ogden Merritt from Savannah. Old man Merritt makes the Merritt safety razors. This fella's crazy about her. Been chasing after her all year.

"She's a wild baby," continued Clark, "but I like her. So does everybody. But she sure does do crazy stunts. She usually gets out alive, but she's got scars all over her reputation from one thing or another she's done."

"That so?" Jim passed over his glass. "That's good corn."

"Not so bad. Oh, she's a wild one. Shoots craps, say, boy! And she do like her highballs. Promised I'd give her one later on."

"She in love with this—Merritt?"

"Damned if I know. Seems like all the best girls around here marry fellas and go off somewhere."

He poured himself one more drink and carefully corked the bottle.

"Listen, Jim, I got to go dance and I'd be much obliged if you just stick this corn right on your hip as long as you're not dancing. If a man notices I've had a drink he'll come up and ask me and before I know it it's all gone and somebody else is having my good time."

So Nancy Lamar was going to marry. This toast of a town was to become the private property of an individual in white trousers—and all because white trousers' father had made a better razor than his neighbor. As they descended the stairs Jim found the idea inexplicably depressing. For the first time in his life he felt a vague and romantic yearning. A picture of her began to form in his imagination—Nancy walking boylike and debonaire along the street, taking an orange as tithe from a worshipful fruit-dealer, charging "a dope" on a mythical account at Soda Sam's, assembling a convoy of beaux and then driving off in triumphal state for an afternoon of splashing and singing.

The Jelly-bean walked out on the porch to a deserted corner, dark between the moon on the lawn and the single lighted door of the ballroom. There he found a chair and, lighting a cigarette, drifted into the thoughtless reverie that was his usual mood. Yet now it was a reverie made sensuous by the night and by the hot smell of damp powder puffs, tucked in the fronts of low dresses and distilling a thousand rich scents to float out through the open door. The music itself, blurred by a loud trombone, became hot and shadowy, a languorous overtone to the scraping of many shoes and slippers.

Suddenly the square of yellow light that fell through the door was obscured by a dark figure. A girl had come out of the dressing-room and was standing on the porch not more than ten feet away. Jim heard a low-breathed "doggone" and then she turned and saw him. It was Nancy Lamar.

Jim rose to his feet.

"Howdy?"

"Hello—" She paused, hesitated and then approached. "Oh, it's—Jim Powell."

He bowed slightly, tried to think of a casual remark.

"Do you suppose," she began quickly, "I mean—do you know anything about gum?"

"What?"

"I've got gum on my shoe. Some utter ass left his or her gum on the floor and of course I stepped in it."

Jim blushed, inappropriately.

"Do you know how to get it off?" she demanded petulantly. "I've tried a knife. I've tried every damn thing in the dressing-room. I've tried soap and water—and even perfume and I've ruined my powder-puff trying to make it stick to that."

Jim considered the question in some agitation.

"Why—I think maybe gasoline—"

The words had scarcely left his lips when she grasped his hand and pulled him at a run off the low veranda, over a flower bed and at a gallop toward a group of cars parked in the moonlight by the first hole of the golf course.

"Turn on the gasoline," she commanded breathlessly.

"What?"

"For the gum of course. I've got to get it off. I can't dance with gum on."

Obediently Jim turned to the cars and began inspecting them with a view to obtaining the desired solvent. Had she demanded a cylinder he would have done his best to wrench one out.

"Here," he said after a moment's search. "Here's one that's easy. Got a handkerchief?"

"It's upstairs wet. I used it for the soap and water."

Jim laboriously explored his pockets.

"Don't believe I got one either."

"Doggone it! Well, we can turn it on and let it run on the ground."

He turned the spout; a dripping began.

"More!"

He turned it on fuller. The dripping became a flow and formed an oily pool that glistened brightly, reflecting a dozen tremulous moons on its quivering bosom.

"Ah," she sighed contentedly, "let it all out. The only thing to do is to wade in it."

In desperation he turned on the tap full and the pool suddenly widened sending tiny rivers and trickles in all directions.

"That's fine. That's something like."

Raising her skirts she stepped gracefully in.

"I know this'll take it off," she murmured.

Jim smiled.

"There's lots more cars."

She stepped daintily out of the gasoline and began scraping her slippers, side and bottom, on the running-board of the automobile. The Jelly-bean contained himself no longer. He bent double with explosive laughter and after a second she joined in.

"You're here with Clark Darrow, aren't you?" she asked as they walked back toward the veranda.

"Yes."

"You know where he is now?"

"Out dancin', I reckon."

"The deuce. He promised me a highball."

"Well," said Jim, "I guess that'll be all right. I got his bottle right here in my pocket."

She smiled at him radiantly.

"I guess maybe you'll need ginger ale though," he added.

"Not me. Just the bottle."

"Sure enough?"

She laughed scornfully.

"Try me. I can drink anything any man can. Let's sit down."

She perched herself on the side of a table and he dropped into one of the wicker chairs beside her. Taking out the cork she held the flask to her lips and took a long drink. He watched her fascinated.

"Like it?"

She shook her head breathlessly.

"No, but I like the way it makes me feel. I think most people are that way."

Jim agreed.

"My daddy liked it too well. It got him."

"American men," said Nancy gravely, "don't know how to drink."

"What?" Jim was startled.

"In fact," she went on carelessly, "they don't know how to do anything very well. The one thing I regret in my life is that I wasn't born in England."

"In England?"

"Yes. It's the one regret of my life that I wasn't."

"Do you like it over there."

"Yes. Immensely. I've never been there in person, but I've met a lot of Englishmen who were over here in the army, Oxford and Cambridge men—you know, that's like Sewanee and University of Georgia are here—and of course I've read a lot of English novels."

Jim was interested, amazed.

"D' you ever hear of Lady Diana Manners?" she asked earnestly.

No, Jim had not.

"Well, she's what I'd like to be. Dark, you know, like me, and wild as sin. She's the girl who rode her horse up the steps of some cathedral or church or something and all the novelists made their heroines do it afterwards."

Jim nodded politely. He was out of his depths.

"Pass the bottle," suggested Nancy. "I'm going to take another little one. A little drink wouldn't hurt a baby.

"You see," she continued, again breathless after a draught. "People over there have style. Nobody has style here. I mean the boys here aren't really worth dressing up for or doing sensational things for. Don't you know?"

"I suppose so—I mean I suppose not," murmured Jim.

"And I'd like to do 'em an' all. I'm really the only girl in town that has style."

She stretched out her arms and yawned pleasantly.

"Pretty evening."

"Sure is," agreed Jim.

"Like to have boat," she suggested dreamily. "Like to sail out on a silver lake, say the Thames, for instance. Have champagne and caviare sandwiches along. Have about eight people. And one of the men would jump overboard to amuse the party and get drowned like a man did with Lady Diana Manners once."

"Did he do it to please her?"

"Didn't mean drown himself to please her. He just meant to jump overboard and make everybody laugh."

"I reckin they just died laughin' when he drowned."

"Oh, I suppose they laughed a little," she admitted. "I imagine she did, anyway. She's pretty hard, I guess—like I am."

"You hard?"

"Like nails." She yawned again and added, "Give me a little more from that bottle."

Jim hesitated but she held out her hand defiantly.

"Don't treat me like a girl," she warned him. "I'm not like any girl *you* ever saw." She considered. "Still, perhaps you're right. You got—you got old head on young shoulders."

She jumped to her feet and moved toward the door. The Jelly-bean rose also.

"Good-bye," she said politely, "good-bye. Thanks, Jelly-bean."

Then she stepped inside and left him wide-eyed upon the porch.

3

At twelve o'clock a procession of cloaks issued single file from the women's dressing-room and, each one pairing with a coated beau like dancers meeting in a cotillion figure, drifted through the door with sleepy happy laughter—through the door into the dark where autos backed and snorted and parties called to one another and gathered around the water-cooler.

Jim, sitting in his corner, rose to look for Clark. They had met at eleven; then Clark had gone in to dance. So, seeking him, Jim wandered into the soft-drink stand that had once been a bar. The room was deserted except for a sleepy Negro dozing behind the counter and two boys lazily fingering a pair of dice at one of the tables. Jim was about to leave when he saw Clark coming in. At the same moment Clark looked up.

"Hi, Jim!" he commanded. "C'mon over and help us with this bottle. I guess there's not much left, but there's one all around."

Nancy, the man from Savannah, Marylyn Wade, and Joe Ewing were lolling and laughing in the doorway. Nancy caught Jim's eye and winked at him humorously.

They drifted over to a table and arranging themselves around it waited for the waiter to bring ginger ale. Jim, faintly ill at ease, turned his eyes on Nancy, who had drifted into a nickel crap game with the two boys at the next table.

"Bring them over here," suggested Clark.

Joe looked around.

"We don't want to draw a crowd. It's against club rules."

"Nobody's around," insisted Clark, "except Mr. Taylor. He's walking up and down like a wild-man trying to find out who let all the gasoline out of his car."

There was a general laugh.

"I bet a million Nancy got something on her shoe again. You can't park when she's around."

"O Nancy, Mr. Taylor's looking for you!"

Nancy's cheeks were glowing with excitement over the game. "I haven't seen his silly little flivver in two weeks."

Jim felt a sudden silence. He turned and saw an individual of uncertain age standing in the doorway.

Clark's voice punctuated the embarrassment.

"Won't you join us, Mr. Taylor?"

"Thanks."

Mr. Taylor spread his unwelcome presence over a chair.

"Have to, I guess. I'm waiting till they dig me up some gasoline. Somebody got funny with my car."

His eyes narrowed and he looked quickly from one to the other. Jim wondered what he had heard from the doorway—tried to remember what had been said.

"I'm right tonight," Nancy sang out, "and my four bits is in the ring."

"Faded!" snapped Taylor suddenly.

"Why, Mr. Taylor, I didn't know you shot craps!" Nancy was overjoyed to find that he had seated himself and instantly covered her bet. They had openly disliked each other since the night she had definitely discouraged a series of rather pointed advances.

"All right, babies, do it for your mamma. Just one little seven." Nancy was *cooing* to the dice. She rattled them with a brave underhand flourish, and rolled them out on the table.

"Ah-h! I suspected it. And now again with the dollar up."

Five passes to her credit found Taylor a bad loser. She was making it personal, and after each success Jim watched triumph flutter across her face. She was doubling with each throw—such luck could scarcely last.

"Better go easy," he cautioned her timidly.

"Ah, but watch this one," she whispered. It was eight on the dice and she called her number.

"Little Ada, this time we're going South."

Ada from Decatur rolled over the table. Nancy was flushed and half-hysterical, but her luck was holding. She drove the pot up and up, refusing to drag. Taylor was drumming with his fingers on the table, but he was in to stay.

Then Nancy tried for a ten and lost the dice. Taylor seized them avidly. He shot in silence, and in the hush of excitement the clatter of one pass after another on the table was the only sound.

Now Nancy had the dice again, but her luck had broken.

An hour passed. Back and forth it went. Taylor had been at it again—and again and again. They were even at last—Nancy lost her ultimate five dollars.

"Will you take my check," she said quickly, "for fifty, and we'll shoot it all?" Her voice was a little unsteady and her hand shook as she reached to the money.

Clark exchanged an uncertain but alarmed glance with Joe Ewing. Taylor shot again. He had Nancy's check.

"How 'bout another?" she said wildly. "Jus' any bank will do—money everywhere as a matter of fact."

Jim understood—the "good old corn" he had given her—the "good old corn" she had taken since. He wished he dared interfere—a girl of that age and position would hardly have two bank accounts. When the clock struck two he contained himself no longer.

"May I—can't you let me roll 'em for you?" he suggested, his low, lazy voice a little strained.

Suddenly sleepy and listless, Nancy flung the dice down before him.

"All right—old boy! As Lady Diana Manners says, 'Shoot 'em, Jelly-bean,—My luck's gone."

"Mr. Taylor," said Jim, carelessly, "we'll shoot for one of those there checks against the cash."

Half an hour later Nancy swayed forward and clapped him on the back.

"Stole my luck, you did." She was nodding her head sagely.

Jim swept up the last check and putting it with the others tore them into confetti and scattered them on the floor. Someone started singing, and Nancy kicking her chair backward rose to her feet.

"Ladies and gentlemen," she announced. "Ladies—that's you Marylyn. I want to tell the world that Mr. Jim Powell, who is a well-known Jelly-bean of this city, is an exception to a great rule—'lucky in dice—unlucky in love.' He's lucky in dice, and as matter of fact I—I *love* him. Ladies and gentlemen, Nancy

Lamar, famous dark-haired beauty often featured in the *Herald* as one th' most popular members of younger set as other girls are often featured in this particular case. Wish to announce—wish to announce, anyway, Gentlemen—" She tipped suddenly. Clark caught her and restored her balance.

"My error," she laughed, "she stoops to—stoops to—anyways— We'll drink to Jelly-bean . . . Mr. Jim Powell, King of the Jelly-beans."

And a few minutes later as Jim waited hat in hand for Clark in the darkness of that same corner of the porch where she had come searching for gasoline, she appeared suddenly beside him.

"Jelly-bean," she said, "are you here, Jelly-bean? I think—" and her slight unsteadiness seemed part of an enchanted dream—"I think you deserve one of my sweetest kisses for that, Jelly-bean."

For an instant her arms were around his neck—her lips were pressed to his.

"I'm a wild part of the world, Jelly-bean, but you did me a good turn."

Then she was gone, down the porch, over the cricket-loud lawn. Jim saw Merritt come out the front door and say something to her angrily—saw her laugh and, turning away, walk with averted eyes to his car. Marylyn and Joe followed, singing a drowsy song about a Jazz baby.

Clark came out and joined Jim on the steps. "All pretty lit, I guess," he yawned. "Merritt's in a mean mood. He's certainly off Nancy."

Over east along the golf course a faint rug of gray spread itself across the feet of the night. The party in the car began to chant a chorus as the engine warmed up.

"Good-night everybody," called Clark.

"Good-night, Clark."

"Good-night."

There was a pause, and then a soft, happy voice added,

"Good-night, Jelly-bean."

The car drove off to a burst of singing. A rooster on a farm across the way took up a solitary mournful crow, and behind them a last Negro waiter turned out the porch light. Jim and Clark strolled over toward the Ford, their shoes crunching raucously on the gravel drive.

"Oh boy!" sighed Clark softly, "how you can set those dice!"

It was still too dark for him to see the flush on Jim's thin cheeks—or to know that it was a flush of unfamiliar shame.

4

Over Tilly's garage a bleak room echoed all day to the rumble and snorting down-stairs and the singing of the Negro washers as they turned the hose on the cars outside. It was a cheerless square of a room, punctuated with a bed and a battered table on which lay half a dozen books—Joe Miller's "Slow Train thru Arkansas," "Lucille," in an old edition very much annotated in an old-fashioned hand; "The Eyes of the World," by Harold Bell Wright, and an ancient prayer-book of the Church of England with the name Alice Powell and the date 1831 written on the fly-leaf.

The East, gray when the Jelly-bean entered the garage, became a rich and vivid blue as he turned on his solitary electric light. He snapped it out again, and going to the window rested his elbows on the sill and stared into the deepening morning. With the awakening of his emotions, his first perception was a sense of futility, a dull ache at the utter grayness of his life. A wall had sprung up suddenly around him hedging him in, a wall as definite and tangible as the white wall of his bare room. And with his perception of this wall all that had been the romance of his existence, the casualness, the light-hearted improvidence, the miraculous open-handedness of life faded out. The Jelly-bean strolling up Jackson Street humming a lazy song, known at every shop and street stand, cropful of easy greeting and local wit, sad sometimes for only the sake of sadness and the flight of time—that Jelly-bean was suddenly vanished. The very name was a reproach, a triviality. With a flood of insight he knew that Merritt must despise him, that even Nancy's kiss in the dawn would have awakened not jealousy but only a contempt for Nancy's so lowering herself. And on his part the Jelly-bean had used for her a dingy subterfuge learned from the garage. He had been her moral laundry; the stains were his.

As the gray became blue, brightened and filled the room, he crossed to his bed and threw himself down on it, gripping the edges fiercely.

"I love her," he cried aloud, "God!"

As he said this something gave way within him like a lump melting in his throat. The air cleared and became radiant with dawn, and turning over on his face he began to sob dully into the pillow.

In the sunshine of three o'clock Clark Darrow chugging painfully along Jackson Street was hailed by the Jelly-bean, who stood on the curb with his fingers in his vest pockets.

"Hi!" called Clark, bringing his Ford to an astonishing stop alongside. "Just get up?"

The Jelly-bean shook his head.

"Never did go to bed. Felt sorta restless, so I took a long walk this morning out in the country. Just got into town this minute."

"Should think you *would* feel restless. I been feeling thataway all day—"

"I'm thinkin' of leavin' town," continued the Jelly-bean, absorbed by his own thoughts. "Been thinkin' of goin' up on the farm, and takin' a little that work off Uncle Dun. Reckin I been bummin' too long."

Clark was silent and the Jelly-bean continued:

"I reckin maybe after Aunt Mamie dies I could sink that money of mine in the farm and make somethin' out of it. All my people originally came from that part up there. Had a big place."

Clark looked at him curiously.

"That's funny," he said. "This—this sort of affected me the same way."

The Jelly-bean hesitated.

"I don't know," he began slowly, "somethin' about—about that girl last night talkin' about a lady named Diana Manners—an English lady, sorta got me thinkin'!" He drew himself up and looked oddly at Clark, "I had a family once," he said defiantly.

Clark nodded.

"I know."

"And I'm the last of 'em," continued the Jelly-bean, his voice rising slightly, "and I ain't worth shucks. Name they call me by means jelly—weak and wobbly like. People who weren't nothin' when my folks was a lot turn up their noses when they pass me on the street."

Again Clark was silent.

"So I'm through. I goin' today. And when I come back to this town it's going to be like a gentleman."

Clark took out his handkerchief and wiped his damp brow.

"Reckon you're not the only one it shook up," he admitted gloomily. "All this thing of girls going round like they do is going to stop right quick. Too bad, too, but everybody'll have to see it that-away."

"Do you mean," demanded Jim in surprise, "that all that's leaked out?"

"Leaked out? How on earth could they keep it secret. It'll be announced in the papers tonight. Doctor Lamar's got to save his name somehow."

Jim put his hands on the sides of the car and tightened his long fingers on the metal.

"Do you mean Taylor investigated those checks?"

It was Clark's turn to be surprised.

"Haven't you heard what happened?"

Jim's startled eyes were answer enough.

"Why," announced Clark dramatically, "those four got another bottle of corn, got tight and decided to shock the town—so Nancy and that fella Merritt were married in Rockville at seven o'clock this morning."

A tiny indentation appeared in the metal under the Jelly-bean's fingers.

"Married?"

"Sure enough. Nancy sobered up and rushed back into town, crying and frightened to death—claimed it'd all been a mistake. First Doctor Lamar went wild and was going to kill Merritt, but finally they got it patched up some way, and Nancy and Merritt went to Savannah on the two-thirty train."

Jim closed his eyes and with an effort overcame a sudden sickness.

"It's too bad," said Clark philosophically. "I don't mean the wedding—reckon that's all right, though I don't guess Nancy cared a darn about him. But it's a crime for a nice girl like that to hurt her family that way."

The Jelly-bean let go the car and turned away. Again something was going on inside him, some inexplicable but almost chemical change.

"Where you going?" asked Clark.

The Jelly-bean turned and looked dully back over his shoulder.

"Got to go," he muttered. "Been up too long; feelin' right sick."

"Oh."

The street was hot at three and hotter still at four, the April dust seeming to enmesh the sun and give it forth again as a world-old joke forever played on an eternity of afternoons. But at half past four a first layer of quiet fell and the shades lengthened under the awnings and heavy foliaged trees. In this heat nothing mattered. All life was weather, a waiting through the hot where events had no significance for the cool that was soft and caressing like a woman's hand on a tired forehead. Down in Georgia there is a feeling—perhaps inarticulate—that this is the greatest wisdom of the South—so after a while the Jelly-bean turned into a pool-hall on Jackson Street where he was sure to find a congenial crowd who would make all the old jokes—the ones he knew.

F. SCOTT FITZGERALD is credited with practically inventing the Jazz Age and the flapper. Much of his popular fiction and personal life did a good deal to foster this illusion. But he was a gifted and serious writer: a precise and beautiful stylist, a master of the short story, and a novelist whose depth, range, and moral vision were increasing when he died in Hollywood in 1940.

Born in St. Paul, Minnesota, in 1896, Fitzgerald's boyhood and Princeton years encouraged his ideals of wealth, success, beauty, and romantic love. While stationed in Alabama during World War I, he met Zelda Sayre, and as soon as his first book, a novel of college life called *This Side of Paradise,* was published, he married her. Their extravagant life together inspired his second novel, *The Beautiful and Damned.* In 1925 *The Great Gatsby* won critical praise and brought letters of admiration from Edith Wharton, T. S. Eliot, and other literary figures, many of whom joined the circle of friends that included Hemingway, Ring Lardner, and Edmund Wilson. Fitzgerald was writing a novel about a movie producer, *The Last Tycoon,* at the time of his death. His letters, published in 1963 and 1965, reveal a gift for zany humor as well as a touching concern for his friends and daughter.

He introduced "The Jelly-bean" thus in *Tales of the Jazz Age:* "This is a Southern story, with the scene laid in the small city of Tarleton, Georgia. I have a profound affection for Tarleton, but somehow whenever I write a story about it I receive letters from all over the South denouncing me in no uncertain terms. 'The Jelly-bean' . . . drew its full share of these admonitory notes.

"It was written under strange circumstances shortly after my first novel was published, and, moreover, it was the first story in which I had a collaborator. For, finding that I was unable to manage the crap-shooting episode, I turned it over to my wife, who, as a Southern girl, was presumably an expert on the technique of that great sectional pastime."

ISAAC BABEL

Awakening

All the folk in our circle—brokers, shopkeepers, clerks in banks and steamship offices—used to have their children taught music. Our fathers, seeing no other escape from their lot, had thought up a lottery, building it on the bones of little children. Odessa more than other towns was seized by the craze. And in fact, in the course of ten years or so our town supplied the concert platforms of the world with infant prodigies. From Odessa came Mischa Elman, Zimbalist, Gabrilowitsch. Odessa witnessed the first steps of Jascha Heifetz.

When a lad was four or five, his mother took the puny creature to Zagursky's. Mr. Zagursky ran a factory of infant prodigies, a factory of Jewish dwarfs in lace collars and patent-leather pumps. He hunted them out in the slums of the Moldavanka, in the evil-smelling courtyards of the Old Market. Mr. Zagursky charted the first course, then the children were shipped off to Professor Auer in St. Petersburg. A wonderful harmony dwelt in the souls of those wizened creatures with their swollen blue hands. They became famous virtuosi. My father decided that I should emulate them. Though I had, as a matter of fact, passed the age limit set for infant prodigies, being now in my fourteenth year, my shortness and lack of strength made it possible to pass me off as an eight-year-old. Herein lay father's hope.

I was taken to Zagursky's. Out of respect for my grandfather, Mr. Zagursky agreed to take me on at the cut rate of a rouble a lesson. My grandfather Leivi-Itzkhok was the laughing-stock of the town, and its chief adornment. He used to walk about the streets in a top hat and old boots, dissipating doubt in the darkest of cases. He would be asked what a Gobelin was, why the Jacobins betrayed Robespierre, how you made artificial silk, what a Caesarean section was. And my grandfather could answer these questions. Out of respect for his learning and craziness, Mr. Zagursky only charged us a rouble a lesson. And he had the devil of a time with me, fearing my grandfather, for with me there was nothing to be done. The sounds dripped from my fiddle like iron filings, causing even me excruciating agony, but father wouldn't give in. At home there was no talk save of Mischa Elman, exempted by the Czar himself from military service. Zimbalist, father would have us know, had been presented to the King of England and had played at Buckingham Palace. The parents of Gabrilowitsch had bought two houses in

St. Petersburg. Infant prodigies brought wealth to their parents, but though my father could have reconciled himself to poverty, fame he must have.

"It's not possible," people feeding at his expense would insinuate, "it's just not possible that the grandson of such a grandfather . . ."

But what went on in my head was quite different. Scraping my way through the violin exercises, I would have books by Turgenev or Dumas on my music stand. Page after page I devoured as I deedled away. In the daytime I would relate impossible happenings to the kids next door; at night I would commit them to paper. In our family, composition was a hereditary occupation. Grandfather Leivi-Itzkhok, who went cracked as he grew old, spent his whole life writing a tale entitled "The Headless Man." I took after him.

Three times a week, laden with violin case and music, I made my reluctant way to Zagursky's place on Witte (formerly Dvoryanskaya) Street. There Jewish girls aflame with hysteria sat along the wall awaiting their turn, pressing to their feeble knees violins exceeding in dimensions the exalted persons they were to play to at Buckingham Palace.

The door to the sanctum would open, and from Mr. Zagursky's study there would stagger big-headed, freckled children with necks as thin as flower stalks and an epileptic flush on their cheeks. The door would bang to, swallowing up the next dwarf. Behind the wall, straining his throat, the teacher sang and waved his baton. He had ginger curls and frail legs, and sported a big bow tie. Manager of a monstrous lottery, he populated the Moldavanka and the dark culs-de-sac of the Old Market with the ghosts of pizzicato and cantilena. Afterward old Professor Auer lent these strains a diabolical brilliance.

In this crew I was quite out of place. Though like them in my dwarfishness, in the voice of my forebears I perceived inspiration of another sort.

The first step was difficult. One day I left home laden like a beast of burden with violin case, violin, music, and twelve roubles in cash—payment for a month's tuition. I was going along Nezhin Street; to get to Zagursky's I should have turned into Dvoryanskaya, but instead of that I went up Tiraspolskaya and found myself at the harbor. The allotted time flew past in the part of the port where ships went after quarantine. So began my liberation. Zagursky's saw me no more: affairs of greater moment occupied my thoughts. My pal Nemanov and I got into the habit of slipping aboard the *S.S. Kensington* to see an old salt named Trottyburn. Nemanov was a year younger than I. From the age of eight onward he had been doing the most ingenious business deals you can imagine. He had a wonderful head for that kind of thing, and later on amply fulfilled his youthful promise. Now he is a New York millionaire, director of General Motors, a company no less powerful than Ford. Nemanov took me along with him because I silently obeyed all his orders. He used to buy pipes smuggled in by Mr. Trottyburn. They were made in Lincoln by the old sailor's brother.

"Gentlemen," Mr. Trottyburn would say to us, "take my word, the pets must be made with your own hands. Smoking a factory-made pipe—might as well shove an enema in your mouth. Do you know who Benvenuto Cellini was? He was a grand lad. My brother in Lincoln could tell you about him. Live and let live is my brother's motto. He's got it into his head that you just has to make the pets with your own hands, and not with no one else's. And who are we to say him no, gen'lemen?"

Nemanov used to sell Trottyburn's pipes to bank-managers, foreign consuls, well-to-do Greeks. He made a hundred percent on them.

The pipes of the Lincolnshire master breathed poetry. In each one of them thought was invested, a drop of eternity. A little yellow eye gleamed in their mouthpieces, and their cases were lined with satin. I tried to picture the life in Old England of Matthew Trottyburn, the last master-pipemaker, who refused to swim with the tide.

"We can't but agree, gen'lemen, that the pets has to be made with your own hands."

The heavy waves by the sea wall swept me further and further away from our house, impregnated with the smell of leeks and Jewish destiny. From the harbor I migrated to the other side of the breakwater. There on a scrap of sandspit dwelt the boys from Primorskaya Street. Trouserless from morn till eve, they dived under wherries, sneaked coconuts for dinner, and awaited the time when boats would arrive from Kherson and Kamenka laden with watermelons, which melons it would be possible to break open against moorings.

To learn to swim was my dream. I was ashamed to confess to those bronzed lads that, born in Odessa, I had not seen the sea till I was ten, and at fourteen didn't know how to swim.

How slow was my acquisition of the things one needs to know! In my childhood, chained to the Gemara, I had led the life of a sage. When I grew up I started climbing trees.

But swimming proved beyond me. The hydrophobia of my ancestors—Spanish rabbis and Frankfurt moneychangers—dragged me to the bottom. The waves refused to support me. I would struggle to the shore pumped full of salt water and feeling as though I had been flayed, and return to where my fiddle and music lay. I was fettered to the instruments of my torture, and dragged them about with me. The struggle of rabbis versus Neptune continued till such time as the local water-god took pity on me. This was Yefim Nikitich Smolich, proofreader of the *Odessa News*. In his athletic breast there dwelt compassion for Jewish children, and he was the god of a rabble of rickety starvelings. He used to collect them from the bug-infested joints on the Moldavanka, take them down to the sea, bury them in the sand, do gym with them, dive with them, teach them songs.

Roasting in the perpendicular sunrays, he would tell them tales about fishermen and wild beasts. To grownups Nikitich would explain that he was a natural philospher. The Jewish kids used to roar with laughter at his tales, squealing and snuggling up to him like so many puppies. The sun would sprinkle them with creeping freckles, freckles of the same color as lizards.

Silently, out of the corner of his eye, the old man had been watching my duel with the waves. Seeing that the thing was hopeless, that I should simply never learn to swim, he included me among the permanent occupants of his heart. That cheerful heart of his was with us there all the time; it never went careering off anywhere else, never knew covetousness and never grew disturbed. With his sunburned shoulders, his superannuated gladiator's head, his bronzed and slightly bandy legs, he would lie among us on the other side of the mole, lord and master of those melon-sprinkled, paraffin-stained waters. I came to love that man, with the love that only a lad suffering from hysteria and headaches can feel for a real man. I was always at his side, always trying to be of service to him.

He said to me:

"Don't you get all worked up. You just strengthen your nerves. The swimming will come of itself. How do you mean, the water won't hold you? Why shouldn't it hold you?"

Seeing how drawn I was to him, Nikitich made an exception of me alone of all his disciples. He invited me to visit the clean and spacious attic where he lived in an ambience of straw mats, showed me his dogs, his hedgehog, his tortoise, and his pigeons. In return for this wealth I showed him a tragedy I had written the day before.

"I was sure you did a bit of scribbling," said Nikitich. "You've the look. You're looking in that direction all the time; no eyes for anywhere else."

He read my writings, shrugged a shoulder, passed a hand through his stiff gray curls, paced up and down the attic.

"One must suppose," he said slowly, pausing after each word, "one must suppose that there's a spark of the divine fire in you."

We went out into the street. The old man halted, struck the pavement with his stick, and fastened his gaze upon me.

"Now what is it you lack? Youth's no matter—it'll pass with the years. What you lack is a feeling for nature."

He pointed with his stick at a tree with a reddish trunk and a low crown.

"What's that tree?"

I didn't know.

"What's growing on that bush?"

I didn't know this either. We walked together across the little square on the Alexandrovsky Prospect. The old man kept poking his stick at trees; he would seize me by the shoulder when a bird flew past, and he made me listen to the various kinds of singing.

"What bird is that singing?"

I knew none of the answers. The names of trees and birds, their division into species, where birds fly away to, on which side the sun rises, when the dew falls thickest—all these things were unknown to me.

"And you dare to write! A man who doesn't live in nature, as a stone does or an animal, will never in all his life write two worthwhile lines. Your landscapes are like descriptions of stage props. In heaven's name, what have your parents been thinking of for fourteen years?"

What *had* they been thinking of? Of protested bills of exchange, of Mischa Elman's mansions. I didn't say anything to Nikitich about that, but just kept mum.

At home, over dinner, I couldn't touch my food. It just wouldn't go down.

"A feeling for nature," I thought to myself. "Goodness, why did that never enter my head? Where am I to find someone who will tell me about the way birds sing and what trees are called? What do I know about such things? I might perhaps recognize lilac, at any rate when it's in bloom. Lilac and acacia—there are acacias along De Ribas and Greek Streets."

At dinner father told a new story about Jascha Heifetz. Just before he got to Robinat's he had met Mendelssohn, Jascha's uncle. It appeared that the lad was getting eight hundred roubles a performance. Just work out how much that comes to at fifteen concerts a month!

I did, and the answer was twelve thousand a month. Multiplying and carrying four in my head, I glanced out of the window. Across the cement courtyard, his cloak swaying in the breeze, his ginger curls poking out from under his soft hat, leaning on his cane, Mr. Zagursky, my music teacher, was advancing. It must be admitted he had taken his time in spotting my truancy. More than three months had elapsed since the day when my violin had grounded on the sand by the breakwater.

Mr. Zagursky was approaching the main entrance. I dashed to the back door, but the day before it had been nailed up for fear of burglars. Then I locked myself in the privy. In half an hour the whole family had assembled outside the door. The women were weeping. Aunt Bobka, exploding with sobs, was rubbing her fat shoulder against the door. Father was silent. Finally he started speaking, quietly and distinctly as he had never before spoken in his life.

"I am an officer," said my father. "I own real estate. I go hunting. Peasants pay me rent. I have entered my son in the Cadet Corps. I have no need to worry about my son."

He was silent again. The women were sniffling. Then a terrible blow descended on the privy door. My father was hurling his whole body against it, stepping back and then throwing himself forward.

"I am an officer," he kept wailing. "I go hunting. I'll kill him. This is the end."

The hook sprang from the door, but there was still a bolt hanging onto a single nail. The women were rolling about on the floor, grasping father by the legs. Crazy, he was trying to break loose. Father's mother came over, alerted by the hubbub.

"My child," she said to him in Hebrew, "our grief is great. It has no bounds. Only blood was lacking in our house. I do not wish to see blood in our house."

Father gave a groan. I heard his footsteps retreating. The bolt still hung by its last nail.

I sat it out in my fortress till nightfall. When all had gone to bed, Aunt Bobka took me to grandmother's. We had a long way to go. The moonlight congealed on bushes unknown to me, on trees that had no name. Some anonymous bird emitted a whistle and was extinguished, perhaps by sleep. What bird was it? What was it called? Does dew fall in the evening? Where is the constellation of the Great Bear? On what side does the sun rise?

We were going along Post Office Street. Aunt Bobka held me firmly by the hand so that I shouldn't run away. She was right to. I was thinking of running away.

—Translated by Walter Morison

ISAAC BABEL was born in the Jewish ghetto of Odessa, the great Russian Black Sea port, in 1894. His father was a shopkeeper whose ambitions for his son are reflected in "Awakening," which is quite autobiographical in feeling, if not in actual fact. Official anti-Semitism in Russia shadowed Babel's youth. Small for his age, artistic in nature, he received traditional Jewish schooling in Odessa and then left his family to live in Kiev. At 21 he moved to St. Petersburg (now Leningrad), where he lived in a cellar on a street named for Russia's greatest poet, Pushkin. Maxim Gorky, the novelist, liked Babel and in 1916 published two of his stories in his literary magazine.

Babel served in the Czar's army on the Rumanian front and later under a Cossack general in Poland. The Cossacks, the crack guard regiments of the highest class, appealed strongly to him for their style, passion, and straightforwardness. His book *Red Cavalry* is about a Jew in a Cossack regiment, and the Cossack appears like a motif in much of his work.

In 1937 Babel was arrested in Russia for unknown reasons. He died in a concentration camp in 1939 or 1940.

WILLIAM FAULKNER

Two Soldiers

Me and Pete would go down to Old Man Killegrew's and listen to his radio. We would wait until after supper, after dark, and we would stand outside Old Man Killegrew's parlor window, and we could hear it because Old Man Killegrew's wife was deaf, and so he run the radio as loud as it would run, and so me an Pete could hear it plain as Old Man Killegrew's wife could, I reckon, even standing outside with the window closed.

And that night I said, "What? Japanese? What's a pearl harbor?" and Pete said, "Hush."

And so we stood there, it was cold, listening to the fellow in the radio talking, only I couldn't make no heads nor tails neither out of it. Then the fellow said that would be all for a while, and me and Pete walked back up the road to home, and Pete told me what it was. Because he was nigh twenty and he had done finished the Consolidated last June and he knowed a heap: about them Japanese dropping bombs on Pearl Harbor and that Pearl Harbor was across the water.

"Across what water?" I said. "Across that Government reservoy up at Oxford?"

"Naw," Pete said. "Across the big water. The Pacific Ocean."

We went home. Maw and pap was already asleep, and me and Pete laid in the bed, and I still couldn't understand where it was, and Pete told me again—the Pacific Ocean.

"What's the matter with you?" Pete said. "You're going on nine years old. You been in school now ever since September. Ain't you learned nothing yet?"

"I reckon we ain't got as fer as the Pacific Ocean yet," I said.

We was still sowing the vetch then that ought to been all finished by the fifteenth of November, because pap was still behind, just like he had been ever since me and Pete had knowed him. And we had firewood to git in, too, but every night me and Pete would go down to Old Man Killegrew's and stand outside his parlor window in the cold and listen to his radio; then we would come back home and lay in the bed and Pete would tell me what it was. That is, he would tell me for a while. Then he wouldn't tell me. It was like he didn't want to talk about it no more. He would tell me to shut up because he wanted to go to sleep, but he never wanted to go to sleep.

He would lay there, a heap stiller than if he was asleep, and it would be something, I could feel it coming out of him, like he was mad at me even, only I knowed he wasn't thinking about me, or like he was worried about something, and it wasn't that neither, because he never had nothing to worry about. He never got behind like pap, let alone stayed behind. Pap give him ten acres when he graduated from the Consolidated and me and Pete both reckoned pap was durn glad to get shut of at least ten acres, less to have to worry with himself; and Pete had them ten acres all sowed to vetch and busted out and bedded for the winter, and so it wasn't that. But it was something. And still we would go down to Old Man Killegrew's every night and listen to his radio, and they was at it in the Philippines now, but General MacArthur was holding um. Then we would come back home and lay in the bed, and Pete wouldn't tell me nothing or talk at all. He would just lay there still as a ambush and when I would touch him, his side or his leg would feel hard and still as iron, until after a while I would go to sleep.

Then one night—it was the first time he had said nothing to me except to jump on me about not chopping enough wood at the wood tree where we was cutting—he said, "I got to go."

"Go where?" I said.

"To that war," Pete said.

"Before we even finish gettin' in the firewood?"

"Firewood, hell," Pete said.

"All right," I said. "When we going to start?"

But he wasn't even listening. He laid there, hard and still as iron in the dark. "I got to go," he said. "I jest ain't going to put up with no folks treating the Unity States that way."

"Yes," I said. "Firewood or no firewood, I reckon we got to go."

This time he heard me. He laid still again, but it was a different kind of still.

"You?" he said. "To a war?"

"You'll whup the big uns and I'll whup the little uns," I said.

Then he told me I couldn't go. At first I thought he just

never wanted me tagging after him, like he wouldn't leave me go with him when he went sparking them girls of Tull's. Then he told me the Army wouldn't leave me go because I was too little, and then I knowed he really meant it and that I couldn't go nohow noways. And somehow I hadn't believed until then that he was going himself, but now I knowed he was and that he wasn't going to leave me go with him a-tall.

"I'll chop the wood and tote the water for you-all then!" I said. "You got to have wood and water!"

Anyway, he was listening to me now. He wasn't like iron now.

He turned onto his side and put his hand on my chest because it was me that was laying straight and hard on my back now.

"No," he said. "You got to stay here and help pap."

"Help him what?" I said. "He ain't never caught up nohow. He can't get no further behind. He can sholy take care of this little shirttail of a farm while me and you are whupping them Japanese. I got to go too. If you got to go, then so have I."

"No," Pete said. "Hush now. Hush." And he meant it, and I knowed he did. Only I made sho from his own mouth. I quit.

"So I just can't go then," I said.

"No," Pete said. "You just can't go. You're too little, in the first place, and in the second place—"

"All right," I said. "Then shut up and leave me go to sleep."

So he hushed then and laid back. And I laid there like I was already asleep, and pretty soon he was asleep and I knowed it was the wanting to go to the war that had worried him and kept him awake, and now that he had decided to go, he wasn't worried any more.

The next morning he told maw and pap. Maw was all right. She cried.

"No," she said, crying, "I don't want him to go. I would rather go myself in his place, if I could. I don't want to save the country. Them Japanese could take it and keep it, so long as they left me and my family and my children alone. But I remember my brother Marsh in that other war. He had to go to that one when he wasn't but nineteen, and our mother couldn't understand it then any more than I can now. But she told Marsh if he had to go, he had to go. And so, if Pete's got to go to this one, he's got to go to it. Jest don't ask me to understand why."

But pap was the one. He was the feller. "To the war?" he said. "Why, I just don't see a bit of use in that. You ain't old enough for the draft, and the country ain't being invaded. Our President in Washington, D. C., is watching the conditions and he will notify us. Besides, in that other war your ma just mentioned, I was drafted and sent clean to Texas and was held there nigh eight months until they finally quit fighting. It seems to me that that, along with your Uncle Marsh who received a actual wound on the battlefields of France, is enough for me and mine to have to do to protect the country, at least in my lifetime. Besides, what'll I do for help on the farm with you gone? It seems to me I'll get mighty far behind."

"You been behind as long as I can remember," Pete said. "Anyway, I'm going. I got to."

"Of course he's got to go," I said. "Them Japanese—"

"You hush your mouth!" maw said, crying. "Nobody's talking to you! Go and get me a armful of wood! That's what you can do!"

So I got the wood. And all the next day, while me and Pete and pap was getting in as much wood as we could in that time because Pete said how pap's idea of plenty of wood was one more stick laying against the wall that maw ain't put on the fire yet, maw was getting Pete ready to go. She washed and mended his clothes and cooked him a shoe box of vittles. And that night me and Pete laid in the bed and listened to her packing his grip and crying, until after a while Pete got up in his nightshirt and went back there, and I could hear them talking, until at last maw said, "You got to go, and so I want you to go. But I don't understand it, and I won't never, and so don't expect me to." And Pete come back and got into the bed again and laid again still and hard as iron on his back, and then he said, and he wasn't talking to me, he wasn't talking to nobody: "I got to go. I just got to."

"Sho you got to," I said. "Them Japanese—" He turned over hard, he kind of surged over onto his side, looking at me in the dark.

"Anyway, you're all right," he said. "I expected to have more trouble with you than with all the rest of them put together."

"I reckon I can't help it neither," I said. "But maybe it will run a few years longer and I can get there. Maybe someday I will jest walk in on you."

"I hope not," Pete said. "Folks don't go to wars for fun. A man don't leave his maw crying just for fun."

"Then why are you going?" I said.

"I got to," he said. "I just got to. Now you go on to sleep. I got to ketch that early bus in the morning."

"All right," I said. "I hear tell Memphis is a big place. How will you find where the Army's at?"

"I'll ask somebody where to go to join it," Pete said. "Go on to sleep now."

"Is that what you'll ask for? Where to join the Army?" I said.

"Yes," Pete said. He turned onto his back again. "Shut up and go to sleep."

We went to sleep. The next morning we et breakfast by lamplight because the bus would pass at six o'clock. Maw wasn't crying now. She jest looked grim and busy, putting breakfast on the table while we et it. Then she finished packing Pete's grip except he never wanted to take no grip to the war, but maw said decent folks never went nowhere, not even to a war, without a change of clothes and something to tote them in. She put in the shoe box of fried chicken and biscuits and she put the Bible in, too, and then it was time to go. We didn't know until then that maw wasn't going to the bus. She jest brought Pete's cap and overcoat, and still she didn't cry no more, she jest stood with her hands on Pete's shoulders and she didn't move, but somehow, and jest holding Pete's shoulders, she looked as hard and fierce as when Pete had turned toward me in the bed last night and tole me that anyway I was all right.

"They could take the country and keep the country, so long as they never bothered me and mine," she said. Then she said, "Don't never forget who you are. You ain't rich and the rest of the world outside of Frenchman's Bend never heard of you. But your blood is good as any blood anywhere, and don't you never forget it."

Then she kissed him, and then we was out of the house, with pap toting Pete's grip whether Pete wanted him to or not. There wasn't no dawn even yet, not even after we had stood on the highway by the mailbox, a while. Then we seen the lights of the bus coming and I was watching the bus until it come up and Pete flagged it, and then, sho enough, there was daylight—it had started while I wasn't watching. And now me and Pete expected pap to say something else foolish, like he done before, about how Uncle Marsh getting wounded in France and that trip to Texas pap taken in 1918 ought to be enough to save the Unity States in 1942, but he never. He done all right too. He jest said, "Good-by, son. Always remember what your ma told you and write her whenever you find the time." Then he shaken Pete's hand, and Pete looked at me a minute and put his hand on my head and rubbed my head durn nigh hard enough to wring my neck off and jumped into the bus, and the feller wound the door shut and the bus began to hum, then it was moving, humming and grinding and whining louder and louder; it was going fast, with two little red lights behind it that never seemed to get no littler, but just seemed to be running together until pretty soon they would touch and jest be one light. But they never did, and then the bus was gone, and even like it was, I could have pretty nigh busted out crying, nigh to nine years old and all.

Me and pap went back to the house. All that day we worked at the wood tree, and so I never had no good chance until about middle of the afternoon. Then I taken my slingshot and I would have liked to took all my bird eggs, too, because Pete had give me his collection and he holp me with mine, and he would like to git the box out and look at them as good as I would, even if he was nigh twenty years old. But the box was too big to tote a long ways and have to worry with, so I just taken the shikepoke egg, because it was the best un, and wropped it up good into a matchbox and hid it and the slingshot under the corner of the barn. Then we et supper and went to bed, and I thought then how if I would 'a' had to stayed in that room and that bed like that even for one more night, I jest couldn't 'a' stood it. Then I could hear pap snoring, but I never heard no sound from maw, whether she was asleep or not, and I don't reckon she was. So I taken my shoes and drapped them out the window, and then I clumb out like I used to watch Pete do when he was still jest seventeen and pap held that he was too young yet to be tomcatting around at night, and wouldn't leave him out, and I put on my shoes and went to the barn and got the slingshot and the shikepoke egg and went to the highway.

It wasn't cold, it was jest durn confounded dark, and that highway stretched on in front of me like, without nobody using it, it had stretched out half again as fer just like a man does when he lays down, so that for a time it looked like full sun was going to ketch me before I had finished them twenty-two miles to Jefferson. But it didn't. Daybreak was jest starting when I walked up the hill into town. I could smell breakfast cooking in the cabins and I wished I had thought to brought me a cold biscuit, but that was too late now. And Pete had told me Memphis was a piece beyond Jefferson, but I never knowed it was no eighty miles. So I stood there on that empty square, with daylight coming and coming and the street lights still burning and that Law looking down at me, and me still eighty miles from Memphis, and it had took me all night to walk jest twenty-two miles, and so, by the time I got to Memphis at that rate, Pete would 'a' done already started for Pearl Harbor.

"Where do you come from?" the Law said.

And I told him again. "I got to git to Memphis. My brother's there."

"You mean you ain't got any folks around here?" the Law said. "Nobody but that brother? What are you doing way off down here and your brother in Memphis?"

And I told him again, "I got to git to Memphis. I ain't got no time to waste talking about it and I ain't got time to walk it. I got to git there today."

"Come on here," the Law said.

We went down another street. And there was the bus, just like when Pete got into it yestiddy morning, except there wasn't no lights on it now and it was empty. There was a regular bus dee-po like a railroad dee-po, with a ticket counter and a feller behind it, and the Law said, "Set down over there," and I set down on the bench, and the Law said, "I want to use your telephone," and he talked in the telephone a minute and put it down and said to the feller behind the ticket counter, "Keep your eye on him. I'll be back as soon as Mrs. Habersham can arrange to get herself up and dressed." He went out. I got up and went to the ticket counter.

"I want to go to Memphis," I said.

"You bet," the feller said. "You set down on the bench now. Mr. Foote will be back in a minute."

"I don't know no Mr. Foote," I said. "I want to ride that bus to Memphis."

"You got some money?" he said. "It'll cost you seventy-two cents."

I taken out the matchbox and unwropped the shikepoke egg. "I'll swap you this for a ticket to Memphis," I said.

"What's that?" he said.

"It's a shikepoke egg," I said. "You never seen one before. It's worth a dollar. I'll take seventy-two cents fer it."

"No," he said, "the fellers that own that bus insist on a cash basis. If I started swapping tickets for bird eggs and livestock and such, they would fire me. You go and set down on the bench now, like Mr. Foote—"

I started for the door, but he caught me, he put one hand on the ticket counter and jumped over it and caught up with me and reached his hand out to ketch my shirt. I whupped out my pocketknife and snapped it open.

"You put a hand on me and I'll cut it off," I said.

I tried to dodge him and run at the door, but he could move quicker than any grown man I ever see, quick as Pete almost. He cut me off and stood with his back against the door and one foot raised a little, and there wasn't no other way to get out. "Get back on that bench and stay there," he said.

And there wasn't no other way out. And he stood there with his back against the door. So I went back to the bench. And then it seemed like to me that dee-po was full of folks. There was that Law again, and there was two ladies in fur coats and their faces already painted. But they still looked like they had got up in a hurry and they still never liked it, a old one and a young one, looking down at me.

"He hasn't got a overcoat!" the old one said. "How in the world did he ever get down here by himself?"

"I ask you," the Law said. "I couldn't get nothing out of him except his brother is in Memphis and he wants to get back up there."

"That's right," I said. "I got to git to Memphis today."

"Of course you must," the old one said. "Are you sure you can find your brother when you get to Memphis?"

"I reckon I can," I said. "I ain't got but one and I have knowed him all my life. I reckon I will know him again when I see him."

The old one looked at me. "Somehow he doesn't look like he lives in Memphis," she said.

"He probably don't," the Law said. "You can't tell though.

He might live anywhere, overhalls or not. This day and time they get scattered overnight from he—hope to breakfast; boys and girls, too, almost before they can walk good. He might have been in Missouri or Texas either yestiddy, for all we know. But he don't seem to have any doubt his brother is in Memphis. All I know to do is send him up there and leave him look."

"Yes," the old one said.

The young one set down on the bench by me and opened a hand satchel and taken out a artermatic writing pen and some papers.

"Now, honey," the old one said, "we're going to see that you find your brother, but we must have a case history for our files first. We want to know your name and your brother's name and where you were born and when your parents died."

"I don't need no case history neither," I said. "All I want is to git to Memphis. I got to get there today."

"You see?" the Law said. He said it almost like he enjoyed it. "That's what I told you."

"You're lucky, at that, Mrs. Habersham," the bus feller said. "I don't think he's got a gun on him, but he can open that knife da—I mean, fast enough to suit any man."

But the old one just stood there looking at me.

"Well," she said. "Well. I really don't know what to do."

"I do," the bus feller said. "I'm going to give him a ticket out of my own pocket, as a measure of protecting the company against riot and bloodshed. And when Mr. Foote tells the city board about it, it will be a civic matter and they will not only reimburse me, they will give me a medal too. Hey, Mr. Foote?"

But never nobody paid him no mind. The old one still stood looking down at me. She said "Well," again. Then she taken a dollar from her purse and give it to the bus feller. "I suppose he will travel on a child's ticket, won't he?"

"Wellum," the bus feller said. "I just don't know what the regulations would be. Likely I will be fired for not crating him and marking the crate Poison. But I'll risk it."

Then they were gone. Then the Law come back with a sandwich and give it to me.

"You're sure you can find that brother?" he said.

"I ain't yet convinced why not," I said. "If I don't see Pete first, he'll see me. He knows me too."

Then the Law went out for good, too, and I et the sandwich. Then more folks come in and bought tickets, and then the bus feller said it was time to go, and I got into the bus just like Pete done, and we was gone.

I seen all the towns. I seen all of them. When the bus got to going good, I found out I was jest about wore out for sleep. But there was too much I hadn't never saw before. We run out of Jefferson and run past fields and woods, then we would run into another town and out of that un and past fields and woods again, and then into another town with stores and gins and water tanks, and we run along by the railroad for a spell and I seen the signal arm move, and then I seen the train and then some more towns, and I was jest about plumb wore out for sleep, but I couldn't risk it. Then Memphis begun. It seemed like, to me, it went on for miles. We would pass a patch of stores and I would think that was sholy it and the bus would even stop. But it wouldn't be Memphis yet and we would go on again past water tanks and smokestacks on top of the mills, and if they was gins and sawmills, I never knowed there was that many and I never seen any that big, and where they got enough cotton and logs to run um I don't know.

Then I see Memphis. I knowed I was right this time. It was standing up into the air. It looked like about a dozen whole towns bigger than Jefferson was set up on one edge in a field, standing up into the air higher than ara hill in all Yoknapatawpha County. Then we was in it, with the bus stopping ever' few feet, it seemed like to me, and cars rushing past on both sides of it and the street crowded with folks from ever'where in town that day, until I didn't see how there could 'a' been nobody left in Mis'sippi a-tall to even sell me a bus ticket, let alone write out no case histories. Then the bus stopped. It was another bus deepo, a heap bigger than the one in Jefferson. And I said, "All right. Where do folks join the Army?"

"What?" the bus feller said.

And I said it again, "Where do folks join the Army?"

"Oh," he said. Then he told me how to get there. I was afraid at first I wouldn't ketch on how to do in a town big as Memphis. But I caught on all right. I never had to ask but twice more. Then I was there, and I was durn glad to git out of all them rushing cars and shoving folks and all that racket for a spell, and I thought, It won't be long now, and I thought how if there was any kind of a crowd there that had done already joined the Army, too, Pete would likely see me before I seen him. And so I walked into the room. And Pete wasn't there.

He wasn't even there. There was a soldier with a big arrerhead on his sleeve, writing, and two fellers standing in front of him, and there was some more folks there, I reckon. It seems to me I remember some more folks there.

I went to the table where the soldier was writing, and I said, "Where's Pete?" and he looked up and I said, "My brother. Pete Grier. Where is he?"

"What?" the soldier said. "Who?"

And I told him again. "He joined the Army yestiddy. He's going to Pearl Harbor. So am I. I want to ketch him. Where you all got him?" Now they were all looking at me, but I never paid them no mind. "Come on," I said. "Where is he?"

The soldier had quit writing. He had both hands spraddled out on the table. "Oh," he said. "You're going, too, hah?"

"Yes," I said. "They got to have wood and water. I can chop it and tote it. Come on. Where's Pete?"

The soldier stood up. "Who let you in here?" he said. "Go on. Beat it."

I be dog if he couldn't move faster than the bus feller even. He never come over the table, he come around it, he was on me almost before I knowed it, so that I jest had time to jump back and whup out my pocketknife and snap it open and hit one lick, and he hollered and jumped back and grabbed one hand with the other and stood there cussing and hollering.

One of the other fellers grabbed me from behind, and I hit at him with the knife, but I couldn't reach him.

Then both of the fellers had me from behind, and then another soldier come out of a door at the back. He had a belt with a britching strop over one shoulder.

"What the hell is this?" he said.

"That little son cut me with a knife!" the first soldier hollered. When he said that, I tried to get at him again, but both them fellers was holding me, two against one, and the soldier with the backing strop said, "Here, here. Put your knife up, feller. None of us are armed. A man don't knife-fight folks that are barehanded." I could begin to hear him then. He sounded jest like Pete talked to me. "Let him go," he said. They let me go. "Now what's all the trouble about?" And I told him. "I see," he said. "And you come up to see if he was all right before he left."

"No," I said. "I came to—"

But he had already turned to where the first soldier was wropping a handkerchief around his hand.

"Have you got him?" he said. The first soldier went back to the table and looked at some papers.

"Here he is," he said. "He enlisted yestiddy. He's in a detachment leaving this morning for Little Rock." He had a watch stropped on his arm. He looked at it. "The train leaves in about fifty minutes. If I know country boys, they're probably all down there at the station right now."

"Get him up here," the one with the backing strop said. "Phone the station. Tell the porter to get him a cab. And you come with me," he said.

It was another office behind that un, with jest a table and some chairs. We set there while the soldier smoked, and it wasn't long; I knowed Pete's feet soon as I heard them. Then the first soldier opened the door and Pete come in. He never had no soldier clothes on. He looked jest like he did when he got on the bus yestiddy morning, except it seemed to me like it was at least a week, so much had happened, and I had done had to do so much traveling. He come in and there he was, looking at me like he hadn't never left home, except that here we was in Memphis, on the way to Pearl Harbor.

And I told him, "You got to have wood and water to cook with. I can chop it and tote it for you-all."

"No," Pete said. "You're going back home."

"No, Pete," I said. "I got to go too. I got to. It hurts my heart, Pete."

"No," Pete said. He looked at the soldier. "I jest don't know what could have happened to him, lootenant," he said. "He never drawed a knife on anybody before in his life." He looked at me. "What did you do it for?"

"I don't know," I said. "I jest had to. I jest had to git here. I jest had to find you."

"Well, don't you never do it again, you hear?" Pete said. "You put that knife in your pocket and you keep it there. If I ever again hear of you drawing it on anybody, I'm coming back from wherever I am at and whup the fire out of you. You hear me?"

"I would pure cut a throat if it would bring you back to stay," I said. "Pete," I said. "Pete."

"No," Pete said. Now his voice wasn't hard and quick no more, it was almost quiet, and I knowed now I wouldn't never change him. "You must go home. You must look after maw, and I am depending on you to look after my ten acres. I want you to go back home. Today. Do you hear?"

"I hear," I said.

"Can he get back home by himself?" the soldier said.

"He come up here by himself," Pete said.

"I can get back, I reckon," I said. "I don't live in but one place. I don't reckon it's moved."

Pete taken a dollar out of his pocket and give it to me.

"That'll buy your bus ticket right to our mailbox," he said. "I want you to mind the lootenant. He'll send you to the bus. And you go back home and you take care of maw and look after my ten acres and keep that durn knife in your pocket. You hear me?"

"Yes, Pete," I said.

"All right," Pete said. "Now I got to go." He put his hand on my head again. But this time he never wrung my neck. He just laid his hand on my head a minute. And then I be dog if he didn't lean down and kiss me, and I heard his feet and then the door, and I never looked up and that was all, me setting there, rubbing the place where Pete kissed me and the soldier throwed back in his chair, looking out the window and coughing. He reached into his pocket and handed something to me without looking around. It was a piece of chewing gum.

"Much obliged," I said. "Well, I reckon I might as well start back. I got a right fer piece to go."

"Wait," the soldier said. Then he telephoned again and I said again I better start back, and he said again, "Wait. Remember what Pete told you."

So we waited, and then another lady come in, old, too, in a fur coat, too, but she smelled all right, she never had no artermatic writing pen nor no case history neither. She come in and the soldier got up, and she looked around quick until she saw me, and come and put her hand on my shoulder light and quick and easy as maw herself might 'a' done it.

"Come on," she said. "Let's go home to dinner."

"Nome," I said. "I got to ketch the bus to Jefferson."

"I know. There's plenty of time. We'll go home and eat dinner first."

She had a car. And now we was right down in the middle of all them other cars. We was almost under the busses, and all them crowds of people on the street close enough to where I could have talked to them if I had knowed who they was. After a while she stopped the car. "Here we are," she said, and I looked at it, and if all that was her house, she sho had a big family. But all of it wasn't. We crossed a hall with trees growing in it and went into a little room without nothing in it but a nigger dressed up in a uniform a heap shinier than them soldiers had, and the nigger shut the door, and then I hollered, "Look out!" and grabbed, but it was all right; that whole little room jest went right on up and stopped and the door opened and we was in another hall, and the lady unlocked a door and we went in, and there was another soldier, a old feller, with a britching strop, too, and a silver-colored bird on each shoulder.

"Here we are," the lady said. "This is Colonel McKellogg. Now, what would you like for dinner?"

"I reckon I'll jest have some ham and eggs and coffee," I said.

She had done started to pick up the telephone. She stopped. "Coffee?" she said. "When did you start drinking coffee?"

"I don't know," I said. "I reckon it was before I could remember."

"You're about eight, aren't you?" she said.

"Nome," I said. "I'm eight and ten months. Going on eleven months."

She telephoned then. Then we set there and I told them how Pete had jest left that morning for Pearl Harbor and I had aimed to go with him, but I would have to go back home to take care of maw and look after Pete's ten acres, and she said how they had a little boy about my size, too, in a school in the East. Then a nigger, another one, in a short kind of shirttail coat, rolled a kind of wheelbarrer in. It had my ham and eggs and a glass of milk and a piece of pie, too, and I thought I was hungry. But when I taken the first bite I found out I couldn't swallow it, and I got up quick.

"I got to go," I said.

"Wait," she said.

"I got to go," I said.

"Just a minute," she said. "I've already telephoned for the

car. It won't be but a minute now. Can't you drink the milk even? Or maybe some of your coffee?"

"Nome," I said. "I ain't hungry. I'll eat when I git home." Then the telephone rung. She never even answered it.

"There," she said. "There's the car." And we went back down in that 'ere little moving room with the dressed-up nigger. This time it was a big car with a soldier driving it. I got into the front with him. She give the soldier a dollar. "He might get hungry," she said. "Try to find a decent place for him."

"O.K., Mrs. McKellogg," the soldier said.

Then we was gone again. And now I could see Memphis good, bright in the sunshine, while we was swinging around it. And first thing I knowed, we was back on the same highway the bus run on this morning—the patches of stores and them big gins and sawmills, and Memphis running on for miles, it seemed like to me, before it begun to give out. Then we was running again between the fields and woods, running fast now, and except for that soldier, it was like I hadn't never been to Memphis a-tall. We was going fast now. At this rate, before I knowed it we would be home again, and I thought about me riding up to Frenchman's Bend in this big car with a soldier running it, and all of a sudden I begun to cry. I never knowed I was fixing to, and I couldn't stop it. I set there by that soldier, crying. We was going fast.

WILLIAM FAULKNER, born in 1897, came from an established Mississippi family. His great-grandfather was a colonel in the Confederate army, a plantation owner, and a novelist; and from childhood William Faulkner wanted to be a writer, too. He attended the University of Mississippi for about a year, then was in and out of various jobs in his home town, Oxford.

Mississippi supplied his books' locale—the mythical Yoknapatawpha County—and his great-grandfather and other citizens of Oxford became their characters. *Sartoris, The Sound and the Fury, Sanctuary,* and *Absalom, Absalom!* are some of his best-known novels, and in them he created an entire world, peopled it with families, gave it a history. Many of his short stories are masterpieces, including the famous "The Bear" and "Two Soldiers," and display enormous variety of subject and technique.

Faulkner worked in Hollywood at times as a writer for films, and the State Department sent him on cultural missions to France, Japan, and Brazil. But mostly he lived in Mississippi with his wife and children. In 1949 he was given the Nobel Prize. One of the world's major writers of fiction, Faulkner died in 1962.

SAKI

Cousin Teresa

Basset Harrowcluff returned to the home of his fathers, after an absence of four years, distinctly well pleased with himself. He was only thirty-one, but he had put in some useful service in an out-of-the-way, though not unimportant, corner of the world. He had quieted a province, kept open a trade route, enforced the tradition of respect which is worth the ransom of many kings in out-of-the-way regions, and done the whole business on rather less expenditure than would be requisite for organizing a charity in the home country. In Whitehall and places where they think, they doubtless thought well of him. It was not inconceivable, his father allowed himself to imagine, that Basset's name might figure in the next list of Honors.

Basset was inclined to be rather contemptuous of his half-brother, Lucas, whom he found feverishly engrossed in the same medley of elaborate futilities that had claimed his whole time and energies, such as they were, four years ago, and almost as far back before that as he could remember. It was the contempt of the man of action for the man of activities, and it was probably reciprocated. Lucas was an over-well nourished individual, some nine years Basset's senior, with a coloring that would have been accepted as a sign of intensive culture in an asparagus, but probably meant in this case mere abstention from exercise. His hair and forehead furnished a recessional note in a personality that was in all other respects obtrusive and assertive. There was certainly no Semitic blood in Lucas's parentage, but his appearance contrived to convey at least a suggestion of Jewish extraction. Clovis Sangrail, who knew most of his associates by sight, said it was undoubtedly a case of protective mimicry.

Two days after Basset's return, Lucas frisked in to lunch in a state of twittering excitement that could not be restrained even for the immediate consideration of soup, but had to be verbally discharged in spluttering competition with mouthfuls of vermicelli.

"I've got hold of an idea for something immense," he babbled, "something that is simply It."

Basset gave a short laugh that would have done equally well as a snort, if one had wanted to make the exchange. His half-brother was in the habit of discovering futilities that were "simply It" at frequently recurring intervals. The discovery generally meant that he flew up to town, preceded by glowingly worded telegrams, to see some one connected with the stage or the publishing world, got together one or two momentous luncheon parties, flitted in and out of "Gambrinus" for one or two evenings, and returned home with an air of subdued importance and the asparagus tint slightly intensified. The great idea was generally forgotten a few weeks later in the excitement of some new discovery.

"The inspiration came to me whilst I was dressing," announced Lucas; "it will be *the* thing in the next music-hall *revue*. All London will go mad over it. It's just a couplet; of course there will be other words, but they won't matter. Listen:

Cousin Teresa takes out Caesar,
Fido, Jock, and the big borzoi.

A lilting, catchy sort of refrain, you see, and big-drum business on the two syllables of bor-zoi. It's immense. And I've thought out all the business of it; the singer will sing the first verse alone, then during the second verse Cousin Teresa will walk through, followed by four wooden dogs on wheels; Caesar will be an Irish terrier, Fido a black poodle, Jock a fox-terrier, and the borzoi, of course, will be a borzoi. During the third verse Cousin Teresa will come on alone, and the dogs will be drawn across by themselves from the opposite wing; then Cousin Teresa will catch on to the singer and go off-stage in one direction, while dogs' procession goes off in the other, crossing *en route,* which is always very effective. There'll be a lot of applause there, and for the fourth verse Cousin Teresa will come on in sables and the dogs will all have coats on. Then I've got a great idea for the fifth verse; each of the dogs will be led on by a Nut, and Cousin Teresa will come on from the opposite side, crossing *en route,* always effective, and then she turns round and leads the whole lot of them off on a string, and all the time every one singing like mad:

Cousin Teresa takes out Caesar
Fido, Jock, and the big borzoi.

Tum-Tum! Drum business on the two last syllables. I'm so excited, I shan't sleep a wink tonight. I'm off tomorrow by the ten-fifteen. I've wired to Hermanova to lunch with me."

If any of the rest of the family felt any excitement over the creation of Cousin Teresa, they were signally successful in concealing the fact.

"Poor Lucas does take his silly little ideas seriously," said Colonel Harrowcluff afterwards in the smoking-room.

"Yes," said his younger son, in a slightly less tolerant tone, "in a day or two he'll come back and tell us that his sensational masterpiece is above the heads of the public, and in about three weeks' time he'll be wild with enthusiasm over a scheme to dramatize the poems of Herrick or something equally promising."

And then an extraordinary thing befell. In defiance of all precedent Lucas's glowing anticipations were justified and endorsed by the course of events. If Cousin Teresa was above the heads of the public, the public heroically adapted itself to her altitude. Introduced as an experiment at a dull moment in a new *revue,* the success of the item was unmistakable; the calls were so insistent and uproarious that even Lucas's ample devisings of additional "business" scarcely sufficed to keep pace with the demand. Packed houses on successive evenings confirmed the verdict of the first night audience, stalls and boxes filled significantly just before the turn came on, and emptied significantly after the last *encore* had been given. The manager tearfully acknowledged that Cousin Teresa was It. Stage hands and supers and program sellers acknowledged it to one another without the least reservation. The name of the *revue* dwindled to secondary importance, and vast letters of electric blue blazoned the words "Cousin Teresa" from the front of the great palace of pleasure. And of course, the magic of the famous refrain laid its spell all over the Metropolis. Restaurant proprietors were obliged to provide the members of their orchestras with painted wooden dogs on wheels, in order that the much-demanded and always conceded melody should be rendered with the necessary spectacular effects, and the crash of bottles and forks on the tables at the mention of the big borzoi usually drowned the sincerest efforts of drum or cymbals. Nowhere and at no time could one get away from the double thump that brought up the rear of the refrain; revelers reeling home at night banged it on doors and hoardings, milkmen clashed their cans to its cadence, messenger boys hit smaller messenger boys resounding double smacks on the same principle. And the more thoughtful circles of the great city were not deaf to the claims and significance of the popular melody. An enterprising and emancipated preacher discoursed from his pulpit on the inner meaning of "Cousin Teresa," and Lucas Harrowcluff was invited to lecture on the subject of his great achievement to members of the Young Men's Endeavor League, the Nine Arts Club, and other learned and willing-to-learn bodies. In Society it seemed to be the one thing people really cared to talk about; men and women of middle age and average education might be seen together in corners earnestly discussing, not the question whether Serbia should have an outlet on the Adriatic, or the possibilities of a British success in international polo contests, but the more absorbing topic of the problematic Aztec or Nilotic origin of the Teresa *motif.*

"Politics and patriotism are so boring and so out of date," said a revered lady who had some pretensions to oracular utterance; "we are too cosmopolitan nowadays to be really moved by them. That is why one welcomes an intelligible production like 'Cousin Teresa,' that has a genuine message for one. One can't understand the message all at once, of course, but one felt from the very first that it was there. I've been to see it eighteen times and I'm going again tomorrow and on Thursday. One can't see it often enough."

"It would be rather a popular move if we gave this Harrowcluff person a knighthood or something of the sort," said the Minister reflectively.

"Which Harrowcluff?" asked his secretary.

"Which? There is only one, isn't there?" said the Minister; "the 'Cousin Teresa' man, of course. I think every one would be pleased if we knighted him. Yes, you can put him down on the list of certainties—under the letter L."

"The letter L," said the secretary, who was new to his job: "does that stand for Liberalism or liberality?"

Most of the recipients of Ministerial favor were expected to qualify in both of those subjects.

"Literature," explained the Minister.

And thus, after a fashion, Colonel Harrowcluff's expectation of seeing his son's name in the list of Honors was gratified.

SAKI (Hector Hugh Munro) had a childhood dominated by two tyrannical maiden aunts, much like the unhappy lives of the little boys in his haunting stories "Sredni Vashtar" and "The Lumber Room." He was born in 1870 in Burma, where his father was inspector-general of police; but in 1872 he, his brother, and his sister were sent to live with the aunts in England.

He began writing as a journalist—both satirist and foreign correspondent. As a correspondent he spent six years in the Balkans, Warsaw, St. Petersburg, and Paris. When he was 38, he settled in London to write the Saki stories and a novel, *The Unbearable Bassington.* In 1914, when World War I broke out, he went to France as a corporal. He was killed by a sniper's bullet in 1916.

Saki is most remembered for his eerie tales of childhood and for his clever-young-man heroes, Reginald and Clovis. "Cousin Teresa," one of Saki's most lighthearted stories, is about the triumph of silliness over diligence, a theme in much of his work, where childlike games defeat all that is pretentious and dull in the adult world: a final revenge on the aunts.

THOMAS HARDY

A Tragedy of Two Ambitions

The shouts of the village-boys came in at the window, accompanied by broken laughter from loungers at the inn-door; but the brothers Halborough worked on.

They were sitting in a bedroom of the master-millwright's house, engaged in the untutored reading of Greek and Latin. It was no tale of Homeric blows and knocks, Argonautic voyaging, or Theban family woe that inflamed their imaginations and spurred them onward. They were plodding away at the Greek Testament, immersed in a chapter of the idiomatic and difficult Epistle to the Hebrews.

The Dog-day sun in its decline reached the low ceiling with slanting sides, and the shadows of the great goat's-willow swayed and interchanged upon the walls like a spectral army maneuvering. The open casement which admitted the remoter sounds now brought the voice of someone close at hand. It was their sister, a pretty girl of fourteen, who stood in the court below.

"I can see the tops of your heads! What's the use of staying up there? I like you not to go out with the street-boys; but do come and play with me!"

They treated her as an inadequate interlocutor, and put her off with some slight word. She went away disappointed. Presently there was a dull noise of heavy footsteps at the side of the house, and one of the brothers sat up. "I fancy I hear him coming," he murmured, his eyes on the window.

A man in the light drab clothes of an old-fashioned country tradesman approached from round the corner, reeling as he came. The elder son flushed with anger, rose from his books, and descended the stairs. The younger sat on, till, after the lapse of a few minutes, his brother re-entered the room.

"Did Rosa see him?"

"No."

"Nor anybody?"

"No."

"What have you done with him?"

"He's in the straw-shed. I got him in with some trouble, and he has fallen asleep. I thought this would be the explanation of his absence! No stones dressed for Miller Kench, the great wheel of the saw-mills waiting for new float-boards, even the poor folk not able to get their wagons wheeled."

"What *is* the use of poring over this!" said the younger, shutting up Donnegan's *Lexicon* with a slap. "O if we had only been able to keep mother's nine hundred pounds, what we could have done!"

"How well she had estimated the sum necessary! Four hundred and fifty each, she thought. And I have no doubt that we could have managed, with care."

This loss of the nine hundred pounds was the thorn of their crown. It was a sum which their mother had amassed with great exertion and self-denial, by adding to a chance legacy such other small amounts as she could lay hands on from time to time; and she had intended with the hoard to indulge the dear wish of her heart—that of sending her sons, Joshua and Cornelius, to one of the Universities, having been informed that from four hundred to four hundred and fifty each might carry them through their terms with such great economy as she knew she could trust them to practice. But she had died a year or two before this time, worn out by too keen a strain towards these ends; and the money, coming unreservedly into the hands of their father, had been nearly dissipated. With its exhaustion went all opportunity and hope of a university degree for the sons.

"It drives me mad when I think of it," said Joshua, the elder. "And here we work and work in our own bungling way, and the utmost we can hope for is a term of years as national schoolmasters, and possible admission to a Theological college, and ordination as despised licentiates."

The anger of the elder was reflected as simple sadness in the face of the other. "We can preach the Gospel as well without a hood on our surplices as with one," he said with feeble consolation.

"Preach the Gospel—true," said Joshua with a slight pursing of mouth. "But we can't rise!"

"Let us make the best of it, and grind on."

The other was silent, and they drearily bent over their books.

The cause of all this gloom, the millwright Halborough,

now snoring in the shed, had been a thriving master-machinist, notwithstanding his free and careless disposition, till a taste for a more than adequate quantity of strong liquor took hold of him; since when his habits had interfered with his business sadly. Already millers went elsewhere for their gear, and only one set of hands was now kept going, though there were formerly two. Already he found a difficulty in meeting his men at the week's end, and though they had been reduced in number there was barely enough work to do for those who remained.

The sun dropped lower and vanished, the shouts of the village ceased to resound, darkness cloaked the students' bedroom, and all the scene outwardly breathed peace. None knew of the fevered youthful ambitions that throbbed in two breasts within the quiet creeper-covered walls of the millwright's house.

In a few months the brothers left the village of their birth to enter themselves as students in a training college for schoolmasters; first having placed their young sister Rosa under as efficient a tuition at a fashionable watering-place as the means at their disposal could command.

2

A man in semi-clerical dress was walking along the road which led from the railway-station into a provincial town. As he walked he read persistently, only looking up once now and then to see that he was keeping on the foot-track and to avoid other passengers. At those moments, whoever had known the former students at the millwright's would have perceived that one of them, Joshua Halborough, was the peripatetic reader here.

What had been simple force in the youth's face was energized judgment in the man's. His character was gradually writing itself out in his countenance. That he was watching his own career with deeper and deeper interest, that he continually "heard his days before him," and cared to hear little else, might have been hazarded from what was seen there. His ambitions were, in truth, passionate, yet controlled; so that the germs of many more plans than ever blossomed to maturity had place in him; and forward visions were kept purposely in twilight, to avoid distraction.

Events so far had been encouraging. Shortly after assuming the mastership of his first school he had obtained an introduction to the Bishop of a diocese far from his native county, who had looked upon him as a promising young man and taken him in hand. He was now in the second year of his residence at the theological college of the cathedral-town, and would soon be presented for ordination.

He entered the town, turned into a back street, and then into a yard, keeping his book before him till he set foot under the arch of the latter place. Round the arch was written "National School," and the stonework of the jambs was worn away as nothing but boys and the waves of ocean will wear it. He was soon amid the sing-song accents of the scholars.

His brother Cornelius, who was the schoolmaster here, laid down the pointer with which he was directing attention to the Capes of Europe, and came forward.

"That's his brother Jos!" whispered one of the sixth-standard boys. "He's going to be a pa'son. He's now at college."

"Corney is going to be one too, when he's saved enough money," said another.

After greeting his brother, whom he had not seen for several months, the junior began to explain his system of teaching geography.

But Halborough the elder took no interest in the subject. "How about your own studies?" he asked. "Did you get the books I sent?"

Cornelius had received them, and he related what he was doing.

"Mind you work in the morning. What time do you get up?"

The younger replied: "Half-past five."

"Half-past four is not a minute too soon this time of the year. There is no time like the morning for construing. I don't know why, but when I feel even too dreary to read a novel I can translate—there is something mechanical about it I suppose. Now, Cornelius, you are rather behindhand, and have some heavy reading before you if you mean to get out of this next Christmas."

"I am afraid I have."

"We must soon sound the Bishop. I am sure you will get a title without difficulty when he has heard all. The sub-dean, the principal of my college, says that the best plan will be for you to come there when his lordship is present at an examination, and he'll get you a personal interview with him. Mind you make a good impression upon him. I found in my case that that was everything, and doctrine almost nothing. You'll do for a deacon, Corney, if not for a priest."

The younger remained thoughtful. "Have you heard from Rosa lately?" he asked; "I had a letter this morning."

"Yes. The little minx writes rather too often. She is homesick—though Brussels must be an attractive place enough. But she must make the most of her time over there. I thought a year would be enough for her, after that high-class school at Sandbourne, but I have decided to give her two, and make a good job of it, expensive as the establishment is."

Their two rather harsh faces had softened directly they began to speak of their sister, whom they loved more ambitiously than they loved themselves.

"But where is the money to come from, Joshua?"

"I have already got it." He looked round, and finding that some boys were near withdrew a few steps. "I have borrowed it at five per cent from the farmer who used to occupy the farm next our field. You remember him."

"But about paying him?"

"I shall pay him by degrees out of my stipend. No, Cornelius, it was no use to do the thing by halves. She promises to be a most attractive, not to say beautiful, girl. I have seen that for years; and if her face is not her fortune, her face and her brains together will be, if I observe and contrive aright. That she should be, every inch of her, an accomplished and refined woman, was indispensable for the fulfilment of her destiny, and for moving onwards and upwards with us; and she'll do it, you will see. I'd half starve myself rather than take her away from that school now."

They looked round the school they were in. To Cornelius it was natural and familiar enough, but to Joshua, with his limited human sympathies, who had just dropped in from a superior sort of place, the sight jarred unpleasantly, as being that of something he had left behind. "I shall be glad when you are out of this," he said, "and in your pulpit, and well through your first sermon."

"You may as well say inducted into my fat living, while you are about it."

"Ah, well—don't think lightly of the Church. There's a fine work for any man of energy in the Church, as you'll find," he said fervidly. "Torrents of infidelity to be stemmed, new views of old subjects to be expounded, truths in spirit to be substituted for truths in the letter. . . ." He lapsed into reverie with the vision of his career, persuading himself that it was ardor for Christianity which spurred him on, and not pride of place. He had shouldered a body of doctrine, and was prepared to defend it tooth and nail, solely for the honor and glory that warriors win.

"If the Church is elastic, and stretches to the shape of the time, she'll last, I suppose," said Cornelius. "If not—. Only think, I bought a copy of Paley's *Evidences,* best edition, broad margins, excellent preservation, at a bookstall the other day for —ninepence; and I thought that at this rate Christianity must be in rather a bad way."

"No, no!" said the other almost angrily. "It only shows that such defenses are no longer necessary. Men's eyes can see the truth without extraneous assistance. Besides, we are in for Christianity, and must stick to her whether or no. I am just now going right through Pusey's *Library of the Fathers.*"

"You'll be a bishop, Joshua, before you have done!"

"Ah!" said the other bitterly, shaking his head. "Perhaps I might have been—I might have been! But where is my D.D. or LL.D.; and how be a bishop without that kind of appendage? Archbishop Tillotson was the son of a Sowerby clothier, but he was sent to Clare College. To hail Oxford or Cambridge as *alma mater* is not for me—for us! My God! when I think of what we should have been—what fair promise has been blighted by that cursed, worthless—"

"Hush, hush! . . . But I feel it, too, as much as you. I have seen it more forcibly lately. You should have obtained your degree long before this time—possibly fellowship—and I should have been on my way to mine."

"Don't talk of it," said the other. "We must do the best we can."

They looked out of the window sadly, through the dusty panes, so high up that only the sky was visible. By degrees the haunting trouble loomed again, and Cornelius broke the silence with a whisper: "He has called on me!"

The living pulses died on Joshua's face, which grew arid as a clinker. "When was that?" he asked quickly.

"Last week."

"How did he get here—so many miles?"

"Came by railway. He came to ask for money."

"Ah!"

"He says he will call on you."

Joshua replied resignedly. The theme of their conversation spoiled his buoyancy for that afternoon. He returned in the evening, Cornelius accompanying him to the station; but he did not read in the train which took him back to the Fountall Theological College, as he had done on the way out. That ineradicable trouble still remained as a squalid spot in the expanse of his life. He sat with the other students in the cathedral choir next day; and the recollection of the trouble obscured the purple splendor thrown by the panes upon the floor.

It was afternoon. All was as still in the Close as a cathedral-green can be between the Sunday services, and the incessant cawing of the rooks was the only sound. Joshua Halborough had finished his ascetic lunch, and had gone into the library, where he stood for a few moments looking out of the large window facing the green. He saw walking slowly across it a man in a fustian coat and a battered white hat with a much-ruffled nap, having upon his arm a tall gypsy-woman wearing long brass earrings. The man was staring quizzically at the west front of the cathedral, and Halborough recognized in him the form and features of his father. Who the woman was he knew not. Almost as soon as Joshua became conscious of these things, the sub-dean, who was also the principal of the college, and of whom the young man stood in more awe than of the Bishop himself, emerged from the gate and entered a path across the Close. The pair met the dignitary, and to Joshua's horror his father turned and addressed the sub-dean.

What passed between them he could not tell. But as he stood in a cold sweat he saw his father place his hand familiarly on the sub-dean's shoulder; the shrinking response of the latter, and his quick withdrawal, told his feeling. The woman seemed to say nothing, but when the sub-dean had passed by they came on towards the college gate.

Halborough flew along the corridor and out at a side door, so as to intercept them before they could reach the front entrance, for which they were making. He caught them behind a clump of laurel.

"By Jerry, here's the very chap! Well, you're a fine fellow, Jos, never to send your father as much as a twist o' baccy on such an occasion, and to leave him to travel all these miles to find ye out!"

"First, who is this?" said Joshua Halborough with pale dignity, waving his hands towards the buxom woman with the great earrings.

"Dammy, the mis'ess! Your step-mother! Didn't you know I'd married? She helped me home from market one night, and we came to terms, and struck the bargain. Didn't we, Selinar?"

"Oi, by the great Lord an' we did!" simpered the lady.

"Well, what sort of a place is this you are living in?" asked the millwright. "A kind of house-of-correction, apparently?"

Joshua listened abstractedly, his features set to resignation. Sick at heart he was going to ask them if they were in want of any necessary, any meal, when his father cut him short by saying, "Why, we've called to ask ye to come round and take pot-luck with us at the Cock-and-Bottle, where we've put up for the day, on our way to see mis'ess's friends at Binegar Fair, where they'll be lying under canvas for a night or two. As for the victuals at the Cock I can't testify to 'em at all; but for the drink, they've the rarest drop of Old Tom that I've tasted for many a year."

"Thanks; but I am a teetotaller; and I have lunched," said Joshua, who could fully believe his father's testimony to the gin, from the odor of his breath. "You see we have to observe regular habits here; and I couldn't be seen at the Cock-and-Bottle just now."

"O dammy, then don't come, your reverence. Perhaps you won't mind standing treat for those who can be seen there?"

"Not a penny," said the younger firmly. "You've had enough already."

"Thank you for nothing. By the bye, who was that spindle-legged, shoe-buckled parson feller we met by now? He seemed to think we should poison him!"

Joshua remarked coldly that it was the principal of his college, guardedly inquiring, "Did you tell him whom you were come to see?"

His father did not reply. He and his strapping gypsy wife—if she were his wife—stayed no longer, and disappeared in the direction of the High Street. Joshua Halborough went back to the library. Determined as was his nature, he wept hot tears upon the books, and was immeasurably more wretched that afternoon than the unwelcome millwright. In the evening he sat down and wrote a letter to his brother, in which, after stating what had happened, and expatiating upon this new disgrace in the gypsy wife, he propounded a plan for raising money sufficient to induce the couple to emigrate to Canada. "It is our only chance," he said. "The case as it stands is maddening. For a successful painter, sculptor, musician, author, who takes society by storm, it is no drawback, it is sometimes even a romantic recommendation, to hail from outcasts and profligates. But for a clergyman of the Church of England! Cornelius, it is fatal! To succeed in the Church, people must believe in you, first of all, as a gentleman, secondly as a man of means, thirdly as a scholar, fourthly as a preacher, fifthly, perhaps, as a Christian—but always first as a gentleman, with all their heart and soul and strength. I would have faced the fact of being a small machinist's son, and have taken my chance, if he'd been in any sense respectable and decent. The essence of Christianity is humility, and by the help of God I would have brazened it out. But this terrible vagabondage and disreputable connection! If he does not accept my terms and leave the country, it will extinguish us and kill me. For how can we live, and relinquish our high aim, and bring down our dear sister Rosa to the level of a gypsy's stepdaughter?"

3

There was excitement in the parish of Narrobourne one day. The congregation had just come out from morning service, and the whole conversation was of the new curate, Mr. Halborough, who had officiated for the first time, in the absence of the rector.

Never before had the feeling of the villagers approached a level which could be called excitement on such a matter as this.

The droning which had been the rule in that quiet old place for a century seemed ended at last. They repeated the text to each other as a refrain: "O Lord, be thou my helper!" Not within living memory till today had the subject of the sermon formed the topic of conversation from the church door to churchyard gate, to the exclusion of personal remarks on those who had been present, and on the week's news in general.

The thrilling periods of the preacher hung about their minds all that day. The parish being steeped in indifferentism, it happened that when the youths and maidens, middle-aged and old people, who had attended church that morning, recurred as by a fascination to what Halborough had said, they did so more or less indirectly, and even with the subterfuge of a light laugh that was not real, so great was their shyness under the novelty of their sensations.

What was more curious than that these unconventional villagers should have been excited by a preacher of a new school after forty years of familiarity with the old hand who had had charge of their souls, was the effect of Halborough's address upon the occupants of the manorhouse pew, including the owner of the estate. These thought they knew how to discount the mere sensational sermon, how to minimize flash oratory to its bare proportions; but they had yielded like the rest of the assembly to the charm of the newcomer.

Mr. Fellmer, the landowner, was a young widower, whose mother, still in the prime of life, had returned to her old position in the family mansion since the death of her son's wife in the year after her marriage, at the birth of a fragile little girl. From the date of his loss to the present time, Fellmer had led an inactive existence in the seclusion of the parish; a lack of motive seemed to leave him listless. He had gladly reinstated his mother in the gloomy house, and his main occupation now lay in stewarding his estate, which was not large. Mrs. Fellmer, who had sat beside him under Halborough this morning, was a cheerful, straightforward woman, who did her marketing and her almsgiving in person, was fond of old-fashioned flowers, and walked about the village on very wet days visiting the parishioners. These, the only two great ones of Narrobourne, were impressed by Joshua's eloquence as much as the cottagers.

Halborough had been briefly introduced to them on his arrival some days before, and, their interest being kindled, they waited a few moments till he came out of the vestry, to walk down the churchyard-path with him. Mrs. Fellmer spoke warmly of the sermon, of the good fortune of the parish in his advent, and hoped he had found comfortable quarters.

Halborough, faintly flushing, said that he had obtained very fair lodgings in the roomy house of a farmer, whom he named.

She feared he would find it very lonely, especially in the evenings, and hoped they would see a good deal of him. When would he dine with them? Could he not come that day—it must be so dull for him the first Sunday evening in country lodgings?

Halborough replied that it would give him much pleasure, but that he feared he must decline. "I am not altogether alone," he said. "My sister, who has just returned from Brussels, and who felt, as you do, that I should be rather dismal by myself, has accompanied me hither to stay a few days till she has put my rooms in order and set me going. She was too fatigued to come to church, and is waiting for me now at the farm."

"Oh, but bring your sister—that will be still better! I shall be delighted to know her. How I wish I had been aware! Do you tell her, please, that we had no idea of her presence."

Halborough assured Mrs. Fellmer that he would certainly bear the message; but as to her coming he was not so sure. The real truth was, however, that the matter would be decided by him, Rosa having an almost filial respect for his wishes. But he was uncertain as to the state of her wardrobe, and had determined that she should not enter the manorhouse at a disadvantage that evening, when there would probably be plenty of opportunities in the future of her doing so becomingly.

He walked to the farm in long strides. This, then, was the outcome of his first morning's work as curate here. Things had gone fairly well with him. He had been ordained; he was in a comfortable parish, where he would exercise almost sole supervision, the rector being infirm. He had made a deep impression at starting, and the absence of a hood seemed to have done him no harm. Moreover, by considerable persuasion and payment, his father and the dark woman had been shipped off to Canada, where they were not likely to interfere greatly with his interests.

Rosa came out to meet him. "Ah! you should have gone to church like a good girl," he said.

"Yes—I wished I had afterwards. But I do so hate church as a rule that even your preaching was underestimated in my mind. It was too bad of me!"

The girl who spoke thus playfully was fair, tall, and sylph-like, in a muslin dress, and with just the coquettish *désinvolture* which an English girl brings home from abroad, and loses again after a few months of native life. Joshua was the reverse of playful; the world was too important a concern for him to indulge in light moods. He told her in decided, practical phraseology of the invitation.

"Now, Rosa, we must go—that's settled—if you've a dress that can be made fit to wear all on the hop like this. You didn't, of course, think of bringing an evening dress to such an out-of-the-way place?"

But Rosa had come from the wrong city to be caught napping in those matters. "Yes, I did," said she. "One never knows what may turn up."

"Well done! Then off we go at seven."

The evening drew on, and at dusk they started on foot, Rosa pulling up the edge of her skirt under her cloak out of the way of the dews, so that it formed a great wind-bag all round her, and carrying her satin shoes under her arm. Joshua would not let her wait till she got indoors before changing them, as she proposed, but insisted on her performing that operation under a tree, so that they might enter as if they had not walked. He was nervously formal about such trifles, while Rosa took the whole proceeding—walk, dressing, dinner, and all—as a pastime. To Joshua it was a serious step in life.

A more unexpected kind of person for a curate's sister was never presented at a dinner. The surprise of Mrs. Fellmer was unconcealed. She had looked forward to a Dorcas, or Martha, or Rhoda at the outside, and a shade of misgiving crossed her face. It was possible that, had the young lady accompanied by her brother to church, there would have been no dining at Narrobourne House that day.

Not so with the young widower, her son. He resembled a sleeper who had awaked in a summer noon expecting to find it only dawn. He could scarcely help stretching his arms and yawning in their faces, so strong was his sense of being suddenly aroused to an unforeseen thing. When they had sat down to table he at first talked to Rosa somewhat with the air of a ruler in the land; but the woman lurking in the acquaintance soon brought him to his level, and the girl from Brussels saw him looking at her mouth, her hands, her contour, as if he could not quite comprehend how they got created; then he dropped into the more satisfactory stage which discerns no particulars.

He talked but little; she said much. The homeliness of the Fellmers, to her view, though they were regarded with such awe down here, quite disembarrassed her. The squire had become so unpracticed, had dropped so far into the shade during the last year or so of his life, that he had almost forgotten what the world contained till this evening reminded him. His mother, after her first moments of doubt, appeared to think that he must be left to his own guidance, and gave her attention to Joshua.

With all his foresight and doggedness of aim, the result of that dinner exceeded Halborough's expectations. In weaving his ambitions he had viewed his sister Rosa as a slight, bright thing to be helped into notice by his abilities; but it now began to dawn upon him that the physical gifts of nature to her might do more for them both than nature's intellectual gifts to himself. While he was patiently boring the tunnel Rosa seemed about to fly over the mountain.

He wrote the next day to his brother, now occupying his own old rooms in the theological college, telling him exultingly of the unanticipated *début* of Rosa at the manorhouse. The next post brought him a reply of congratulation, dashed with the counteracting intelligence that his father did not like Canada—that his wife had deserted him, which made him feel so dreary that he thought of returning home.

In his recent satisfaction at his own successes Joshua Halborough had well-nigh forgotten his chronic trouble—latterly screened by distance. But it now returned upon him; he saw more in this brief announcement than his brother seemed to see. It was the cloud no bigger than a man's hand.

4

The following December, a day or two before Christmas, Mrs. Fellmer and her son were walking up and down the broad gravel path which bordered the east front of the house. Till within the last half-hour the morning had been a drizzling one, and they had just emerged for a short turn before luncheon.

"You see, dear mother," the son was saying, "it is the peculiarity of my position which makes her appear to me in such a desirable light. When you consider how I have been crippled at starting, how my life has been maimed; that I feel anything like publicity distasteful, that I have no political ambition, and that my chief aim and hope lie in the education of the little thing Annie has left me, you must see how desirable a wife like Miss Halborough would be, to prevent my becoming a mere vegetable."

"If you adore her, I suppose you must have her!" replied his mother with dry indirectness. "But you'll find that she will not be content to live on here as you do, giving her whole mind to a young child."

"That's just where we differ. Her very disqualification, that of being a nobody, as you call it, is her recommendation in my eyes. Her lack of influential connections limits her ambition. From what I know of her, a life in this place is all that she would wish for. She would never care to go outside the park-gates if it were necessary to stay within."

"Being in love with her, Albert, and meaning to marry her, you invent your practical reasons to make the case respectable. Well, do as you will; I have no authority over you, so why should you consult me? You mean to propose on this very occasion, no doubt. Don't you, now?"

"By no means. I am merely revolving the idea in my mind. If on further acquaintance she turns out to be as good as she has hitherto seemed—well, I shall see. Admit, now, that you like her."

"I readily admit it. She is very captivating at first sight. But as a step-mother to your child! You seem mighty anxious, Albert, to get rid of me!"

"Not at all. And I am not so reckless as you think. I don't make up my mind in a hurry. But the thought having occurred to me, I mention it to you at once, mother. If you dislike it, say so."

"I don't say anything. I will try to make the best of it if you are determined. When does she come?"

"Tomorrow."

All this time there were great preparations in train at the curate's, who was now a householder. Rosa, whose two or three weeks' stay on two occasions earlier in the year had so affected the squire, was coming again, and at the same time her younger brother Cornelius, to make up a family party. Rosa, who journeyed from the Midlands, could not arrive till late in the evening, but Cornelius was to get there in the afternoon, Joshua going out to meet him in his walk across the fields from the railway.

Everything being ready in Joshua's modest abode he started on his way, his heart buoyant and thankful, if ever it was in his life. He was of such good report himself that his brother's path into holy orders promised to be unexpectedly easy; and he longed to compare experiences with him, even though there was on hand a more exciting matter still. From his youth he had held that, in old-fashioned country places, the Church conferred social prestige up to a certain point at a cheaper price than any other profession or pursuit; and events seemed to be proving him right.

He had walked about half an hour when he saw Cornelius coming along the path; and in a few minutes the two brothers met. The experiences of Cornelius had been less immediately interesting than those of Joshua, but his personal position was satisfactory, and there was nothing to account for the singularly subdued manner that he exhibited, which at first Joshua set down to the fatigue of over-study; and he proceeded to the subject of Rosa's arrival in the evening, and the probable consequences of this her third visit. "Before next Easter she'll be his wife, my boy," said Joshua with grave exultation.

Cornelius shook his head. "She comes too late!" he returned.

"What do you mean?"

"Look here." He produced the Fountall paper, and placed his finger on a paragraph, which Joshua read. It appeared under the report of Petty Sessions, and was a commonplace case of disorderly conduct, in which a man was sent to prison for seven days for breaking windows in that town.

"Well?" said Joshua.

"It happened during an evening that I was in the street; and the offender is our father."

"Not—how—I sent him more money on his promising to stay in Canada?"

"He is home, safe enough." Cornelius in the same gloomy tone gave the remainder of his information. He had witnessed the scene, unobserved of his father, and had heard him say that he was on his way to see his daughter, who was going to marry a rich gentleman. The only good fortune attending the untoward incident was that the millwright's name had been printed as Joshua Alborough.

"Beaten! We are to be beaten on the eve of our expected victory!" said the elder brother. "How did he guess that Rosa was likely to marry? Good Heaven! Cornelius, you seem doomed to bring bad news always, do you not!"

"I do," said Cornelius. "Poor Rosa!"

It was almost in tears, so great was their heartsickness and shame, that the brothers walked the remainder of the way to Joshua's dwelling. In the evening they set out to meet Rosa, bringing her to the village in a fly; and when she had come into the house, and was sitting down with them, they almost forgot their secret anxiety in contemplating her, who knew nothing about it.

Next day the Fellmers came, and the two or three days after that were a lively time. That the squire was yielding to his impulses—making up his mind—there could be no doubt. On Sunday Cornelius read the lessons, and Joshua preached. Mrs. Fellmer was quite maternal towards Rosa, and it appeared that she had decided to welcome the inevitable with a good grace. The pretty girl was to spend yet another afternoon with the elder lady, superintending some parish treat at the house in observance of Christmas, and afterwards to stay on to dinner, her brothers to fetch her in the evening. They were also invited to dine, but they could not accept owing to an engagement.

The engagement was of a somber sort. They were going to meet their father, who would that day be released from Fountall Gaol, and try to persuade him to keep away from Narrobourne. Every exertion was to be made to get him back to Canada, to his old home in the Midlands—anywhere, so that he would not impinge disastrously upon their courses, and blast their sister's prospects of the auspicious marriage which was just then hanging in the balance.

As soon as Rosa had been fetched away by her friends at the manorhouse her brothers started on their expedition, without waiting for dinner or tea. Cornelius, to whom the millwright always addressed his letters when he wrote any, drew from his pocket and reread as he walked the curt note which had led to this journey being undertaken; it was dispatched by their father the night before, immediately upon his liberation, and stated that he was setting out for Narrobourne at the moment of writing; that having no money he would be obliged to walk all the way; that he calculated on passing through the intervening town of Ivell about six on the following day, where he should sup at the Castle Inn, and where he hoped they would meet him with a carriage-and-pair, or some other such conveyance, that he might not disgrace them by arriving like a tramp.

"That sounds as if he gave a thought to our position," said Cornelius.

Joshua knew the satire that lurked in the paternal words, and said nothing. Silence prevailed during the greater part of their journey. The lamps were lighted in Ivell when they entered the streets, and Cornelius, who was quite unknown in this neighborhood, and who, moreover, was not in clerical attire, decided that he should be the one to call at the Castle Inn. Here, in answer to his inquiry under the darkness of the archway, they told him that such a man as he had described left the house about a quarter of an hour earlier, after making a meal in the kitchen-settle. He was rather the worse for liquor.

"Then," said Joshua, when Cornelius joined him outside with this intelligence, "we must have met and passed him! And now that I think of it, we did meet some one who was unsteady in his gait, under the trees on the other side of Hendford Hill, where it was too dark to see him."

They rapidly retraced their steps; but for a long stretch of the way home could discern nobody. When, however, they had gone about three-quarters of the distance, they became conscious of an irregular footfall in front of them, and could see a whitish figure in the gloom. They followed dubiously. The figure met another wayfarer—the single one that had been encountered upon this lonely road—and they distinctly heard him ask the way to Narrobourne. The stranger replied—what was quite true —that the nearest way was by turning in at the stile by the next bridge, and following the footpath which branched thence across the meadows.

When the brothers reached the stile they also entered the path, but did not overtake the subject of their worry till they had crossed two or three meads, and the lights from Narrobourne manorhouse were visible before them through the trees. Their father was no longer walking; he was seated against the wet bank of an adjoining hedge. Observing their forms he shouted, "I'm going to Narrobourne; who may you be?"

They went up to him, and revealed themselves, reminding him of the plan which he had himself proposed in his note, that they should meet him at Ivell.

"By Jerry, I'd forgot it!" he said. "Well, what do you want me to do?" His tone was distinctly quarrelsome.

A long conversation followed, which became embittered at the first hint from them that he should not come to the village. The millwright drew a quart bottle from his pocket, and challenged them to drink if they meant friendly and called themselves men. Neither of the two had touched alcohol for years, but for once they thought it best to accept, so as not to needlessly provoke him.

"What's in it?" said Joshua.

"A drop of weak gin-and-water. It won't hurt ye. Drink from the bottle." Joshua did so, and his father pushed up the bottom of the vessel so as to make him swallow a good deal in spite of himself. It went down into his stomach like molten lead.

"Ha, ha, that's right!" said old Halborough. "But 'twas raw spirit—ha, ha!"

"Why should you take me in so!" said Joshua, losing his self-command, try as he would to keep calm.

"Because you took me in, my lad, in banishing me to that cursed country under pretense that it was for my good. You were a pair of hypocrites to say so. It was done to get rid of me—no more nor less. But, by Jerry, I'm a match for ye now! I'll spoil your souls for preaching. My daughter is going to be married to the squire here. I've heard the news—I saw it in a paper!"

"It is premature—"

"I know it is true; and I'm her father, and I shall give her away, or there'll be a hell of a row, I can assure ye! Is that where the gennleman lives?"

Joshua Halborough writhed in impotent despair. Fellmer had not yet positively declared himself, his mother was hardly won round; a scene with their father in the parish would demolish as fair a palace of hopes as was ever builded. The millwright rose. "If that's where the squire lives I'm going to call. Just arrived from Canady with her fortune—ha, ha! I wish no harm to the gennleman, and the gennleman will wish no harm to me. But I like to take my place in the family, and stand upon my rights, and lower people's pride!"

"You've succeeded already! Where's that woman you took with you—"

"Woman! She was my wife as lawful as the Constitution—a sight more lawful than your mother was till some time after you were born!"

Joshua had for many years before heard whispers that his father had cajoled his mother in their early acquaintance, and had made somewhat tardy amends; but never from his father's lips till now. It was the last stroke, and he could not bear it. He sank back against the hedge. "It is over!" he said. "He ruins us all!"

The millwright moved on, waving his stick triumphantly, and the two brothers stood still. They could see his drab figure stalking along the path, and over his head the lights from the conservatory of Narrobourne House, inside which Albert Fellmer might possibly be sitting with Rosa at that moment, holding her hand, and asking her to share his home with him.

The staggering whitey-brown form, advancing to put a blot on all this, had been diminishing in the shade; and now suddenly disappeared beside a weir. There was the noise of a flounce in the water.

"He has fallen in!" said Cornelius, starting forward to run for the place at which his father had vanished.

Joshua, awaking from the stupefied reverie into which he had sunk, rushed to the other's side before he had taken ten steps. "Stop, stop, what are you thinking of?" he whispered hoarsely, grasping Cornelius's arm.

"Pulling him out!"

"Yes, yes—so am I. But—wait a moment—"

"But, Joshua!"

"Her life and happiness, you know—Cornelius—and your reputation and mine—and our chance of rising together, all three—"

He clutched his brother's arm to the bone; and as they stood breathless the splashing and floundering in the weir continued; over it they saw the hopeful lights from the manorhouse conservatory winking through the trees as their bare branches waved to and fro.

The floundering and splashing grew weaker, and they could hear gurgling words: "Help—I'm drownded! Rosie—Rosie!"

"We'll go—we *must* save him. O Joshua!"

"Yes, yes! we must!"

Still they did not move, but waited, holding each other, each thinking the same thought. Weights of lead seemed to be affixed to their feet, which would no longer obey their wills. The mead became silent. Over it they fancied they could see figures moving in the conservatory. The air up there seemed to emit gentle kisses.

Cornelius started forward at last, and Joshua almost simultaneously. Two or three minutes brought them to the brink of the stream. At first they could see nothing in the water, though it was not so deep nor the night so dark but that their father's light kerseymere coat would have been visible if he had lain at the bottom. Joshua looked this way and that.

"He has drifted into the culvert," he said.

Below the footbridge of the weir the stream suddenly narrowed to half its width, to pass under a barrel arch or culvert constructed for wagons to cross into the middle of the mead in haymaking time. It being at present the season of high water the arch was full to the crown, against which the ripples clucked every now and then. At this point he had just caught sight of a pale object slipping under. In a moment it was gone.

They went to the lower end, but nothing emerged. For a long time they tried at both ends to effect some communication with the interior, but to no purpose.

"We ought to have come sooner!" said the conscience-stricken Cornelius, when they were quite exhausted, and dripping wet.

"I suppose we ought," replied Joshua heavily. He perceived his father's walking-stick on the bank; hastily picking it up he stuck it into the mud among the sedge. Then they went on.

"Shall we—say anything about this accident?" whispered Cornelius as they approached the door of Joshua's house.

"What's the use? It can do no good. We must wait until he is found."

They went indoors and changed their clothes; after which they started for the manorhouse, reaching it about ten o'clock. Besides their sister there were only three guests; an adjoining landowner and his wife, and the infirm old rector.

Rosa, although she had parted from them so recently,

grasped their hands in an ecstatic, brimming, joyful manner, as if she had not seen them for years. "You look pale," she said.

The brothers answered that they had had a long walk, and were somewhat tired. Everybody in the room seemed charged full with some sort of interesting knowledge: the squire's neighbor and his wife looked wisely around; and Fellmer himself played the part of host with a preoccupied bearing which approached fervor. They left at eleven, not accepting the carriage offered, the distance being so short and the roads dry. The squire came rather farther into the dark with them than he need have done, and wished Rosa good-night in a mysterious manner, slightly apart from the rest.

When they were walking along Joshua said, with a desperate attempt at joviality, "Rosa, what's going on?"

"O, I—" she began between a gasp and a bound. "He—"

"Never mind—if it disturbs you."

She was so excited that she could not speak connectedly at first, the practiced air which she had brought home with her having disappeared. Calming herself she added, "I am not disturbed, and nothing has happened. Only he said he wanted to ask me *something*, some day; and I said never mind that now. He hasn't asked yet, and is coming to speak to you about it. He would have done so tonight, only I asked him not to be in a hurry. But he will come tomorrow, I am sure!"

5

It was summer-time, six months later, and mowers and haymakers were at work in the meads. The manorhouse, being opposite them, frequently formed a peg for conversation during these operations; and the doings of the squire, and the squire's young wife, the curate's sister—who was at present the admired of most of them, and the interest of all—met with their due amount of criticism.

Rosa was happy, if ever woman could be said to be so. She had not learnt the fate of her father, and sometimes wondered —perhaps with a sense of relief—why he did not write to her from his supposed home in Canada. Her brother Joshua had been presented to a living in a small town, shortly after her marriage, and Cornelius had thereupon succeeded to the vacant curacy of Narrobourne.

These two had awaited in deep suspense the discovery of their father's body; and yet the discovery had not been made. Every day they expected a man or a boy to run up from the meads with the intelligence; but he had never come. Days had accumulated to weeks and months; the wedding had come and gone: Joshua had tolled and read himself in at his new parish; and never a shout of amazement over the millwright's remains.

But now, in June, when they were mowing the meads, the hatches had to be drawn and the water let out of its channels for the convenience of the mowers. It was thus that the discovery was made. A man, stooping low with his scythe, caught a view of the culvert lengthwise, and saw something entangled in the recently bared weeds of its bed. A day or two after there was an inquest; but the body was unrecognizable. Fish and flood had been busy with the millwright; he had no watch or marked article which could be identified; and a verdict of the accidental drowning of a person unknown settled the matter.

As the body was found in Narrobourne parish, there it had to be buried. Cornelius wrote to Joshua, begging him to come and read the service, or to send someone; he himself could not do it. Rather than let in a stranger Joshua came, and silently scanned the coroner's order handed him by the undertaker:—

"I, Henry Giles, Coroner for the Mid-Division of Outer Wessex, do hereby order the Burial of the Body now shown to the Inquest Jury as the Body of an Adult Male Person Unknown . . . ," etc.

Joshua Halborough got through the service in some way, and rejoined his brother Cornelius at his house. Neither accepted an invitation to lunch at their sister's; they wished to discuss parish matters together. In the afternoon she came down, though they had already called on her, and had not expected to see her again. Her bright eyes, brown hair, flowery bonnet, lemon-colored gloves, and flush beauty, were like an irradiation into the apartment, which they in their gloom could hardly bear.

"I forgot to tell you," she said, "of a curious thing which happened to me a month or two before my marriage—something which I have thought may have had a connection with the accident to the poor man you have buried today. It was on the evening I was at the manorhouse waiting for you to fetch me; I was in the winter-garden with Albert, and we were sitting silent together, when we fancied we heard a cry. We opened the door, and while Albert ran to fetch his hat, leaving me standing there, the cry was repeated, and my excited senses made me think I heard my own name. When Albert came back all was silent, and we decided that it was only a drunken shout, and not a cry for help. We both forgot the incident, and it never has occurred to me till since the funeral today that it might have been this stranger's cry. The name of course was only fancy, or he might have had a wife or child with a name something like mine, poor man!"

When she was gone the brothers were silent till Cornelius said, "Now mark this, Joshua. Sooner or later she'll know."

"How?"

"From one of us. Do you think human hearts are iron-cased safes, that you suppose we can keep this secret forever?"

"Yes, I think they are, sometimes," said Joshua.

"No. It will out. We shall tell."

"What, and ruin her—kill her? Disgrace her children, and pull down the whole auspicious house of Fellmer about out ears? No! May I—drown where he was drowned before I do it! Never, never. Surely you can say the same, Cornelius!"

Cornelius seemed fortified, and no more was said. For a

long time after that day he did not see Joshua, and before the next year was out a son and heir was born to the Fellmers. The villagers rang the three bells every evening for a week and more, and were made merry by Mr. Fellmer's ale; and when the christening came on Joshua paid Narrobourne another visit.

Among all the people who assembled on that day the brother clergymen were the least interested. Their minds were haunted by a spirit in kerseymere. In the evening they walked together in the fields.

"She's all right," said Joshua. "But here are you doing journey-work, Cornelius, and like to continue at it till the end of the day, as far as I can see. I, too, with my petty living—what am I after all? . . . To tell the truth, the Church is a poor forlorn hope for people without influence, particularly when their enthusiasm begins to flag. A social regenerator has a better chance outside, where he is unhampered by dogma and tradition. As for me, I would rather have gone on mending mills, with my crust of bread and liberty."

Almost automatically they had bent their steps along the margin of the river; they now paused. They were standing on the brink of the well-known weir. There were the hatches, there was the culvert; they could see the pebbly bed of the stream through the pellucid water. The notes of the church-bells were audible, still jangled by the enthusiastic villagers.

"Why see—it was there I hid his walking-stick!" said Joshua, looking towards the sedge. The next moment, during a passing breeze, something flashed white on the spot to which the attention of Cornelius was drawn.

From the sedge rose a straight little silver-poplar, and it was the leaves of this sapling which caused the flicker of whiteness.

"His walking-stick has grown!" Joshua added. "It was a rough one—cut from the hedge, I remember."

At every puff of wind the tree turned white, till they could not bear to look at it; and they walked away.

"I see him every night," Cornelius murmured. . . . "Ah,

we read our *Hebrews* to little account, Jos! "Ὑπέμεινε σταυρὸν, αἰσχύνης καταφρονήσας. To have *endured* the cross, *despising* the shame—there lay greatness! But now I often feel that I should like to put an end to trouble here in this self-same spot."

"I have thought of it myself," said Joshua.

"Perhaps we shall, some day," murmured his brother.

"Perhaps," said Joshua moodily.

With that contingency to consider in the silence of their nights and days they bent their steps homewards.

THOMAS HARDY spent most of his life in Wessex, the harsh moor country of southern England that is the locale of all his books. He was born there in 1840, and when he died in 1928, his heart was buried there, while his ashes were placed next to those of Charles Dickens in Westminster Abbey.

Hardy's education was poor—he attended school for eight years—and for a time he worked as an architect. At 31 he published his first book, under the editorial guidance of George Meredith, who was a reader for Hardy's publisher. He wrote numerous stories and articles and ten novels, among them *The Return of the Native, Tess of the D'Urbervilles,* and *Jude the Obscure.* He also composed nearly a thousand poems.

His work is often described as "fatalistic," but he was deeply concerned with character—its relationship to fate and to the causes of unhappiness. "A Tragedy of Two Ambitions," from *Life's Little Ironies,* deals, like Hardy's most mature work, with human responsibility.

JAMES AGEE

Rufus

When breakfast was over he wandered listlessly into the sitting room and looked all around, but he did not see any place where he would like to sit down. He felt deeply idle and empty and at the same time gravely exhilarated, as if this were the morning of his birthday, except that this day seemed even more particularly his own day. There was nothing in the way it looked which was not ordinary, but it was filled with a noiseless and invisible kind of energy. He could see his mother's face while she told them about it and hear her voice, over and over, and silently, over and over, while he looked around the sitting room and through the window into the street, words repeated themselves. He's dead. He died last night while I was asleep and now it was already morning. He has already been dead since way last night and I didn't even know until I woke up. He has been dead all night while I was asleep and now it is morning and I am awake but he is still dead and he will stay right on being dead all afternoon and all night and all tomorrow while I am asleep again and wake up again and go to sleep again and he can't come back home again ever any more but I will see him once more before he is taken away. Dead now. He died last night while I was asleep and now it is already morning.

A boy went by with his books in a strap.

Two girls went by with their satchels.

He went to the hat rack and took his satchel and his hat and started back down the hall to the kitchen to get his lunch; then he remembered his new cap. But it was upstairs. It would be in Mama's and Daddy's room, he could remember when she took it off his head. He did not want to go in for it where she was lying down and now he realized, too, that he did not want to wear it. He would like to tell her good-bye before he went to school, but he did not want to go in and see her lying down and looking like that. He kept on towards the kitchen. He would tell Aunt Hannah good-bye instead.

She was at the sink washing dishes and Catherine sat on a kitchen chair watching her. He looked all around but he could not see any lunch. I guess she doesn't know about lunch, he reflected. She did not seem to realize that he was there so, after a moment, he said, "Good-bye."

"What-*is*-it?" she said and turned her lowered head, peering. "Why, Rufus!" she exclaimed, in such a tone that he wondered what he had done. "You're not going to *school,*" she said, and now he realized that she was not mad at him.

"I can stay out of school?"

"Of course you can. You must. Today and tomorrow as well and—for a sufficient time. A few days. Now put up your things, and stay right in this house, child."

He looked at her and said to himself: but then they can't see me; but he knew there was no use begging her; already she was busy with the dishes again.

He went back along the hall towards the hat rack. In the first moment he had been only surprised and exhilarated not to have to go to school, and something of this sense of privilege remained, but almost immediately he was also disappointed. He could now see vividly how they would all look up when he came into the schoolroom and how the teacher would say something nice about his father and about him, and he knew that on this day everybody would treat him well, and even look up to him, for something had happened to him today which had not happened to any other boy in school, any other boy in town. They might even give him part of their lunches.

He felt even more profoundly empty and idle than before.

He laid down his satchel on the seat of the hat rack, but he kept his hat on. She'll spank me, he thought. Even worse, he could foresee her particular, crackling kind of anger. I won't let her find out, he told himself. Taking great care to be silent, he let himself out the front door.

The air was cool and gray and here and there along the street, shapeless and watery sunlight strayed and vanished. Now that he was in this outdoor air he felt even more listless and powerful; he was alone, and the silent, invisible energy was everywhere. He stood on the porch and supposed that everyone he saw passing knew of an event so famous. A man was walking quickly up the street and as Rufus watched him, and waited for the man to meet his eyes, he felt a great quiet lifting within him of pride and of shyness, and he felt his face break into a smile, and then an uncontrollable grin, which he knew he must try to make sober again; but the man walked past without looking at him, and so did the next man who walked past in the other direction. Two schoolboys passed whose faces he knew, so he knew that they must know his, but they did not even seem to see him. Arthur and Alvin Tripp came down their front steps and along the far sidewalk and now he was sure, and came down his own front steps and halfway out to the sidewalk, but then he stopped, for now, although both of them looked across into his eyes, and he into theirs, they did not cross the street to him or even say hello, but kept on their way, still looking into his eyes with a kind of shy curiosity, even when their heads were turned almost backwards on their necks, and he turned his own head slowly, watching them go by, but when he saw that they were not going to speak he took care not to speak either.

What's the matter with them, he wondered, and still watched them; and even now, far down the street, Arthur kept turning his head, and for several steps Alvin walked backwards.

What are they mad about?

Now they no longer looked around, and now he watched them vanish under the hill.

Maybe they don't know, he thought. Maybe the others don't know, either.

He came out to the sidewalk.

Maybe everybody knew. Or maybe he knew something of great importance which nobody else knew. The alternatives were not at all distinct in his mind; he was puzzled, but no less proud and expectant than before. My daddy's dead, he said to himself slowly, and then, shyly, he said it aloud: "My daddy's dead." Nobody in sight seemed to have heard; he had said it to nobody in particular. "My daddy's dead," he said again, chiefly for his own benefit. It sounded powerful, solid, and entirely creditable, and he knew that if need be he would tell people. He watched a large, slow man come towards him and waited for the man to look at him and acknowledge the fact first, but when the man was just ahead of him, and still did not appear even to have seen him, he told him, "My daddy's dead," but the man did not seem to hear him, he just swung on by. He took care to tell the next man sooner and the man's face looked almost as if he were dodging a blow but he went on by, looking back a few steps later with a worried face; and after a few steps more he turned and came slowly back.

"What was that you said, sonny?" he asked; he was frowning slightly.

"My daddy's dead," Rufus said, expectantly.

"You mean that sure enough?" the man asked.

"He died last night when I was asleep and now he can't come home ever any more."

The man looked at him as if something hurt him.

"Where do you live, sonny?"

"Right here"; he showed with his eyes.

"Do your folks know you out here wandern round?"

He felt his stomach go empty. He looked frankly into his eyes and nodded quickly.

The man just looked at him and Rufus realized: He doesn't believe me. How do they always know?

"You better just go on back in the house, son," he said. "They won't like you being out here on the street." He kept looking at him, hard.

Rufus looked into his eyes with reproach and apprehension, and turned in at his walk. The man still stood there. Rufus went on slowly up his steps, and looked around. The man was on his way again but at the moment Rufus looked around, he did too, and now he stopped again.

He shook his head and said, in a friendly voice which made Rufus feel ashamed, "How would your daddy like it, you out here telling strangers how he's dead?"

Rufus opened the door, taking care not to make a sound, and stepped in and silently closed it, and hurried into the sitting room. Through the curtains he watched the man. He still stood there, lighting a cigarette, but now he started walking again. He looked back once and Rufus felt, with a quailing of shame and fear, he sees me; but the man immediately looked away again and Rufus watched him until he was out of sight.

How would your daddy like it?

He thought of the way they teased him and did things to him, and how mad his father got when he just came home. He thought how different it would be today if he only didn't have to stay home from school.

He let himself out again and stole back between the houses to the alley, and walked along the alley, listening to the cinders cracking under each step, until he came near the sidewalk. He was not in front of his own home now, or even on Highland Avenue; he was coming into the side street down from his home, and he felt that here nobody would identify him with his home and send him back to it. What he could see from the mouth of the alley was much less familiar to him, and he took the last few steps which brought him out onto the sidewalk with deliberation and shyness. He was doing something he had been told not to do.

He looked up the street and he could see the corner he knew so well, where he always met the others so unhappily, and, farther away, the corner around which his father always disappeared on the way to work, and first appeared on his way home from work. He felt it would be good luck that he would not be meeting them at that corner. Slowly, uneasily, he turned his head, and looked down the side street in the other direction; and there they were: three together, and two along the far side of the street, and one alone, farther off, and another alone, farther off, and, without importance to him, some girls here and there, as well. He knew the faces of all of these boys well, though he was not sure of any of their names. The moment he saw them all he was sure they saw him, and sure that they knew. He stood still and waited for them, looking from one to another of them, into their eyes, and step by step at their several distances, each of them at all times looking into his eyes and knowing, they came silently nearer. Waiting, in silence, during those many seconds before the first of them came really near him, he felt that it was so long to wait, and be watched so closely and silently, and to watch back, that he wanted to go back into the alley and not be seen by them or by anybody else, and yet at the same time he knew that they were all approaching him with the realization that something had happened to him that had not happened to any other boy in town, and that now at last they were bound to think well of him; and the nearer they came but were yet at a distance, the more the gray, sober air was charged with the great energy and with a sense of glory and of danger, and the deeper and more exciting the silence became, and the more tall, proud, shy and exposed he felt; so that as they came still nearer he once again felt his face break into a wide smile, with which he had nothing to do, and, feeling that there was something deeply wrong in such a smile, tried his best to quieten his face and told them, shyly and proudly, "My daddy's dead."

Of the first three who came up, two merely looked at him and the third said, "Huh! Betcha he ain't"; and Rufus, astounded that they did not know and that they should disbelieve him, said, "Why he is so!"

"Where's your satchel at?" said the boy who had spoken. "You're just making up a lie so you can lay out of school."

"I am not laying out," Rufus replied. "I was going to school and my Aunt Hannah told me I didn't have to go to school today or tomorrow or not till—not for a few days. She said I mustn't. So I am not laying out. I'm just staying out."

And another of the boys said, "That's right. If his daddy is dead he don't have to go back to school till after the funerl."

While Rufus had been speaking two other boys had crossed over to join them and now one of them said, "He don't have to. He can lay out cause his daddy got killed," and Rufus looked at the boy gratefully and the boy looked back at him, it seemed to Rufus, with deference.

But the first boy who had spoken said, resentfully, "How do *you* know?"

And the second boy, while his companion nodded, said, "Cause my daddy seen it in the paper. Can't your daddy read the paper?"

The paper, Rufus thought; it's even in the paper! And he looked wisely at the first boy. And the first boy, interested enough to ignore the remark against his father, said, "Well how did he get killed, then?" and Rufus, realizing with respect that it was even more creditable to get killed than just to die, took a deep breath and said, "Why, he was . . ."; but the boy whose father had seen it in the paper was already talking, so he listened, instead, feeling as if all this were being spoken for him, and on his behalf, and in his praise, and feeling it all the more as he looked from one silent boy to the next and saw that their eyes were constantly on him. And Rufus listened, too, with as much interest as they did, while the boy said with relish, "In his ole Tin Lizzie, that's how. He was driving along in his ole Tin Lizzie and it hit a rock and throwed him out in the ditch and run up a eight-foot bank and then fell back and turned over and over and landed right on top of him *whomph* and mashed every bone in his body, that's all. And somebody come and found him and he was dead already time they got there, that's how."

"He was instantly killed," Rufus began, and expected to go ahead and correct some of the details of the account, but nobody seemed to hear him, for two other boys had come up and just as he began to speak one of them said, "Your daddy got his name in the paper didn't he, and you too," and he saw that now all the boys looked at him with new respect.

"He's dead," he told them. "He got killed."

"That's what my daddy says," one of them said, and the other said, "What you get for driving a auto when you're drunk, that's what my dad says," and the two of them looked gravely at the other boys, nodding, and at Rufus.

"What's drunk?" Rufus asked.

"What's drunk?" one of the boys mocked incredulously: "Drunk is fulla good ole whiskey"; and he began to stagger about in circles with his knees weak and his head lolling. "At's what drunk is."

"Then he wasn't," Rufus said.

"How do *you* know?"

"He wasn't drunk because that wasn't how he died. The wheel hit a rock and the other wheel, the one you steer with, just hit him on the chin, but it hit him so hard it killed him. He was instantly killed."

"What's instantly killed?" one of them asked.

"What do you care?" another said.

"Right off like that," an older boy explained, snapping his fingers. Another boy joined the group. Thinking of what instantly meant, and how his father's name was in the paper and his own too, and how he had got killed, not just died, he was not listening to them very clearly for a few moments, and then, all of a sudden, he began to realize that he was the center of everything and that they all knew it and that they waited to hear him tell the true account of it.

"I don't know nothing about no chin," the boy whose father saw it in the paper was saying. "Way I heard it he was a-drivin along in his ole Tin Lizzie and he hit a rock and old Tin Lizzie run off the road and thowed him out and run up a eight-foot bank and turned over and over and fell back down on top of him *whomp.*"

"How do *you* know?" an older boy was saying. "You wasn't there. 'Anybody here knows it's *him.*" And he pointed at Rufus and Rufus was startled from his reverie.

"Why?" asked the boy who had just come up.

"Cause it's his daddy," one of them explained.

"It's my daddy," Rufus said.

"What happened?" asked still another boy, at the fringe of the group.

"My daddy got killed," Rufus said.

"His daddy got killed," several of the others explained.

"My daddy says he bets he was drunk."

"Good old whiskey!"

"Shut up, what's *your* daddy know about it."

"Was he drunk?"

"No," Rufus said.

"No," two others said.

"Let *him* tell it."

"Yeah, *you* tell it."

"Anybody here ought to know, it's him."

"Come on and tell us."

"Good old whiskey."

"Shut your mouth."

"Well come on and tell us, then."

They became silent and all of them looked at him. Rufus looked back into their eyes in the sudden deep stillness. A man walked by, stepping into the gutter to skirt them.

Rufus said, quietly, "He was coming home from Grampa's last night, Grampa Follet. He's very sick and Daddy had to go up way in the middle of the night to see him, and he was hurrying as fast as he could to get back home because he was so late. And there was a cotter pin worked loose."

"What's a cotter pin?"

"Shut up."

"A cotter pin is what holds things together underneath, that you steer with. It worked loose and fell out so that when one of the front wheels hit a loose rock it wrenched the wheel and he couldn't steer and the auto ran down off the road with an awful bump and they saw where the wheel you steer with hit him right on the chin and he was instantly killed. He was thrown all the way out of the auto and it ran up an eight-foot emb—embackment and then it rolled back down and it was upside down beside him when they found him. There was not a mark on his body. Only a little tiny blue mark right on the end of the chin and another on his lip."

In the silence he could see the auto upside down with its wheels in the air and his father lying beside it with the little blue marks on his chin and on his lip.

"Heck," one of them said, "how can *that* kill anybody?"

He felt a kind of sullen stirring among the others, and he felt that he was not believed, or that they did not think very well of his father for being killed so easily.

"It was just exactly the way it just happened to hit him, Uncle Andrew says. He says it was just a chance in a million. It gave him a concush, con, concush—it did something to his brain that killed him."

"Just a chance in a million," one of the older boys said gravely, and another gravely nodded.

"A million trillion," another said.

"Knocked him crazy as a loon," another cried, and with a waggling forefinger he made a rapid blubbery noise against his loose lower lip.

"Shut yer Goddamn mouth," an older boy said coldly. "Ain't you got no sense at all?"

"Way I heard it, ole Tin Lizzie just rolled right back on top of him *whomp*."

This account of it was false, Rufus was sure, but it seemed to him more exciting than his own, and more creditable to his father and to him, and nobody could question, scornfully, whether that could kill, as they could of just a blow on the chin; so he didn't try to contradict. He felt that he was lying, and in some way being disloyal as well, but he said only, "He was instantly killed. He didn't have to feel any pain."

"Never even knowed what hit him," a boy said quietly. "That's what my dad says."

"No," Rufus said. It had not occurred to him that way. "I guess he didn't." Never even knowed what hit him. Knew.

"Reckon that old Tin Lizzie is done for now. Huh?"

He wondered if there was some meanness behind calling it an old Tin Lizzie. "I guess so," he said.

"Good old waggin, but she done broke down."

His father sang that.

"No more joy rides in that old Tin Lizzie, huh, Rufus?"

"I guess not," Rufus replied shyly.

He began to realize that for some moments now a bell, the school bell, had been weltering on the dark gray air; he realized it because at this moment the last of its reverberations were fading.

"Last bell," one of the boys said in sudden alarm.

"Come on, we're goana get hell," another said; and within another second Rufus was watching them all run dwindling away up the street, and around the corner into Highland Avenue, as fast as they could go, and all round him the morning was empty and still. He stood still and watched the corner for almost half a minute after the fattest of them, and then the smallest, had disappeared; then he walked slowly back along the alley, hearing once more the sober crumbling of the cinders under each step, and up through the narrow side yard between the houses, and up the steps of the front porch.

In the paper! He looked for it beside the door, but it was not there. He listened carefully, but he could not hear anything. He let himself quietly through the front door, at the moment his Aunt Hannah came from the sitting room into the front hall. She wore a cloth over her hair and in her hands she was carrying the smoking stand. She did not see him at first and he saw how fierce and lonely her face looked. He tried to make himself small but just then she wheeled on him, her lenses flashing, and exclaimed, "Rufus Follet, where on earth have you been!" His stomach quailed, for her voice was so angry it was as if it were crackling with sparks.

"Outdoors."

"Where, outdoors! I've been looking for you all over the place."

"Just out. Back in the alley."

"Didn't you hear me calling you?"

He shook his head.

"I shouted until my voice was hoarse."

He kept shaking his head. "Honest," he said.

"Now listen to me carefully. You mustn't go outdoors today. Stay right here inside this house, do you understand?"

He nodded. He felt suddenly that he had done an awful thing.

"I know it's hard to," she said more gently, "but you've got to. Help Catherine with her coloring. Read a book. You promise?"

"Yes'm."

"And don't do anything to disturb your mother."

"No'm."

She went on down the hall and he watched her. What was she doing with the pipes and the ashtrays, he wondered. He considered sneaking behind her, for he knew that she could not see at all well, yet he would be sure to get caught, for her hearing was very sharp. All the same, he sneaked along to the back of the hall and watched her empty the ashes into the garbage pail and rap out the pipes against its rim. Then she stood with the pipes in her hand, looking around uncertainly; finally she put the pipes and the ashtrays on the cupboard shelf, and set the smoking stand in the corner of the kitchen behind the stove. He went back along the hall on tiptoe and into the sitting room.

Catherine sat in the little chair by the side window with a picture book on her knees. Her crayons were all over the window sill and she was working intently with an orange crayon. She looked up when he came in and looked down again and kept on working.

He did not want to help her, he wanted to be by himself

and see if he could find the paper with the names in it, but he felt that he ought to try to be good, for by now he felt a dark uneasiness about something, he was not quite sure what, that he had done. He walked over to her. "I'll help you," he said.

"No," Catherine said, without even looking up. It was the Mother Goose book and with her orange crayon she was scrawling all over the cow which jumped over the moon, inside and outside the lines of the cow.

"Aunt Hannah says to," he said, disgusted to see what she was doing to the cow.

"No," Catherine said, and again she did not look up or stop scrawling for a second.

"That ain't no color for a cow," he said. "Whoever saw an orange cow?" She made no reply, but he could see that her face was getting red. "Besides, you're not even coloring inside the cow," he said. "Just look at that. You're just running that crayon around all over the place and it isn't even the right color." She bore down even harder and harder with the crayon and pushed it in a wider and wider tangle of lines and all of a sudden it snapped and the long part rolled to the floor. "See now, you busted it," Rufus said.

"Leave me alone!" She tried to draw with the stub of the crayon but it was too short, and the paper got in the way. She looked along the window sill and selected a brown crayon.

"What you goana do with that brown one?" Rufus said. "You already got all that orange all over everything, what you goana do with that brown one?" Catherine took the brown crayon and made a brutal tangle of dark lines all over the orange lines. "Now all you did is just spoil it," Rufus said. "You don't know how to draw!"

"*Quit* it!" Catherine yelled, and all of a sudden she was crying. He heard his Aunt Hannah's sharp voice from the kitchen: "Rufus?"

"He was furious with Catherine. "Crybaby," he whispered with cold hatred: "Tattletale!"

And there was Aunt Hannah at the door, just as mad as a hornet. "Now, what's the matter? What have you done to her!" She walked straight at him.

It wasn't fair. How did she know he was doing anything? With a feeling of real righteousness he talked back: "I didn't do one single thing to her. She was just messing everything up on her picture and I tried to help her like you told me to and all of a sudden she started to cry."

"What did he do, Catherine?"

"He wouldn't let me alone."

"Why good night, I never even touched you and you're a liar if you say I did!"

All of a sudden he felt himself gripped by the shoulders and shaken and he turned his rattling head from his sister to look into his Aunt Hannah's freezing glare.

"Now you just listen to me," she said. "Are you listening?" she sputtered. *"Are you listening?"* she said still more intensely.

"Yes," he managed to get out, though the word was all shaken up.

"I don't want to spank you on this day of all days, but if I hear you say one more rough thing like that to your sister I'll give you a spanking you'll remember to your dying day, do you hear me? *Do you hear me?"*

"Yes."

"And if you tease her or make her cry just one more time I'll—I'll turn the whole matter over to your Uncle Andrew and we'll see what *he'll* do about it. Do you want me to call him? He's upstairs this minute! Shall I call him?" She stopped shaking him and looked at him. "Shall I?" He shook his head; he was terrified. "All right, but this is my last warning. Do you understand?"

"Yes'm."

"Now if you can't play with Catherine in peace like a decent boy just—stay by yourself. Look at some pictures. Read a book. But you be quiet. And good. Do you hear me?"

"Yes'm."

"Very well." She stood up and her joints snapped. "Come with me, Catherine," she said. "Let's bring your crayons." And she helped Catherine gather up the crayons and the stubs from the window sill and from the carpet. Catherine's face was still red but she was not crying any more. As she passed Rufus she gave him a glance filled with satisfaction, and he answered it with a glance of helpless malevolence.

He listened towards the upstairs. If his Uncle Andrew had overheard this, there would really be trouble. But there was no evidence that he had. Rufus felt weak in the knees and in the stomach. He went over to the chair beside the fireplace and sat down.

It was mean to pester Catherine like that but he hadn't wanted to do anything for her anyway. And why did she have to holler like that and bring Aunt Hannah running? He remembered the way her face got red and he knew that he had really been mean to her and he was sorry. But what did she holler for, like a regular crybaby? He would be very careful today, but sooner or later he sure would get back on her. Darn crybaby. Tattletale.

The others really did pay him some attention, though. Anybody here ought to know, it's him. His daddy got killed. Yeah *you* tell it. Come on and tell us. Just a chance in a million. A million trillion. Never even knowed, knew, what hit him. Shut yer Goddamn mouth. Ain't you got no sense at all?

Instantly killed.

Concussion, that was it. Concussion of the brain.

Knocked him crazy as a loon, bibblibblebble.

Shut yer Goddam mouth.

But there was something that made him feel wrong.

Ole Tin Lizzie.

What you get for driving a auto when you're drunk, that's what my dad says.

Good old whiskey.

Something he did.

Ole Tin Lizzie just rolled back down on top of him *whomp.*

Didn't either.

He didn't say it didn't. Not clear enough.

Heck, how can that kill anybody?

Did, though. Just a chance in a million. Million trillion. Instantly killed.

Worse than that, he did.

What.

How would your daddy like it?

He would like me to be with them without them teasing; looking up to me.

How would your daddy like it?

Like what?

Going out in the street like that when he is dead.

Out in the street like what?

Showing off to people because he is dead.

He wants me to get along with them.

So I tell them he is dead and they look up to me, they don't tease me.

Showing off because he's dead, that's all you can show off about. Any other thing they'd tease me and I wouldn't fight back.

How would your daddy like it?

But he likes me to get along with them. That's why I—went out—showed off.

He felt so uneasy, deep inside his stomach, that he could not think about it any more. He wished he hadn't done it. He wished he could go back and not do anything of the kind. He wished his father could know about it and tell him that yes he was bad but it was all right he didn't mean to be bad. He was glad his father didn't know because if his father knew he would think even worse of him than ever. But if his father's soul was around, always, watching over them, then he knew. And that was worst of anything because there was no way to hide from a soul, and no way to talk to it, either. He just knows, and it couldn't say anything to him, and he couldn't say anything to it. It couldn't whip him either, but it could sit and look at him and be ashamed of him.

"I didn't mean it," he said aloud. "I didn't mean to do bad."

I wanted to show you my cap, he added, silently.

He looked at his father's morsechair.

Not a mark on his body.

He still looked at the chair. With a sense of deep stealth and secrecy he finally went over and stood beside it. After a few moments, and after listening most intently, to be sure that nobody was near, he smelled of the chair, its deeply hollowed seat, the arms, the back. There was only a cold smell of tobacco and, high along the back, a faint smell of hair. He thought of the ashtray on its weighted strap on the arm; it was empty. He ran his finger inside it; there was only a dim smudge of ash. There was nothing like enough to keep in his pocket or wrap up in a paper. He looked at his finger for a moment and licked it; his tongue tasted of darkness.

JAMES AGEE's death at the age of 45 ended the career of a great and poetic writer. He wrote fiction, non-fiction, poetry, screenplays and film criticism with equal art. *A Death in the Family* is his most famous book, but millions remember his screenplays for "The African Queen" and "The Quiet One" and his television film biography, "Mr. Lincoln," which was repeated three times on *Omnibus.* His movie criticism (for *Time, Life,* and other periodicals) and five of his screenplays have been collected in two volumes called *Agee On Film.* Whether writing a poem, an essay on Chaplin, or a report about Alabama sharecroppers (*Let Us Now Praise Famous Men*), he always produced distinguished work.

Agee was born in 1909 in Knoxville, Tennessee (the setting for *A Death in the Family*), and attended St. Andrew's School, Exeter, and Harvard, where he was editor of the *Advocate*. "Rufus" is a chapter from *A Death in the Family,* which received the Pulitzer Prize in 1958, three years after Agee's death.

EVELYN WAUGH

Charles's Holiday

I returned home for the Long Vacation without plans and without money. To cover end-of-term expenses I had sold my Omega screen to Collins for ten pounds, of which I now kept four; my last cheque overdrew my account by a few shillings, and I had been told that, without my father's authority, I must draw no more. My next allowance was not due until October. I was thus faced with a bleak prospect and, turning the matter over in my mind, I felt something not far off remorse for the prodigality of the preceding weeks.

I had started the term with my battels paid and over a hundred pounds in hand. All that had gone, and not a penny paid out where I could get credit. There had been no reason for it, no great pleasure unattainable else; it had gone in ducks and drakes. Sebastian often chid me with extravagance, but I resented his censure for a large part of my money went on and with him. His own finances were perpetually, vaguely distressed. "It's all done by lawyers," he said helplessly, "and I suppose they embezzle a lot. Anyway, I never seem to get much. Of course, Mummy would give me anything I asked for."

"Then why don't you ask her for a proper allowance?"

"Oh, Mummy likes everything to be a present. She's so sweet," he said, adding one more line to the picture I was forming of her.

Now Sebastian had disappeared into that other life of his where I was not asked to follow, and I was left, instead, forlorn and regretful.

How ungenerously in later life we disclaim the virtuous moods of our youth, living in retrospect long, summer days of unreflecting dissipation, Dresden figures of pastoral gaiety! Our wisdom, we prefer to think, is all of our own gathering, while, if the truth be told, it is, most of it, the last coin of a legacy that dwindles with time. There is no candor in a story of early manhood which leaves out of account the home-sickness for nursery morality, the regrets and resolutions of amendment, the black hours which, like zero on the roulette table, turn up with roughly calculable regularity.

Thus I spent the first afternoon at home, wandering from room to room, looking from the plate-glass windows in turn on the garden and the street, in a mood of vehement self-reproach.

My father, I knew, was in the house, but his library was inviolable, and it was not until just before dinner that he appeared to greet me. He was then in his late fifties, but it was his idiosyncrasy to seem much older than his years; to see him one might have put him at seventy, to hear him speak at nearly eighty. He came to me now, with the shuffling mandarin-tread which he affected, and a shy smile of welcome. When he dined at home—and he seldom dined elsewhere—he wore a frogged velvet smoking suit of the kind which had been fashionable many years before and was to be so again, but, at that time, was a deliberate archaism.

"My dear boy, they never told me you were here. Did you have a very exhausting journey? They gave you tea? You are well? I have just made a somewhat audacious purchase from Sonerschein's—a terra-cotta bull of the fifth century. I was examining it and forgot your arrival. Was the carriage *very* full? You had a corner seat?" (He traveled so rarely himself that to hear of others doing so always excited his solicitude.) "Hayter brought you the evening paper? There is no news, of course—such a lot of nonsense."

Dinner was announced. My father from long habit took a book with him to the table and then, remembering my presence, furtively dropped it under his chair. "What do you like to drink? Hayter, what have we for Mr. Charles to drink?"

"There's some whiskey."

"There's whiskey. Perhaps you like something else? What else have we?"

"There isn't anything else in the house, sir."

"There's nothing else. You must tell Hayter what you would like and he will get it in. I never keep any wine now. I am forbidden it and no one comes to see me. But while you are here, you must have what you like. You are here for long?"

"I'm not quite sure, Father."

"It's a *very* long vacation," he said wistfully. "In my day we used to go on what were called 'reading parties,' always in mountainous areas. Why? Why," he repeated petulantly, "should alpine scenery be thought conducive to study?"

"I thought of putting in some time at an art school—in the life class."

"My dear boy, you'll find them all shut. The students go to Barbizon or such places and paint in the open air. There was an institution in my day called a 'sketching club'—mixed sexes" (snuffle), "bicycles" (snuffle), "pepper-and-salt knickerbockers, holland umbrellas and, it was popularly thought, free love." (Snuffle) "*Such* a lot of nonsense. I expect they still go on. You might try that."

"One of the problems of the vacation is money, Father."

"Oh, I shouldn't worry about a thing like that at your age."

"You see, I've run rather short."

"Yes?" said my father without any sound of interest.

"In fact I don't quite know how I'm going to get through the next two months."

"Well, I'm the worst person to come to for advice. I've never been 'short,' as you so painfully call it. And yet what else could you say? Hard up? Penurious? Distressed? Embarrassed? Stonybroke?" (Snuffle) "On the rocks? In Queer Street? Let us say you are in Queer Street and leave it at that. Your grandfather once said to me, 'Live within your means, but if you do get into difficulties, come to me. Don't go to the Jews.' Such a lot of nonsense. You try. Go to those gentlemen in Jermyn Street who offer advances on note of hand only. My dear boy, they won't give you a sovereign."

"Then what do you suggest my doing?"

"Your cousin Melchior was imprudent with his investments and got into a very queer street. *He* went to Australia."

I had not seen my father so gleeful since he found two pages of second-century papyrus between the leaves of a Lombardic breviary.

"Hayter, I've dropped my book."

It was recovered for him from under his feet and propped against the epergne. For the rest of dinner he was silent save for an occasional snuffle of merriment which could not, I thought, be provoked by the work he read.

Presently we left the table and sat in the garden-room; and there, plainly, he put me out of his mind; his thoughts, I knew, were far away, in those distant ages where he moved at ease, where time passed in centuries and all the figures were defaced and the names of his companions were corrupt readings of words of quite other meaning. He sat in an attitude which to anyone else would have been one of extreme discomfort, askew in his upright armchair, with his book held high and obliquely to the light. Now and then he took a gold pencil case from his watch-chain and made an entry in the margin. The windows were open to the summer night; the ticking of the clocks, the distant murmur of traffic on the Bayswater Road, and my father's regular turning of the pages were the only sounds. I had thought it impolitic to smoke a cigar while pleading poverty; now in desperation I went to my room and fetched one. My father did not look up. I pierced it, lit it, and with renewed confidence said, "Father, you surely don't want me to spend the whole vacation here with you?"

"Eh?"

"Won't you find it rather a bore having me at home for so long?"

"I trust I should not betray such an emotion even if I felt it," said my father mildly and turned back to his book.

The evening passed. Eventually all over the room clocks of diverse pattern musically chimed eleven. My father closed his book and removed his spectacles, "You are very welcome, my dear boy," he said. "Stay as long as you find it convenient." At the door he paused and turned back. "Your cousin Melchior worked his passage to Australia *before the mast.*" (Snuffle) "What, I wonder, is 'before the mast'?"

During the sultry week that followed my relations with my father deteriorated sharply. I saw little of him during the day;

he spent hours on end in the library; now and then he emerged and I would hear him calling over the banisters: "Hayter. Call me a cab." Then he would be away, sometimes for half an hour or less, sometimes for a whole day; his errands were never explained. Often I saw trays going up to him at odd hours, laden with meager nursery snacks—rusks, glasses of milk, bananas and so forth. If we met in a passage or on the stairs he would look at me vacantly and say "Ah-ha" or "Very warm," or "Splendid, splendid," but in the evening, when he came to the garden-room in his velvet smoking suit, he always greeted me formally.

The dinner table was our battlefield.

On the second evening I took my book with me to the dining-room. His mild and wandering eye fastened on it with sudden attention, and as we passed through the hall he surreptitiously left his own on a side table. When we sat down he said plaintively: "I do think, Charles, you might talk to me. I've had a very exhausting day. I was looking forward to a little conversation."

"Of course, Father. What shall we talk about?"

"Cheer me up. Take me out of myself"; (petulantly) "tell me all about the new plays."

"But I haven't been to any."

"You should, you know, you really should. It's not natural in a young man to spend all his evenings at home."

"Well, Father, as I told you, I haven't much money to spare for theatre-going."

"My dear boy, you must not let money become your master in this way. Why, at your age, your cousin Melchior was part owner of a musical piece. It was one of his few happy ventures. You should go to the play as part of your education. If you read the lives of eminent men you will find that quite half of them made their first acquaintance with drama from the gallery. I am told there is no pleasure like it. It is there that you find the real critics and devotees. It is called 'sitting with the gods.' The expense is nugatory, and even while you wait for admission in the street you are diverted by 'buskers.' We will sit with the gods together one night. How do you find Mrs. Abel's cooking?"

"Rather insipid."

"It was inspired by my sister Philippa. She gave Mrs. Abel ten menus, and they have never been varied. When I am alone I do not notice what I eat, but now that you are here, we must have a change. What would you like? What is in season? Are you fond of lobsters? Hayter, tell Mrs. Abel to give us lobsters to-morrow night."

Dinner that evening consisted of a white, tasteless soup, overfried fillets of sole with a pink sauce, lamb cutlets propped against a cone of mashed potato, stewed pears in jelly standing on a kind of sponge cake.

"It is purely out of respect for your Aunt Philippa that I dine at this length. She laid it down that a three-course dinner was middle-class. 'If you once let the servants get their way,' she said, 'you will find yourself dining nightly off a single chop.' There is nothing I should like more. In fact, that is exactly what I do when I go to my club on Mrs. Abel's evening out. But your aunt ordained that at home I must have soup and three courses; some nights it is fish, meat and savory, on others it is meat, sweet, savory—there are a number of possible permutations.

"It is remarkable how some people are able to put their opinions in lapidary form; your aunt had that gift.

"It is odd to think that she and I once dined together nightly—just as you and I do, my boy. Now *she* made unremitting efforts to take me out of myself. She used to tell me about her reading. It was in *her* mind to make a home with me, you know. She thought I should get into funny ways if I was left on my own. Perhaps I *have* got into funny ways. Have I? But it didn't do. I got her out in the end."

There was an unmistakable note of menace in his voice as he said this.

It was largely by reason of my Aunt Philippa that I now found myself so much a stranger in my father's house. After my mother's death she came to live with my father and me, no doubt, as he said, with the idea of making her home with us. I knew nothing, then, of the nightly agonies at the dinner table. My aunt made herself my companion, and I accepted her without question. That was for a year. The first change was that she re-opened her house in Surrey which she had meant to sell, and lived there during my school terms, coming to London only for a few days' shopping and entertainment. In the summer we went to lodgings together at the sea-side. Then in my last year at school she left England. *"I got her out in the end,"* he said with derision and triumph of that kindly lady, and he knew that I heard in the words a challenge to myself.

As we left the dining-room my father said, "Hayter, have you said anything yet to Mrs. Abel about the lobsters I ordered for tomorrow?"

"No, sir."

"Do not do so."

"Very good, sir."

And when we reached our chairs in the garden-room he said: "I wonder whether Hayter had any intention of mentioning lobsters. I rather think not. Do you know, I believe he thought I was *joking?*"

Next day, by chance, a weapon came to hand. I met an old acquaintance of school days, a contemporary of mine named Jorkins. I never had much liking for Jorkins. Once, in my Aunt Philippa's day, he had come to tea, and she had condemned him as being probably charming at heart, but unattractive at first sight. Now I greeted him with enthusiasm and asked him to dinner. He came and showed little alteration. My father must have been warned by Hayter that there was a guest, for instead of his velvet suit he wore a tail coat; this, with a back waistcoat, very high collar, and very narrow white tie, was his evening dress; he wore it with an air of melancholy as though it were court mourning, which he had assumed in early youth and, finding the style sympathetic, had retained. He never possessed a dinner jacket.

"Good evening, good evening. So nice of you to come all this way."

"Oh, it wasn't far," said Jorkins, who lived in Sussex Square.

"Science annihilates distance," said my father disconcertingly. "You are over here on business?"

"Well, I'm *in* business, if that's what you mean."

"I had a cousin who was in business—you wouldn't know him; it was before your time. I was telling Charles about him only the other night. He has been much in my mind. He came," my father paused to give full weight to the bizarre word—"a *cropper*."

Jorkins giggled nervously. My father fixed him with a look of reproach.

"You find his misfortune the subject of mirth? Or perhaps the word I used was unfamiliar; *you* no doubt would say that he 'folded up.' "

My father was master of the situation. He had made a little fantasy for himself, that Jorkins should be an American, and throughout the evening he played a delicate, one-sided parlor-game with him, explaining any peculiarly English terms that occurred in the conversation, translating pounds into dollars, and courteously deferring to him with such phrases as "Of course, by *your* standards . . ."; "All this must seem very parochial to Mr. Jorkins"; "In the vast spaces to which *you* are accustomed . . ." so that my guest was left with the vague sense that there was a misconception somewhere as to his identity, which he never got the chance of explaining. Again and again during dinner he sought my father's eye, thinking to read there the simple statement that this form of address was an elaborate joke, but met instead a look of such mild benignity that he was left baffled.

Once I thought my father had gone too far, when he said:

"I am afraid that, living in London, you must sadly miss your national game."

"My national game?" asked Jorkins, slow in the uptake, but scenting that here, at last, was the opportunity for clearing the matter up.

My father glanced from him to me and his expression changed from kindness to malice; then back to kindness again as he turned once more to Jorkins. It was the look of a gambler who lays down fours against a full house. "Your national game," he said gently, "*cricket,*" and he snuffled uncontrollably, shaking all over and wiping his eyes with his napkin. "Surely, working in the City, you find your time on the cricket-field greatly curtailed?"

At the door of the dining-room he left us. "Good night, Mr. Jorkins," he said. "I hope you will pay us another visit when you next 'cross the herring pond.' "

"I say, what did your governor mean by that? He seemed almost to think I was American."

"He's rather odd at times."

"I mean all that about advising me to visit Westminster Abbey. It seemed rum."

"Yes. I can't quite explain."

"I almost thought he was pulling my leg," said Jorkins in puzzled tones.

My father's counter-attack was delivered a few days later. He sought me out and said, "Mr. Jorkins is still here?"

"No, Father, of course not. He only came to dinner."

"Oh, I hoped he was staying with us. Such a *versatile* young man. But you will be dining in?"

"Yes."

"I am giving a little dinner party to diversify the rather monotonous series of your evenings at home. You think Mrs. Abel is up to it? No. But our guests are not exacting. Sir Cuthbert and Lady Orme-Herrick are what might be called the nucleus. I hope for a little music afterwards. I have included in the invitations some young people for you."

My presentiments of my father's plan were surpassed by the actuality. As the guests assembled in the room which my father, without self-consciousness, called "the Gallery," it was plain to me that they had been carefully chosen for my discomfort. The "young people" were Miss Gloria Orme-Herrick, a student of the cello; her fiancé, a bald young man from the British Museum; and a monoglot Munich publisher. I saw my father snuffling at me from behind a case of ceramics as he stood with them. That evening he wore, like a chivalric badge of battle, a small red rose in his button-hole.

Dinner was long and chosen, like the guests, in a spirit of careful mockery. It was not of Aunt Philippa's choosing, but had been reconstructed from a much earlier period, long before he was of an age to dine downstairs. The dishes were ornamental in appearance and regularly alternated in color between red and white. They and the wine were equally tasteless. After dinner my father led the German publisher to the piano and then, while he played, left the dining-room to show Sir Cuthbert Orme-Herrick the Etruscan bull in the gallery.

It was a gruesome evening, and I was astonished to find, when at last the party broke up, that it was only a few minutes after eleven. My father helped himself to a glass of barley-water and said: "What very dull friends I have! You know, without the spur of your presence I should never have roused myself to invite them. I have been very negligent about entertaining lately. Now that you are paying me such a long visit, I will have many such evenings. You liked Miss Gloria Orme-Herrick?"

"No."

"No? Was it her little mustache you objected to or her very large feet? Do you think she enjoyed herself?"

"No."

"That was my impression also. I doubt if any of our guests will count this as one of their happiest evenings. That young foreigner played atrociously, I thought. Where can I have met him? And Miss Constantia Smethwick—where can I have met *her?* But the obligations of hospitality must be observed. As long as you are here, you shall not be dull."

Strife was internecine during the next fortnight, but I suffered the more, for my father had greater reserves to draw on and a wider territory for maneuver, while I was pinned to my bridgehead between the uplands and the sea. He never declared his war aims; and I do not to this day know whether they were purely punitive—whether he had really at the back of his mind some geopolitical idea of getting me out of the country, as Aunt Philippa had been driven to Bordighera and my cousin Melchior to Darwin, or whether, as seems most likely, he fought for the sheer love of a battle, in which indeed he shone.

I received one letter from Sebastian, a conspicuous object which was brought to me in my father's presence one day when he was lunching at home; I saw him look curiously at it and bore it away to read in solitude. It was written on, and enveloped in, heavy late-Victorian mourning paper, black-coroneted and black-bordered. I read it eagerly:—

BRIDESHEAD CASTLE
WILTSHIRE

Dearest Charles,—

I found a box of this paper at the back of a bureau so I must write to you as I am mourning for my lost innocence. It never looked like living. The doctors despaired of it from the start.

Soon I am off to Venice to stay with my papa in his palace of sin. I wish you were coming. I wish you were here.

I am never quite alone. Members of my family keep turning up and collecting luggage and going away again, but the white raspberries are ripe.

I have a good mind not to take Aloysius to Venice. I don't want him to meet a lot of horrid Italian bears and pick up bad habits.

Love or what you will.

S.

I knew his letters of old; I had had them at Ravenna; I should not have been disappointed; but that day as I tore the stiff sheet across and let it fall into the basket, and gazed resentfully across the grimy gardens and irregular backs of Bayswater, at the jumble of soil pipes and fire-escapes and protuberant little conservatories, I saw, in my mind's eye, the pale face of Anthony Blanche, peering through the straggling leaves as it had peered through the candle flames at Thame, and heard, above the murmur of traffic, his clear tones . . . "You mustn't blame Sebastian if at times he seems a little insipid. . . . When I hear him talk I am reminded of that in some ways nauseating picture of 'Bubbles.' . . . Boredom . . . like a cancer in the breast. . . ."

For days after that I thought I hated Sebastian; then one Sunday afternoon a telegram came from him, which dispelled that shadow, adding a new and darker one of its own.

My father was out and returned to find me in a condition of feverish anxiety. He stood in the hall with his Panama hat still on his head and beamed at me.

"You'll never guess how I have spent the day; I have been to the Zoo. It was most agreeable; the animals seem to enjoy the sunshine so much."

"Father, I've got to leave at once."

"Yes?"

"A great friend of mine—he's had a terrible accident. I must go to him at once. Hayter's packing for me, now. There's a train in half an hour."

I showed him the telegram, which read simply: GRAVELY INJURED COME AT ONCE. SEBASTIAN.

"Well," said my father. "I'm sorry you are upset. Reading this message I should not say that the accident was as serious as you seem to think—otherwise it would hardly be signed by the victim himself. Still, of course, he may well be fully conscious but blind or paralyzed with a broken back. Why exactly is your presence so necessary? You have no medical knowledge. You are not in holy orders. Do you hope for a legacy?"

"I told you, he is a great friend."

"Well, Orme-Herrick is a great friend of mine, but I should not go tearing off to his deathbed on a warm Sunday afternoon. I should doubt whether Lady Orme-Herrick would welcome me. However, I see you have no such doubts. I shall miss you, my dear boy, but do not hurry back on my account."

EVELYN WAUGH, the son of an English publisher and the brother of Alec Waugh, novelist and author of travel books, was born in 1898. A slim, blond, brilliant Senior History Scholar at Oxford, he became known there for his fashionable playboy manner. After Oxford he studied art and worked as a journalist, and in 1928 he published his first book, a study of Rossetti. He then turned to satiric fiction about postwar London society. In *A Handful of Dust* (1934) and *Brideshead Revisited* (1945) he turned to more serious themes, but all of his novels have the gloss of cleverness and the delight in humorous or ironical social relations that can be seen in this selection from *Brideshead Revisited.* Even Waugh's lightest work has the touch of a great English stylist.

His later books include travel sketches and *The Loved One* (1948), a macabre satire on America that was recently made into a film.

Waugh lived a conservative country life for many years. He converted to Roman Catholicism in 1930. On Easter Day, 1966, he died at his Gloucestershire home, surrounded by his wife and children.

HENRY JAMES

The Marriages

1

"Won't you stay a little longer?" the hostess said, holding the girl's hand and smiling. "It's too early for everyone to go; it's too absurd." Mrs. Churchley inclined her head to one side and looked gracious; she held up to her face, in a vague, protecting, sheltering way, an enormous fan of red feathers. Everything about her, to Adela Chart, was enormous. She had big eyes, big teeth, big shoulders, big hands, big rings and bracelets, big jewels of every sort and many of them. The train of her crimson dress was longer than any other; her house was huge; her drawing room, especially now that the company had left it, looked vast, and it offered to the girl's eyes a collection of the largest sofas and chairs, pictures, mirrors, and clocks that she had ever beheld. Was Mrs. Churchley's fortune also large, to account for so many immensities? Of this Adela could know nothing, but she reflected, while she smiled sweetly back at their entertainer, that she had better try to find out. Mrs. Churchley had at least a high-hung carriage drawn by the tallest horses, and in the Row she was to be seen perched on a mighty hunter. She was high and expansive herself, though not exactly fat; her bones were big, her limbs were long, and she had a loud, hurrying voice, like the bell of a steamboat. While she spoke to his daughter she had the air of hiding from Colonel Chart, a little shyly, behind the wide ostrich fan. But Colonel Chart was not a man to be either ignored or eluded.

"Of course everyone is going on to something else," he said. "I believe there are a lot of things tonight."

"And where are *you* going?" Mrs. Churchley asked, dropping her fan and turning her bright, hard eyes on the Colonel.

"Oh, I don't do that sort of thing!" he replied, in a tone of resentment just perceptible to his daughter. She saw in it that he thought Mrs. Churchley might have done him a little more justice. But what made the honest soul think that she was a person to look to for a perception of fine shades? Indeed the shade was one that it might have been a little difficult to seize—the difference between "going on" and coming to a dinner of twenty people. The pair were in mourning; the second year had not lightened it for Adela, but the Colonel had not objected to dining with Mrs. Churchley, any more than he had objected, at Easter, to going down to the Millwards', where he had met her, and where the girl had her reasons for believing him to have known he should meet her. Adela was not clear about the occasion of their original meeting, to which a certain mystery attached. In Mrs. Churchley's exclamation now there was the fullest concurrence in Colonel Chart's idea; she didn't say, "Ah, yes, dear friend, I understand!" but this was the note of sympathy she plainly wished to sound. It immediately made Adela say to her, "Surely you must be going on somewhere yourself."

"Yes, you must have a lot of places," the Colonel observed, looking at her shining raiment with a sort of invidious directness. Adela could read the tacit implication: "You're not in sorrow, in desolation."

Mrs. Churchley turned away from her at this, waiting just a moment before answering. The red fan was up again, and this time it sheltered her from Adela. "I'll give everything up—for *you,*" were the words that issued from behind it. "*Do* stay a little. I always think this is such a nice hour. One can really talk," Mrs. Churchley went on. The Colonel laughed; he said it wasn't fair. But their hostess continued, to Adela, "Do sit down; it's the only time to have any talk." The girl saw her father sit down, but she wandered away, turning her back and pretending to look at a picture. She was so far from agreeing with Mrs. Churchley that it was an hour she particularly disliked. She was conscious of the queerness, the shyness, in London, of the gregarious flight of guests, after a dinner, the general *sauve qui peut* and panic fear of being left with the host and hostess. But personally she always felt the contagion, always conformed to the flurry. Besides, she felt herself turning red now, flushed with a conviction that had come over her and that she wished not to show.

Her father sat down on one of the big sofas with Mrs. Churchley; fortunately he was also a person with a presence that could hold its own. Adela didn't care to sit and watch them while they made love, as she crudely formulated it, and she cared still less to join in their conversation. She wandered further away, went into another of the bright, "handsome," rather nude rooms—they were like women dressed for a ball—where the displaced chairs, at awkward angles to each other, seemed to retain the attitudes of bored talkers. Her heart beat strangely, but she continued to make a pretense of looking at the pictures on the walls and the ornaments on the tables, while she hoped that, as she preferred it, it would be also the course that her father would like best. She hoped "awfully," as she would have said, that he wouldn't think her rude. She was a person of courage, and he was a kind, an intensely good-natured man; nevertheless, she was a good deal afraid of him. At home it had always been a religion with them to be nice to the people he liked. How, in the old days, her mother, her incomparable mother, so clever, so unerring, so perfect—how in the precious days her mother had practiced that art! Oh, her mother, her irrecoverable mother! One of the pictures that she was looking at swam before her eyes. Mrs. Churchley, in the natural course, would have begun immediately to climb staircases. Adela could see the high, bony shoulders and the long, crimson tail and the universal coruscating nod wriggle their businesslike way through the rest of the night. Therefore she *must* have had her reasons for detaining them. There were mothers who thought everyone wanted to marry their eldest son, and the girl asked herself if *she* belonged to the class of daughters who thought everyone wanted to marry their father. Her companions left her alone; and though she didn't want to be near them, it angered her that Mrs. Churchley didn't call her. That proved that she was conscious of the situation. She would have called her, only Colonel Chart had probably murmured, "Don't." That proved that he also was conscious. The time was really not long—ten minutes at the most elapsed—when he cried out, gaily, pleasantly, as if with a little jocular reproach, "I say, Adela, we must release this dear lady!" He spoke, of course, as if it had been Adela's fault that they lingered. When they took leave she gave Mrs. Churchley, without intention and without defiance, but from the simple sincerity of her anxiety, a longer look into the eyes than she had ever given her before. Mrs. Churchley's onyx pupils reflected the question; they seemed to say: "Yes, I *am,* if that's what you want to know!"

What made the case worse, what made the girl more sure, was the silence preserved by her companion in the brougham, on their way home. They rolled along in the June darkness from Prince's Gate to Seymour Street, each looking out of a window in conscious dumbness; watching without seeing the hurry of the London night, the flash of lamps, the quick roll on the wood of hansoms and other broughams. Adela had expected that her father would say something about Mrs. Churchley; but when he said nothing, it was, strangely, still more as if he had spoken. In Seymour Street he asked the footman if Mr. Godfrey had come in, to which the servant replied that he had come in early and gone straight to his room. Adela had perceived as much, without saying so, by a lighted window in the third story; but she contributed no remark to the question. At the foot of the stairs her father halted a moment, hesitating, as if he had something on his mind; but what it amounted to, apparently, was only the dry "Good night" with which he presently ascended. It was the first time since her mother's death that he had bidden her good night without kissing her. They were a kissing family, and after her mother's death the habit had taken a fresh spring. She had left behind her such a general passion of regret that in kissing each other they seemed to themselves a little to be kissing her. Now, as, standing in the hall, with the stiff watching footman (she could have said to him angrily, "Go away!") planted near her, she looked with unspeakable pain at her father's back while he mounted, the effect was of his having withheld from other and still more sensitive lips the touch of his own.

He was going to his room, and after a moment she heard his door close. Then she said to the servant, "Shut up the house" (she tried to do everything her mother had done, to be a little of what she had been, conscious only of mediocrity), and took her own way upstairs. After she had reached her room she waited, listening, shaken by the apprehension that she should hear her father come out again and go up to Godfrey. He would go up to tell him, to have it over without delay, precisely because it would be so difficult. She asked herself, indeed, why he should tell Godfrey when he had not taken the occasion—their drive home was an occasion—to tell herself. However, she wanted no announcing, no telling; there was such a horrible clearness in her mind that what she now waited for was only to be sure her father wouldn't leave his room. At the end of ten minutes she saw that this particular danger was over, upon which she came out and made her way to Godfrey. Exactly what she wanted to say to him first, if her father counted on the boy's greater indulgence, and before he could say anything, was, "Don't forgive him; don't, don't!"

He was to go up for an examination, poor fellow, and during these weeks his lamp burned till the small hours. It was for the diplomatic service, and there was to be some frightful number of competitors; but Adela had great hopes of him—she believed so in his talents, and she saw, with pity, how hard he worked. This would have made her spare him, not trouble his night, his scanty rest, if anything less dreadful had been at stake. It was a blessing, however, that one could count upon his coolness, young as he was—his bright, good-looking discretion. Moreover, he was the one who would care most. If Leonard was the eldest son—he had, as a matter of course, gone into the army and was in India, on the staff, by good luck, of a governor-general—it was exactly this that would make him comparatively indifferent. His life was elsewhere, and his father and he had been in a measure military comrades, so that he would be deterred by a certain delicacy from protesting; he wouldn't have liked his father to protest in an affair of *his*. Beatrice and Muriel would care, but they were too young to speak, and this was just why her own responsibility was so great.

Godfrey was in working gear—shirt and trousers and slippers and a beautiful silk jacket. His room felt hot, though a window was open to the summer night; the lamp on the table shed its studious light over a formidable heap of textbooks and papers, and the bed showed that he had flung himself down to think out a problem. As soon as she got in she said to him: "Father's going to marry Mrs. Churchley!"

She saw the poor boy's pink face turn pale. "How do you know?"

"I've seen with my eyes. We've been dining there—we've just come home. He's in love with her—she's in love with him; they'll arrange it."

"Oh, I say!" Godfrey exclaimed, incredulous.

"He will, he will, he will!" cried the girl; and with this she burst into tears.

Godfrey, who had a cigarette in his hand, lighted it at one of the candles on the mantelpiece as if he were embarrassed. As Adela, who had dropped into his armchair, continued to sob, he said, after a moment: "He oughtn't to—he oughtn't to."

"Oh, think of mamma—think of mamma!" the girl went on.

"Yes, he ought to think of mamma"; and Godfrey looked at the tip of his cigarette.

"To such a woman as that, after *her!*"

"Dear old mamma!" said Godfrey, smoking.

Adela rose again, drying her eyes. "It's like an insult to her; it's as if he denied her." Now that she spoke of it, she felt herself tremendously exalted. "It's as if he rubbed out at a stroke all the years of their happiness."

"They were awfully happy," said Godfrey.

"Think what she was—think how no one else will ever again be like her!" the girl cried.

"I suppose he's not very happy now," Godfrey continued vaguely.

"Of course he isn't, any more than you and I are; and it's dreadful of him to want to be."

"Well, don't make yourself miserable till you're sure," the young man said.

But his sister showed him confidently that she *was* sure, from the way the pair had behaved together and from her father's attitude on the drive home. If Godfrey had been there, he would have seen everything; it couldn't be explained, but he would have felt. When he asked at what moment the girl had first had her suspicion, she replied that it had all come at once, that evening; or that at least she had had no conscious fear till then. There had been signs for two or three weeks, but she hadn't understood them—ever since the day Mrs. Churchley had dined in Seymour Street. Adela had thought it odd then that her father had wished to invite her, in the quiet way they were living; she was a person they knew so little. He had said something about her having been very civil to him, and that evening, already, she had guessed that he had been to Mrs. Churchley's oftener than she had supposed. Tonight it had come to her clearly that he had been to see her every day since the day she dined with them; every afternoon, about the hour she thought he was at his club. Mrs. Churchley was his club—she was just like a club. At this Godfrey laughed; he wanted to know what his sister knew about clubs. She was slightly disappointed in his laugh, slightly wounded by it, but she knew perfectly what she meant: she meant that Mrs. Churchley was public and florid, promiscuous and mannish.

"Oh, I dare say she's all right," said Godfrey, as if he wanted to get on with his work. He looked at the clock on the mantelshelf; he would have to put in another hour.

"All right to come and take darling mamma's place—to sit where *she* used to sit, to lay her horrible hands on *her* things?" Adela was appalled—all the more that she had not expected it—at her brother's apparent acceptance of such a prospect.

He colored; there was something in her passionate piety

that scorched him. She glared at him with her tragic eyes as if he had profaned an altar. "Oh, I mean nothing will come of it."

"Not if we do our duty," said Adela.

"Our duty?"

"You must speak to him—tell him how we feel; that we shall never forgive him, that we can't endure it."

"He'll think I'm cheeky," returned Godfrey, looking down at his papers, with his back to her and his hands in his pockets.

"Cheeky, to plead for *her* memory?"

"He'll say it's none of my business."

"Then you believe he'll do it?" cried the girl.

"Not a bit. Go to bed!"

"*I*'ll speak to him," said Adela, as pale as a young priestess.

"Don't cry out till you're hurt; wait till he speaks to *you*."

"He won't, he won't!" the girl declared. "He'll do it without telling us."

Her brother had faced round to her again; he started a little at this, and again, at one of the candles, lighted his cigarette, which had gone out. She looked at him a moment; then he said something that surprised her.

"Is Mrs. Churchley very rich?"

"I haven't the least idea. What has that to do with it?"

Godfrey puffed his cigarette. "Does she live as if she were?"

"She has got a lot of showy things."

"Well, we must keep our eyes open," said Godfrey. "And now you *must* let me get on." He kissed his sister, as if to make up for dismissing her, or for his failure to take fire; and she held him a moment, burying her head on his shoulder. A wave of emotion surged through her; she broke out with a wail:

"Ah, why did she leave us? Why did she leave us?"

"Yes, why indeed?" the young man sighed, disengaging himself with a movement of oppression.

2

Adela was so far right as that by the end of the week, though she remained certain, her father had not made the announcement she dreaded. What made her certain was the sense of her changed relations with him—of there being between them something unexpressed; something of which she was as conscious as she would have been of an unhealed wound. When she spoke of this to Godfrey, he said the change was of her own making, that she was cruelly unjust to the governor. She suffered even more from her brother's unexpected perversity; she had had so different a theory about him that her disappointment was almost a humiliation and she needed all her fortitude to pitch her faith lower. She wondered what had happened to him and why he had changed. She would have trusted him to feel right about anything, above all about such a matter as this. Their worship of their mother's memory, their recognition of her sacred place in their past, her exquisite influence in their father's life, his fortunes, his career, in the whole history of the family and welfare of the house—accomplished, clever, gentle, good, beautiful and capable as she had been, a woman whose soft distinction was universally proclaimed, so that on her death one of the Princesses, the most august of her friends, had written Adela such a note about her as princesses were understood very seldom to write: their hushed tenderness over all this was a kind of religion, and also a sort of honor, in falling away from which there was a semblance of treachery. This was not the way people usually felt in London, she knew; but, strenuous, ardent, observant girl as she was, with secrecies of sentiment and dim originalities of attitude, she had already made up her mind that London was no place to look for delicacies. Remembrance there was hammered thin, and to be faithful was to be a bore. The patient dead were sacrificed; they had no shrines, for people were literally ashamed of mourning. When they had hustled all sensibility out of their lives, they invented the fiction that they felt too much to utter. Adela said nothing to her sisters; this reticence was part of the virtue it was her system to exercise for them. *She* was to be their mother, a direct deputy and representative. Before the vision of that other woman parading in such a character, she felt capable of ingenuities and subtleties. The foremost of these was tremulously to watch her father. Five days after they had dined together at Mrs. Churchley's he asked her if she had been to see that lady.

"No indeed, why should I?" Adela knew that he knew she had not been, since Mrs. Churchley would have told him.

"Don't you call on people after you dine with them?" said Colonel Chart.

"Yes, in the course of time. I don't rush off within the week."

Her father looked at her, and his eyes were colder than she had ever seen them, which was probably, she reflected, just the way her own appeared to him. "Then you'll please rush off tomorrow. She's to dine with us on the 12th, and I shall expect your sisters to come down."

Adela stared. "To a dinner party?"

"It's not to be a dinner party. I want them to know Mrs. Churchley."

"Is there to be nobody else?"

"Godfrey, of course. A family party."

The girl asked her brother that evening if *that* was not tantamount to an announcement. He looked at her queerly, and then he said, "*I*'ve been to see her."

"What on earth did you do that for?"

"Father told me he wished it."

"Then he *has* told you?"

"Told me what?" Godfrey asked, while her heart sank with the sense that he was making difficulties for her.

"That they're engaged, of course. What else can all this mean?"

"He didn't tell me that, but I like her."

"*Like* her!" the girl shrieked.

"She's very kind, very good."

"To thrust herself upon us when we hate her? Is that what you call kind? Is that what you call decent?"

"Oh, *I* don't hate her," Godfrey rejoined, turning away as if his sister bored him.

She went the next day to see Mrs. Churchley, with a vague plan of breaking out to her, appealing to her, saying, "Oh, spare us! have mercy on us! let him alone! go away!" But that was not easy when they were face to face. Mrs. Churchley had every intention of getting, as she would have said—she was perpetually using the expression—into touch; but her good intentions were as depressing as a tailor's misfits. She could never understand that they had no place for her vulgar charity; that their life was filled with a fragrance of perfection for which she had no sense fine enough. She was as undomestic as a shopfront and as out of tune as a parrot. She would make them live in the streets, or bring the streets into their lives—it was the same thing. She had evidently never read a book, and she used intonations that Adela had never heard, as if she had been an Australian or an American. She understood everything in a vulgar sense; speaking of Godfrey's visit to her and praising him according to her idea, saying horrid things about him—that he was awfully good-looking, a perfect gentleman, the kind she liked. How could her father, who was after all, in everything else, such a dear, listen to a woman, or endure her, who thought she was pleasing when she called the son of his dead wife a perfect gentleman? What would he have been, pray? Much she knew about what any of them were! When she told Adela she wanted her to like her, the girl thought for an instant her opportunity had come—the chance to plead with her and beg her off. But she presented such an impenetrable surface that it would have been like giving a message to a varnished door. She wasn't a woman, said Adela; she was an address.

When she dined in Seymour Street, the "children," as the girl called the others, including Godfrey, liked her. Beatrice and Muriel stared shyly and silently at the wonders of her apparel (she was brutally overdressed!) without, of course, guessing the danger that tainted the air. They supposed her, in their innocence, to be amusing, and they didn't know, any more than she did herself, that she patronized them. When she was upstairs with them, after dinner, Adela could see her looking around the room at the things she meant to alter; their mother's things, not a bit like her own and not good enough for her. After a quarter of an hour of this, our young lady felt sure she was deciding that Seymour Street wouldn't do at all, the dear old home that had done for their mother for twenty years. Was she plotting to transport them all to her horrible Prince's Gate? Of one thing, at any rate, Adela was certain: her father, at that moment, alone in the dining room with Godfrey, pretending to drink another glass of wine to make time, was coming to the point, was telling the news. When they came upstairs, they both, to her eyes, looked strange: the news had been told.

She had it from Godfrey before Mrs. Churchley left the house, when, after a brief interval, he followed her out of the drawing room on her taking her sisters to bed. She was waiting for him at the door of her room. Her father was then alone with his *fiancée* (the word was grotesque to Adela); it was already as if it were her home.

"What did you say to him?" the girl asked, when her brother had told her.

"I said nothing." Then he added, coloring (the expression of her face was such), "There was nothing to say."

"Is that how it strikes you?" said Adela, staring at the lamp.

"He asked me to speak to her," Godfrey went on.

"To speak to her?"

"To tell her I was glad."

"And did you?" Adela panted.

"I don't know. I said something. She kissed me."

"Oh, how *could* you?" shuddered the girl, covering her face with her hands.

"He says she's very rich," said Godfrey simply.

"Is that why you kissed her?"

"I didn't kiss her. Good night," and the young man, turning his back upon her, went out.

When her brother was gone Adela locked herself in, as if with the fear that she should be overtaken or invaded, and during a sleepless, feverish, memorable night she took counsel of her uncompromising spirit. She saw things as they were, in all the indignity of life. The levity, the mockery, the infidelity, the ugliness, lay as plain as a map before her; it was a world *pour rire,* but she cried about it, all the same. The morning dawned early, or rather it seemed to her that there had been no night, nothing but a sickly, creeping day. But by the time she heard the house stirring again she had determined what to do. When she came down to the breakfast room her father was already in his place, with newspapers and letters; and she expected the first words he would utter to be a rebuke to her for having disappeared, the night before, without taking leave of Mrs. Churchley. Then she saw that he wished to be intensely kind, to make every allowance, to conciliate and console her. He knew that she knew from Godfrey, and he got up and kissed her. He told her as quickly as possible, to have it over, stammering a little, with an "I've a piece of news for you that will probably shock you," yet looking even exaggeratedly grave and rather pompous, to inspire the respect he didn't deserve. When he kissed her she melted, she burst into tears. He held her against him, kissing her again and again, saying tenderly, "Yes, yes, I know, I know." But he didn't know, or he could never have done it. Beatrice and Muriel came in, frightened when they saw her crying, and still more scared when she turned to them with words and an air that were terrible in their comfortable little lives: "Papa's going to be married; he's going to marry Mrs. Churchley!" After staring a moment and seeing their father look as strange, on his side, as Adela, though in a different way, the children also began to cry, so that when the servants arrived, with tea and boiled eggs, these functionaries were greatly embarrassed with their burden, not knowing whether to come in or hang back. They all scraped together a decorum, as soon as the things had been put on the table the Colonel banished the men with a glance. Then he made a little affectionate speech to Beatrice and Muriel, in which he assured them that Mrs. Churchley was the kindest, the most delightful, of women, only wanting to make them happy, only wanting to make him happy, and convinced that he would be if they were and that they would be if he was.

"What do such words mean?" Adela asked herself. She declared privately that they meant nothing, but she was silent, and everyone was silent, on account of the advent of Miss Flynn, the governess, before whom Colonel Chart preferred not to discuss the situation. Adela recognized on the spot that, if things were to go as he wished, his children would practically never again be alone with him. He would spend all his time with Mrs. Churchley till they were married, and then Mrs. Churchley would spend all her time with him. Adela was ashamed of him, and that was horrible—all the more that everyone else would be, all his other friends, everyone who had known her mother. But the public dishonor to that high memory should not be enacted; he should not do as he wished.

After breakfast her father told her that it would give him pleasure if, in a day or two, she would take her sisters to see Mrs. Churchley, and she replied that he should be obeyed. He held her hand a moment, looking at her with an appeal in his eyes which presently hardened into sternness. He wanted to know that she forgave him, but he also wanted to say to her that he expected her to mind what she did, to go straight. She turned away her eyes; she was indeed ashamed of him.

She waited three days, and then she took her sisters to see Mrs. Churchley. That lady was surrounded with callers, as Adela knew she would be; it was her "day" and the occasion the girl preferred. Before this she had spent all her time with her sisters, talking to them about their mother, playing upon their memory of her, making them cry and making them laugh, reminding them of certain hours of their early childhood, telling them anecdotes of her own. None the less she assured them that she believed there was no harm at all in Mrs. Churchley, and that when the time should come she would probably take them out immensely. She saw with smothered irritation that they enjoyed their visit in Prince's Gate; they had never been at anything so "grown-up," nor seen so many smart bonnets and brilliant complexions. Moreover, they were considered with interest, as if, as features of Mrs. Churchley's new life, they had been described in advance and were the heroines of the occasion. There were so many ladies present that Mrs. Churchley didn't talk to them much; but she called them her "chicks" and asked them to hand about tea cups and bread and butter. All this was highly agreeable and indeed intensely exciting to Beatrice and Muriel, who had little round red spots in *their* cheeks when they came away. Adela quivered with the sense that her mother's children were now Mrs. Churchley's "chicks" and features of Mrs. Churchley's life.

It was one thing to have made up her mind, however; it was another thing to make her attempt. It was when she learned from Godfrey that the day was fixed, the 20th of July, only six weeks removed, that she felt the importance of prompt action. She learned everything from Godfrey now, having determined that it would be hypocrisy to question her father. Even her silence was hypocritical, but she couldn't weep and wail. Her father showed extreme tact; taking no notice of her detachment, treating her as if it were a moment of *bouderie* which he was bound to allow her and which would pout itself away. She debated much as to whether she should take Godfrey into her confidence; she would have done so without hesitation if he had not disappointed her. He was so strange and so perversely preoccupied that she could explain it only by the high pressure at which he was living, his anxiety about his "exam." He was in a fidget, in a fever, putting on a spurt to come in first; skeptical moreover about his success and cynical about everything else. He appeared to agree to the general axiom that they didn't want a strange woman thrust into their home, but he found Mrs. Churchley "very jolly as a person to know." He had been to see her by himself; he had been to see her three times. He said to his sister that he would make the most of her now; he should probably be so little in Seymour Street after these days. What Adela at last determined to say to him was that the marriage would never take place. When he asked her what she meant and who was to prevent it, she replied that the interesting couple would give it up themselves, or that Mrs. Churchley at least would after a week or two back out of it.

"That will be really horrid then," Godfrey rejoined. "The only respectable thing, at the point they've come to, is to put it through. Charming for poor father to have the air of being 'chucked.' "

This made her hesitate two days more, but she found answers more valid than any objections. The many-voiced answer to everything—it was like the autumn wind around the house—was the backward affront to her mother. Her mother was dead, but it killed her again. So one morning, at eleven o'clock, when Adela knew her father was writing letters, she went out quietly and, stopping the first hansom she met, drove to Prince's Gate. Mrs. Churchley was at home, and she was shown into the drawing room with the request that she would wait five minutes. She waited, without the sense of breaking down at the last, the impulse to run away, which was what she had expected to have. In the cab and at the door her heart had beat terribly, but now, suddenly, with the game really to play, she found herself lucid and calm. It was a joy to her to feel later that this was the way Mrs. Churchley found her; not confused, not stammering nor prevaricating, only a little amazed at her own courage, conscious of the immense responsibility of her step and wonderfully older than her years. Her hostess fixed her at first with the waiting eyes of a cashier, but after a little, to Adela's surprise, she burst into tears. At this the girl cried herself, but with the secret happiness of believing they were saved. Mrs. Churchley said she would think over what she had been told, and she promised Adela, freely enough and very firmly, not to betray the secret of her visit to the Colonel. They were saved—they were saved: the words sung themselves in the girl's soul as she came downstairs. When the door was opened for her she saw her brother on the step, and they looked at each other in surprise, each finding it on the part of the other an odd hour for Prince's Gate. Godfrey remarked that Mrs. Churchley would have enough of the family, and Adela answered that she would perhaps have too much. None the less the young man went in, while his sister took her way home.

3

Adela Chart saw nothing of her brother for nearly a week; he had more and more his own time and hours, adjusted to his tremendous responsibilities, and he spent whole days at his crammer's. When she knocked at his door, late in the evening, he was not in his room. It was known in the house that he was greatly worried; he was horribly nervous about his ordeal. It was to begin on the 23rd of June, and his father was as worried as himself. The wedding had been arranged in relation to this; they wished poor Godfrey's fate settled first, though it was felt that the nuptials would be darkened if it should not be settled right.

Ten days after her morning visit to Mrs. Churchley Adela began to perceive that there was a difference in the air; but as yet she was afraid to exult. It was not a difference for the better, so that there might be still many hours of pain. Her father, since the announcement of his intended marriage, had been visibly pleased with himself, but that pleasure appeared to have undergone a check. Adela had the impression which the passengers on a great steamer receive when, in the middle of the night, they hear the engines stop. As this impression resolves itself into the general sense that something serious has happened, so the girl asked herself what had happened now. She had expected something serious; but it was as if she couldn't keep still in her cabin—she wanted to go up and see. On the 20th, just before breakfast, her maid brought her a message from her brother. Mr. Godfrey would be obliged if she would speak to him in his room. She went straight up to him, dreading to find him ill, broken down on the eve of his formidable week. This was not the case, however, inasmuch as he appeared to be already at work, to have been at work since dawn. But he was very white, and his eyes had a strange and new expression. Her beautiful young brother looked older; he looked haggard and hard. He met her there as if he had been waiting for her, and he said immediately: "Please to tell me this, Adela: what was the purpose of your visit, the other morning, to Mrs. Churchley—the day I met you at her door?"

She stared—she hesitated. "The purpose? What's the matter? Why do you ask?"

"They've put it off—they've put it off a month."

"Ah, thank God!" said Adela.

"Why do you thank God?" Godfrey exclaimed roughly.

His sister gave a strained, intense smile. "You know I think it's all wrong."

He stood looking at her up and down. "What did you do there? How did you interfere?"

"Who told you I interfered?" she asked, flushing.

"You said something—you did something. I knew you had done it when I saw you come out."

"What I did was my own business."

"Damn your own business!" cried the young man.

She had never in her life been so spoken to, and in advance, if she had been given the choice, she would have said that she would rather die than be so spoken to by Godfrey. But her spirit was high, and for a moment she was as angry as if someone had cut her with a whip. She escaped the blow, but she felt the insult. "And *your* business, then?" she asked. "I wondered what that was when I saw *you*."

He stood a moment longer frowning at her; then, with the exclamation "You've made a pretty mess!" he turned away from her and sat down to his books.

They had put it off, as he said; her father was dry and stiff and official about it. "I suppose I had better let you know that we have thought it best to postpone our marriage till the end of the summer—Mrs. Churchley has so many arrangements to make:" he was not more expansive than that. She neither knew nor greatly cared whether it was her fancy or a reality that he watched her obliquely, to see how she would take these words. She flattered herself that, thanks to Godfrey's preparation, cruel as the form of it had been, she took them very cleverly. She had a perfectly good conscience, for she was now able to judge what odious elements Mrs. Churchley, whom she had not seen since the morning in Prince's Gate, had already introduced into their relations with each other. She was able to infer that her father had not concurred in the postponement, for he was more restless than before, more absent, and distinctly irritable. There was of course still the question of how much of this condition was to be attributed to his solicitude about Godfrey. That young man took occasion to say a horrible thing to his sister: "If I don't pass, it will be your fault." These were dreadful days for the girl, and she asked herself how she could have borne them if the hovering spirit of her mother had not been at her side. Fortunately, she always felt it there, sustaining, commending, sanctifying. Suddenly her father announced to her that he wished her to go immediately, with her sisters, down to Overland, where there was always part of a household and where for a few weeks they would be sufficiently comfortable. The only explanation he gave of this desire was that he wanted them out of the way. "Out of the way of what?" she queried, since, for the time, there were to be no preparations in Seymour Street. She was willing to believe that it was out of the way of his nerves.

She never needed urging, however, to go to Overland, the dearest old house in the world, where the happiest days of her young life had been spent and the silent nearness of her mother always seemed greatest. She was happy again, with Beatrice and Muriel and Miss Flynn, and the air of summer, and the haunted rooms, and her mother's garden, and the talking oaks and the nightingales. She wrote briefly to her father, to give him, as he had requested, an account of things; and he wrote back that, since she was so contented (she didn't remember telling him that), she had better not return to town at all. The rest of the season was not important for her, and he was getting on very well. He mentioned that Godfrey had finished his exam; but, as she knew, there would be a tiresome wait before they could learn the result. Godfrey was going abroad for a month with young Sherard—he had earned a little rest and a little fun. He went abroad without a word to Adela, but in his beautiful little hand he took a chaffing leave of Beatrice. The child showed her sister the letter, of which she was very proud and which contained no message for Adela. This was the worst bitterness of the whole crisis for that young lady—that it exhibited so strangely the creature in the world whom, after her mother, she had loved best.

Colonel Chart had said he would "run down" while his children were at Overland, but they heard no more about it. He only wrote two or three times to Miss Flynn, upon matters in regard to which Adela was surprised that he should not have communicated with herself. Muriel accomplished an upright little letter to Mrs. Churchley—her eldest sister neither fostered nor discouraged the performance—to which Mrs. Churchley replied, after a fortnight, in a meager and, as Adela thought, illiterate fashion, making no allusion to the approach of any closer tie. Evidently the situation had changed; the question of the marriage was dropped, at any rate for the time. This idea gave the girl a singular and almost intoxicating sense of power; she felt as if she were riding a great wave of responsibility. She had chosen and acted, and the greatest could do no more than that. The grand thing was to see one's results, and what else was she doing? These results were in important and opulent lives; the stage was large on which she moved her figures. Such a vision was exciting, and as they had the use of a couple of ponies at Overland she worked off her excitement by a long gallop. A day or two after this, however, came news of which the effect was to rekindle it. Godfrey had come back, the list had been published, he had passed first. These happy tidings proceeded from the young man himself; he announced them by a telegram to Beatrice, who had never in her life before received such a missive and was proportionately inflated. Adela reflected that she herself ought to have felt snubbed, but she was too happy. They were free again, they were themselves, the nightmare of the previous weeks was blown away, the unity and dignity of her father's life were restored, and, to round off her sense of success, Godfrey had achieved his first step toward high distinction. She wrote to him the next day, as frankly and affectionately as if there had been no estrangement between them; and besides telling him that she rejoiced in his triumph, she begged him in charity to let them know exactly how the case stood with regard to Mrs. Churchley.

Late in the summer afternoon she walked through the park to the village with her letter, posted it, and came back. Suddenly, at one of the turns of the avenue, halfway to the house, she saw a young man looking toward her and waiting for her—a young man who proved to be Godfrey, on his march, on foot, across from the station. He had seen her, as he took his short cut, and if he had come down to Overland it was not, apparently, to avoid her. There was none of the joy of his triumph in his face, however, as he came a very few steps to meet her; and although, stiffly enough, he let her kiss him and say, "I'm so glad—I'm so glad!" she felt that this tolerance was not quite the calmness of the rising diplomatist. He turned toward the house with her and walked on a short distance, while she uttered the hope that he had come to stay some days.

"Only till tomorrow morning. They are sending me straight to Madrid. I came down to say good-by; there's a fellow bringing my portmanteau."

"To Madrid? How awfully nice! And it's awfully nice of you to have come," Adela said, passing her hand into his arm.

The movement made him stop, and, stopping, he turned on her, in a flash, a face of something more than suspicion—of passionate reprobation. "What I really came for—you might as well know without more delay—is to ask you a question."

"A question?" Adela repeated with a beating heart.

They stood there, under the old trees, in the lingering light, and, young and fine and fair as they both were, they were in complete superficial accord with the peaceful English scene. A near view, however, would have shown that Godfrey Chart had not come down to Overland to be superficial. He looked deep into his sister's eyes and demanded: "What was it you said that morning to Mrs. Churchley?"

Adela gazed at the ground a moment; then raising her eyes: "If she has told you, why do you ask?"

"She has told me nothing. I've seen for myself."

"What have you seen?"

"She has broken it off—everything's over—father's in the depths."

"In the depths?" the girl quavered.

"Did you think it would make him jolly?" asked her brother.

"He'll get over it; he'll be glad."

"That remains to be seen. You interfered, you invented something, you got round her. I insist on knowing what you did."

Adela felt that she could be obstinate if she wished, and that if it should be a question of organizing a defense, she should find treasures of perversity under her hand. She stood looking down again a moment, and saying to herself, "I could be dumb and dogged if I chose, but I scorn to be." She was not ashamed of what she had done, but she wanted to be clear. "Are you absolutely certain it's broken off?"

"He is, and she is; so that's as good."

"What reason has she given?"

"None at all—or half a dozen; it's the same thing. She has changed her mind—she mistook her feelings—she can't part with her independence; moreover, he has too many children."

"Did he tell you this?" said Adela.

"Mrs. Churchley told me. She has gone abroad for a year."

"And she didn't tell you what I said to her?"

"Why should I take this trouble if she had?"

"You might have taken it to make me suffer," said Adela. "That appears to be what you want to do."

"No, I leave that to *you;* it's the good turn you've done me!" cried the young man, with hot tears in his eyes.

She stared, aghast with the perception that there was some dreadful thing she didn't know; but he walked on, dropping the question angrily and turning his back to her as if he couldn't trust himself. She read his disgust in his averted face, in the way he squared his shoulders and smote the ground with his stick, and she hurried after him and presently overtook him. She accompanied him for a moment in silence; then she pleaded: "What do you mean? What in the world have I done to you?"

"She would have helped me; she was all ready to do it," said Godfrey.

"Helped you in what?" She wondered what he meant; if he had made debts that he was afraid to confess to his father and—of all horrible things—had been looking to Mrs. Churchley to pay. She turned red with the mere apprehension of this and, on the heels of her guess, exulted again at having perhaps averted such a shame.

"Can't you see that I'm in trouble? Where are your eyes, your senses, your sympathy, that you talk so much about? Haven't you seen these six months that I've a cursed worry in my life?"

She seized his arm, she made him stop, she stood looking up at him like a frightened little girl. "What's the matter, Godfrey—what *is* the matter?"

"You've vexed me so—I could strangle you!" he growled. This idea added nothing to her dread; her dread was that he had done some wrong, was stained with some guilt. She uttered it to him with clasped hands, begging him to tell her the worst; but, still more passionately, he cut her short with his own cry: "In God's name, satisfy me! What infernal thing did you do?"

"It was not infernal; it was right. I told her mamma had been wretched," said Adela.

"Wretched? You told her such a lie?"

"It was the only way, and she believed me."

"Wretched how—wretched when—wretched where?" the young man stammered.

"I told her papa had made her so, and that *she* ought to know it. I told her the question troubled me unspeakably, but that I had made up my mind it was my duty to initiate her." Adela paused, with the light of bravado in her face, as if, though struck while she phrased it, with the monstrosity of what she had done, she was incapable of abating a jot of it. "I notified her that he had faults and peculiarities that made mamma's life a long worry—a martyrdom that she hid wonderfully from the world, but that we saw and that I had often pitied. I told her what they were, these faults and peculiarities; I put the dots on the *i*'s. I said it wasn't fair to let another person marry him without a warning. I warned her; I satisfied my conscience. She could do as she liked. My responsibility was over."

Godfrey gazed at her; he listened, with parted lips, incredulous and appalled. "You invented such a tissue of falsities and calumnies, and you talk about your conscience? You stand there in your senses and proclaim your crime?"

"I would have committed any crime that would have rescued us."

"You insult and defame your own father?" Godfrey continued.

"He'll never know it; she took a vow she wouldn't tell him."

"I'll be damned if *I* won't tell him!" Godfrey cried.

Adela felt sick at this, but she flamed up to resent the treachery, as it struck her, of such a menace. "I did right—I did right!" she vehemently declared. "I went down on my knees to pray for guidance, and I saved mamma's memory from outrage. But if I hadn't, if I hadn't"—she faltered for an instant—"I'm not worse than you, and I'm not so bad, for you've done something that you're ashamed to tell me."

Godfrey had taken out his watch; he looked at it with quick intensity, as if he were not hearing nor heeding her. Then, glancing up with his calculating eye, he fixed her long enough to exclaim, with unsurpassable horror and contempt: "You raving maniac!" He turned away from her; he bounded down the avenue in the direction from which they had come, and, while she watched him, strode away across the grass, toward the short cut to the station.

4

Godfrey's portmanteau, by the time Adela got home, had been brought to the house, but Beatrice and Muriel, who had been informed of this, waited for their brother in vain. Their sister said nothing to them about having seen him, and she accepted, after a little, with a calmness that surprised herself, the idea that he had returned to town to denounce her. She believed that would make no difference now—she had done what she had done. She had somehow a faith in Mrs. Churchley. If Mrs. Churchley had broken off, she wouldn't renew. She was a heavy-footed person, incapable of further agility. Adela recognized too that it might well have come over her that there were too many children. Lastly the girl fortified herself with the reflection, grotesque under the circumstances and tending to prove that her sense of humor was not high, that her father, after all, was not a man to be played with. It seemed to her, at any rate, that if she *had* prevented his marriage she could bear anything—bear imprisonment and bread and water, bear lashes and torture, bear even his lifelong reproach. What she could bear least was the wonder of the inconvenience she had inflicted on Godfrey. She had time to turn this over, very vainly, for a succession of days—days more numerous than she had expected, which passed without bringing her from London any summons to come up and take her punishment. She sounded the possible, she compared the degrees of the probable; feeling however that, as a cloistered girl, she was poorly equipped for speculation. She tried to imagine the calamitous things young men might do, and could only feel that such things would naturally be connected either with money or with women. She became conscious that after all she knew almost nothing about either subject. Meanwhile there was no reverberation from Seymour Street—only a sultry silence.

At Overland she spent hours in her mother's garden, where she had grown up, where she considered that she was training for old age, for she meant not to depend upon whist. She loved the place as, had she been a good Catholic, she would have loved the smell of her parish church; and indeed there was in her passion for flowers something of the respect of a religion. They seemed to her the only things in the world that really respected themselves, unless one made an exception for Nutkins, who had been in command all through her mother's time, with whom she had had a real friendship, and who had been affected by their pure example. He was the person left in the world with whom, on the whole, she could talk most intimately about her mother. They never had to name her together—they only said "she"; and Nutkins freely conceded that she had taught him everything he knew. When Beatrice and Muriel said "she" they referred to Mrs. Churchley. Adela had reason to believe that she should never marry, and that some day she should have about a thousand a year. This made her see in the far future a little garden of her own, under a hill, full of rare and exquisite things, where she would spend most of her old age on her knees, with an apron and stout gloves, a pair of shears and a trowel, steeped in the comfort of being thought mad.

One morning, ten days after her scene with Godfrey, upon coming back into the house shortly before lunch, she was met by Miss Flynn with the notification that a lady in the drawing room had been waiting for her for some minutes. "A lady" suggested immediately Mrs. Churchley. It came over Adela that the form in which her penalty was to descend would be a personal explanation with that misdirected woman. The lady had not given her name, and Miss Flynn had not seen Mrs. Churchley; nevertheless, the governess was certain that Adela's surmise was wrong.

"Is she big and dreadful?" the girl asked.

Miss Flynn, who was circumspection itself, hesitated a moment. "She's dreadful, but she's not big." She added that she was not sure she ought to let Adela go in alone; but this young lady felt throughout like a heroine, and it was not for a heroine to shrink from any encounter. Was she not, every instant, in transcendent contact with her mother? The visitor might have no connection whatever with the drama of her father's frustrated marriage; but everything, today, to Adela, was a part of that.

Miss Flynn's description had prepared her for a considerable shock, but she was not agitated by her first glimpse of the person who awaited her. A youngish, well-dressed woman stood there, and silence was between them while they looked at each other. Before either of them had spoken, however, Adela began to see what Miss Flynn had intended. In the light of the drawing-room window the lady was five-and-thirty years of age and had vivid yellow hair. She also had a blue cloth suit with brass buttons, a stick-up collar like a gentleman's, a necktie arranged in a sailor's knot, with a golden pin in the shape of a little lawn-tennis racket, and pearl-gray gloves with big black stitchings. Adela's second impression was that she was an actress; her third was that no such person had ever before crossed that threshold.

"I'll tell you what I've come for," said the apparition. "I've come to ask you to intercede." She was not an actress; an actress would have had a nicer voice.

"To intercede?" Adela was too bewildered to ask her to sit down.

"With your father, you know. He doesn't know, but he'll have to." Her "have" sounded like " 'ave." She explained, with many more such sounds, that she was Mrs. Godfrey, that they had been married seven mortal months. If Godfrey was going abroad, she must go with him, and the only way she could go with him would be for his father to do something. He was afraid of his father—that was clear; he was afraid even to tell him. What she had come down for was to see some other member of the family face to face ("fice to fice" Mrs. Godfrey called it) and try if he couldn't be approached by another side. If no one else would act, then she would just have to act herself. The Colonel would have to do something—that was the only way out of it.

What really happened Adela never quite understood; what seemed to be happening was that the room went round and round. Through the blur of perception accompanying this effect the sharp stabs of her visitor's revelation came to her like the words heard by a patient "going off" under ether. She denied passionately, afterward, even to herself, that she had done anything so abject as to faint; but there was a lapse in her consciousness in relation to Miss Flynn's intervention. This intervention had evidently been active, for when they talked the matter over, later in the day, with bated breath and infinite dissimulation for the schoolroom quarter, the governess had more information, and still stranger, to impart than to receive. She was at any rate under the impression that she had athletically contended, in the drawing room, with the yellow hair, after removing Adela from the scene and before inducing Mrs. Godfrey to withdraw. Miss Flynn had never known a more thrilling day, for all the rest of it, too, was pervaded with agitations and conversations, precautions and alarms. It was given out to Beatrice and Muriel that their sister had been taken suddenly ill, and the governess ministered to her in her room. Indeed, Adela had never found herself less at ease; for this time she had received a blow that she couldn't return. There was nothing to do but to take it, to endure the humiliation of her wound.

At first she declined to take it; it was much easier to consider that her visitor was a monstrous masquerader. On the face of the matter, moreover, it was not fair to believe till one heard; and to hear in such a case was to hear Godfrey himself. Whatever his sister had tried to imagine about him she had not arrived at anything so belittling as an idiotic secret marriage with a dyed and painted hag. Adela repeated this last word as if it gave her some comfort; and indeed where everything was so bad fifteen years of seniority made the case little worse. Miss Flynn was portentous, for Miss Flynn had had it out with the wretch. She had cross-questioned her and had not broken her down. This was the most important hour of Miss Flynn's life; for whereas she usually had to content herself with being humbly and gloomily in the right, she could now be magnanimously and showily so. Her only perplexity was as to what she ought to do—write to Colonel Chart or go up to town to see him. She bloomed with alternatives, never having known the like before. Toward evening Adela was obliged to recognize that Godfrey's worry, of which he had spoken to her, had appeared bad enough to consist even of a low wife, and to remember that, so far from its being inconceivable that a young man in his position should clandestinely take one, she had been present, years before, during her mother's lifetime, when Lady Molesley declared gaily, over a cup of tea, that this was precisely what she expected of her eldest son. The next morning it was the worst possibilities that seemed the clearest; the only thing left with a tatter of dusky comfort being the ambiguity of Godfrey's charge that his sister's action had "done" for him. That was a matter by itself, and she racked her brains for a connecting link between Mrs. Churchley and Mrs. Godfrey. At last she made up her mind that they were related by blood; very likely, though differing in fortune, they were cousins or even sisters. But even then what did her brother mean?

Arrested by the unnatural fascination of opportunity, Miss Flynn received before lunch a telegram from Colonel Chart—an order for dinner and a vehicle; he and Godfrey were to arrive at six o'clock. Adela had plenty of occupation for the interval, for she was pitying her father when she was not rejoicing that her mother had gone too soon to know. She flattered herself she discerned the providential reason of that cruelty now. She found time however still to wonder for what purpose, under the circumstances, Godfrey was to be brought down. She was not unconscious, it is true, that she had little general knowledge of what usually was done with young men in that predicament. One talked about the circumstances, but the circumstances were an abyss. She felt this still more when she found, on her father's arrival, that nothing, apparently, was to happen as she had taken for granted it would. There was a kind of inviolable hush over the whole affair, but no tragedy, no publicity, nothing ugly. The tragedy had been in town, and the faces of the two men spoke of it, in spite of themselves; so that at present there was only a family dinner, with Beatrice and Muriel and the governess, and almost a company tone, the result of the desire to avoid publicity. Adela admired her father; she knew what he was feeling, if Mrs. Godfrey had been at him, and yet she saw him positively gallant. He was very gentle, he never looked at his son, and there were moments when he seemed almost sick with sadness. Godfrey was equally inscrutable and therefore wholly different from what he had been as he stood before her in the park. If he was to start on his career (with such a wife!—wouldn't she utterly blight it?), he was already professional enough to know how to wear a mask.

Before they rose from table the girl was wholly bewildered, so little could she perceive the effects of such large causes. She had nerved herself for a great ordeal, but the air was as sweet as an anodyne. It was constantly plain to her that her father was deadly sad—as pathetic as a creature jilted. He was broken, but he showed no resentment; there was a weight on his heart, but he had lightened it by dressing as immaculately as usual for dinner. She asked herself what immensity of a row there could have been in town to have left his anger so spent. He went through everything, even to sitting with his son after dinner. When they came out together he invited Beatrice and Muriel to the billiard room; and as Miss Flynn discreetly withdrew, Adela was left alone with Godfrey, who was completely changed and not in a rage any more. He was broken, too, but he was not so pathetic as his father. He was only very correct and apologetic; he said to his sister, "I'm awfully sorry *you* were annoyed; it was something I never dreamed of."

She couldn't think immediately what he meant; then she grasped the reference to the yellow hair. She was uncertain, however, what tone to take; perhaps his father had arranged with him that they were to make the best of it. But she spoke her own despair in the way she murmured: "O Godfrey, Godfrey, is it true?"

"I've been the most unutterable donkey—you can say what you like to me. You can't say anything worse than I've said to myself."

"My brother, my brother!" his words made her moan. He hushed her with a movement, and she asked, "What has father said?"

Godfrey looked over her head. "He'll give her six hundred a year."

"Ah, the angel!"

"On condition she never comes near me. She has solemnly promised; and she'll probably leave me alone, to get the money. If she doesn't—in diplomacy—I'm lost." The young man had been turning his eyes vaguely about, this way and that, to avoid meeting hers; but after another instant he gave up the effort, and she had the miserable confession of his glance. "I've been living in hell," he said.

"My brother, my brother!" she repeated.

"I'm not an idiot; yet for her I've behaved like one. Don't ask me—you mustn't know. It was all done in a day, and since then, fancy my condition—fancy my work!"

"Thank God you passed!" cried Adela.

"I would have shot myself if I hadn't. I had an awful day yesterday with father; it was late at night before it was over. I leave England next week. He brought me down here for it to look well—so that the children sha'n't know."

"He's wonderful!" she murmured.

"He's wonderful!" said Godfrey.

"Did *she* tell him?" the girl asked.

"She came straight to Seymour Street from here. She saw him alone first; then he called me in. *That* luxury lasted about an hour."

Adela said, "Poor, poor father!" to this; on which her brother remained silent. Then, after he had remarked that it had been the scene he had lived in terror of all through his cramming, and she had stammered her pity and admiration at such a mixture of anxieties and such a triumph of talent, she demanded: "Have you told him?"

"Told him what?"

"What you said you would—what *I* did."

Godfrey turned away, as if at present he had very little interest in that inferior tribulation. "I was angry with you, but I cooled off. I held my tongue."

Adela clasped her hands. "You thought of mamma!"

"Oh, don't speak of mamma," said the young man tenderly.

It was indeed not a happy moment; and she murmured: "No, if you *had* thought of her"—

This made Godfrey turn back at her, with a little flare in his eyes. "Oh, *then* it didn't prevent. I thought that woman was good. I believed in her."

"Is she *very* bad?" his sister inquired.

"I shall never mention her to you again," Godfrey answered, with dignity.

"You may believe that *I* won't speak of her. So father doesn't know?" she added.

"Doesn't know what?"

"That I said that to Mrs. Churchley."

"I don't think so, but you must find out for yourself."

"I shall find out," said Adela. "But what had Mrs. Churchley to do with it?"

"With *my* misery? I told her. I had to tell someone."

"Why didn't you tell me?"

Godfrey hesitated. "Oh, you take things so beastly hard—you make such rows." Adela covered her face with her hands, and he went on: "What I wanted was comfort—not to be lashed up. I thought I should go mad. I wanted Mrs. Churchley to break it to father, to intercede for me and help him to meet it. She was awfully kind to me; she listened and she understood; she could fancy how it had happened. Without her I shouldn't have pulled through. She liked me, you know," Godfrey dropped. "She said she would do what she could for me; she was full of sympathy and resource; I really leaned on her. But when you cut in, of course it spoiled everything. That's why I was so angry with you. She couldn't do anything then."

Adela dropped her hands, staring; she felt that she had walked in darkness. "So that he had to meet it alone?"

"Dame!" said Godfrey, who had got up his French tremendously.

Muriel came to the door to say papa wished the two others to join them, and the next day Godfrey returned to town. His father remained at Overland, without an intermission, the rest of the summer and the whole of the autumn, and Adela had a chance to find out, as she had said, whether he knew that she had interfered. But in spite of her chance she never found out. He knew that Mrs. Churchley had thrown him over and he knew that his daughter rejoiced in it, but he appeared not to have divined the relation between the two facts. It was strange that one of the matters he was clearest about—Adela's secret triumph—should have been just the thing which, from this time on, justified less and less such a confidence. She was too sorry for him to be consistently glad. She watched his attempts to wind himself up on the subject of shorthorns and drainage, and she favored to the utmost of her ability his intermittent disposition to make a figure in orchids. She wondered whether they mightn't have a few people at Overland; but when she mentioned the idea her father asked what in the world there would be to attract them. It was a confoundedly stupid house, he remarked, with all respect to *her* cleverness. Beatrice and Muriel were mystified; the prospect of going out immensely had faded so utterly away. They were apparently not to go out at all. Colonel Chart was aimless and bored; he paced up and down and went back to smoking, which was bad for him, and looked drearily out of windows, as if on the bare chance that something might arrive. Did he expect Mrs. Churchley to arrive, to relent? It was Adela's belief that she gave no sign. But the girl thought it really remarkable of her not to have betrayed her ingenious young visitor. Adela's judgment of human nature was perhaps harsh, but she believed that many women, under the circumstances, would not have been so forbearing. This lady's conception of the point of honor presented her as rather a higher type than one might have supposed.

Adela knew her father found the burden of Godfrey's folly

very heavy to bear and was incommoded at having to pay the horrible woman six hundred a year. Doubtless he was having dreadful letters from her; doubtless she threatened them all with a hideous exposure. If the matter should be bruited, Godfrey's prospects would collapse on the spot. He thought Madrid very charming and curious, but Mrs. Godfrey was in England, so that his father had to face the music. Adela took a dolorous comfort in thinking that her mother was out of *that*—it would have killed her; but this didn't blind her to the fact that the comfort for her father would perhaps have been greater if he had had someone to talk to about his trouble. He never dreamed of doing so to her, and she felt that she couldn't ask him. In the family life he wanted utter silence about it. Early in the winter he went abroad for ten weeks, leaving her with her sisters in the country, where it was not to be denied that at this time existence had very little savor. She half-expected that her sister-in-law would descend upon her again; but the fear was not justified, and the quietude of such a personage savored terribly of expense. There were sure to be extras. Colonel Chart went to Paris and to Monte Carlo and then to Madrid to see his boy. Adela wondered whether he would meet Mrs. Churchley somewhere, since, if she had gone for a year, she would still be on the Continent. If he should meet her, perhaps the affair would come on again: she caught herself musing over this. Her father brought back no news of her, and seeing him after an interval, she was struck afresh with his jilted and wasted air. She didn't like it; she resented it. A little more and she would have said that that was no way to treat such a man.

They all went up to town in March, and on one of the first days of April she saw Mrs. Churchley in the park. She herself remained apparently invisible to that lady—she herself and Beatrice and Muriel, who sat with her in their mother's old bottle-green landau. Mrs. Churchley, perched higher than ever, rode by without a recognition; but this didn't prevent Adela from going to her before the month was over. As on her great previous occasion, she went in the morning, and she again had the good fortune to be admitted. But this time her visit was shorter, and a week after making it—the week was a desolation—she addressed to her brother at Madrid a letter which contained these words:

"I could endure it no longer—I confessed and retracted; I explained to her as well as I could the falsity of what I said to her ten months ago and the benighted purity of my motives for saying it. I besought her to regard it as unsaid, to forgive me, not to despise me too much, to take pity on poor *perfect* papa and come back to him. She was more good-natured than you might have expected; indeed, she laughed extravagantly. She had never believed me—it was too absurd; she had only, at the time, disliked me. She found me utterly false (she was very frank with me about this), and she told papa that she thought I was horrid. She said she could never live with such a girl, and as I would certainly never marry I must be sent away; in short she quite loathed me. Papa defended me, he refused to sacrifice me, and this led practically to their rupture. Papa gave her up, as it were, for me. Fancy the angel, and fancy what I must try to be to him for the rest of his life! Mrs. Churchley can never come back—she's going to marry Lord Dovedale."

HENRY JAMES was one of a gifted and cultured family that included William James, the scientist and philosopher, Henry's older brother. Born in New York City in 1843, he spent his childhood in the most sophisticated cities of the East—Albany, Newport, New York, Cambridge—and in Europe. He was educated by various tutors and schools here and abroad, and attended Harvard Law School for a year. His contemplative nature and love for complex, cultivated society turned him toward Europe, where he finally settled, moving in the most fashionable circles.

James is famous for his novels about the responses of Americans and Europeans to each other (*The Portrait of a Lady, The American, The Ambassadors, The Golden Bowl*). But all of his fiction reveals his commitment to the ideal of individual conscience. "The Marriages," with Adela's deepening awareness of the consequences of her actions, is ultimately a story about morality. James's heroes and heroines always strive to be fully conscious of their natures, to know themselves, to do "the right thing."

SAMUEL BUTLER

The Watch

Among the servants at the Rectory was a remarkably pretty girl named Ellen. She came from Devonshire, and was the daughter of a fisherman who had been drowned when she was a child. Her mother set up a small shop in the village where her husband had lived, and just managed to make a living. Ellen remained with her till she was fourteen, when she first went out to service. Four years later, when she was about eighteen, but so well grown that she might have passed for twenty, she had been strongly recommended to Christina, who was then in want of a housemaid, and had now been at Battersby about twelve months.

As I have said, the girl was remarkably pretty; she looked the perfection of health and good temper, indeed there was a serene expression upon her face which captivated almost all who saw her; she looked as if matters had always gone well with her and were always going to do so, and as if no conceivable combination of circumstances could put her for long together out of temper either with herself or with anyone else. Her complexion was clear, but high; her eyes were grey and beautifully shaped; her lips were full and restful, with something of an Egyptian Sphinx-like character about them. When I learned that she came from Devonshire I fancied I saw a strain of faraway Egyptian blood in her, for I had heard, though I know not what foundation there was for the story, that the Egyptians made settlements on the coast of Devonshire and Cornwall long before the Romans conquered Britain. Her hair was a rich brown, and her figure—of about the middle height—perfect, but erring if at all on the side of robustness. Altogether she was one of those girls about whom one is inclined to wonder how they can remain unmarried a week or a day longer.

Her face (as indeed faces generally are, though I grant they lie sometimes) was a fair index to her disposition. She was good nature itself, and everyone in the house, not excluding I believe even Theobald himself after a fashion, was fond of her. As for Christina she took the very warmest interest in her, and used to have her into the dining room twice a week, and prepare her for confirmation (for by some accident she had never been confirmed) by explaining to her the geography of Palestine and the routes taken by St. Paul on his various journeys in Asia Minor.

When Bishop Treadwell did actually come down to Battersby and hold a confirmation there (Christina had her wish, he slept at Battersby, and she had a grand dinner party for him, and called him "My Lord" several times), he was so much struck with her pretty face and modest demeanor when he laid his hands upon her that he asked Christina about her. When she replied that Ellen was one of her own servants, the bishop seemed, so she thought or chose to think, quite pleased that so pretty a girl should have found so exceptionally good a situation.

Ernest used to get up early during the holidays so that he might play the piano before breakfast without disturbing his papa and mamma—or rather, perhaps, without being disturbed by them. Ellen would generally be there sweeping the drawing-room floor and dusting while he was playing, and the boy, who was ready to make friends with most people, soon became very fond of her. He was not as a general rule sensitive to the charms of the fair sex, indeed he had hardly been thrown in with any women except his Aunts Allaby, and his Aunt Alethea, his mother, his sister Charlotte and Mrs. Jay; sometimes also he had had to take off his hat to the Miss Skinners, and had felt as if he should sink into the earth on doing so, but his shyness had worn off with Ellen, and the pair had become fast friends.

Perhaps it was well that Ernest was not at home for very long together, but as yet his affection though hearty was quite Platonic. He was not only innocent, but deplorably—I might say guiltily—innocent. His preference was based upon the fact that Ellen never scolded him, but was always smiling and good tempered; besides, she used to like to hear him play, and this gave him additional zest in playing. The morning access to the piano was indeed the one distinct advantage which the holidays had in Ernest's eyes, for at school he could not get at a piano except quasi-surreptitiously at the shop of Mr. Pearsall, the music-seller.

On returning this midsummer he was shocked to find his favorite looking pale and ill. All her good spirits had left her, the roses had fled from her cheek, and she seemed on the point of going into a decline. She said she was unhappy about her mother, whose health was failing, and was afraid she was herself not long for this world. Christina, of course, noticed the change. "I have often remarked," she said, "that those very fresh-colored, healthy-looking girls are the first to break up. I have given her calomel and James's powders repeatedly, and though she does not like it, I think I must show her to Dr. Martin when he next comes here."

"Very well, my dear," said Theobald, and so next time Dr. Martin came Ellen was sent for. Dr. Martin soon discovered what would probably have been apparent to Christina herself if she had been able to conceive of such an ailment in connection with a servant who lived under the same roof as Theobald and herself—the purity of whose married life should have preserved all unmarried people who came near them from any taint of mischief.

When it was discovered that in three or four months more Ellen would become a mother, Christina's natural good nature would have prompted her to deal as leniently with the case as she could, if she had not been panic-stricken lest any mercy on her and Theobald's part should be construed into toleration, however partial, of so great a sin; hereon she dashed off into the conviction that the only thing to do was to pay Ellen her wages, and pack her off on the instant bag and baggage out of the house which purity had more especially and particularly singled out for its abiding city. When she thought of the fearful contamination which Ellen's continued presence even for a week would occasion, she could not hesitate.

Then came the question—horrid thought!—as to who was the partner of Ellen's guilt. Was it, could it be, her own son, her darling Ernest? Ernest was getting a big boy now. She could excuse any young woman for taking a fancy to him; as for himself, why she was sure he was behind no young man of his age in appreciation of the charms of a nice-looking young woman. So long as he was innocent she did not mind this, but oh, if he were guilty!

She could not bear to think of it, and yet it would be mere cowardice not to look such a matter in the face—her hope was in the Lord, and she was ready to bear cheerfully and make the best of any suffering He might think fit to lay upon her. That the baby must be either a boy or girl—this much, at any rate, was clear. No less clear was it that the child, if a boy, would resemble Theobald, and if a girl, herself. Resemblance, whether of body or mind, generally leaped over a generation. The guilt of the parents must not be shared by the innocent offspring of shame—oh! no—and such a child as this would be . . . She was off in one of her reveries at once.

The child was in the act of being consecrated Archbishop of Canterbury when Theobald came in from a visit in the parish, and was told of the shocking discovery.

Christina said nothing about Ernest, and I believe was more than half angry when the blame was laid upon other shoulders. She was easily consoled, however, and fell back on the double reflection, firstly, that her son was pure, and secondly, that she was quite sure he would not have been so had it not been for his religious convictions which had held him back—as, of course, it was only to be expected they would.

Theobald agreed that no time must be lost in paying Ellen her wages and packing her off. So this was done, and less than two hours after Dr. Martin had entered the house Ellen was sitting beside John the coachman, with her face muffled up so that it could not be seen, weeping bitterly as she was being driven to the station.

Ernest had been out all the morning, but came into the yard of the Rectory from the spinney behind the house just as Ellen's things were being put into the carriage. He thought it was Ellen whom he then saw get into the carriage, but as her face had been hidden by her handkerchief he had not been able to see plainly who it was, and dismissed the idea as improbable.

He went to the back-kitchen window, at which the cook was standing peeling the potatoes for dinner, and found her crying bitterly. Ernest was much distressed, for he liked the cook, and, of course, wanted to know what all the matter was, who it was that had just gone off in the pony carriage, and why? The cook told him it was Ellen, but said that no earthly power should make it cross her lips why it was she was going away; when, however, Ernest took her *au pied de la lettre* and asked no further questions, she told him all about it after extorting the most solemn promises of secrecy.

It took Ernest some minutes to arrive at the facts of the case, but when he understood them he leaned against the pump, which stood near the back-kitchen window, and mingled his tears with the cook's.

Then his blood began to boil within him. He did not see that after all his father and mother could have done much otherwise than they actually did. They might perhaps have been less precipitate, and tried to keep the matter a little more quiet, but this would not have been easy, nor would it have mended things very materially. The bitter fact remains that if a girl does certain things she must do them at her peril, no matter how young and pretty she is nor to what temptation she has succumbed. This is the way of the world, and as yet there has been no help found for it.

Ernest could only see what he gathered from the cook, namely, that his favorite, Ellen, was being turned adrift with a matter of three pounds in her pocket, to go she knew not where, and to do she knew not what, and that she had said she should hang or drown herself, which the boy implicitly believed she would.

With greater promptitude than he had shown yet, he reckoned up his money and found he had two shillings and threepence at his command; there was his knife which might sell for a shilling, and there was the silver watch his Aunt Alethea had given him shortly before she died. The carriage had been gone now a full quarter of an hour, and it must have got some distance ahead, but he would do his best to catch it up, and there were short cuts which would perhaps give him a chance. He was off at once, and from the top of the hill just past the Rectory paddock he could see the carriage, looking very small, on a bit of road which showed perhaps a mile and a half in front of him.

One of the most popular amusements at Roughborough was an institution called "the hounds"—more commonly known elsewhere as "hare and hounds," but in this case the hare was a couple of boys who were called foxes, and boys are so particular about correctness of nomenclature where their sports are concerned that I dare not say they played "hare and hounds"; these were "the hounds," and that was all. Ernest's want of muscular strength did not tell against him here; there was no jostling up against boys who, though neither older nor taller than he, were yet more robustly built; if it came to mere endurance he was as good as anyone else, so when his carpentering was stopped he had naturally taken to "the hounds" as his favorite amusement. His lungs thus exercised had become developed, and as a run of six or seven miles across country was not more than he was used to, he did not despair by the help of the short cuts of overtaking the carriage, or at the worst of catching Ellen at the station before the train left. So he ran and ran and ran till his first wind was gone and his second came, and he could breathe more easily. Never with "the hounds" had he run so fast and with so few breaks as now, but with all his efforts and the help of the short cuts he did not catch up with the carriage, and would probably not have done so had not John happened to turn his head and see him running and making signs for the carriage to stop a quarter of a mile off. He was now about five miles from home, and was nearly done up.

He was crimson with his exertion; covered with dust, and with his trousers and coat sleeves a trifle short for him, he cut a poor figure enough as he thrust on Ellen his watch, his knife, and the little money he had. The one thing he implored of her was not to do those dreadful things which she threatened—for his sake if for no other reason.

Ellen at first would not hear of taking anything from him, but the coachman, who was from the north country, sided with Ernest. "Take it, my lass," he said kindly; "take what thou canst get whiles thou canst get it; as for Master Ernest here—he has run well after thee; therefore let him give thee what he is minded."

Ellen did what she was told, and the two parted with many tears, the girl's last words being that she should never forget him, and that they should meet again hereafter, she was sure they should, and then she would repay him.

Then Ernest got into a field by the roadside, flung himself on the grass, and waited under the shadow of a hedge till the carriage should pass on its return from the station and pick him up, for he was dead beat. Thoughts which had already occurred to him with some force now came more strongly before him, and he saw that he had got himself into one mess—or rather into a half a dozen messes—the more.

In the first place he should be late for dinner, and this was one of the offenses on which Theobald had no mercy. Also he should have to say where he had been, and there was a danger of being found out if he did not speak the truth. Not only this, but sooner or later it must come out that he was no longer possessed of the beautiful watch which his dear aunt had given him—and what, pray, had he done with it, or how had he lost it? The reader will know very well what he ought to have done. He should have gone straight home, and if questioned should have said, "I have been running after the carriage to catch our housemaid Ellen, whom I am very fond of; I have given her my watch, my knife, and all my pocket money, so that I have now no pocket money at all and shall probably ask you for some more sooner than I otherwise might have done, and you will also have to buy me a new watch and a knife." But then fancy the consternation which such an announcement would have occasioned! Fancy the scowl and flashing eyes of the infuriated Theobald! "You unprincipled young scoundrel," he would exclaim, "do you mean to vilify your own parents by implying that they have dealt harshly by one whose profligacy has disgraced their house?"

Or he might take it with one of those sallies of sarcastic calm, of which he believed himself to be a master.

"Very well, Ernest, very well: I shall say nothing; you can please yourself; you are not yet twenty-one, but pray act as if you were your own master; your poor aunt doubtless gave you the watch that you might fling it away upon the first improper character you came across; I think I can now understand, however, why she did not leave you her money; and, after all, your godfather may just as well have it as the kind of people on whom you would lavish it if it were yours."

Then his mother would burst into tears and implore him to repent and seek the things belonging to his peace while there was yet time, by falling on his knees to Theobald and assuring him of his unfailing love for him as the kindest and tenderest father in the universe. Ernest could do all this just as well as they could, and now, as he lay on the grass, speeches, some one or other of which was as certain to come as the sun to set, kept running in his head till they confuted the idea of telling the truth by reducing it to an absurdity. Truth might be heroic, but it was not within the range of practical domestic politics.

Having settled then that he was to tell a lie, what lie should be tell? Should he say he had been robbed? He had enough imagination to know that he had not enough imagination to carry him out here. Young as he was, his instinct told him that the best liar is he who makes the smallest amount of lying go the longest way—who husbands it too carefully to waste it where it can be dispensed with. The simplest course would be to say that he had lost the watch, and was late for dinner because he had been looking for it. He had been out for a long walk—he chose the line across the fields that he had actually taken—and the weather being very hot, he had taken off his coat and waistcoat; in carrying them over his arm his watch, his money, and his knife had dropped out of them. He had got nearly home when he found out his loss, and had run back as fast as he could looking along the line he had followed, till at last he had given it up; seeing the carriage coming back from the station, he had let it pick him up and bring him home.

This covered everything, the running and all; for his face still showed that he must have been running hard; the only question was whether he had been seen about the Rectory by any but the servants for a couple of hours or so before Ellen had gone, and this he was happy to believe was not the case; for he had been out except during his few minutes' interview with the cook. His father had been out in the parish; his mother had certainly not come across him, and his brother and sister had also been out with the governess. He knew he could depend upon the cook and the other servants—the coachman would see to this; on the whole, therefore, both he and the coachman thought the story as proposed by Ernest would about meet the requirements of the case.

When Ernest got home and sneaked in through the back door, he heard his father's voice in its angriest tones, inquiring whether Master Ernest had already returned. He felt as Jack must have felt in the story of Jack and the Bean Stalk, when from the oven in which he was hidden he heard the ogre ask his wife what young children she had got for his supper. With much courage, and, as the event proved, with not less courage than discretion, he took the bull by the horns, and announced himself at once as having just come in after having met with a terrible misfortune. Little by little he told his story, and though Theobald stormed somewhat at his "incredible folly and carelessness," he got off better than he expected. Theobald and Christina had indeed at first been inclined to connect his absence from dinner with Ellen's dismissal, but on finding it clear, as Theobald said—everything was always clear with Theobald—that Ernest had not been in the house all the morning, and could therefore have known nothing of what had happened, he was acquitted on this account for once in a way, without a stain upon his character. Perhaps Theobald was in a good temper; he may have seen from the paper that morning that his stocks had been rising; it may have been this or twenty other things, but whatever it was, he did not scold so much as Ernest had expected, and, seeing the boy look exhausted and believing him to be much grieved at the loss of his watch, Theobald actually prescribed a glass of wine after his dinner, which, strange to say, did not choke him, but made him see things more cheerfully than was usual with him.

That night when he said his prayers, he inserted a few paragraphs to the effect that he might not be discovered, and that things might go well with Ellen, but he was anxious and ill at ease. His guilty conscience pointed out to him a score of weak places in his story, through any one of which detection might even yet easily enter. Next day and for many days afterwards he fled when no man was pursuing, and trembled each time he heard his father's voice calling for him. He had already so many causes of anxiety that he could stand little more, and in spite of all his endeavors to look cheerful, even his mother could see that something was preying upon his mind. Then the idea returned to her that, after all, her son might not be innocent in the Ellen matter—and this was so interesting that she felt bound to get as near the truth as she could.

"Come here, my poor, pale-faced, heavy-eyed boy," she said to him one day in her kindest manner; "come and sit down by me, and we will have a little quiet confidential talk together, will we not?"

The boy went mechanically to the sofa. Whenever his mother wanted what she called a confidential talk with him she always selected the sofa as the most suitable ground on which to open her campaign. All mothers do this; the sofa is to them what the dining room is to fathers. In the present case the sofa was particularly well adapted for a strategic purpose, being an old-fashioned one with a high back, mattress, bolsters, and cushions. Once safely penned into one of its deep corners, it was like a dentist's chair, not too easy to get out of again. Here she could get at him better to pull him about, if this should seem desirable, or if she thought fit to cry she could bury her head in the sofa cushion and abandon herself to an agony of grief which seldom failed of its effect. None of her favorite maneuvers were so easily adopted in her usual seat, the armchair on the right-hand side of the fireplace, and so well did her son know from his mother's tone that this was going to be a sofa conversation that he took his place like a lamb as soon as she began to speak and before she could reach the sofa herself.

"My dearest boy," began his mother, taking hold of his hand and placing it within her own, "promise me never to be afraid either of your dear papa or of me; promise me this, my dear, as you love me, promise it to me," and she kissed him again and again and stroked his hair. But with her other hand she still kept hold of his; she had got him and she meant to keep him.

The lad hung down his head and promised. What else could he do?

"You know there is no one, dear, dear Ernest, who loves you so much as your papa and I do; no one who watches so carefully over your interests or who is so anxious to enter into all your little joys and troubles as we are; but, my dearest boy, it grieves me to think sometimes that you have not that perfect love for and confidence in us which you ought to have. You know, my darling, that it would be as much our pleasure as our duty to watch over the development of your moral and spiritual nature, but alas! you will not let us see your moral and spiritual nature. At times we are almost inclined to doubt whether you have a moral and spiritual nature at all. Of your inner life, my dear, we know nothing beyond such scraps as we can glean in spite of you, from little things which escape you almost before you know that you have said them."

The boy winced at this. It made him feel hot and uncomfortable all over. He knew well how careful he ought to be, and yet, do what he could, from time to time his forgetfulness of the part betrayed him into unreserve. His mother saw that he winced, and enjoyed the scratch she had given him. Had she felt confident of victory she had better have foregone the pleasure of touching as it were the eyes at the end of the snail's horns in order to enjoy seeing the snail draw them in again—but she knew that when she had got him well down into the sofa, and held his hand, she had the enemy almost absolutely at her mercy, and could do pretty much what she liked.

"Papa does not feel," she continued, "that you love him with that fullness and unreserve which would prompt you to have no concealment from him, and to tell him everything freely and fearlessly as your most loving earthly friend next only to your Heavenly Father. Perfect love, as we know, casteth out fear; your father loves you perfectly, my darling, but he does not feel as though you loved him perfectly in return. If you fear him it is because you do not love him as he deserves, and I know it sometimes cuts him to the very heart to think that he has earned from you a deeper and more willing sympathy than you display towards him. Oh, Ernest, Ernest, do not grieve one who is so good and noble-hearted by conduct which I can call by no other name than ingratitude."

Ernest could never stand being spoken to in this way by his mother: for he still believed that she loved him, and that he was fond of her and had a friend in her—up to a certain point. But his mother was beginning to come to the end of her tether; she had played the domestic confidence trick upon him times without number already. Over and over again had she wheedled from him all she wanted to know, and afterwards got him into the most horrible scrape by telling the whole to Theobald. Ernest had remonstrated more than once upon these occasions, and had pointed out to his mother how disastrous to him his confidences had been, but Christina had always joined issue with him and showed him in the clearest possible manner that in each case she had been right, and that he could not reasonably complain. Generally it was her conscience that forbade her to be silent, and against this there was no appeal, for we are all bound to follow the dictates of our conscience. Ernest used to have to recite a hymn about conscience. It was to the effect that if you did not pay attention to its voice it would soon leave off speaking. "My mamma's conscience has not left off speaking," said Ernest to one of his chums at Roughborough; "it's always jabbering."

When a boy has once spoken so disrespectfully as this about his mother's conscience it is practically all over between him and her. Ernest through sheer force of habit, of the sofa, and of the return of the associated ideas, was still so moved by the siren's voice as to yearn to sail towards her, and fling himself into her arms, but it would not do; there were other associated ideas that returned also, and the mangled bones of too many murdered confessions were lying whitening round the skirts of his mother's dress to allow him by any possibility to trust her further. So he hung his head and looked sheepish, but kept his own counsel.

"I see, my dearest," continued his mother, "either that I am mistaken, and that there is nothing on your mind, or that you will not unburden yourself to me; but oh, Ernest, tell me at least this much: is there nothing that you repent of, nothing which makes you unhappy in connection with that miserable girl Ellen?"

Ernest's heart failed him. "I am a dead boy now," he said to himself. He had not the faintest conception what his mother was driving at, and thought she suspected about the watch; but he held his ground.

I do not believe he was much more of a coward than his neighbors, only he did not know that all sensible people are cowards when they are off their beat, or when they think they are going to be roughly handled. I believe that if the truth were known, it would be found that even the valiant St. Michael himself tried hard to shirk his famous combat with the dragon; he pretended not to see all sorts of misconduct on the dragon's part; shut his eyes to the eating up of I do not know how many hundreds of men, women, and children whom he had promised to protect; allowed himself to be publicly insulted a dozen times over without resenting it; and in the end, when even an angel could stand it no longer, he shilly-shallied and temporized an unconscionable time before he would fix the day and hour for the encounter. As for the actual combat, it was much such another *wurra-wurra* as Mrs. Allaby had had with the young man who had in the end married her eldest daughter, till after a time, behold, there was the dragon lying dead, while he was himself alive and not very seriously hurt after all.

"I do not know what you mean, Mamma," exclaimed Ernest anxiously and more or less hurriedly. His mother construed his manner into indignation at being suspected, and being rather frightened herself, she turned tail and scuttled off as fast as her tongue could carry her.

"Oh!" she said, "I see by your tone that you are innocent! Oh! oh! how I thank my heavenly Father for this; may He for His dear Son's sake keep you always pure. Your father, my dear"—here she spoke hurriedly but gave him a searching look—"was as pure as a spotless angel when he came to me. Like him, always be self-denying, truly truthful both in word and deed, never forgetful whose son and grandson you are, nor of the name we gave you, of the sacred stream in whose waters your sins were washed out of you through the blood and blessing of Christ," etc.

But Ernest cut this—I will not say short—but a great deal shorter than it would have been if Christina had had her say out, by extricating himself from his mamma's embrace and showing a clean pair of heels. As he got near the purlieus of the kitchen (where he was more at ease) he heard his father calling for his mother, and again his guilty conscience rose against him. "He has found all out now," it cried, "and he is going to tell Mamma—this time I am done for." But there was nothing in it; his father only wanted the key of the cellaret. Then Ernest slunk off into a coppice or spinney behind the Rectory paddock, and consoled himself with a pipe of tobacco. Here in the wood with the summer sun streaming through the trees and a book and his pipe the boy forgot his cares and had an interval of that rest without which I verily believe his life would have been insupportable.

Of course, Ernest was made to look for his lost property, and a reward was offered for it, but it seemed he had wandered a good deal off the path, thinking to find a lark's nest, more than once, and looking for a watch and purse on Battersby piewipes was very like looking for a needle in a bundle of hay; besides, it might have been found and taken by some tramp, or by a magpie, of which there were many in the neighborhood, so that after a week or ten days the search was discontinued, and the unpleasant fact had to be faced that Ernest must have another watch, another knife, and a small sum of pocket money.

It was only right, however, that Ernest should pay half the cost of the watch; this should be made easy for him, for it should be deducted from his pocket money in half-yearly installments extending over two, or even it might be three years. In Ernest's own interests, then, as well as those of his father and mother, it would be well that the watch should cost as little as possible, so it was resolved to buy a second-hand one. Nothing was to be said to Ernest, but it was to be bought, and laid upon his plate as a surprise just before the holidays were over. Theobald would have to go to the county town in a few days, and could then find some second-hand watch which would answer sufficiently well. In the course of time, therefore, Theobald went, furnished with a long list of household commissions, among which was the purchase of a watch for Ernest.

Those, as I have said, were always happy times, when Theobald was away for a whole day certain; the boy was beginning to feel easy in his mind as though God had heard his prayers, and he was not going to be found out. Altogether the day had proved an unusually tranquil one, but, alas! it was not to close as it had begun; the fickle atmosphere in which he lived was never more likely to breed a storm than after such an interval of brilliant calm, and when Theobald returned Ernest had only to look in his face to see that a hurricane was approaching.

Christina saw that something had gone very wrong, and was quite frightened lest Theobald should have heard of some serious money loss; he did not, however, at once unbosom himself, but rang the bell and said to the servant, "Tell Master Ernest I wish to speak to him in the dining room."

Long before Ernest reached the dining room his ill-divining soul had told him that his sin had found him out. What head of a family ever sends for any of its members into the dining room if his intentions are honorable?

When he reached it he found it empty—his father having been called away for a few minutes unexpectedly upon some parish business—and he was left in the same kind of suspense as people are in after they have been ushered into their dentist's anterooom.

Of all the rooms in the house he hated the dining room worst. It was here that he had had to do his Latin and Greek lessons with his father. It had a smell of some particular kind of polish or varnish which was used in polishing the furniture, and neither I nor Ernest can even now come within range of the smell of this kind of varnish without our hearts failing us.

Over the chimney piece there was a veritable old master, one of the few original pictures which Mr. George Pontifex had brought from Italy. It was supposed to be a Salvator Rosa, and had been bought as a great bargain. The subject was Elijah or Elisha (whichever it was) being fed by the ravens in the desert. There were the ravens in the upper-right-hand corner with bread and meat in their beaks and claws, and there was the prophet in question in the lower-left-hand corner looking longingly up towards them. When Ernest was a very small boy it had been a constant matter of regret to him that the food which the ravens carried never actually reached the prophet; he did not understand the limitation of the painter's art, and wanted the meat and the prophet to be brought into direct contact. One day, with the help of some steps which had been left in the room, he had clambered up to the picture and with a piece of bread and butter traced a greasy line right across it from the ravens to Elisha's mouth, after which he had felt more comfortable.

Ernest's mind was drifting back to this youthful escapade when he heard his father's hand on the door, and in another second Theobald entered.

"Oh, Ernest," said he, in an offhand, rather cheery manner, "there's a little matter which I should like you to explain to me, as I have no doubt you very easily can." Thump, thump, thump, went Ernest's heart against his ribs; but his father's manner was so much nicer than usual that he began to think it might be after all only another false alarm.

"It had occurred to your mother and myself that we should like to set you up with a watch again before you went back to school" ("Oh, that's all," said Ernest to himself, quite relieved), "and I have been today to look out for a second-hand one which should answer every purpose so long as you are at school."

Theobald spoke as if watches had half a dozen purposes besides timekeeping, but he could hardly open his mouth without using one or other of his tags, and "answering every purpose" was one of them.

Ernest was breaking out into the usual expression of gratitude, when Theobald continued, "You are interrupting me," and Ernest's heart thumped again.

"You are interrupting me, Ernest. I have not yet done." Ernest was instantly dumb.

"I passed several shops with second-hand watches for sale, but I saw none of a description and price which pleased me, till at last I was shown one which had, so the shopman said, been left with him recently for sale, and which I at once recognized as the one which had been given you by your Aunt Alethea. Even if I had failed to recognize it, as perhaps I might have done, I should have identified it directly it reached my hands, inasmuch as it had 'E. P., a present from A. P.' engraved upon the inside. I need say no more to show that this was the very watch which you told your mother and me that you had dropped out of your pocket."

Up to this time Theobald's manner had been studiously calm, and his words had been uttered slowly, but here he suddenly quickened and flung off the mask as he added the words, "or some such cock-and-bull story, which your mother and I were too truthful to disbelieve. You can guess what must be our feelings now."

Ernest felt that this last home thrust was just. In his less anxious moments he had thought his papa and mamma "green" for the readiness with which they believed him, but he could not deny that their credulity was a proof of their habitual truthfulness of mind. In common justice he must own that it was very dreadful for two such truthful people to have a son as untruthful as he knew himself to be.

"Believing that a son of your mother and myself would be incapable of falsehood I at once assumed that some tramp had picked the watch up and was now trying to dispose of it."

This to the best of my belief was not accurate. Theobald's first assumption had been that it was Ernest who was trying to sell the watch, and it was an inspiration of the moment to say that his magnanimous mind had at once conceived the idea of a tramp.

"You may imagine how shocked I was when I discovered that the watch had been brought for sale by that miserable woman Ellen"—here Ernest's heart hardened a little, and he felt as near an approach to an instinct to turn as one so defenseless could be expected to feel; his father quickly perceived this and continued, "who was turned out of this house in circumstances which I will not pollute your ears by more particularly describing.

"I put aside the horrid conviction which was beginning to

dawn upon me, and assumed that in the interval between her dismissal and her leaving this house, she had added theft to her other sin, and having found your watch in your bedroom had purloined it. It even occurred to me that you might have missed your watch after the woman was gone, and, suspecting who had taken it, had run after the carriage in order to recover it; but when I told the shopman of my suspicions he assured me that the person who left it with him had declared most solemnly that it had been given her by her master's son, whose property it was, and who had a perfect right to dispose of it.

"He told me further that, thinking the circumstances in which the watch was offered for sale somewhat suspicious, he had insisted upon the woman's telling him the whole story of how she came by it, before he would consent to buy it of her.

"He said that at first—as women of that stamp invariably do—she tried prevarication, but on being threatened that she should at once be given into custody if she did not tell the whole truth, she described the way in which you had run after the carriage, till as she said you were black in the face, and insisted on giving her all your pocket money, your knife, and your watch. She added that my coachman, John—whom I shall instantly discharge—was witness to the whole transaction. Now, Ernest, be pleased to tell me whether this appalling story is true or false?"

It never occurred to Ernest to ask his father why he did not hit a man his own size, or to stop him midway in the story with a remonstrance against being kicked when he was down. The boy was too much shocked and shaken to be inventive; he could only drift and stammer out that the tale was true.

"So I feared," said Theobald, "and now, Ernest, be good enough to ring the bell."

When the bell had been answered, Theobald desired that John should be sent for, and when John came Theobald calculated the wages due to him and desired him at once to leave the house.

John's manner was quiet and respectful. He took his dismissal as a matter of course, for Theobald had hinted enough to make him understand why he was being discharged, but when he saw Ernest sitting pale and awestruck on the edge of his chair against the dining-room wall, a sudden thought seemed to strike him, and turning to Theobald he said in a broad northern accent which I will not attempt to reproduce:

"Look here, master, I can guess what all this is about—now before I goes I want to have a word with you."

"Ernest," said Theobald, "leave the room."

"No, Master Ernest, you shan't," said John, planting himself against the door. "Now, master," he continued, "you may do as you please about me. I've been a good servant to you, and I don't mean to say as you've been a bad master to me, but I do say that if you bear hardly on Master Ernest here I have those in the village as 'll hear on't and let me know; and if I do hear on't I'll come back and break every bone in your skin, so there!"

John's breath came and went quickly, as though he would have been well enough pleased to begin the bone-breaking business at once. Theobald turned of an ashen color—not, as he explained afterwards, at the idle threats of a detected and angry ruffian, but at such atrocious insolence from one of his own servants.

"I shall leave Master Ernest, John," he rejoined proudly, "to the reproaches of his own conscience." ("Thank God and thank John," thought Ernest.) "As for yourself, I admit that you have been an excellent servant until this unfortunate business came on, and I shall have much pleasure in giving you a character if you want one. Have you anything more to say?"

"No more nor what I have said," said John sullenly, "but what I've said I means and I'll stick to—character or no character."

"Oh, you need not be afraid about your character, John," said Theobald kindly, "and as it is getting late, there can be no occasion for you to leave the house before tomorrow morning."

To this there was no reply from John, who retired, packed up his things, and left the house at once.

When Christina heard what had happened she said she could condone all except that Theobald should have been subjected to such insolence from one of his own servants through the misconduct of his son. Theobald was the bravest man in the whole world, and could easily have collared the wretch and turned him out of the room, but how far more dignified, how far nobler had been his reply! How it would tell in a novel or upon the stage, for though the stage as a whole was immoral, yet there were doubtless some plays which were improving spectacles. She could fancy the whole house hushed with excitement at hearing John's menace, and hardly breathing by reason of their interest and expectation of the coming answer. Then the actor—probably the great and good Mr. Macready—would say, "I shall leave Master Ernest, John, to the reproaches of his own conscience." Oh, it was sublime! What a roar of applause must follow! Then she should enter herself, and fling her arms about her husband's neck, and call him her lion-hearted husband. When the curtain dropped, it would be buzzed about the house that the scene just witnessed had been drawn from real life, and had actually occurred in the household of the Rev. Theobald Pontifex, who had married a Miss Allaby, etc., etc.

As regards Ernest the suspicions which had already crossed her mind were deepened, but she thought it better to leave the matter where it was. At present she was in a very strong position. Ernest's official purity was firmly established, but at the same time he had shown himself so susceptible that she was able to fuse two contradictory impressions concerning him into a single idea, and consider him as a kind of Joseph and Don Juan in one. This was what she had wanted all along, but her vanity being gratified by the possession of such a son, there was an end of it; the son himself was naught.

No doubt if John had not interfered, Ernest would have

had to expiate his offense with ache, penury, and imprisonment. As it was, the boy was "to consider himself" as undergoing these punishments, and as suffering pangs of unavailing remorse inflicted on him by his conscience into the bargain; but beyond the fact that Theobald kept him more closely to his holiday task, and the continued coldness of his parents, no ostensible punishment was meted out to him. Ernest, however, tells me that he looks back upon this as the time when he began to know that he had a cordial and active dislike for both his parents, which I suppose means that he was now beginning to be aware that he was reaching man's estate.

SAMUEL BUTLER, born in 1835 in Nottinghamshire, England, was a witty and eccentric genius who authorized publication of *The Way of All Flesh* (from which "The Watch" is taken) on his deathbed. This largely autobiographical novel was a bitter attack on the piety and hypocrisy of Victorian family life, and its influence was vast, extending to such modern novelists as Somerset Maugham.

Butler, like his book's hero Ernest Pontifex, was the son of a clergyman, who expected his son to take holy orders after his education at Cambridge. Butler's preference for painting estranged him from his father; he fled to New Zealand and took up sheep farming for five years. Returning to London, he successfully exhibited his paintings and wrote some music.

He became interested in evolution, met Charles Darwin, and was fascinated by the new sciences, even developing his own theories. A student of classical literature, he always maintained a curious belief that the *Odyssey* had been written by a woman. In *Erewhon* (an anagram of "nowhere") he used the "Utopia" device to satirize Victorian society. His *Notebooks* are full of delightful jottings, theories, epigrams, and character sketches, and are usually mentioned among the favorite reading of practicing writers.

JAMES JOYCE

A Little Cloud

Eight years before he had seen his friend off at the North Wall and wished him godspeed. Gallaher had got on. You could tell that at once by his traveled air, his well-cut tweed suit and fearless accent. Few fellows had talents like his and fewer still could remain unspoiled by such success. Gallaher's heart was in the right place and he had deserved to win. It was something to have a friend like that.

Little Chandler's thoughts ever since lunchtime had been of his meeting with Gallaher, of Gallaher's invitation and of the great city London where Gallaher lived. He was called Little Chandler because, though he was but slightly under the average stature, he gave one the idea of being a little man. His hands were white and small, his frame was fragile, his voice was quiet and his manners were refined. He took the greatest care of his fair silken hair and mustache and used perfume discreetly on his handkerchief. The half-moons of his nails were perfect and when he smiled you caught a glimpse of a row of childish white teeth.

As he sat at his desk in the King's Inns he thought what changes those eight years had brought. The friend whom he had known under a shabby and necessitous guise had become a brilliant figure on the London Press. He turned often from his tiresome writing to gaze out of the office window. The glow of a late autumn sunset covered the grass plots and walks. It cast a shower of kindly golden dust on the untidy nurses and decrepit old men who drowsed on the benches; it flickered upon all the moving figures—on the children who ran screaming along the gravel paths and on everyone who passed through the gardens. He watched the scene and thought of life; and (as always happened when he thought of life) he became sad. A gentle melancholy took possession of him. He felt how useless it was to struggle against fortune, this being the burden of wisdom which the ages had bequeathed to him.

He remembered the books of poetry upon his shelves at home. He had been tempted to take one down from the bookshelf and read out something to his wife. But shyness had always held him back; and so the books had remained on their shelves. At times he repeated lines to himself and this consoled him.

When his hour had struck he stood up and took leave of his desk and of his fellow-clerks punctiliously. He emerged from under the feudal arch of the King's Inns, a neat modest figure, and walked swiftly down Henrietta Street. The golden sunset was waning and the air had grown sharp. A horde of grimy children populated the street. They stood or ran in the roadway or crawled up the steps before the gaping doors or squatted like mice upon the thresholds. Little Chandler gave them no thought. He picked his way deftly through all that minute vermin-like life and under the shadow of the gaunt spectral mansions in which the old nobility of Dublin had roistered. No memory of the past touched him, for his mind was full of a present joy.

He had never been in Corless's but he knew the value of the name. He knew that people went there after the theatre to eat oysters and drink liqueurs; and he had heard that the waiters there spoke French and German. Walking swiftly by at night he had seen cabs drawn up before the door and richly dressed ladies, escorted by cavaliers, alight and enter quickly. They wore noisy dresses and many wraps. Their faces were powdered and they caught up their dresses, when they touched earth, like alarmed Atalantas. He had always passed without turning his head to look. It was his habit to walk swiftly in the street even by day and whenever he found himself in the city late at night he hurried on his way apprehensively and excitedly. Sometimes, however, he courted the causes of his fear. He chose the darkest and narrowest streets and, as he walked boldly forward, the silence that was spread about his footsteps troubled him, the wandering, silent figures troubled him; and at times a sound of low fugitive laughter made him tremble like a leaf.

He turned to the right towards Capel Street. Ignatius Gallaher on the London Press! Who would have thought it possible eight years before? Still, now that he reviewed the past, Little Chandler could remember many signs of future greatness in his friend. People used to say that Ignatius Gallaher was wild. Of course, he did mix with a rakish set of fellows at that time, drank freely and borrowed money on all sides. In the end he had got mixed up in some shady affair, some money transaction: at least, that was one version of his flight. But nobody denied him talent. There was always a certain . . . something in Ignatius Gallaher that impressed you in spite of yourself. Even when he was out at elbows and at his wit's end for money he kept up a bold face. Little Chandler remembered (and the remembrance brought a slight flush of pride to his cheek) one of Ignatius Gallaher's sayings when he was in a tight corner:

"Half time now, boys," he used to say light-heartedly. "Where's my considering cap?"

That was Ignatius Gallaher all out; and, damn it, you couldn't but admire him for it.

Little Chandler quickened his pace. For the first time in his life he felt himself superior to the people he passed. For the first time his soul revolted against the dull inelegance of Capel Street. There was no doubt about it: if you wanted to succeed you had to go away. You could do nothing in Dublin. As he crossed Grattan Bridge he looked down the river towards the lower quays and pitied the poor stunted houses. They seemed to him a band of tramps, huddled together along the riverbanks, their old coats covered with dust and soot, stupefied by the panorama of sunset and waiting for the first chill of night to bid them arise, shake themselves and begone. He wondered whether he could write a poem to express his idea. Perhaps Gallaher might be able to get it into some London paper for him. Could he write something original? He was not sure what idea he wished to express but the thought that a poetic moment had touched him took life within him like an infant hope. He stepped onward bravely.

Every step brought him nearer to London, farther from his own sober inartistic life. A light began to tremble on the horizon of his mind. He was not so old—thirty-two. His temperament might be said to be just at the point of maturity. There were so many different moods and impressions that he wished to express in verse. He felt them within him. He tried to weigh his soul to see if it was a poet's soul. Melancholy was the dominant note of his temperament, he thought, but it was a melancholy tempered by recurrences of faith and resignation and simple joy.

If he could give expression to it in a book of poems perhaps men would listen. He would never be popular: he saw that. He could not sway the crowd but he might appeal to a little circle of kindred minds. The English critics, perhaps, would recognize him as one of the Celtic school by reason of the melancholy tone of his poems; besides that, he would put in allusions. He began to invent sentences and phrases from the notice which his book would get. *"Mr. Chandler has the gift of easy and graceful verse."* . . . *"A wistful sadness pervades these poems."* . . . *"The Celtic note."* It was a pity his name was not more Irish-looking. Perhaps it would be better to insert his mother's name before the surname: Thomas Malone Chandler, or better still: T. Malone Chandler. He would speak to Gallaher about it.

He pursued his reverie so ardently that he passed his street and had to turn back. As he came near Corless's his former agitation began to overmaster him and he halted before the door in indecision. Finally he opened the door and entered.

The light and noise of the bar held him at the doorways for a few moments. He looked about him, but his sight was confused by the shining of many red and green wine-glasses. The bar seemed to him to be full of people and he felt that the people were observing him curiously. He glanced quickly to right and left (frowning slightly to make his errand appear serious), but when his sight cleared a little he saw that nobody had turned to look at him: and there, sure enough, was Ignatius Gallaher leaning with his back against the counter and his feet planted far apart.

"'Hallo, Tommy, old hero, here you are! What is it to be? What will you have? I'm taking whisky: better stuff than we get across the water. Soda? Lithia? No mineral? I'm the same. Spoils the flavor. . . . Here, *garçon,* bring us two halves of malt whisky, like a good fellow. . . . Well, and how have you been pulling along since I saw you last? Dear God, how old we're getting! Do you see any signs of aging in me—eh, what? A little grey and thin on the top—what?"

Ignatius Gallaher took off his hat and displayed a large closely cropped head. His face was heavy, pale and clean-shaven. His eyes, which were of bluish slate-color, relieved his unhealthy pallor and shone out plainly above the vivid orange tie he wore. Between these rival features the lips appeared very long and shapeless and colorless. He bent his head and felt with two sympathetic fingers the thin hair at the crown. Little Chandler shook his head as a denial. Ignatius Gallaher put on his hat again.

"It pulls you down," he said, "Press life. Always hurry and scurry, looking for copy and sometimes not finding it: and then, always to have something new in your stuff. Damn proofs and printers, I say, for a few days. I'm deuced glad, I can tell you, to get back to the old country. Does a fellow good, a bit of a holiday. I feel a ton better since I landed again in dear dirty Dublin. . . . Here you are, Tommy. Water? Say when."

Little Chandler allowed his whisky to be very much diluted.

"You don't know what's good for you, my boy," said Ignatius Gallaher. "I drink mine neat."

"I drink very little as a rule," said Little Chandler modestly. "An odd half-one or so when I meet any of the old crowd: that's all."

"Ah, well," said Ignatius Gallaher, cheerfully, "here's to us and to old times and old acquaintance."

They clinked glasses and drank the toast.

"I met some of the old gang today," said Ignatius Gallaher. "O'Hara seems to be in a bad way. What's he doing?"

"Nothing," said Little Chandler. "He's gone to the dogs."

"But Hogan has a good sit, hasn't he?"

"Yes; he's in the Land Commission."

"I met him one night in London and he seemed to be very flush. . . . Poor O'Hara! Booze, I suppose?"

"Other things, too," said Little Chandler shortly.

Ignatius Gallaher laughed.

"Tommy," he said, "I see you haven't changed an atom. You're the very same serious person that used to lecture me on Sunday mornings when I had a sore head and a fur on my tongue. You'd want to knock about a bit in the world. Have you never been anywhere even for a trip?"

"I've been to the Isle of Man," said Little Chandler.

Ignatius Gallaher laughed.

"The Isle of Man!" he said, "Go to London or Paris: Paris, for choice. That'd do you good."

"Have you seen Paris?"

"I should think I have! I've knocked about there a little."

"And is it really so beautiful as they say?" asked Little Chandler.

He sipped a little of his drink while Ignatius Gallaher finished his boldly.

"Beautiful?" said Ignatius Gallaher, pausing on the word and on the flavor of his drink. "It's not so beautiful, you know. Of course, it is beautiful. . . . But it's the life of Paris; that's the thing. Ah, there's no city like Paris for gaiety, movement, excitement. . . ."

Little Chandler finished his whisky and, after some trouble, succeeded in catching the barman's eye. He ordered the same again.

"I've been to the Moulin Rouge," Ignatius Gallaher continued when the barman had removed their glasses, "and I've been to all the Bohemian cafés. Hot stuff! Not for a pious chap like you, Tommy."

Little Chandler said nothing until the barman returned with two glasses: then he touched his friend's glass lightly and reciprocated the former toast. He was beginning to feel somewhat disillusioned. Gallaher's accent and way of expressing himself did not please him. There was something vulgar in his friend which he had not observed before. But perhaps it was only the result of living in London amid the bustle and competition of the Press. The old personal charm was still there under this new gaudy manner. And, after all, Gallaher had lived, he had seen the world. Little Chandler looked at his friend enviously.

"Everything in Paris is gay," said Ignatius Gallaher. "They believe in enjoying life—and don't you think they're right? If you want to enjoy yourself properly you must go to Paris. And, mind you, they've a great feeling for the Irish there. When they heard I was from Ireland they were ready to eat me, man."

Little Chandler took four or five sips from his glass.

"Tell me," he said, "is it true that Paris is so . . . immoral as they say?"

Ignatius Gallaher made a catholic gesture with his right arm.

"Every place is immoral," he said. "Of course you do find spicy bits in Paris. Go to one of the students' balls, for instance. That's lively, if you like, when the *cocottes* begin to let themselves loose. You know what they are, I suppose?"

"I've heard of them," said Little Chandler.

Ignatius Gallaher drank off his whisky and shook his head.

"Ah," he said, "you may say what you like. There's no woman like the Parisienne—for style, for go."

"Then it is an immoral city," said Little Chandler, with timid insistence— "I mean, compared with London or Dublin?"

"London!" said Ignatius Gallaher. "It's six of one and half-a-dozen of the other. You ask Hogan, my boy. I showed him a bit about London when he was over there. He'd open your eye. . . . I say, Tommy, don't make punch of that whisky: liquor up."

"No, really. . . ."

"Oh, come on, another one won't do you any harm. What is it? The same again, I suppose?"

"Well . . . all right."

"*François,* the same again. . . . Will you smoke, Tommy?"

Ignatius Gallaher produced his cigar-case. The two friends lit their cigars and puffed at them in silence until their drinks were served.

"I'll tell you my opinion," said Ignatius Gallaher, emerging after some time from the clouds of smoke in which he had taken refuge, "it's a rum world. Talk of immorality! I've heard of cases —what am I saying?—I've known them: cases of . . . immorality. . . ."

Ignatius Gallaher puffed thoughtfully at his cigar and then, in a calm historian's tone, he proceeded to sketch for his friend some pictures of the corruption which was rife abroad. He summarized the vices of many capitals and seemed inclined to award the palm to Berlin. Some things he could not vouch for (his friends had told him), but of others he had had personal experience. He spared neither rank nor caste. He revealed many of the secrets of religious houses on the Continent and described some of the practices which were fashionable in high society and ended by telling, with details, a story about an English duchess —a story which he knew to be true. Little Chandler was astonished.

"Ah, well," said Ignatius Gallaher, "here we are in old jog-along Dublin where nothing is known of such things."

"How dull you must find it," said Little Chandler, "after all the other places you've seen!"

"Well," said Ignatius Gallaher, "it's a relaxation to come over here, you know. And, after all, it's the old country, as they say, isn't it? You can't help having a certain feeling for it. That's human nature. . . . But tell me something about yourself. Hogan told me you had . . . tasted the joys of connubial bliss. Two years ago, wasn't it?"

Little Chandler blushed and smiled.

"Yes," he said. "I was married last May twelve months."

"I hope it's not too late in the day to offer my best wishes," said Ignatius Gallaher. "I didn't know your address or I'd have done so at the time."

He extended his hand, which Little Chandler took.

"Well, Tommy," he said, "I wish you and yours every joy in life, old chap, and tons of money, and may you never die till I shoot you. And that's the wish of a sincere friend, an old friend. You know that?"

"I know that," said Little Chandler.

"Any youngsters?" said Ignatius Gallaher.

Little Chandler blushed again.

"We have one child," he said.

"Son or daughter?"

"A little boy."

Ignatius Gallaher slapped his friend sonorously on the back.

"Bravo," he said, "I wouldn't doubt you, Tommy."

Little Chandler smiled, looked confusedly at his glass and bit his lower lip with three childishly white front teeth.

"I hope you'll spend an evening with us," he said, "before you go back. My wife will be delighted to meet you. We can have a little music and—"

"Thanks awfully, old chap," said Ignatius Gallaher, "I'm sorry we didn't meet earlier. But I must leave tomorrow night."

"Tonight, perhaps . . . ?"

"I'm awfully sorry, old man. You see I'm over here with another fellow, clever young chap he is too, and we arranged to go to a little card party. Only for that . . ."

"O, in that case . . ."

"But who knows?" said Ignatius Gallaher considerately. "Next year I may take a little skip over here now that I've broken the ice. It's only a pleasure deferred."

"Very well," said Little Chandler, "the next time you come we must have an evening together. That's agreed now, isn't it?"

"Yes, that's agreed," said Ignatius Gallaher. "Next year if I come, *parole d'honneur.*"

"And to clinch the bargain," said Little Chandler, "we'll just have one more now."

Ignatius Gallaher took out a large gold watch and looked at it.

"Is it to be the last?" he said. "Because you know, I have an a.p."

"O, yes, positively," said Little Chandler.

"Very well, then," said Ignatius Gallaher, "let us have another one as a *deoc an doruis*—that's good vernacular for a small whisky, I believe."

Little Chandler ordered the drinks. The blush which had risen to his face a few moments before was establishing itself. A trifle made him blush at any time: and now he felt warm and excited. Three small whiskies had gone to his head and Gallaher's strong cigar had confused his mind, for he was a delicate and abstinent person. The adventure of meeting Gallaher after eight years, of finding himself with Gallaher in Corless's surrounded by lights and noise, of listening to Gallaher's stories and of sharing for a brief space Gallaher's vagrant and triumphant life, upset the equipoise of his sensitive nature. He felt acutely the contrast between his own life and his friend's, and it seemed to him unjust. Gallaher was his inferior in birth and education. He was sure that he could do something better than his friend had ever done, or could ever do, something higher than mere tawdry journalism if he only got the chance. What was it that stood in his way? His unfortunate timidity! He wished to vindicate himself in some way, to assert his manhood. He saw behind Gallaher's refusal of his invitation. Gallaher was only patronizing him by his friendliness just as he was patronizing Ireland by his visit.

The barman brought their drinks. Little Chandler pushed one glass towards his friend and took up the other boldly.

"Who knows?" he said, as they lifted their glasses. "When you come next year I may have the pleasure of wishing long life and happiness to Mr. and Mrs. Ignatius Gallaher."

Ignatius Gallaher in the act of drinking closed one eye expressively over the rim of his glass. When he had drunk he smacked his lips decisively, set down his glass and said:

"No blooming fear of that, my boy. I'm going to have my fling first and see a bit of life and the world before I put my head in the sack—if I ever do."

"Some day you will," said Little Chandler calmly.

Ignatius Gallaher turned his orange tie and slate-blue eyes full upon his friend.

"You think so?" he said.

"You'll put your head in the sack," repeated Little Chandler stoutly, "like everyone else if you can find the girl."

He had slightly emphasized his tone and he was aware that he had betrayed himself; but, though the color had heightened in his cheek, he did not flinch from his friend's gaze. Ignatius Gallaher watched him for a few moments and then said:

"If ever it occurs, you may bet your bottom dollar there'll be no mooning and spooning about it. I mean to marry money. She'll have a good fat account at the bank or she won't do for me."

Little Chandler shook his head.

"Why, man alive," said Ignatius Gallaher, vehemently, "do you know what it is? I've only to say the word and tomorrow I can have the woman and the cash. You don't believe it? Well, I know it. There are hundreds—what am I saying?—thousands of rich Germans and Jews, rotten with money, that'd only be too glad. . . . You wait a while, my boy. See if I don't play my cards properly. When I go about a thing I mean business, I tell you. You just wait."

He tossed his glass to his mouth, finished his drink and laughed loudly. Then he looked thoughtfully before him and said in a calmer tone:

"But I'm in no hurry. They can wait. I don't fancy tying myself up to one woman, you know."

He imitated with his mouth the act of tasting and made a wry face.

"Must get a bit stale, I should think," he said.

Little Chandler sat in the room off the hall, holding a child in his arms. To save money they kept no servant but Annie's young sister Monica came for an hour or so in the morning and an hour or so in the evening to help. But Monica had gone home long ago. It was a quarter to nine. Little Chandler had come home late for tea and, moreover, he had forgotten to bring Annie home the parcel of coffee from Bewley's. Of course she was in a bad humor and gave him short answers. She said she would do without any tea but when it came near the time at which the shop at the corner closed she decided to go out herself for a quarter of a pound of tea and two pounds of sugar. She put the sleeping child deftly in his arms and said:

"Here. Don't waken him."

A little lamp with a white china shade stood upon the table and its light fell over a photograph which was enclosed in a frame of crumpled horn. It was Annie's photograph. Little Chandler looked at it, pausing at the thin tight lips. She wore the pale blue summer blouse which he had brought her home as a present one Saturday. It had cost him ten and elevenpence; but what an agony of nervousness it had cost him! How he had suffered that day, waiting at the shop door until the shop was empty, standing at the counter and trying to appear at his ease while the girl piled ladies' blouses before him, paying at the desk and forgetting to take up the odd penny of his change, being called back by the cashier, and finally, striving to hide his blushes as he left the shop by examining the parcel to see if it was securely tied. When he brought the blouse home Annie kissed him and said it was very pretty and stylish; but when she heard the price she threw the blouse on the table and said it was a regular swindle to charge ten and elevenpence for it. At first she wanted to take it back but when she tried it on she was delighted with it, especially with the make of the sleeves, and kissed him and said he was very good to think of her.

Hm! . . .

He looked coldly into the eyes of the photograph and they answered coldly. Certainly they were pretty and the face itself was pretty. But he found something mean in it. Why was it so unconscious and ladylike? The composure of the eyes irritated him. They repelled him and defied him: there was no passion in them, no rapture. He thought of what Gallaher had said about rich Jewesses. Those dark Oriental eyes, he thought, how full they are of passion, of voluptuous longing! . . . Why had he married the eyes in the photograph?

He caught himself up at the question and glanced nervously round the room. He found something mean in the pretty furniture which he had bought for his house on the hire system. Annie had chosen it herself and it reminded him of her. It too was prim and pretty. A dull resentment against his life awoke within him. Could he not escape from his little house? Was it too late for him to try to live bravely like Gallaher? Could he go to London? There was the furniture still to be paid for. If he could only write a book and get it published, that might open the way for him.

A volume of Byron's poems lay before him on the table. He opened it cautiously with his left hand lest he should waken the child and began to read the first poem in the book:

Hushed are the winds and still the evening gloom,
Not e'en a Zephyr wanders through the grove,
Whilst I return to view my Margaret's tomb
And scatter flowers on the dust I love.

He paused. He felt the rhythm of the verse about him in the room. How melancholy it was! Could he, too, write like that, express the melancholy of his soul in verse? There were so many things he wanted to describe: his sensation of a few hours before on Grattan Bridge, for example. If he could get back again into that mood. . . .

The child awoke and began to cry. He turned from the

page and tried to hush it: but it would not be hushed. He began to rock it to and fro in his arms but its wailing cry grew keener. He rocked it faster while his eyes began to read the second stanza:

Within this narrow cell reclines her clay,
That clay where once . . .

It was useless. He couldn't read. He couldn't do anything. The wailing of the child pierced the drum of his ear. It was useless, useless! He was a prisoner for life. His arms trembled with anger and suddenly bending to the child's face he shouted: "Stop!"

The child stopped for an instant, had a spasm of fright and began to scream. He jumped up from his chair and walked hastily up and down the room with the child in his arms. It began to sob piteously, losing its breath for four or five seconds, and then bursting out anew. The thin walls of the room echoed the sound. He tried to soothe it but it sobbed more convulsively. He looked at the contracted and quivering face of the child and began to be alarmed. He counted seven sobs without a break between them and caught the child to his breast in fright. If it died! . . .

The door was burst open and a young woman ran in, panting.

"What is it? What is it?" she cried.

The child, hearing its mother's voice, broke out into a paroxysm of sobbing.

"It's nothing, Annie . . . it's nothing. . . . He began to cry . . ."

She flung her parcels on the floor and snatched the child from him.

"What have you done to him?" she cried, glaring into his face.

Little Chandler sustained for one moment the gaze of her

eyes and his heart closed together as he met the hatred in them. He began to stammer:

"It's nothing. . . . He . . . he began to cry. . . . I couldn't . . . I didn't do anything. . . . What?"

Giving no heed to him she began to walk up and down the room, clasping the child tightly in her arms and murmuring:

"'My little man! My little mannie! Was 'ou frightened, love? . . . There now, love! There now! . . . Lambabaun! Mama's little lamb of the world! . . . There now!"

Little Chandler felt his cheeks suffused with shame and he stood back out of the lamplight. He listened while the paroxysm of the child's sobbing grew less and less; and tears of remorse started to his eyes.

JAMES JOYCE was one of fifteen children born to Mary Jane Murray and Stanislaus Joyce, a Dublin medical student and municipal politician. Joyce received a classical Jesuit education and planned to combine writing with a career in medicine. He was too poverty-stricken to afford medical school, however; and he supported himself and his wife, Norah, in their first years of marriage by teaching school and working in Trieste as a Berlitz language instructor.

In 1914, largely through the help of Ezra Pound, *A Portrait of the Artist as a Young Man* was serialized in a magazine. The same year, *Dubliners,* a collection of stories that includes "A Little Cloud," was published after nine years of rejections. The Joyces moved to Paris in 1920, and in 1922 *Ulysses* was published, to a clamorous, hostile reception that mellowed to apathy when *Finnegans Wake* followed. Joyce's dreamlike probing of the subconscious and the multiple meanings of his scholarly, idiomatic language make his novels among the most difficult works of fiction to read. But he has since been recognized as one of the few authentic geniuses ever to write in English.

Joyce's life was a painful struggle. Afflicted with glaucoma, he was for many years nearly blind in spite of numerous operations. He died in 1941 in Zurich, Switzerland.

PHILIP ROTH

Defender of the Faith

In May of 1945, only a few weeks after the fighting had ended in Europe, I was rotated back to the States, where I spent the remainder of the war with a training company at Camp Crowder, Missouri. Along with the rest of the Ninth Army, I had been racing across Germany so swiftly during the late winter and spring that when I boarded the plane, I couldn't believe its destination lay to the west. My mind might inform me otherwise, but there was an inertia of the spirit that told me we were flying to a new front, where we would disembark and continue our push eastward—eastward until we'd circled the globe, marching through villages along whose twisting, cobbled streets crowds of the enemy would watch us take possession of what, up till then, they'd considered their own. I had changed enough in two years not to mind the trembling of the old people, the crying of the very young, the uncertainty and fear in the eyes of the once arrogant. I had been fortunate enough to develop an infantryman's heart, which, like his feet, at first aches and swells but finally grows horny enough for him to travel the weirdest paths without feeling a thing.

Captain Paul Barrett was my C.O. in Camp Crowder. The day I reported for duty, he came out of his office to shake my hand. He was short, gruff, and fiery, and—indoors or out—he wore his polished helmet liner pulled down to his little eyes. In Europe, he had received a battlefield commission and a serious chest wound, and he'd been returned to the States only a few months before. He spoke easily to me, and at the evening formation he introduced me to the troops. "Gentlemen," he said, "Sergeant Thurston, as you know, is no longer with this company. Your new first sergeant is Sergeant Nathan Marx, here. He is a veteran of the European theater, and consequently will expect to find a company of soldiers here, and not a company of *boys.*"

I sat up late in the orderly room that evening, trying half-heartedly to solve the riddle of duty rosters, personnel forms, and morning reports. The Charge of Quarters slept with his mouth open on a mattress on the floor. A trainee stood reading the next day's duty roster, which was posted on the bulletin board just inside the screen door. It was a warm evening, and I could hear radios playing dance music over in the barracks. The trainee, who had been staring at me whenever he thought I wouldn't notice, finally took a step in my direction.

"Hey, Sarge—we having a G.I. party tomorrow night?" he asked. A G.I. party is a barracks cleaning.

"You usually have them on Friday nights?" I asked him.

"Yes," he said, and then he added, mysteriously, "that's the whole thing."

"Then you'll have a G.I. party."

He turned away, and I heard him mumbling. His shoulders were moving, and I wondered if he was crying.

"What's your name, soldier?" I asked.

He turned, not crying at all. Instead, his green-speckled eyes, long and narrow, flashed like fish in the sun. He walked over to me and sat on the edge of my desk. He reached out a hand. "Sheldon," he said.

"Stand on your feet, Sheldon."

Getting off the desk, he said, "Sheldon Grossbart." He smiled at the familiarity into which he'd led me.

"You against cleaning the barracks Friday night, Grossbart?" I said. "Maybe we shouldn't have G.I. parties. Maybe we should get a maid." My tone startled me. I felt I sounded like every top sergeant I had ever known.

"No, Sergeant." He grew serious, but with a seriousness that seemed to be only the stifling of a smile. "It's just—G.I. parties on Friday night of all nights."

He slipped up onto the corner of the desk again—not quite sitting, but not quite standing, either. He looked at me with those speckled eyes flashing, and then made a gesture with his hand. It was very slight—no more than a movement back and forth of the wrist—and yet it managed to exclude from our affairs everything else in the orderly room, to make the two of us the center of the world. It seemed, in fact, to exclude everything even about the two of us except our hearts.

"Sergeant Thurston was one thing," he whispered, glancing at the sleeping C.Q., "but we thought that with you here things might be a little different."

"We?"

"The Jewish personnel."

"Why?" I asked, harshly. "What's on your mind?" Whether

I was still angry at the "Sheldon" business, or now at something else, I hadn't time to tell, but clearly I was angry.

"We thought you—Marx, you know, like Karl Marx. The Marx Brothers. Those guys are all—M-a-r-x. Isn't that how *you* spell it, Sergeant?"

"M-a-r-x."

"Fishbein said—" He stopped. "What I mean to say, Sergeant—" His face and neck were red, and his mouth moved but no words came out. In a moment, he raised himself to attention, gazing down at me. It was as though he had suddenly decided he could expect no more sympathy from me than from Thurston, the reason being that I was of Thurston's faith, and not his. The young man had managed to confuse himself as to what my faith really was, but I felt no desire to straighten him out. Very simply, I didn't like him.

When I did nothing but return his gaze, he spoke, in an altered tone. "You see, Sergeant," he explained to me, "Friday nights, Jews are supposed to go to services."

"Did Sergeant Thurston tell you you couldn't go to them when there was a G.I. party?"

"No."

"Did he say you had to stay and scrub the floors?"

"No, Sergeant."

"Did the Captain say you had to stay and scrub the floors?"

"That isn't it, Sergeant. It's the other guys in the barracks." He leaned toward me. "They think we're goofing off. But we're not. That's when Jews go to services, Friday night. We have to."

"Then go."

"But the other guys make accusations. They have no right."

"That's not the Army's problem, Grossbart. It's a personal problem you'll have to work out yourself."

"But it's un*fair*."

I got up to leave. "There's nothing I can do about it," I said.

Grossbart stiffened, and stood in front of me. "But this is a matter of *religion,* sir."

"Sergeant," I said.

"I mean 'Sergeant,' " he said, almost snarling.

"Look, go see the chaplain. You want to see Captain Barrett, I'll arrange an appointment."

"No, no. I don't want to make trouble, Sergeant. That's the first thing they throw up to you. I just want my rights!"

"Damn it, Grossbart, stop whining. You have your rights. You can stay and scrub floors or you can go to shul—"

The smile swam in again. Spittle gleamed at the corners of his mouth. "You mean church, Sergeant."

"I mean shul, Grossbart!"

I walked past him and went outside. Near me, I heard the scrunching of a guard's boots on gravel. Beyond the lighted windows of the barracks, young men in T shirts and fatigue pants were sitting on their bunks, polishing their rifles. Suddenly there was a light rustling behind me. I turned and saw Grossbart's dark frame fleeing back to the barracks, racing to tell his Jewish friends that they were right—that, like Karl and Harpo, I was one of them.

The next morning, while chatting with Captain Barrett, I recounted the incident of the previous evening. Somehow, in the telling, it must have seemed to the Captain that I was not so much explaining Grossbart's position as defending it. "Marx, I'd fight side by side with a nigger if the fella proved to me he was a man. I pride myself," he said, looking out the window, "that I've got an open mind. Consequently, Sergeant, nobody gets special treatment here, for the good *or* the bad. All a man's got to do is prove himself. A man fires well on the range, I give him a weekend pass. He scores high in P.T., he gets a weekend pass. He *earns* it." He turned from the window and pointed a finger at me. "You're a Jewish fella, am I right, Marx?"

"Yes, sir."

"And I admire you. I admire you because of the ribbons on your chest. I judge a man by what he shows me on the field of battle, Sergeant. It's what he's got *here,*" he said, and then, though I expected he would point to his heart, he jerked a thumb toward the buttons straining to hold his blouse across his belly. "Guts," he said.

"O.K., sir. I only wanted to pass on to you how the men felt."

"Mr. Marx, you're going to be old before your time if you worry about how the men feel. Leave that stuff to the chaplain—that's his business, not yours. Let's us train these fellas to shoot straight. If the Jewish personnel feels the other men are accusing them of goldbricking—well, I just don't know. Seems awful funny that suddenly the Lord is calling so loud in Private Grossman's ear he's just got to run to church."

"Synagogue," I said.

"Synagogue is right, Sergeant. I'll write that down for handy reference. Thank you for stopping by."

That evening, a few minutes before the company gathered outside the orderly room for the chow formation, I called the C.Q., Corporal Robert LaHill, in to see me. LaHill was a dark, burly fellow whose hair curled out of his clothes wherever it could. He had a glaze in his eyes that made one think of caves and dinosaurs. "LaHill," I said, "when you take the formation, remind the men that they're free to attend church services *whenever* they are held, provided they report to the orderly room before they leave the area."

LaHill scratched his wrist, but gave no indication that he'd heard or understood.

"LaHill," I said, "*church*. You remember? Church, priest, Mass, confession."

He curled one lip into a kind of smile; I took it for a signal that for a second he had flickered back up into the human race.

"Jewish personnel who want to attend services this evening are to fall out in front of the orderly room at 1900," I said.

Then, as an afterthought, I added, "By order of Captain Barrett."

A little while later, as the day's last light—softer than any I had seen that year—began to drop over Camp Crowder, I heard LaHill's thick, inflectionless voice outside my window: "Give me your ears, troopers. Toppie says for me to tell you that at 1900 hours all Jewish personnel is to fall out in front, here, if they want to attend the Jewish Mass."

At seven o'clock, I looked out the orderly-room window and saw three soldiers in starched khakis standing on the dusty quadrangle. They looked at their watches and fidgeted while they whispered back and forth. It was getting dimmer, and alone on the otherwise deserted field, they looked tiny. When I opened the door, I heard the noises of the G.I. party coming from the surrounding barracks—bunks being pushed to the walls, faucets pounding water into buckets, brooms whisking at the wooden floors, cleaning the dirt away for Saturday's inspection. Big puffs of cloth moved round and round on the windowpanes. I walked outside, and the moment my foot hit the ground I thought I heard Grossbart call to the others, "'Ten-*hut!*" Or maybe, when they all three jumped to attention, I imagined I heard the command.

Grossbart stepped forward. "Thank you, sir," he said.

" 'Sergeant,' Grossbart," I reminded him. "You call officers 'sir.' I'm not an officer. You've been in the Army three weeks—you know that."

He turned his palms out at his sides to indicate that, in truth, he and I lived beyond convention. "Thank you, anyway," he said.

"Yes," a tall boy behind him said. "Thanks a lot."

And the third boy whispered, "Thank you," but his mouth barely fluttered, so that he did not alter by more than a lip's movement his posture of attention.

"For what?" I asked.

Grossbart snorted happily. "For the announcement. The Corporal's announcement. It helped. It made it—"

"Fancier." The tall boy finished Grossbart's sentence.

Grossbart smiled. "He means formal, sir. Public," he said to me. "Now it won't seem as though we're just taking off—goldbricking because the work has begun."

"It was by order of Captain Barrett," I said.

"Aaah, but you pull a little weight," Grossbart said. "So we thank you." Then he turned to his companions. "Sergeant Marx, I want you to meet Larry Fishbein."

The tall boy stepped forward and extended his hand. I shook it. "You from New York?" he asked.

"Yes."

"Me, too." He had a cadaverous face that collapsed inward from his cheekbone to his jaw, and when he smiled—as he did at the news of our communal attachment—revealed a mouthful of bad teeth. He was blinking his eyes a good deal, as though he were fighting back tears. "What borough?" he asked.

I turned to Grossbart. "It's five after seven. What time are services?"

"Shul," he said, smiling, "is in ten minutes. I want you to meet Mickey Halpern. This is Nathan Marx, our sergeant."

The third boy hopped forward. "Private Michael Halpern." He saluted.

"Salute officers, Halpern," I said. The boy dropped his hand, and, on its way down, in his nervousness, checked to see if his shirt pockets were buttoned.

"Shall I march them over, sir?" Grossbart asked. "Or are you coming along?"

From behind Grossbart, Fishbein piped up. "Afterward, they're having refreshments. A ladies' auxiliary from St. Louis, the rabbi told us last week."

"The chaplain," Halpern whispered.

"You're welcome to come along," Grossbart said.

To avoid his plea, I looked away, and saw, in the windows

of the barracks, a cloud of faces staring out at the four of us. "Hurry along, Grossbart," I said.

"O.K., then," he said. He turned to the others. "Double time, *march!*"

They started off, but ten feet away Grossbart spun around and, running backward, called to me, "Good *shabbus,* sir!" And then the three of them were swallowed into the alien Missouri dusk.

Even after they had disappeared over the parade ground, whose green was now a deep blue, I could hear Grossbart singing the double-time cadence, and as it grew dimmer and dimmer, it suddenly touched a deep memory—as did the slant of the light—and I was remembering the shrill sounds of a Bronx playground where, years ago, beside the Grand Concourse, I had played on long spring evenings such as this. It was a pleasant memory for a young man so far from peace and home, and it brought so many recollections with it that I began to grow exceedingly tender about myself. In fact, I indulged myself in a reverie so strong that I felt as though a hand were reaching down inside me. It had to reach so very far to touch me! It had to reach past those days in the forests of Belgium, and past the dying I'd refused to weep over; past the nights in German farmhouses whose books we'd burned to warm us; past endless stretches when I had shut off all softness I might feel for my fellows, and had managed even to deny myself the posture of a conqueror—the swagger that I, as a Jew, might well have worn as my boots whacked against the rubble of Wesel, Münster, and Braunschweig.

But now one night noise, one rumor of home and time past, and memory plunged down through all I had anesthetized, and came to what I suddenly remembered was myself. So it was not altogether curious that, in search of more of me, I found myself following Grossbart's tracks to Chapel No. 3, where the Jewish services were being held.

I took a seat in the last row, which was empty. Two rows in

front of me sat Grossbart, Fishbein, and Halpern, holding little white Dixie cups. Each row of seats was raised higher than the one in front of it, and I could see clearly what was going on. Fishbein was pouring the contents of his cup into Grossbart's, and Grossbart looked mirthful as the liquid made a purple arc between Fishbein's hand and his. In the glaring yellow light, I saw the chaplain standing on the platform at the front; he was chanting the first line of the responsive reading. Grossbart's prayer book remained closed on his lap; he was swishing the cup around. Only Halpern responded to the chant by praying. The fingers of his right hand were spread wide across the cover of his open book. His cap was pulled down low onto his brow, which made it round, like a yarmulke. From time to time, Grossbart wet his lips at the cup's edge; Fishbein, his long yellow face a dying light bulb, looked from here to there, craning forward to catch sight of the faces down the row, then of those in front of him, then behind. He saw me, and his eyelids beat a tattoo. His elbow slid into Grossbart's side, his neck inclined toward his friend, he whispered something, and then, when the congregation next responded to the chant, Grossbart's voice was among the others. Fishbein looked into his book now, too; his lips, however, didn't move.

Finally, it was time to drink the wine. The chaplain smiled down at them as Grossbart swigged his in one long gulp, Halpern sipped, meditating, and Fishbein faked devotion with an empty cup. "As I look down amongst the congregation"—the chaplain grinned at the word—"this night, I see many new faces, and I want to welcome you to Friday-night services here at Camp Crowder. I am Major Leo Ben Ezra, your chaplain." Though an American, the chaplain spoke deliberately—syllable by syllable, almost—as though to communicate, above all, with the lip readers in his audience. "I have only a few words to say before we adjourn to the refreshment room, where the kind ladies of the Temple Sinai, St. Louis, Missouri, have a nice setting for you."

Applause and whistling broke out. After another momentary grin, the chaplain raised his hands, palms out, his eyes flicking upward a moment, as if to remind the troops where they were and Who Else might be in attendance. In the sudden silence that followed, I thought I heard Grossbart cackle, "Let the goyim clean the floors!" Were those the words? I wasn't sure, but Fishbein, grinning, nudged Halpern. Halpern looked dumbly at him, then went back to his prayer book, which had been occupying him all through the rabbi's talk. One hand tugged at the black kinky hair that stuck out under his cap. His lips moved.

The rabbi continued. "It is about the food that I want to speak to you for a moment. I know, I know, I know," he intoned, wearily, "how in the mouths of most of you the *trafe* food tastes like ashes. I know how you gag, some of you, and how your parents suffer to think of their children eating foods unclean and offensive to the palate. What can I tell you? I can only say, close your eyes and swallow as best you can. Eat what you must to live, and throw away the rest. I wish I could help more. For those of you who find this impossible, may I ask that you try and try, but then come to see me in private. If your revulsion is so great, we will have to seek aid from those higher up."

A round of chatter rose and subsided. Then everyone sang "Ain Kelohainu"; after all those years, I discovered I still knew the words. Then, suddenly, the service over, Grossbart was upon me. "Higher up? He means the General?"

"Hey, Shelley," Fishbein said, "he means God." He smacked his face and looked at Halpern. "How high can you go!"

"Sh-h-h!" Grossbart said. "What do you think, Sergeant?"

"I don't know," I said. "You better ask the chaplain."

"I'm going to. I'm making an appointment to see him in private. So is Mickey."

Halpern shook his head. "No, no, Sheldon—"

"You have rights, Mickey," Grossbart said. "They can't push us around."

"It's O.K.," said Halpern. "It bothers my mother, not me."

Grossbart looked at me. "Yesterday he threw up. From the hash. It was all ham and God knows what else."

"I have a cold—that was why," Halpern said. He pushed his yarmulke back into a cap.

"What about you, Fishbein?" I asked. "You kosher, too?"

He flushed. "A little. But I'll let it ride. I have a very strong stomach, and I don't eat a lot anyway." I continued to look at him, and he held up his wrist to reinforce what he'd just said; his watch strap was tightened to the last hole, and he pointed that out to me.

"But services are important to you?" I asked him.

He looked at Grossbart. "Sure, sir."

" 'Sergeant.' "

"Not so much at home," said Grossbart, stepping between us, "but away from home it gives one a sense of his Jewishness."

"We have to stick together," Fishbein said.

I started to walk toward the door; Halpern stepped back to make way for me.

"That's what happened in Germany," Grossbart was saying, loud enough for me to hear. "They didn't stick together. They let themselves get pushed around."

I turned. "Look, Grossbart. This is the Army, not summer camp."

He smiled. "So?"

Halpern tried to sneak off, but Grossbart held his arm.

"Grossbart, how old are you?" I asked.

"Nineteen."

"And you?" I said to Fishbein.

"The same. The same month, even."

"And what about him?" I pointed to Halpern, who had by now made it safely to the door.

"Eighteen," Grossbart whispered. "But like he can't tie his shoes or brush his teeth himself. I feel sorry for him."

"I feel sorry for all of us, Grossbart," I said, "but just act like a man. Just don't overdo it."

"Overdo what, sir?"

"The 'sir' business, for one thing. Don't overdo that," I said.

I left him standing there. I passed by Halpern, but he did not look at me. Then I was outside, but, behind, I heard Grossbart call, "Hey, Mickey, my *leben,* come on back. Refreshments!"

"Leben!" My grandmother's word for me!

One morning a week later, while I was working at my desk, Captain Barrett shouted for me to come into his office. When I entered, he had his helmet liner squashed down so far on his head that I couldn't even see his eyes. He was on the phone, and when he spoke to me, he cupped one hand over the mouthpiece. "Who the hell is Grossbart?"

"Third platoon, Captain," I said. "A trainee."

"What's all this stink about food? His mother called a goddam congressman about the food." He uncovered the mouthpiece and slid his helmet up until I could see his bottom eyelashes. "Yes, sir," he said into the phone. "Yes, sir. I'm still here, sir. I'm asking Marx, here, right now—"

He covered the mouthpiece again and turned his head back toward me. "Lightfoot Harry's on the phone," he said, between his teeth. "This congressman calls General Lyman, who calls Colonel Sousa, who calls the Major, who calls me. They're just dying to stick this thing on me. Whatsa matter?" He shook the phone at me. "I don't feed the troops? What the hell is this?"

"Sir, Grossbart is strange—" Barrett greeted that with a mockingly indulgent smile. I altered my approach. "Captain, he's a very orthodox Jew, and so he's only allowed to eat certain foods."

"He throws up, the congressman said. Every time he eats something, his mother says, he throws up!"

"He's accustomed to observing the dietary laws, Captain."

"So why's his old lady have to call the White House?"

"Jewish parents, sir—they're apt to be more protective than you expect. I mean, Jews have a very close family life. A boy goes away from home, sometimes the mother is liable to get very upset. Probably the boy mentioned something in a letter, and his mother misinterpreted."

"I'd like to punch him one right in the mouth," the Captain said. "There's a goddam war on, and he wants a silver platter!"

"I don't think the boy's to blame, sir. I'm sure we can straighten it out by just asking him. Jewish parents worry—"

"All parents worry, for Christ's sake. But they don't get on their high horse and start pulling strings—"

I interrupted, my voice higher, tighter than before. "The home life, Captain, is very important—but you're right, it may sometimes get out of hand. It's a very wonderful thing, Captain, but because it's so close, this kind of thing . . ."

He didn't listen any longer to my attempt to present both myself and Lightfoot Harry with an explanation for the letter. He turned back to the phone. "Sir?" he said. "Sir—Marx, here, tells me Jews have a tendency to be pushy. He says he thinks we can settle it right here in the company. . . . Yes, sir. . . . I *will* call back, sir, soon as I can." He hung up. "Where are the men, Sergeant?"

"On the range."

With a whack on the top of his helmet, he crushed it down over his eyes again, and charged out of his chair. "We're going for a ride," he said.

The Captain drove, and I sat beside him. It was a hot spring day, and under my newly starched fatigues I felt as though my armpits were melting down onto my sides and chest. The roads were dry, and by the time we reached the firing range, my teeth felt gritty with dust, though my mouth had been shut the whole trip. The Captain slammed the brakes on and told me to get the hell out and find Grossbart.

I found him on his belly, firing wildly at the five-hundred-feet target. Waiting their turns behind him were Halpern and Fishbein. Fishbein, wearing a pair of steel-rimmed G.I. glasses I hadn't seen on him before, had the appearance of an old peddler who would gladly have sold you his rifle and the cartridges that were slung all over him. I stood back by the ammo boxes, waiting for Grossbart to finish spraying the distant targets. Fishbein straggled back to stand near me.

"Hello, Sergeant Marx," he said.

"How are you?" I mumbled.

"Fine, thank you. Sheldon's really a good shot."

"I didn't notice."

"I'm not so good, but I think I'm getting the hang of it now. Sergeant, I don't mean to, you know, ask what I shouldn't —" The boy stopped. He was trying to speak intimately, but the noise of the shooting forced him to shout at me.

"What is it?" I asked. Down the range, I saw Captain Barrett standing up in the jeep, scanning the line for me and Grossbart.

"My parents keep asking and asking where we're going," Fishbein said. "Everybody says the Pacific. I don't care, but my parents—If I could relieve their minds, I think I could concentrate more on my shooting."

"I don't know where, Fishbein. Try to concentrate anyway."

"Sheldon says you might be able to find out."

"I don't know a thing, Fishbein. You just take it easy, and don't let Sheldon—"

"*I'm* taking it easy, Sergeant. It's at home—"

Grossbart had finished on the line, and was dusting his fatigues with one hand. I called to him. "Grossbart, the Captain wants to see you."

He came toward us. His eyes blazed and twinkled. "Hi!"

"Don't point that goddam rifle!" I said.

"I wouldn't shoot you, Sarge." He gave me a smile as wide as a pumpkin, and turned the barrel aside.

"Damn you, Grossbart, this is no joke! Follow me."

I walked ahead of him, and had the awful suspicion that, behind me, Grossbart was *marching,* his rifle on his shoulder, as though he were a one-man detachment. At the jeep, he gave the Captain a rifle salute. "Private Sheldon Grossbart, sir."

"At ease, Grossman." The Captain sat down, slid over into the empty seat, and, crooking a finger, invited Grossbart closer.

"Bart, sir. Sheldon Gross*bart.* It's a common error." Grossbart nodded at me; *I* understood, he indicated. I looked away just as the mess truck pulled up to the range, disgorging a half-dozen K.P.s with rolled-up sleeves. The mess sergeant screamed at them while they set up the chow-line equipment.

"Grossbart, your mama wrote some congressman that we don't feed you right. Do you know that?" the Captain said.

"It was my father, sir. He wrote to Representative Franconi that my religion forbids me to eat certain foods."

"What religion is that, Grossbart?"

"Jewish."

" 'Jewish, *sir,*' " I said to Grossbart.

"Excuse me, sir. Jewish, sir."

"What have you been living on?" the Captain asked. "You've been in the Army a month already. You don't look to me like you're falling to pieces."

"I eat because I have to, sir. But Sergeant Marx will testify to the fact that I don't eat one mouthful more than I need to in order to survive."

"Is that so, Marx?" Barrett asked.

"I've never seen Grossbart eat, sir," I said.

"But you heard the rabbi," Grossbart said. "He told us what to do, and I listened."

The Captain looked at me. "Well, Marx?"

"I still don't know what he eats and doesn't eat, sir."

Grossbart raised his arms to plead with me, and it looked for a moment as though he were going to hand me his weapon to hold. "But, Sergeant—"

"Look, Grossbart, just answer the Captain's questions," I said sharply.

Barrett smiled at me, and I resented it. "All right, Grossbart," he said. "What is it you want? The little piece of paper? You want out?"

"No, sir. Only to be allowed to live as a Jew. And for the others, too."

"What others?"

"Fishbein, sir, and Halpern."

"They don't like the way we serve, either?"

"Halpern throws up, sir. I've seen it."

"I thought *you* throw up."

"Just once, sir. I didn't know the sausage was sausage."

"We'll give menus, Grossbart. We'll show training films about the food, so you can identify when we're trying to poison you."

Grossbart did not answer. The men had been organized into two long chow lines. At the tail end of one, I spotted Fishbein—or, rather, his glasses spotted me. They winked sunlight back at me. Halpern stood next to him, patting the inside of his collar with a khaki handkerchief. They moved with the line as it began to edge up toward the food. The mess sergeant was still screaming at the K.P.'s For a moment, I was actually terrified by the thought that somehow the mess sergeant was going to become involved in Grossbart's problem.

"Marx," the Captain said, "you're a Jewish fella—am I right?"

I played straight man. "Yes, sir."

"How long you been in the Army? Tell this boy."

"Three years and two months."

"A year in combat, Grossbart. Twelve goddam months in combat all through Europe. I admire this man." The Captain snapped a wrist against my chest. "Do you hear him peeping about the food? Do you? I want an answer, Grossbart. Yes or no."

"No, sir."

"And why not? He's a Jewish fella."

"Some things are more important to some Jews than other things to other Jews."

Barrett blew up. "Look, Grossbart. Marx, here, is a good man—a goddam hero. When you were in high school, Sergeant Marx was killing Germans. Who does more for the Jews—you, by throwing up over a lousy piece of sausage, a piece of first-cut meat, or Marx, by killing those Nazi bastards? If I was a Jew, Grossbart, I'd kiss this man's feet. He's a goddam hero, and *he* eats what we give him. Why do you have to cause trouble is what I want to know! What is it you're buckin' for—a discharge?"

"No, sir."

"I'm talking to a wall, Sergeant, get him out of my way." Barrett swung himself back into the driver's seat. "I'm going to see the chaplain." The engine roared, the jeep spun around in a whirl of dust, and the Captain was headed back to camp.

For a moment, Grossbart and I stood side by side, watching the jeep. Then he looked at me and said, "I don't want to start trouble. That's the first thing they toss up to us."

When he spoke, I saw that his teeth were white and straight, and the sight of them suddenly made me understand that Grossbart actually did have parents—that once upon a time someone had taken little Sheldon to the dentist. He was their son. Despite all the talk about his parents, it was hard to believe in Grossbart as a child, an heir—as related by blood to anyone, mother, father, or, above all, to me. This realization led me to another.

"What does your father do, Grossbart?" I asked as we started to walk back toward the chow line.

"He's a tailor."

"An American?"

"Now, yes. A son in the Army," he said, jokingly.

"And your mother?" I asked.

He winked. "A *ballabusta.* She practically sleeps with a dustcloth in her hand."

"She's also an immigrant?"

"All she talks is Yiddish, still."

"And your father, too?"

"A little English. 'Clean,' 'Press,' 'Take the pants in.' That's the extent of it. But they're good to me."

"Then, Grossbart—" I reached out and stopped him. He turned toward me, and when our eyes met, his seemed to jump back, to shiver in their sockets. "Grossbart—you were the one who wrote that letter, weren't you?"

It took only a second or two for his eyes to flash happy again. "Yes." He walked on, and I kept pace. "It's what my father *would* have written if he had known how. It was his name, though. *He* signed it. He even mailed it. I sent it home. For the New York postmark."

I was astonished, and he saw it. With complete seriousness, he thrust his right arm in front of me. "Blood is blood, Sergeant," he said, pinching the blue vein in his wrist.

"What the hell *are* you trying to do, Grossbart?" I asked. "I've seen you eat. Do you know that? I told the Captain I don't know what you eat, but I've seen you eat like a hound at chow."

"We work hard, Sergeant. We're in training. For a furnace to work, you've got to feed it coal."

"Why did you say in the letter that you threw up all the time?"

"I was really talking about Mickey there. I was talking *for* him. He would never write, Sergeant, though I pleaded with him. He'll waste away to nothing if I don't help. Sergeant, I used my name—my father's name—but it's Mickey, and Fishbein, too, I'm watching out for."

"You're a regular Messiah, aren't you?"

We were at the chow line now.

"That's a good one, Sergeant," he said, smiling. "But who knows? Who can tell? Maybe you're the Messiah—a little bit. What Mickey says is the Messiah is a collective idea. He went to Yeshiva, Mickey, for a while. He says *together* we're the Messiah. Me a little bit, you a little bit. You should hear that kid talk, Sergeant, when he gets going."

"Me a little bit, you a little bit," I said. "You'd like to believe that, wouldn't you, Grossbart? That would make everything so clean for you."

"It doesn't seem too bad a thing to believe, Sergeant. It only means we should all *give* a little, is all."

I walked off to eat my rations with the other noncoms.

Two days later, a letter addressed to Captain Barrett passed over my desk. It had come through the chain of command—from the office of Congressman Franconi, where it had been received, to General Lyman, to Colonel Sousa, to Major Lamont, now to Captain Barrett. I read it over twice. It was dated May 14, the day Barrett had spoken with Grossbart on the rifle range.

Dear Congressman:

First let me thank you for your interest in behalf of my son, Private Sheldon Grossbart. Fortunately, I was able to speak with Sheldon on the phone the other night, and I think I've been able to solve our problem. He is, as I mentioned in my last letter, a very religious boy, and it was only with the greatest difficulty that I could persuade him that the religious thing to do—what God Himself would want Sheldon to do—would be to suffer the pangs of religious remorse for the good of his country and all mankind. It took some doing, Congressman, but finally he saw the light. In fact, what he said (and I wrote down the words on a scratch pad so as never to forget), what he said was "I guess you're right, Dad. So many millions of my fellow-Jews gave up their lives to the enemy, the least I can do is live for a while minus a bit of my heritage so as to help end this struggle and regain for all the children of God dignity and humanity." That, Congressman, would make any father proud.

By the way, Sheldon wanted me to know—and to pass on to you—the name of a soldier who helped him reach this decision: SERGEANT NATHAN MARX. Sergeant Marx is a combat veteran who is Sheldon's first sergeant. This man helped Sheldon over some of the first hurdles he's had to face in the Army, and is in part responsible for Sheldon's changing his mind about the dietary laws. I know Sheldon would appreciate any recognition Marx could receive.

Thank you and good luck. I look forward to seeing your name on the next election ballot.

Respectfully,
Samuel E. Grossbart

Attached to the Grossbart communiqué was another, addressed to General Marshall Lyman, the post commander, and signed by Representative Charles E. Franconi, of the House of Representatives. The communiqué informed General Lyman that Sergeant Nathan Marx was a credit to the U.S. Army and the Jewish people.

What was Grossbart's motive in recanting? Did he feel he'd gone too far? Was the letter a strategic retreat—a crafty attempt to strengthen what he considered our alliance? Or had he actually changed his mind, via an imaginary dialogue between Grossbart *père* and Grossbart *fils?* I was puzzled, but only for a few days—that is, only until I realized that, whatever his reasons, he had actually decided to disappear from my life; he was going to allow himself to become just another trainee. I saw him at inspection, but he never winked; at chow formations, but he never flashed me a sign. On Sundays, with the other trainees, he would sit around watching the noncoms' softball team, for which I pitched, but not once did he speak an unnecessary word to me. Fishbein and Halpern retreated, too—at Grossbart's command, I was sure. Apparently he had seen that wisdom lay in turning back before he plunged over into the ugliness of privilege undeserved. Our separation allowed me to forgive him our past encounters, and, finally, to admire him for his good sense.

Meanwhile, free of Grossbart, I grew used to my job and my administrative tasks. I stepped on a scale one day, and discovered I had truly become a noncombatant; I had gained seven pounds. I found patience to get past the first three pages of a book. I thought about the future more and more, and wrote letters to girls I'd known before the war. I even got a few answers. I sent away to Columbia for a Law School catalogue. I continued to follow the war in the Pacific, but it was not my war. I thought I could see the end, and sometimes, at night, I dreamed that I was walking on the streets of Manhattan—Broadway, Third Avenue, 116th Street, where I had lived the three years I attended Columbia. I curled myself around these dreams and I began to be happy.

And then, on Saturday, when everybody was away and I was alone in the orderly room reading a month-old copy of the *Sporting News,* Grossbart reappeared.

"You a baseball fan, Sergeant?"

I looked up. "How are you?"

"Fine," Grossbart said. "They're making a soldier out of me."

"How are Fishbein and Halpern?"

"Coming along," he said. "We've got no training this afternoon. They're at the movies."

"How come you're not with them?"

"I wanted to come over and say hello."

He smiled—a shy, regular-guy smile, as though he and I well knew that our friendship drew its sustenance from unexpected visits, remembered birthdays, and borrowed lawnmowers. At first it offended me, and then the feeling was swallowed by the general uneasiness I felt at the thought that everyone on the post was locked away in a dark movie theater and I was here alone with Grossbart. I folded up my paper.

"Sergeant," he said, "I'd like to ask a favor. It is a favor, and I'm making no bones about it."

He stopped, allowing me to refuse him a hearing—which, of course, forced me into a courtesy I did not intend. "Go ahead."

"Well, actually it's two favors."

I said nothing.

"The first one's about these rumors. Everybody says we're going to the Pacific."

"As I told your friend Fishbein, I don't know," I said. "You'll just have to wait to find out. Like everybody else."

"You think there's a chance of any of us going East?"

"Germany?" I said. "Maybe."

"I meant New York."

"I don't think so, Grossbart. Offhand."

"Thanks for the information, Sergeant," he said.

"It's not information, Grossbart. Just what I surmise."

"It certainly would be good to be near home. My parents—you know." He took a step toward the door and then turned back. "Oh, the other thing. May I ask the other?"

"What is it?"

"The other thing is—I've got relatives in St. Louis, and they say they'll give me a whole Passover dinner if I can get down there. God, Sergeant, that'd mean an awful lot to me."

I stood up. "No passes during basic, Grossbart."

"But we're off from now till Monday morning, Sergeant. I could leave the post and no one would even know."

"I'd know. You'd know."

"But that's all. Just the two of us. Last night, I called my aunt, and you should have heard her. 'Come—come,' she said. 'I got gefilte fish, *chrain*—the works!' Just a day, Sergeant. I'd take the blame if anything happened."

"The Captain isn't here to sign a pass."

"You could sign."

"Look, Grossbart—"

"Sergeant, for two months, practically, I've been eating *trafe* till I want to die."

"I thought you'd made up your mind to live with it. To be minus a little bit of heritage."

He pointed a finger at me. "You!" he said. "That wasn't for you to read."

"I read it. So what?"

"That letter was addressed to a congressman."

"Grossbart, don't feed me any baloney. You *wanted* me to read it."

"Why are you persecuting me, Sergeant?"

"Are you kidding!"

"I've run into this before," he said, "but never from my own!"

"Get out of here, Grossbart! Get the hell out of my sight!"

He did not move. "Ashamed, that's what you are," he said. "So you take it out on the rest of us. They say Hitler himself was half a Jew. Hearing you, I wouldn't doubt it."

"What are you trying to do with me, Grossbart?" I asked him. "What are you after? You want me to give you special privileges, to change the food, to find out about your orders, to give you weekend passes."

"You even talk like a goy!" Grossbart shook his fist. "Is this just a weekend pass I'm asking for? Is a Seder sacred, or not?"

Seder! It suddenly occurred to me that Passover had been celebrated weeks before. I said so.

"That's right," he replied. "Who says no? A month ago—and I was in the field eating hash! And now all I ask is a simple favor. A Jewish boy I thought would understand. My aunt's willing to go out of her way—to make a Seder a month later. . . ." He turned to go, mumbling.

"Come back here!" I called. He stopped and looked at me.

"Grossbart, why can't you be like the rest? Why do you have to stick out like a sore thumb?"

"Because I'm a Jew, Sergeant. I *am* different. Better, maybe not. But different."

"This is a war, Grossbart. For the time being *be* the same."

"I refuse."

"What?"

"I refuse. I can't stop being me, that's all there is to it." Tears came to his eyes. "It's a hard thing to be a Jew. But now I understand what Mickey says—it's a harder thing to stay one." He raised a hand sadly toward me. "Look at *you*."

"Stop crying!"

"Stop this, stop that, stop the other thing! *You* stop, Sergeant. Stop closing your heart to your own!" And, wiping his face with his sleeve, he ran out the door. "The least we can do for one another—the least . . ."

An hour later, looking out of the window, I saw Grossbart headed across the field. He wore a pair of starched khakis and carried a little leather ditty bag. I went out into the heat of the day. It was quiet; not a soul was in sight except, over by the mess hall, four K.P.'s sitting around a pan, sloped forward from their waists, gabbing and peeling potatoes in the sun.

"Grossbart!" I called.

He looked toward me and continued walking.

"Grossbart, get over here!"

He turned and came across the field. Finally, he stood before me.

"Where are you going?" I asked.

"St. Louis. I don't care."

"You'll get caught without a pass."

"So I'll get caught without a pass."

"You'll go to the stockade."

"I'm *in* the stockade." He made an about-face and headed off.

I let him go only a step or two. "Come back here," I said,

and he followed me into the office, where I typed out a pass and signed the Captain's name, and my own initials after it.

He took the pass and then, a moment later, reached out and grabbed my hand. "Sergeant, you don't know how much this means to me."

"O.K.," I said. "Don't get in any trouble."

"I wish I could show you how much this means to me."

"Don't do me any favors. Don't write any more congressmen for citations."

He smiled. "You're right. I won't. But let me do something."

"Bring me a piece of that gefilte fish. Just get out of here."

"I will!" he said. "With a slice of carrot and a little horseradish. I won't forget."

"All right. Just show your pass at the gate. And don't tell *anybody.*"

"I won't. It's a month late, but a good Yom Tov to you."

"Good Yom Tov, Grossbart," I said.

"You're a good Jew, Sergeant. You like to think you have a hard heart, but underneath you're a fine, decent man. I mean that."

Those last three words touched me more than any words from Grossbart's mouth had the right to. "All right, Grossbart," I said. "Now call me 'sir,' and get the hell out of here."

He ran out the door and was gone. I felt very pleased with myself; it was a great relief to stop fighting Grossbart, and it had cost me nothing. Barrett would never find out, and if he did, I could manage to invent some excuse. For a while, I sat at my desk, comfortable in my decision. Then the screen door flew back and Grossbart burst in again. "Sergeant!" he said. Behind him I saw Fishbein and Halpern, both in starched khakis, both carrying ditty bags like Grossbart's.

"Sergeant, I caught Mickey and Larry coming out of the movies. I almost missed them."

"Grossbart—did I say tell no one?" I said.

"But my aunt said I could bring friends. That I should, in fact."

"I'm the Sergeant, Grossbart—not your aunt!"

Grossbart looked at me in disbelief. He pulled Halpern up by his sleeve. "Mickey, tell the Sergeant what this would mean to you."

Halpern looked at me and, shrugging, said, "A lot."

Fishbein stepped forward without prompting. "This would mean a great deal to me and my parents, Sergeant Marx."

"No!" I shouted.

Grossbart was shaking his head. "Sergeant, I could see you denying me, but how you can deny Mickey, a Yeshiva boy—that's beyond me."

"I'm not denying Mickey anything," I said. "You just pushed a little too hard, Grossbart. *You* denied him."

"I'll give him my pass, then," Grossbart said. "I'll give him my aunt's address and a little note. At least let him go."

In a second, he had crammed the pass into Halpern's pants pocket. Halpern looked at me, and so did Fishbein. Grossbart was at the door, pushing it open. "Mickey, bring me a piece of gefilte fish, at least," he said, and then he was outside again.

The three of us looked at one another, and then I said, "Halpern, hand that pass over."

He took it from his pocket and gave it to me. Fishbein had now moved to the doorway, where he lingered. He stood there for a moment with his mouth slightly open, and then he pointed to himself. "And me?" he asked.

His utter ridiculousness exhausted me. I slumped down in my seat and felt pulses knocking at the back of my eyes. "Fishbein," I said, "you understand I'm not trying to deny you anything, don't you? If it was my Army, I'd serve gefilte fish in the mess hall. I'd sell *kugel* in the PX, honest to God."

Halpern smiled.

"You understand, don't you, Halpern?"

"Yes, Sergeant."

"And you, Fishbein? I don't want enemies. I'm just like you—I want to serve my time and go home. I miss the same things you miss."

"Then, Sergeant," Fishbein said, "why don't you come, too?"

"Where?"

"To St. Louis. To Shelly's aunt. We'll have a regular Seder. Play hide-the-matzoh." He gave me a broad, black-toothed smile.

I saw Grossbart again, on the other side of the screen.

"Pst!" He waved a piece of paper. "Mickey, here's the address. Tell her I couldn't get away."

Halpern did not move. He looked at me, and I saw the shrug moving up his arms into his shoulders again. I took the cover off my typewriter and made out passes for him and Fishbein. "Go," I said. "The three of you."

I thought Halpern was going to kiss my hand.

That afternoon, in a bar in Joplin, I drank beer and listened with half an ear to the Cardinal game. I tried to look squarely at what I'd become involved in, and began to wonder if perhaps the struggle with Grossbart wasn't as much my fault as his. What was I that I had to *muster* generous feelings? Who was I to have been feeling so grudging, so tight-hearted? After all, I wasn't being asked to move the world. Had I a right, then, or a reason, to clamp down on Grossbart, when that meant clamping down on Halpern, too? And Fishbein—that ugly, agreeable soul? Out of the many recollections of my childhood that had tumbled over me these past few days I heard my grandmother's voice: "What are you making a *tsimmes?*" It was what she would ask my mother when, say, I had cut myself while doing something I shouldn't have done, and her daughter was busy bawling me out. I needed a hug and a kiss, and my mother would moralize. But my grandmother knew—mercy overrides justice. I should have known it, too. Who was Nathan Marx to be such a penny pincher with kindness? Surely, I thought, the Messiah Himself—if He should ever come—won't niggle over nickels and dimes. God willing, He'll hug and kiss.

The next day, while I was playing softball over on the parade ground, I decided to ask Bob Wright, who was noncom in charge of Classification and Assignment, where he thought our trainees would be sent when their cycle ended, in two weeks. I asked casually, between innings, and he said, "They're pushing them all into the Pacific. Shulman cut the orders on your boys the other day."

The news shocked me, as though I were the father of Halpern, Fishbein, and Grossbart.

That night, I was just sliding into sleep when someone tapped on my door. "Who is it?" I asked.

"Sheldon."

He opened the door and came in. For a moment, I felt his presence without being able to see him. "How was it?" I asked.

He popped into sight in the near-darkness before me. "Great, Sergeant." Then he was sitting on the edge of the bed. I sat up.

"How about you?" he asked. "Have a nice weekend?"

"Yes."

"The others went to sleep." He took a deep, paternal breath. We sat silent for a while, and a homey feeling invaded my ugly little cubicle; the door was locked, the cat was out, the children were safely in bed.

"Sergeant, can I tell you something? Personal?"

I did not answer, and he seemed to know why. "Not about me. About Mickey. Sergeant, I never felt for anybody like I feel for him. Last night I heard Mickey in the bed next to me. He was crying so, it could have broken your heart. Real sobs."

"I'm sorry to hear that."

"I had to talk to him to stop him. He held my hand, Sergeant—he wouldn't let it go. He was almost hysterical. He kept saying if he only knew where we were going. Even if he knew it *was* the Pacific, that would be better than nothing. Just to know."

Long ago, someone had taught Grossbart the sad rule that only lies can get the truth. Not that I couldn't believe in the fact of Halpern's crying; his eyes *always* seemed red-rimmed. But, fact or not, it became a lie when Grossbart uttered it. He was entirely strategic. But then—it came with the force of indictment—so was I! There are strategies of aggression, but there are strategies of retreat as well. And so, recognizing that I myself had not been without craft and guile, I told him what I knew. "It is the Pacific."

He let out a small gasp, which was not a lie. "I'll tell him. I wish it was otherwise."

"So do I."

He jumped on my words. "You mean you think you could do something? A change, maybe?"

"No, I couldn't do a thing."

"Don't you know anybody over at C. and A.?"

"Grossbart, there's nothing I can do," I said. "If your orders are for the Pacific, then it's the Pacific."

"But Mickey—"

"Mickey, you, me—everybody, Grossbart. There's nothing to be done. Maybe the war'll end before you go. Pray for a miracle."

"But—"

"Good night, Grossbart." I settled back, and was relieved to feel the springs unbend as Grossbart rose to leave. I could see him clearly now; his jaw had dropped, and he looked like a dazed prizefighter. I noticed for the first time a little paper bag in his hand.

"Grossbart." I smiled. "My gift?"

"Oh, yes, Sergeant. Here—from all of us." He handed me the bag. "It's egg roll."

"Egg roll?" I accepted the bag and felt a damp grease spot on the bottom. I opened it, sure that Grossbart was joking.

"We thought you'd probably like it. You know—Chinese egg roll. We thought you'd probably have a taste for—"

"Your aunt served egg roll?"

"She wasn't home."

"Grossbart, she invited you. You told me she invited you and your friends."

"I know," he said. "I just reread the letter. *Next* week."

I got out of bed and walked to the window. "Grossbart," I said. But I was not calling to him.

"What?"

"What are you, Grossbart? Honest to God, what are you?"

I think it was the first time I'd asked him a question for which he didn't have an immediate answer.

"How can you do this to people?" I went on.

"Sergeant, the day away did us all a world of good. Fishbein, you should see him, he *loves* Chinese food."

"But the Seder," I said.

"We took second best, Sergeant."

Rage came charging at me. I didn't sidestep. "Grossbart, you're a liar!" I said. "You're a schemer and a crook. You've got no respect for anything. Nothing at all. Not for me, for the truth—not even for poor Halpern! You use us all—"

"Sergeant, Sergeant, I feel for Mickey. Honest to God, I do. I *love* Mickey. I try—"

"You try! You feel!" I lurched toward him and grabbed his shirt front. I shook him furiously. "Grossbart, get out! Get out and stay the hell away from me. Because if I see you, I'll make your life miserable. *You understand that?*"

"Yes."

I let him free, and when he walked from the room, I wanted to spit on the floor where he had stood. I couldn't stop the fury. It engulfed me, owned me, till it seemed I could only rid myself of it with tears or an act of violence. I snatched from the bed the bag Grossbart had given me and, with all my strength, threw it out the window. And the next morning, as the men policed the area around the barracks, I heard a great cry go up from one of the trainees, who had been anticipating only his morning handful of cigarette butts and candy wrappers. "Egg roll!" he shouted. "Holy Christ, Chinese goddam egg roll!"

A week later, when I read the orders that had come down from C. and A., I couldn't believe my eyes. Every single trainee was to be shipped to Camp Stoneman, California, and from there to the Pacific—every trainee but one. Private Sheldon Grossbart. He was to be sent to Fort Monmouth, New Jersey. I read the mimeographed sheet several times. Dee, Farrell, Fishbein, Fuselli, Fylypowycz, Glinicki, Gromke, Gucwa, Halpern, Hardy, Helebrandt, right down to Anton Zygadlo—all were to be headed West before the month was out. All except Grossbart. He had pulled a string, and I wasn't it.

I lifted the phone and called C. and A.

The voice on the other end said smartly, "Corporal Shulman, sir."

"Let me speak to Sergeant Wright."

"Who is this calling, sir?"

"Sergeant Marx."

And, to my surprise, the voice said, *"Oh!"* Then, "Just a minute, Sergeant."

Shulman's *"Oh!"* stayed with me while I waited for Wright to come to the phone. Why *"Oh!"*? Who was Shulman? And then, so simply, I knew I'd discovered the string that Grossbart had pulled. In fact, I could hear Grossbart the day he'd discovered Shulman in the PX, or in the bowling alley, or maybe even at services. "Glad to meet you. Where you from? Bronx? Me, too. Do you know So-and-So? And So-and-So? Me, too! You work at C. and A.? Really? Hey, how's chances of getting East? Could you do something? Change something? Swindle, cheat, lie? We gotta help each other, you know. If the Jews in Germany . . ."

Bob Wright answered the phone. "How are you, Nate? How's the pitching arm?"

"Good. Bob, I wonder if you could do me a favor." I heard clearly my own words, and they so reminded me of Grossbart that I dropped more easily than I could have imagined into what I had planned. "This may sound crazy, Bob, but I got a kid here on orders to Monmouth who wants them changed. He had a brother killed in Europe, and he's hot to go to the Pacific. Says he'd feel like a coward if he wound up Stateside. I don't know, Bob—can anything be done? Put somebody else in the Monmouth slot?"

"Who?" he asked cagily.

"Anybody. First guy in the alphabet. I don't care. The kid just asked if something could be done."

"What's his name?"

"Grossbart, Sheldon."

Wright didn't answer.

"Yeah," I said. "He's a Jewish kid, so he thought I could help him out. You know."

"I guess I can do something," he finally said. "The Major hasn't been around here for weeks. Temporary duty to the golf course. I'll try, Nate, that's all I can say."

"I'd appreciate it, Bob. See you Sunday." And I hung up, perspiring.

The following day, the corrected orders appeared: Fishbein, Fuselli, Fylypowcyz, Glinicki, Gromke, Grossbart, Gucwa, Halpern, Hardy . . . Lucky Private Harley Alton was to go to Fort Monmouth, New Jersey, where, for some reason or other, they wanted an enlisted man with infantry training.

After chow that night, I stopped back at the orderly room to straighten out the guard-duty roster. Grossbart was waiting for me. He spoke first.

"You son of a bitch!"

I sat down at my desk, and while he glared at me, I began to make the necessary alterations in the duty roster.

"What do you have against me?" he cried. "Against my family? Would it kill you for me to be near my father, God knows how many months he has left to him?"

"Why so?"

"His heart," Grossbart said. "He hasn't had enough troubles in a lifetime, you've got to add to them. I curse the day I ever met you, Marx! Shulman told me what happened over there. There's no limit to your anti-Semitism, is there? The damage you've done here isn't enough. You have to make a special phone call! You really want me dead!"

I made the last few notations in the duty roster and got up to leave. "Good night, Grossbart."

"You owe me an explanation!" He stood in my path.

"Sheldon, you're the one who owes explanations."

He scowled. "To *you?*"

"To me, I think so—yes. Mostly to Fishbein and Halpern."

"That's right, twist things around. I owe nobody nothing, I've done all I could do for them. Now I think I've got the right to watch out for myself."

"You call this watching out for me—what you did?"

"No. For all of us."

I pushed him aside and started for the door. I heard his furious breathing behind me, and it sounded like steam rushing from an engine of terrible strength.

"You'll be all right," I said from the door. And, I thought, so would Fishbein and Halpern be all right, even in the Pacific, if only Grossbart continued to see—in the obsequiousness of the one, the soft spirituality of the other—some profit for himself.

I stood outside the orderly room, and I heard Grossbart weeping behind me. Over in the barracks, in the lighted windows, I could see the boys in their T shirts sitting on their bunks talking about their orders, as they'd been doing for the past two days. With a kind of quiet nervousness, they polished shoes, shined belt buckles, squared away underwear, trying as best they could to accept their fate. Behind me, Grossbart swallowed hard, accepting his. And then, resisting with all my will an impulse to turn and seek pardon for my vindictiveness, I accepted my own.

PHILIP ROTH was born in Newark, New Jersey on March 19, 1933. He graduated from Bucknell University at 21 and received his Master's degree a year later from the University of Chicago.

In a remarkably short time, his emerging talent was recognized by both critics and the public. His stories were anthologized in *Best American Short Stories 1956, 1959, 1960* and also appeared in magazines like *The New Yorker* and *Harper's.* A collection, *Goodbye Columbus,* received the National Book Award in 1960.

In 1959 Roth was awarded a Guggenheim fellowship, and in 1960 he joined the Iowa Writers' Workshop, whose faculty has at different times included Vance Bourjaily, Hortense Calisher, and Kurt Vonnegut. *Letting Go,* his first novel, appeared in 1962, and a second, *When She Was Young,* was published early in 1967. Currently, Philip Roth is teaching at the State University of New York.

"Defender of the Faith," from *Goodbye Columbus,* reveals Roth's characteristic concern with the condition of being both Jewish and American.

WILLIAM SAROYAN

The Daring Young Man on the Flying Trapeze

1 SLEEP

Horizontally wakeful amid universal widths, practising laughter and mirth, satire, the end of all, of Rome and yes of Babylon, clenched teeth, remembrance, much warmth volcanic, the streets of Paris, the plains of Jericho, much gliding as of reptile in abstraction, a gallery of watercolors, the sea and the fish with eyes, symphony, a table in the corner of the Eiffel Tower, jazz at the opera house, alarm clock and the tap dancing of doom, conversation with a tree, the river Nile, Cadillac coupe to Kansas, the roar of Dostoyevsky, and the dark sun.

This earth, the face of one who lived, the form without the weight, weeping upon snow, white music, the magnified flower twice the size of the universe, black clouds, the caged panther staring, deathless space, Mr. Eliot with rolled sleeves baking bread, Flaubert and Guy de Maupassant, a wordless rhyme of early meaning, Finlandia, mathematics highly polished and slick as a green onion to the teeth, Jerusalem, the path to paradox.

The deep song of man, the sly whisper of someone unseen but vaguely known, hurricane in the cornfield, a game of chess, hush the queen, the king, Karl Franz, black Titanic, Mr. Chaplin weeping, Stalin, Hitler, a multitude of Jews, tomorrow is Monday, no dancing in the streets.

O swift moment of life: it is ended, the earth is again now.

2 WAKEFULNESS

He (the living) dressed and shaved, grinning at himself in the mirror. Very unhandsome, he said; where is my tie? (He had but one.) Coffee and a gray sky, Pacific Ocean fog, the drone of a passing streetcar, people going to the city, time again, the day, prose and poetry. He moved swiftly down the stairs to the street and began to talk, thinking suddenly, *It is only in sleep that we may know that we live. There only, in that living death, do we meet ourselves and the far earth, God and the saints, the names of our fathers; the substance of remote moments; it is there that the centuries merge in the moment, that the vast becomes the tiny, tangible atom of eternity.*

He walked into the day as alertly as might be, making a definite noise with his heels, perceiving with his eyes the superficial truth of streets and structures, the trivial truth of reality. Helplessly his mind sang. *He flies through the air with the greatest of ease; the daring young man on the flying trapeze;*

then laughed with all the might of his being. It was really a splendid morning: gray, cold, and cheerless, a morning for inward vigor; ah, Edgar Guest, he said, how I long for your music.

In the gutter he saw a coin which proved to be a penny dated 1923, and placing it in the palm of his hand he examined it closely, remembering that year and thinking of Lincoln whose profile was stamped upon the coin. There was almost nothing a man could do with a penny. I will purchase a motorcar, he thought. I will dress myself in the fashion of a fop, visit the hotel strumpets, drink and dine, and then return to the quiet. Or I will drop the coin into a slot and weigh myself.

It was good to be poor, and the Communists—but it was dreadful to be hungry. What appetites they had, how fond they were of food! Empty stomachs. He remembered how greatly he needed food. Every meal was bread and coffee and cigarettes, and now he had no more bread. Coffee without bread could never honestly serve as supper, and there were no weeds in the park that could be cooked as spinach is cooked.

If the truth were known, he was half starved, and yet there was still no end of books he ought to read before he died. He remembered the young Italian in a Brooklyn hospital, a small sick clerk named Mollica, who had said desperately, I would like to see California once before I die. And he thought earnestly, I ought at least to read *Hamlet* once again; or perhaps *Huckleberry Finn.*

It was then that he became thoroughly awake: at the thought of dying. Now wakefulness was a state in the nature of a sustained shock. A young man could perish rather unostentatiously, he thought; and already he was very nearly starved. Water and prose were fine, they filled much inorganic space, but they were inadequate. If there were only some work he might do for money, some trivial labor in the name of commerce. If they would only allow him to sit at a desk all day and add trade figures, subtract and multiply and divide, then perhaps he would not die. He would buy food, all sorts of it: untasted delicacies from Norway, Italy, and France; all manner of beef, lamb, fish, cheese; grapes, figs, pears, apples, melons, which he would worship when he had satisfied his hunger. He would place a bunch of red grapes on a dish beside two black figs, a large yellow pear, and a green apple. He would hold a cut melon to his nostrils for hours. He would buy great brown loaves of French bread, vegetables of all sorts, meat; he would buy life.

From a hill he saw the city standing majestically in the east, great towers, dense with his kind, and there he was suddenly outside of it all, almost definitely certain that he should never gain admittance, almost positive that somehow he had ventured upon the wrong earth, or perhaps into the wrong age, and now a young man of twenty-two was to be permanently ejected from it. This thought was not saddening. He said to himself, sometime soon I must write *An Application for Permission to Live.* He accepted the thought of dying without pity for himself or for man, believing that he would at least sleep another night. His rent for another day was paid; there was yet another tomorrow. And after that he might go where other homeless men went. He might even visit the Salvation Army—sing to God and Jesus (unlover of my soul), be saved, eat and sleep. But he knew that he would not. His life was a private life. He did not wish to destroy this fact. Any other alternative would be better.

Through the air on the flying trapeze, his mind hummed. Amusing it was, astoundingly funny. A trapeze to God, or to nothing, a flying trapeze to some sort of eternity; he prayed objectively for strength to make the flight with grace.

I have one cent, he said. It is an American coin. In the evening I shall polish it until it glows like a sun, and I shall study the words.

He was now walking in the city itself, among living men. There were one or two places to go. He saw his reflection in the plate-glass windows of stores and was disappointed with his appearance. He seemed not at all as strong as he felt; he seemed, in fact, a trifle infirm in every part of his body, in his neck, his shoulders, arms, trunk, and knees. This will never do, he said, and with an effort he assembled all his disjointed parts and became tensely, artificially erect and solid.

He passed numerous restaurants with magnificent discipline, refusing even to glance into them, and at last reached a building which he entered. He rose in an elevator to the seventh floor, moved down a hall, and, opening a door, walked into the office of an employment agency. Already there were two dozen young men in the place; he found a corner where he stood waiting his turn to be interviewed. At length he was granted this great privilege and was questioned by a thin, scatterbrained miss of fifty.

Now tell me, she said; what can you do?

He was embarrassed. I can write, he said pathetically.

You mean your penmanship is good? Is that it? said the elderly maiden.

Well, yes, he replied. But I mean that I can write.

Write what? said the miss, almost with anger.

Prose, he said simply.

There was a pause. At last the lady said:

Can you use a typewriter?

Of course, said the young man.

All right, went on the miss, we have your address; we will get in touch with you. There is nothing this morning, nothing at all.

It was much the same at the other agency, except that he was questioned by a conceited young man who closely resembled a pig. From the agencies he went to the large department stores: there was a good deal of pomposity, some humiliation on his part, and finally the report that work was not available. He did not feel displeased, and strangely did not even feel that he was personally involved in all the foolishness. He was a living young man who was in need of money with which to go on being one, and there was no way of getting it except by working for it; and there was no work. It was purely an abstract problem which he wished for the last time to attempt to solve. Now he was pleased that the matter was closed.

He began to perceive the definiteness of the course of his life. Except for moments, it had been largely artless, but now at the last minute he was determined that there should be as little imprecision as possible.

He passed countless stores and restaurants on his way to the Y.M.C.A. where he helped himself to paper and ink and began to compose his *Application*. For an hour he worked on this document, then suddenly, owing to the bad air in the place and to hunger, he became faint. He seemed to be swimming away from himself with great strokes, and hurriedly left the building. In the Civic Center Park, across from the Public Library Building, he drank almost a quart of water and felt himself refreshed. An old man was standing in the center of the brick boulevard surrounded by sea gulls, pigeons, and robins. He was taking handfuls of bread crumbs from a large paper sack and tossing them to the birds with a gallant gesture.

Dimly he felt impelled to ask the old man for a portion of the crumbs, but he did not allow the thought even nearly to reach consciousness; he entered the Public Library and for an hour read Proust, then, feeling himself to be swimming away again, he rushed outdoors. He drank more water at the fountain in the park and began the long walk to his room.

I'll go and sleep some more, he said; there is nothing else to do. He knew now that he was much too tired and weak to deceive himself about being all right, and yet his mind seemed somehow still lithe and alert. It, as if it were a separate entity, persisted in articulating impertinent pleasantries about his very real physical suffering. He reached his room early in the afternoon and immediately prepared coffee on the small gas range. There was no milk in the can, and the half pound of sugar he had purchased a week before was all gone; he drank a cup of the hot black fluid, sitting on his bed and smiling.

From the Y.M.C.A. he had stolen a dozen sheets of letter paper upon which he hoped to complete his document, but now the very notion of writing was unpleasant to him. There was nothing to say. He began to polish the penny he had found in the morning, and this absurd act somehow afforded him great enjoyment. No American coin can be made to shine so brilliantly as a penny. How many pennies would he need to go on living? Wasn't there something more he might sell? He looked about the bare room. No. His watch was gone; also his books. All those fine books; nine of them for eighty-five cents. He felt ill and ashamed for having parted with his books. His best suit he had sold for two dollars, but that was all right. He didn't mind at all about clothes. But the books. That was different. It made him very angry to think that there was no respect for men who wrote.

He placed the shining penny on the table, looking upon it with the delight of a miser. How prettily it smiles, he said. Without reading them he looked at the words, *E Pluribus Unum One Cent United States of America,* and turning the penny over, he saw Lincoln and the words, *In God We Trust Liberty 1923.* How beautiful it is, he said.

He became drowsy and felt a ghastly illness coming over his blood, a feeling of nausea and distintegration. Bewildered, he stood beside his bed, thinking *there is nothing to do but sleep.* Already he felt himself making great strides through the fluid of the earth, swimming away to the beginning. He fell face down upon the bed, saying, I ought first at least to give the coin to some child. A child could buy any number of things with a penny.

Then swiftly, neatly, with the grace of the young man on the trapeze, he was gone from his body. For an eternal moment he was all things at once: the bird, the fish, the rodent, the reptile, and man. An ocean of print undulated endlessly and darkly before him. The city burned. The herded crowd rioted. The earth circled away, and knowing that he did so, he turned his lost face to the empty sky and became dreamless, unalive, perfect.

WILLIAM SAROYAN's literary career began in 1933 with this remarkable story, "The Daring Young Man on the Flying Trapeze." He wrote it one day when he was 25 years old, and it was his first published work. Since then he has written hundreds of stories and several novels and plays, among them *My Name Is Aram* (1940), *The Human Comedy* (1943), and *The Time of Your Life* (1939), awarded a Pulitzer Prize which the author refused to accept, saying the play was no better than any of his other work.

Born in the Armenian section of Fresno, California, in 1908, Saroyan had a childhood marked by truancy, several years in an orphanage, avid reading, and the irrepressible love of life that illuminates all his work. Mr. Saroyan now shuttles spiritedly between Paris, London, New York, San Francisco, and his Fresno home.

LIONEL TRILLING

Of This Time, Of That Place

It was a fine September day. By noon it would be summer again, but now it was true autumn with a touch of chill in the air. As Joseph Howe stood on the porch of the house in which he lodged, ready to leave for his first class of the year, he thought with pleasure of the long indoor days that were coming. It was a moment when he could feel glad of his profession.

On the lawn the peach tree was still in fruit and young

Hilda Aiken was taking a picture of it. She held the camera tight against her chest. She wanted the sun behind her, but she did not want her own long morning shadow in the foreground. She raised the camera, but that did not help, and she lowered it, but that made things worse. She twisted her body to the left, then to the right. In the end she had to step out of the direct line of the sun. At last she snapped the shutter and wound the film with intense care.

Howe, watching her from the porch, waited for her to finish and called a good morning. She turned, startled, and almost sullenly lowered her glance. In the year Howe had lived at the Aikens', Hilda had accepted him as one of her family, but since his absence of the summer she had grown shy. Then suddenly she lifted her head and smiled at him, and the humorous smile confirmed the pleasure in the day. She picked up her bookbag and set off for school.

The handsome houses on the streets to the college were not yet fully awake, but they looked very friendly. Howe went by the Bradby house where he would be a guest this evening at the first dinner party of the year. When he had gone the length of the picket fence, the whitest in town, he turned back. Along the path there was a fine row of asters and he went through the gate and picked one for his buttonhole. The Bradbys would be pleased if they happened to see him invading their lawn and the knowledge of this made him even more comfortable.

He reached the campus as the hour was striking. The students were hurrying to their classes. He himself was in no hurry. He stopped at his dime cubicle of an office and lit a cigarette. The prospect of facing his class had suddenly presented itself to him and his hands were cold; the lawful seizure of power he was about to make seemed momentous. Waiting did not help. He put out his cigarette, picked up a pad of theme paper, and went to his classroom.

As he entered, the rattle of voices ceased, and the twenty-odd freshmen settled themselves and looked at him appraisingly.

Their faces seemed gross, his heart sank at their massed impassivity, but he spoke briskly.

"My name is Howe," he said, and turned and wrote it on the blackboard. The carelessness of the scrawl confirmed his authority. He went on, "My office is 412 Slemp Hall, and my office-hours are Monday, Wednesday, and Friday from eleven-thirty to twelve-thirty."

He wrote, "M., W., F., 11:30-12:30." He said, "I'll be very glad to see any of you at that time. Or if you can't come then, you can arrange with me for some other time."

He turned again to the blackboard and spoke over his shoulder. "The text for the course is Jarman's *Modern Plays,* revised edition. The Co-op has it in stock." He wrote the name, underlined "revised edition" and waited for it to be taken down in the new notebooks.

When the bent heads were raised again he began his speech of prospectus. "It is hard to explain—" he said, and paused as they composed themselves. "It is hard to explain what a course like this is intended to do. We are going to try to learn something about modern literature and something about prose composition."

As he spoke, his hands warmed and he was able to look directly at the class. Last year on the first day the faces had seemed just as cloddish, but as the term wore on they became gradually alive and quite likable. It did not seem possible that the same thing could happen again.

"I shall not lecture in this course," he continued. "Our work will be carried on by discussion and we will try to learn by an exchange of opinion. But you will soon recognize that my opinion is worth more than anyone else's here."

He remained grave as he said it, but two boys understood and laughed. The rest took permission from them and laughed too. All Howe's private ironies protested the vulgarity of the joke, but the laughter made him feel benign and powerful.

When the little speech was finished, Howe picked up the

pad of paper he had brought. He announced that they would write an extemporaneous theme. Its subject was traditional, "Who I am and why I came to Dwight College." By now the class was more at ease and it gave a ritualistic groan of protest. Then there was a stir as fountain pens were brought out and the writing-arms of the chairs were cleared, and the paper was passed about. At last, all the heads bent to work, and the room became still.

Howe sat idly at his desk. The sun shone through the tall clumsy windows. The cool of the morning was already passing. There was a scent of autumn and of varnish and the stillness of the room was deep and oddly touching. Now and then a student's head was raised and scratched in the old, elaborate students' pantomime that calls the teacher to witness honest intellectual effort.

Suddenly a tall boy stood within the frame of the open door. "Is this," he said, and thrust a large nose into a college catalogue, "is this the meeting place of English IA? The section instructed by Dr. Joseph Howe?"

He stood on the very sill of the door, as if refusing to enter until he was perfectly sure of his rights. The class looked up from work, found him absurd and gave a low mocking cheer.

The teacher and the new student, with equal pointedness, ignored the disturbance. Howe nodded to the boy, who pushed his head forward and then jerked it back in a wide elaborate arc to clear his brow of a heavy lock of hair. He advanced into the room and halted before Howe, almost at attention. In a loud, clear voice he announced, "I am Tertan, Ferdinand R., reporting at the direction of Head of Department Vincent."

The heraldic formality of this statement brought forth another cheer. Howe looked at the class with a sternness he could not really feel, for there was indeed something ridiculous about this boy. Under his displeased regard the rows of heads dropped to work again. Then he touched Tertan's elbow, led him up to the desk and stood so as to shield their conversation from the class.

"We are writing an extemporaneous theme," he said. "The subject is 'Who I am and why I came to Dwight College.' "

He stripped a few sheets from the pad and offered them to the boy. Tertan hesitated and then took the paper, but he held it only tentatively. As if with the effort of making something clear, he gulped and a slow smile fixed itself on his face. It was at once knowing and shy.

"Professor," he said, "to be perfectly fair to my classmates" —he made a large gesture over the room—"and to you"—he inclined his head to Howe—"this would not be for me an extemporaneous subject."

Howe tried to understand. "You mean you've already thought about it—you've heard we always give the same subject? That doesn't matter."

Again the boy ducked his head and gulped. It was the gesture of one who wishes to make a difficult explanation with perfect candor. "Sir," he said, and made the distinction with great care, "the topic I did not expect, but I have given much ratiocination to the subject."

Howe smiled and said, "I don't think that's an unfair advantage. Just go ahead and write."

Tertan narrowed his eyes and glanced sidewise at Howe. His strange mouth smiled. Then in quizzical acceptance, he ducked his head, threw back the heavy, dank lock, dropped into a seat with a great loose noise and began to write rapidly.

The room fell silent again and Howe resumed his idleness. When the bell rang, the students who had groaned when the task had been set now groaned again because they had not finished. Howe took up the papers, and held the class while he made the first assignment. When he dismissed it, Tertan bore down on him, his slack mouth held ready for speech.

"Some professors," he said, "are pedants. They are Dry-asdusts. However some professors are free souls and creative spirits. Kant, Hegel, and Nietzsche were all professors." With this pronouncement he paused. "It is my opinion," he continued, "that you occupy the second category."

Howe looked at the boy in surprise and with good-natured irony, "With Kant, Hegel, and Nietzsche?"

Not only Tertan's hand and head, but his whole awkward body waved away the stupidity. "It is the kind and not the quantity of the kind," he said sternly.

Rebuked, Howe said as simply and seriously as he could, "It would be nice to think so." He added, "Of course I am not a professor."

This was clearly a disappointment but Tertan met it. "In the French sense," he said with composure. "Generically, a teacher."

Suddenly he bowed. It was such a bow, Howe fancied, as a stage-director might teach an actor playing a medieval student who takes leave of Abelard—stiff, solemn, with elbows close to the body and feet together. Then, quite as suddenly, he turned and left.

A queer fish, and as soon as Howe reached his office, he sifted through the batch of themes and drew out Tertan's. The boy had filled many sheets with his unformed headlong scrawl. "Who am I?" he had begun. "Here, in a mundane, not to say commercialized academe, is asked the question which from time long immemorably out of mind has accreted doubts and thoughts in the psyche of man to pester him as nuisance. Whether in St. Augustine (or Austin as sometimes called) or Miss Bashkirtsieff or Frederic Amiel or Empedocles, or in less lights of the intellect than these, this posed question has been ineluctable."

Howe took out his pencil. He circled "academe" and wrote "vocab." in the margin. He underlined "time long immemorably out of mind" and wrote "Diction!" But this seemed inadequate for what was wrong. He put down his pencil and read ahead to discover the principle of error in the theme. "Today as ever, in spite of gloomy prophets of the dismal science (economics) the question is uninvalidated. Out of the starry depths of heaven hurtles this spear of query demanding to be caught on the shield of the mind ere it pierces the skull and the limbs be unstrung."

Baffled but quite caught, Howe read on. "Materialism, by which is meant the philosophic concept and not the moral idea, provides no aegis against the question which lies beyond the tangible (metaphysics). Existence without alloy is the question presented. Environment and heredity relegated aside, the rags and old clothes of practical life discarded, the name and the instrumentality of livelihood do not, as the prophets of the dismal science insist on in this connection, give solution to the interrogation which not from the professor merely but veritably from the cosmos is given. I think, therefore I am (cogito etc.) but who am I? Tertan I am, but what is Tertan? Of this time, of that place, of some parentage, what does it matter?"

Existence without alloy: the phrase established itself. Howe put aside Tertan's paper and at random picked up another. "I am Arthur U. Casebeer, Jr.," he read. "My father is Arthur J. Casebeer and my grandfather was Arthur J. Casebeer before him. My mother is Nina Wimble Casebeer. Both of them are college graduates and my father is in insurance. I was born in St. Louis eighteen years ago and we still make our residence there."

Arthur J. Casebeer, who knew who he was, was less interesting than Tertan, but more coherent. Howe picked up Tertan's paper again. It was clear that none of the routine marginal comments, no "sent. str." or "punct." or "vocab." could cope with this torrential rhetoric. He read ahead, contenting himself with underscoring the errors against the time when he should have the necessary "conference" with Tertan.

It was a busy and official day of cards and sheets, arrangements and small decisions, and it gave Howe pleasure. Even when it was time to attend the first of the weekly Convocations he felt the charm of the beginning of things when intention is still innocent and uncorrupted by effort. He sat among the young instructors on the platform, and joined in their humorous complaints at having to assist at the ceremony, but actually he got a clear satisfaction from the ritual of prayer and prosy speech, and even from wearing his academic gown. And when the Convocation was over the pleasure continued as he crossed the campus, exchanging greetings with men he had not seen since the spring. They were people who did not yet, and perhaps never would, mean much to him, but in a year they had grown amiably to be part of his life. They were his fellow-townsmen.

The day had cooled again at sunset, and there was a bright chill in the September twilight. Howe carried his voluminous gown over his arm, he swung his doctoral hood by its purple neckpiece, and on his head he wore his mortarboard with its heavy gold tassel bobbing just over his eye. These were the weighty and absurd symbols of his new profession and they pleased him. At twenty-six Joseph Howe had discovered that he was neither so well off nor so bohemian as he had once thought. A small income, adequate when supplemented by a sizable cash legacy, was genteel poverty when the cash was all spent. And the literary life—the room at the Lafayette, or the small apartment without a lease, the long summers on the Cape, the long afternoons and the social evenings—began to weary him. His writing filled his mornings and should perhaps have filled his life, yet it did not. To the amusement of his friends, and with a certain sense that he was betraying his own freedom, he had used the last of his legacy for a year at Harvard. The small but respectable reputation of his two volumes of verse had proved useful—he continued at Harvard on a fellowship and when he emerged as Doctor Howe he received an excellent appointment, with prospects, at Dwight.

He had his moments of fear when all that had ever been said of the dangers of the academic life had occurred to him. But after a year in which he had tested every possibility of corruption and seduction he was ready to rest easy. His third volume of verse, most of it written in his first years of teaching, was not only ampler but, he thought, better than its predecessors.

There was a clear hour before the Bradby dinner party, and Howe looked forward to it. But he was not to enjoy it, for lying with his mail on the hall table was a copy of this quarter's issue of *Life and Letters,* to which his landlord subscribed. Its severe cover announced that its editor, Frederic Woolley, had this month contributed an essay called "Two Poets," and Howe, picking it up, curious to see who the two poets might be, felt his own name start out at him with cabalistic power—Joseph Howe. As he continued to turn the pages his hand trembled.

Standing in the dark hall, holding the neat little magazine, Howe knew that his literary contempt for Frederic Woolley meant nothing, for he suddenly understood how he respected Woolley in the way of the world. He knew this by the trembling of his hand. And of the little world as well as the great, for although the literary groups of New York might dismiss Woolley, his name carried high authority in the academic world. At Dwight it was even a revered name, for it had been here at the college that Frederic Woolley had made the distinguished scholarly career from which he had gone on to literary journalism. In middle life he had been induced to take the editorship of *Life and Letters,* a literary monthly not widely read but heavily endowed, and in its pages he had carried on the defense of what he sometimes called the older values. He was not without wit, he had great knowledge and considerable taste, and even in the full movement of the "new" literature he had won a certain respect for his refusal to accept it. In France, even in England, he would have been connected with a more robust tradition of conservatism, but America gave him an audience not much better than genteel. It was known in the college that to the subsidy of *Life and Letters* the Bradbys contributed a great part.

As Howe read, he saw that he was involved in nothing less than an event. When the Fifth Series of *Studies in Order and*

Value came to be collected, this latest of Frederic Woolley's essays would not be merely another step in the old direction. Clearly and unmistakably, it was a turning point. All his literary life Woolley had been concerned with the relation of literature to morality, religion, and the private and delicate pieties, and he had been unalterably opposed to all that he had called "inhuman humanitarianism." But here, suddenly, dramatically late, he had made an about-face, turning to the public life and to the humanitarian politics he had so long despised. This was the kind of incident the histories of literature make much of. Frederic Woolley was opening for himself a new career and winning a kind of new youth. He contrasted the two poets, Thomas Wormser, who was admirable, Joseph Howe, who was almost dangerous. He spoke of the "precious subjectivism" of Howe's verse. "In times like ours," he wrote, "with millions facing penury and want, one feels that the qualities of the *tour d'ivoire* are well-nigh inhuman, nearly insulting. The *tour d'ivoire* becomes the *tour d'ivresse,* and it is not self-intoxicated poets that our people need." The essay said more: "The problem is one of meaning. I am not ignorant that the creed of the esoteric poets declares that a poem does not and should not *mean* anything, that it *is* something. But poetry is what the poet makes, and if he is a true poet he makes what his society needs. And what is needed now is the tradition in which Mr. Wormser writes, the true tradition of poetry. The Howes do no harm, but they do no good when positive good is demanded of all responsible men. Or do the Howes indeed do no harm? Perhaps Plato would have said they do, that in some ways theirs is the Phrygian music that turns men's minds from the struggle. Certainly it is true that Thomas Wormser writes in the lucid Dorian mode which sends men into battle with evil."

It was easy to understand why Woolley had chosen to praise Thomas Wormser. The long, lilting lines of *Corn Under Willows* hymned, as Woolley put it, the struggle for wheat in the Iowa fields, and expressed the real lives of real people. But why out of the dozen more notable examples he had chosen Howe's little volume as the example of "precious subjectivism" was hard to guess. In a way it was funny, this multiplication of himself into "the Howes." And yet this becoming the multiform political symbol by whose creation Frederic Woolley gave the sign of a sudden new life, this use of him as a sacrifice whose blood was necessary for the rites of rejuvenation, made him feel oddly unclean.

Nor could Howe get rid of a certain practical resentment. As a poet he had a special and respectable place in the college life. But it might be another thing to be marked as the poet of a willful and selfish obscurity.

As he walked to the Bradbys', Howe was a little tense and defensive. It seemed to him all the world knew of the "attack" and agreed with it. And, indeed, the Bradbys had read the essay but Professor Bradby, a kind and pretentious man, said, "I see my old friend knocked you about a bit, my boy," and his wife Eugenia looked at Howe with her childlike blue eyes and said, "I shall *scold* Frederic for the untrue things he wrote about you. You aren't the least obscure." They beamed at him. In their genial snobbery they seemed to feel that he had distinguished himself. He was the leader of Howeism. He enjoyed the dinner party as much as he had thought he would.

And in the following days, as he was more preoccupied with his duties, the incident was forgotten. His classes had ceased to be mere groups. Student after student detached himself from the mass and required or claimed a place in Howe's awareness. Of them all it was Tertan who first and most violently signaled his separate existence. A week after classes had begun Howe saw his silhouette on the frosted glass of his office door. It was motionless for a long time, perhaps stopped by the problem of whether or not to knock before entering. Howe called, "Come in!" and Tertan entered with his shambling stride.

He stood beside the desk, silent and at attention. When Howe asked him to sit down, he responded with a gesture of head and hand, as if to say that such amenities were beside the point. Nevertheless, he did take the chair. He put his ragged, crammed briefcase between his legs. His face, which Howe now observed fully for the first time, was confusing, for it was made up of florid curves, the nose arched in the bone and voluted in the nostril, the mouth loose and soft and rather moist. Yet the face was so thin and narrow as to seem the very type of asceticism. Lashes of unusual length veiled the eyes and, indeed, it seemed as if there were a veil over the whole countenance. Before the words actually came, the face screwed itself into an attitude of preparation for them.

"You can confer with me now?" Tertan said.

"Yes. I'd be glad to. There are several things in your two themes I want to talk to you about." Howe reached for the packet of themes on his desk and sought for Tertan's. But the boy was waving them away.

"These are done perforce," he said. "Under the pressure of your requirement. They are not significant; mere duties." Again his great hand flapped vaguely to dismiss his themes. He leaned forward and gazed at his teacher.

"You are," he said, "a man of letters? You are a poet?" It was more declaration than question.

"I should like to think so," Howe said.

At first Tertan accepted the answer with a show of appreciation, as though the understatement made a secret between himself and Howe. Then he chose to misunderstand. With his shrewd and disconcerting control of expression, he presented to Howe a puzzled grimace. "What does that mean?" he said.

Howe retracted the irony. "Yes. I am a poet." It sounded strange to say.

"That," Tertan said, "is a wonder." He corrected himself with his ducking head. "I mean that is wonderful."

Suddenly, he dived at the miserable briefcase between his legs, put it on his knees, and began to fumble with the catch, all intent on the difficulty it presented. Howe noted that his suit was worn thin, his shirt almost unclean. He became aware, even, of a vague and musty odor of garments worn too long in unaired rooms. Tertan conquered the lock and began to concentrate upon a search into the interior. At last he held in his hand what he was after, a torn and crumpled copy of *Life and Letters.*

"I learned it from here," he said, holding it out.

Howe looked at him sharply, his hackles a little up. But the boy's face was not only perfectly innocent, it even shone with a conscious admiration. Apparently nothing of the import of the essay had touched him except the wonderful fact that his teacher was a "man of letters." Yet this seemed too stupid, and Howe, to test it, said, "The man who wrote that doesn't think it's wonderful."

Tertan made a moist hissing sound as he cleared his throat of saliva. His head, oddly loose on his neck, wove a pattern of contempt in the air. "A critic," he said, "who admits *prima facie* that he does not understand." Then he said grandly, "It is the inevitable fate."

It was absurd, yet Howe was not only aware of the absurdity but of a tension suddenly and wonderfully relaxed. Now that the "attack" was on the table between himself and this strange boy, and subject to the boy's funny and absolutely certain contempt, the hidden force of his feeling was revealed to him in the very moment that it vanished. All unsuspected, there had been a film over the world, a transparent but discoloring haze of danger. But he had no time to stop over the brightened aspect of things. Tertan was going on. "I also am a man of letters. Putative."

"You have written a good deal?" Howe meant to be more than polite, and he was surprised at the tenderness he heard in his words.

Solemnly the boy nodded, threw back the dank lock, and sucked in a deep, anticipatory breath. "First, a work of homiletics, which is a defense of the principles of religious optimism against the pessimism of Schopenhauer and the humanism of Nietzsche."

"Humanism? Why do you call it humanism?"

"It is my nomenclature for making a deity of man," Tertan replied negligently. "Then three fictional works, novels. And numerous essays in science, combating materialism. Is it your duty to read these if I bring them to you?"

Howe answered simply. "No, it isn't exactly my duty, but I shall be happy to read them."

Tertan stood up and remained silent. He rested his bag on the chair. With a certain compunction—for it did not seem entirely proper that, of two men of letters, one should have the right to blue-pencil the other, to grade him or to question the quality of his "sentence structure"—Howe reached for Tertan's papers. But before he could take them up, the boy suddenly made his bow-to-Abelard, the stiff inclination of the body with the hands seeming to emerge from the scholar's gown. Then he was gone.

But after his departure something was still left of him. The timbre of his curious sentences, the downright finality of so quaint a phrase as "It is the inevitable fate" still rang in the air. Howe gave the warmth of his feeling to the new visitor who stood at the door announcing himself with the genteel clearing of the throat.

"Doctor Howe, I believe?" the student said. A large hand advanced into the room and grasped Howe's hand. "Blackburn, sir, Theodore Blackburn, vice-president of the Student Council. A great pleasure, sir."

Out of a pair of ruddy cheeks a pair of small eyes twinkled good-naturedly. The large face, the large body were not so much fat as beefy and suggested something "typical"—monk, politician, or innkeeper.

Blackburn took the seat beside Howe's desk. "I may have seemed to introduce myself in my public capacity, sir," he said.

"But it is really as an individual that I came to see you. That is to say, as one of your students to be."

He spoke with an English intonation and went on, "I was once an English major, sir."

For a moment Howe was startled, for the roast-beef look of the boy and the manner of his speech gave a second's credibility to one sense of his statement. Then the collegiate meaning of the phrase asserted itself, but some perversity made Howe say what was really not in good taste even with so forward a student, "Indeed? What regiment?"

Blackburn stared and then gave a little pouf-pouf of laughter. He waved the misapprehension away. "*Very* good, sir. It certainly is an ambiguous term." He chuckled in appreciation of Howe's joke, then cleared his throat to put it aside. "I look forward to taking your course in the romantic poets, sir," he said earnestly. "To me the romantic poets are the very crown of English literature."

Howe made a dry sound, and the boy, catching some meaning in it, said, "Little as I know them, of course. But even Shakespeare, who is so dear to us of the Anglo-Saxon tradition, is in a sense but the preparation for Shelley, Keats, and Byron. And Wadsworth."

Almost sorry for him, Howe dropped his eyes. With some embarrassment, for the boy was not actually his student, he said softly, "Wordsworth."

"Sir?"

"Wordsworth, not Wadsworth. You said Wadsworth."

"Did I, sir?" Gravely he shook his head to rebuke himself for the error. "Wordsworth, of course—slip of the tongue." Then, quite in command again, he went on. "I have a favor to ask of you, Doctor Howe. You see, I began my college course as an English major,"—he smiled—"as I said."

"Yes?"

"But after my first year I shifted. I shifted to the social sciences. Sociology and government—I find them stimulating and very *real.*" He paused, out of respect for reality. "But now I find that perhaps I have neglected the other side."

"The other side?" Howe said.

"Imagination, fancy, culture. A well-rounded man." He trailed off as if there were perfect understanding between them. "And so, sir, I have decided to end my senior year with your course in the romantic poets."

His voice was filled with an indulgence which Howe ignored as he said flatly and gravely, "But that course isn't given until the spring term."

"Yes, sir, and that is where the favor comes in. Would you let me take your romantic prose course? I can't take it for credit, sir, my program is full, but just for background it seems to me that I ought to take it. I do hope," he concluded in a manly way, "that you will consent."

"Well, it's no great favor, Mr. Blackburn. You can come if you wish, though there's not much point in it if you don't do the reading."

The bell rang for the hour and Howe got up.

"May I begin with this class, sir?" Blackburn's smile was candid and boyish.

Howe nodded carelessly and together, silently, they walked to the classroom down the hall. When they reached the door Howe stood back to let his student enter, but Blackburn moved adroitly behind him and grasped him by the arm to urge him over the threshold. They entered with Blackburn's hand firmly on Howe's biceps, the student inducting the teacher into his own room. Howe felt a surge of temper rise in him and almost violently disengaged his arm and walked to the desk, while Blackburn found a seat in the front row and smiled at him.

2

The question was, At whose door must the tragedy be laid? All night the snow had fallen heavily and only now was abating in sparse little flurries. The windows were valanced high with white. It was very quiet; something of the quiet of the world had reached the class, and Howe found that everyone was glad to talk or listen. In the room there was a comfortable sense of pleasure in being human.

Casebeer believed that the blame for the tragedy rested with heredity. Picking up the book he read, "The sins of the fathers are visited on their children." This opinion was received with general favor. Nevertheless, Johnson ventured to say that the fault was all Pastor Manders' because the Pastor had made Mrs. Alving go back to her husband and was always hiding the truth. To this Hibbard objected with logic enough, "Well then, it was really all her husband's fault. He *did* all the bad things." De Witt, his face bright with an impatient idea, said that the fault was all society's. "By society I don't mean upper-crust society," he said. He looked around a little defiantly, taking in any members of the class who might be members of upper-crust society. "Not in that sense. I mean the social unit."

Howe nodded and said, "Yes, of course."

"If the society of the time had progressed far enough in science," De Witt went on, "then there would be no problem for Mr. Ibsen to write about. Captain Alving plays around a little, gives way to perfectly natural biological urges, and he gets a social disease, a venereal disease. If the disease is cured, no problem. Invent salvarsan and the disease is cured. The problem of heredity disappears and li'l Oswald just doesn't get paresis. No paresis, no problem—no problem, no play."

This was carrying the ark into battle, and the class looked at De Witt with respectful curiosity. It was his usual way and on the whole they were sympathetic with his struggle to prove to Howe that science was better than literature. Still, there was something in his reckless manner that alienated them a little.

"Or take birth-control, for instance," De Witt went on. "If Mrs. Alving had some knowledge of contraception, she wouldn't have had to have li'l Oswald at all. No li'l Oswald, no play."

The class was suddenly quieter. In the back row Stettenhover swung his great football shoulders in a righteous sulking gesture, first to the right, then to the left. He puckered his mouth ostentatiously. Intellect was always ending up by talking dirty.

Tertan's hand went up, and Howe said, "Mr. Tertan." The boy shambled to his feet and began his long characteristic gulp. Howe made a motion with his fingers, as small as possible, and Tertan ducked his head and smiled in apology. He sat down. The class laughed. With more than half the term gone, Tertan had not not been able to remember that one did not rise to speak. He seemed unable to carry on the life of the intellect without this mark of respect for it. To Howe the boy's habit of rising seemed to accord with the formal shabbiness of his dress. He never wore the casual sweaters and jackets of his classmates. Into the free and comfortable air of the college classroom he brought the stuffy sordid strictness of some crowded, metropolitan high school.

"Speaking from one sense," Tertan began slowly, "there is no blame ascribable. From the sense of determinism, who can say where the blame lies? The preordained is the preordained and it cannot be said without rebellion against the universe, a palpable absurdity."

In the back row Stettenhover slumped suddenly in his seat, his heels held out before him, making a loud, dry, disgusted sound. His body sank until his neck rested on the back of his chair. He folded his hands across his belly and looked significantly out of the window, exasperated not only with Tertan, but with Howe, with the class, with the whole system designed to encourage this kind of thing. There seemed a certain insolence in the movement and Howe flushed. As Tertan continued to speak, Howe stalked casually toward the window and placed himself in the line of Stettenhover's vision. He stared at the great fellow, who pretended not to see him. There was so much power in the big body, so much contempt in the Greek-athlete face under the crisp Greek-athlete curls, that Howe felt almost physical fear. But at last Stettenhover admitted him to focus and under his disapproving gaze sat up with slow indifference. His eyebrows raised high in resignation, he began to examine his hands. Howe relaxed and turned his attention back to Tertan.

"Flux of existence," Tertan was saying, "produces all things, so that judgment wavers. Beyond the phenomena, what? But phenomena are adumbrated and to them we are limited."

Howe saw it for a moment as perhaps it existed in the boy's mind—the world of shadows which are cast by a great light upon a sudden reality as in the old myth of the Cave. But the little brush with Stettenhover had tired him, and he said irritably, "But come to the point, Mr. Tertan."

He said it so sharply that some of the class looked at him curiously. For three months he had gently carried Tertan through his verbosities, to the vaguely respectful surprise of the other students, who seemed to conceive that there existed between this strange classmate and their teacher some special understanding from which they were content to be excluded. Tertan looked at him mildly, and at once came brilliantly to the point. "This is the summation of the play," he said and took up his book and read, " 'Your poor father never found any outlet for the overmastering joy of life that was in him. And I brought no holiday into his home, either. Everything seemed to turn upon duty and I am afraid I made your poor father's home unbearable to him, Oswald.' Spoken by Mrs. Alving."

Yes that was surely the "summation" of the play and Tertan had hit it, as he hit, deviously and eventually, the literary point of almost everything. But now, as always, he was wrapping it away from sight. "For most mortals," he said, "there are only joys of biological urgings, gross and crass, such as the sensuous Captain Alving. For certain few there are the transmutations beyond these to a contemplation of the utter whole."

Oh, the boy was mad. And suddenly the word, used in hyperbole, intended almost for the expression of exasperated admiration, became literal. Now that the word was used, it became simply apparent to Howe that Tertan was mad.

It was a monstrous word and stood like a bestial thing in the room. Yet it so completely comprehended everything that had puzzled Howe, it so arranged and explained what for three months had been perplexing him that almost at once its horror became domesticated. With this word Howe was able to understand why he had never been able to communicate to Tertan the value of a single criticism or correction of his wild verbose themes. Their conferences had been frequent and long but had done nothing to reduce to order the splendid confusion of the boy's ideas. Yet, impossible though its expression was, Tertan's incandescent mind could always strike for a moment into some dark corner of thought.

And now it was suddenly apparent that it was not a faulty rhetoric that Howe had to contend with. With his new knowledge he looked at Tertan's face and wondered how he could have so long deceived himself. Tertan was still talking, and the class had lapsed into a kind of patient unconsciousness, a coma of respect for words which, for all that most of them knew, might be profound. Almost with a suffusion of shame, Howe believed that in some dim way the class had long ago had some intimation of Tertan's madness. He reached out as decisively as he could to seize the thread of Tertan's discourse before it should be entangled further.

"Mr. Tertan says that the blame must be put upon whoever kills the joy of living in another. We have been assuming that Captain Alving was a wholly bad man, but what if we assume that he became bad only because Mrs. Alving, when they were first married, acted toward him in the prudish way she says she did?"

It was a ticklish idea to advance to freshmen and perhaps not profitable. Not all of them were following.

"That would put the blame on Mrs. Alving herself, whom most of you admire. And she herself seems to think so." He glanced at his watch. The hour was nearly over. "What do you think, Mr. De Witt?"

De Witt rose to the idea; he wanted to know if society couldn't be blamed for educating Mrs. Alving's temperament in the wrong way. Casebeer was puzzled, Stettenhover continued to look at his hands until the bell rang.

Tertan, his brows louring in thought, was making as always for a private word. Howe gathered his books and papers to leave quickly. At this moment of his discovery and with the knowledge still raw, he could not engage himself with Tertan. Tertan sucked in his breath to prepare for speech and Howe made ready for the pain and confusion. But at that moment Casebeer detached himself from the group with which he had been conferring and which he seemed to represent. His constituency remained at a tactful distance. The mission involved the time of an assigned essay. Casebeer's presentation of the plea—it was based on the freshmen's heavy duties at the fraternities during Carnival Week—cut across Tertan's preparations for speech. "And so some of us fellows thought," Casebeer concluded with heavy solemnity, "that we could do a better job, give our minds to it more, if we had more time."

Tertan regarded Casebeer with mingled curiosity and revulsion. Howe not only said that he would postpone the assignment but went on to talk about the Carnival, and even drew the waiting constituency into the conversation. He was conscious of Tertan's stern and astonished stare, then of his sudden departure.

Now that the fact was clear, Howe knew that he must act on it. His course was simple enough. He must lay the case before the Dean. Yet he hesitated. His feeling for Tertan must now, certainly, be in some way invalidated. Yet could he, because of a word, hurry to assign to official and reasonable solicitude what had been until this moment, so various and warm? He could at least delay and, by moving slowly, lend a poor grace to the necessary, ugly act of making his report.

It was with some notion of keeping the matter in his own hands that he went to the Dean's office to look up Tertan's records. In the outer office the Dean's secretary greeted him brightly, and at his request brought him the manila folder with the small identifying photograph pasted in the corner. She laughed. "He was looking for the birdie in the wrong place," she said.

Howe leaned over her shoulder to look at the picture. It was as bad as all the Dean's-office photographs were, but it differed from all that Howe had ever seen. Tertan, instead of looking into the camera, as no doubt he had been bidden, had, at the moment of exposure, turned his eyes upward. His mouth, as though conscious of the trick played on the photographer, had the sly superior look that Howe knew.

The secretary was fascinated by the picture. "What a funny boy," she said. "He looks like Tartuffe!"

And so he did, with the absurd piety of the eyes and the conscious slyness of the mouth and the whole face bloated by the bad lens.

"Is he *like* that?" the secretary said.

"Like Tartuffe? No."

From the photograph there was little enough comfort to be had. The records themselves gave no clue to madness, though they suggested sadness enough. Howe read of a father, Stanislaus Tertan, born in Budapest and trained in engineering in Berlin, once employed by the Hercules Chemical Corporation—this was one of the factories that dominated the sound end of the town—but now without employment. He read of a mother Erminie (Youngfellow) Tertan, born in Manchester, educated at a Normal School at Leeds, now housewife by profession. The family lived on Greenbriar Street which Howe knew as a row of once elegant homes near what was now the factory district. The old mansion had long ago been divided into small and primitive apartments. Of Ferdinand himself there was little to learn. He lived with his parents, had attended a Detroit high school and had transferred to the local school in his last year. His rating for intelligence, as expressed in numbers, was high, his scholastic record was remarkable, he held a college scholarship for his tuition.

Howe laid the folder on the secretary's desk. "Did you find what you wanted to know?" she asked.

The phrases from Tertan's momentous first theme came back to him. "Tertan I am, but what is Tertan? Of this time, of that place, of some parentage, what does it matter?"

"No, I didn't find it," he said.

Now that he had consulted the sad, half-meaningless record he knew all the more firmly that he must not give the matter out of his hands. He must not release Tertan to authority. Not that he anticipated from the Dean anything but the greatest kindness for Tertan. The Dean would have the experience and skill which he himself could not have. One way or another the Dean could answer the question. "What is Tertan?" Yet this was precisely what he feared. He alone could keep it still a question. Some sure instinct told him that he must not surrender the question to a clean official desk in a clear official light to be dealt with, settled and closed.

He heard himself saying, "Is the Dean busy at the moment? I'd like to see him."

His request came thus unbidden, even forbidden, and it was one of the surprising and startling incidents of his life. Later when he reviewed the events, so disconnected in themselves, or so merely odd, of the story that unfolded for him that year, it was over this moment, on its face the least notable, that he paused longest. It was frequently to be with fear and never without a certainty of its meaning in his own knowledge of himself that he would recall this simple, routine request, and the feeling of shame and freedom it gave him as he sent everything down the official chute. In the end, of course, no matter what he did to "protect" Tertan, he would have had to make the same request and lay the matter on the Dean's clean desk. But it would always be a landmark of his life that, at the very moment when he was rejecting the official way, he had been, without will or intention, so gladly drawn to it.

After the storm's last delicate flurry, the sun had come out. Reflected by the new snow, it filled the office with a golden light which was almost musical in the way it made all the commonplace objects shine with a sudden sad and noble significance. And the light, now that he noticed it, made the utterance of his perverse and unwanted request even more momentous.

The secretary consulted the engagement pad. "He'll be free any minute. Don't you want to wait in the parlor?"

She threw open the door of the large and pleasant room in which the Dean held his Committee meetings, and in which his visitors waited. It was designed with a homely elegance on the masculine side of the eighteenth-century manner. There was a small coal fire in the grate and the handsome mahogany table was strewn with books and magazines. The large windows gave on the snowy lawn, and there was such a fine width of window that the white casements and walls seemed at this moment but a continuation of the snow, the snow but an extension of casement and walls. The outdoors seemed taken in and made safe, the indoors seemed luxuriously freshened and expanded.

Howe sat down by the fire and lighted a cigarette. The room had its intended effect upon him. He felt comfortable and relaxed, yet nicely organized, some young diplomatic agent of the eighteenth century, the newly fledged Swift carrying out Sir William Temple's business. The rawness of Tertan's case quite vanished. He crossed his legs and reached for a magazine.

It was that famous issue of *Life and Letters* that his idle hand found and his blood raced as he sifted through it, and the shape of his own name, Joseph Howe, sprang out at him, still cabalistic in its power. He tossed the magazine back on the table as the door of the Dean's office opened and the Dean ushered out Theodore Blackburn.

"Ah, Joseph!" the Dean said.

Blackburn said, "Good morning, Doctor." Howe winced at the title and caught the flicker of amusement over the Dean's face. The Dean stood with his hand high on the door-jamb and Blackburn, still in the doorway, remained standing almost under the long arm.

Howe nodded briefly to Blackburn, snubbing his eager deference. "Can you give me a few minutes?" he said to the Dean.

"All the time you want. Come in." Before the two men could enter the office, Blackburn claimed their attention with a long full "er." As they turned to him, Blackburn said, "Can *you* give *me* a few minutes, Doctor Howe?" His eyes sparkled at the little audacity he had committed, the slightly impudent play with hierarchy. Of the three of them Blackburn kept himself the lowest, but he reminded Howe of his subaltern relation to the Dean.

"I mean, of course," Blackburn went on easily, "when you've finished with the Dean."

"I'll be in my office shortly," Howe said, turned his back on the ready "Thank you, sir," and followed the Dean into the inner room.

"Energetic boy," said the Dean. "A bit beyond himself but very energetic. Sit down."

The Dean lighted a cigarette, leaned back in his chair, sat easy and silent for a moment, giving Howe no signal to go ahead with business. He was a young Dean, not much beyond forty, a tall handsome man with sad, ambitious eyes. He had been a Rhodes scholar. His friends looked for great things from him, and it was generally said that he had notions of education which he was not yet ready to try to put into practice.

His relaxed silence was meant as a compliment to Howe. He smiled and said, "What's the business, Joseph?"

"Do you know Tertan—Ferdinand Tertan, a freshman?"

The Dean's cigarette was in his mouth and his hands were clasped behind his head. He did not seem to search his memory for the name. He said, "What about him?"

Clearly the Dean knew something, and he was waiting for Howe to tell him more. Howe moved only tentatively. Now that he was doing what he had resolved not to do, he felt more guilty at having been so long deceived by Tertan and more need to be loyal to his error.

"He's a strange fellow," he ventured. He said stubbornly, "In a strange way he's very brilliant." He concluded, "But very strange."

The springs of the Dean's swivel chair creaked as he came out of his sprawl and leaned forward to Howe. "Do you mean he's so strange that it's something you could give a name to?"

Howe looked at him stupidly. "What do you mean?" he said.

"What's his trouble?" the Dean said more neutrally.

"He's very brilliant, in a way. I looked him up and he has a top intelligence rating. But somehow, and it's hard to explain just how, what he says is always on the edge of sense and doesn't quite make it."

The Dean looked at him and Howe flushed up. The Dean had surely read Woolley on the subject of "the Howes" and the *tour d'ivresse*. Was that quick glance ironical?

The Dean picked up some papers from his desk, and Howe could see that they were in Tertan's impatient scrawl. Perhaps the little gleam in the Dean's glance had come only from putting facts together.

"He sent me this yesterday," the Dean said. "After an interview I had with him. I haven't been able to do more than glance at it. When you said what you did, I realized there was something wrong."

Twisting his mouth, the Dean looked over the letter. "You seem to be involved," he said without looking up. "By the way, what did you give him at mid-term?"

Flushing, setting his shoulders, Howe said firmly, "I gave him A-minus."

The Dean chuckled. "Might be a good idea if some of our nicer boys went crazy—just a little." He said, "Well," to conclude the matter and handed the papers to Howe. "See if this is the same thing you've been finding. Then we can go into the matter again."

Before the fire in the parlor, in the chair that Howe had been occupying, sat Blackburn. He sprang to his feet as Howe entered.

"I said my office, Mr. Blackburn." Howe's voice was sharp. Then he was almost sorry for the rebuke, so clearly and naively did Blackburn seem to relish his stay in the parlor, close to authority.

"I'm in a bit of a hurry, sir," he said, "and I did want to be sure to speak to you, sir."

He was really absurd, yet fifteen years from now he would have grown up to himself, to the assurance and mature beefiness. In banks, in consular offices, in brokerage firms, on the bench, more seriously affable, a little sterner, he would make use of his ability to be administered by his job. It was almost reassuring. Now he was exercising his too-great skill on Howe. "I owe you an apology, sir," he said.

Howe knew that he did, but he showed surprise.

"I mean, Doctor, after your having been so kind about letting me attend your class, I stopped coming." He smiled in deprecation. "Extracurricular activities take up so much of my time. I'm afraid I undertook more than I could perform."

Howe had noticed the absence and had been a little irritated by it after Blackburn's elaborate plea. It was an absence that might be interpreted as a comment on the teacher. But there was only one way for him to answer. "You've no need to apologize," he said. "It's wholly your affair."

Blackburn beamed. "I'm so glad you feel that way about it,

sir. I was worried you might think I had stayed away because I was influenced by—" he stopped and lowered his eyes.

Astonished, Howe said, "Influenced by what?"

"Well, by—" Blackburn hesitated and for answer pointed to the table on which lay the copy of *Life and Letters.* Without looking at it, he knew where to direct his hand. "By the unfavorable publicity, sir." He hurried on. "And that brings me to another point, sir. I am secretary of Quill and Scroll, sir, the student literary society, and I wonder if you would address us. You could read your own poetry, sir, and defend your own point of view. It would be very interesting."

It was truly amazing. Howe looked long and cruelly into Blackburn's face, trying to catch the secret of the mind that could have conceived this way of manipulating him, this way so daring and inept—but not entirely inept—with its malice so without malignity. The face did not yield its secret. Howe smiled broadly and said, "Of course I don't think you were influenced by the unfavorable publicity."

"I'm still going to take—regularly, for credit—your romantic poets course next term," Blackburn said.

"Don't worry, my dear fellow, don't worry about it."

Howe started to leave and Blackburn stopped him with, "But about Quill, sir?"

"Suppose we wait until next term? I'll be less busy then."

And Blackburn said, "Very good, sir, and thank you."

In his office the little encounter seemed less funny to Howe, was even in some indeterminate way disturbing. He made an effort to put it from his mind by turning to what was sure to disturb him more, the Tertan letter read in the new interpretation. He found what he had always found, the same florid leaps beyond fact and meaning, the same headlong certainty. But as his eye passed over the familiar scrawl it caught his own name, and for the second time that hour he felt the race of his blood.

"The Paraclete," Tertan had written to the Dean, "from a Greek word meaning to stand in place of, but going beyond the primitive idea to mean traditionally the helper, the one who comforts and assists, cannot without fundamental loss be jettisoned. Even if taken no longer in the supernatural sense, the concept remains deeply in the human consciousness inevitably. Humanitarianism is no reply, for not every man stands in the place of every other man for this other comrade's comfort. But certain are chosen out of the human race to be the consoler of some other. Of these, for example, is Joseph Barker Howe, Ph.D.—of intellects not the first yet of true intellect and lambent instructions, given to that which is intuitive and irrational, not to what is logical in the strict word, what is judged by him is of the heart and not of the head. Here is one chosen, in that he chooses himself to stand in the place of another for comfort and consolation. To him more than another I give my gratitude, with all respect to our Dean who reads this, a noble man, but merely dedicated, not consecrated. But not in the aspect of the Paraclete only is Dr. Joseph Barker Howe established, for he must be the Paraclete to another aspect of himself, that which is driven and persecuted by the lack of understanding in the world at large, so that he himself embodies the full history of man's tribulations and, overflowing upon others, notably the present writer, is the ultimate end."

This was love. There was no escaping it. Try as Howe might to remember that Tertan was mad and all his emotions invalidated, he could not destroy the effect upon him of his student's stern, affectionate regard. He had betrayed not only a power of mind but a power of love. And however firmly he held before his attention the fact of Tertan's madness, he could do nothing to banish the physical sensation of gratitude he felt. He had never thought of himself as "driven and persecuted" and he did not now. But still he could not make meaningless his sensation of gratitude. The pitiable Tertan sternly pitied him, and comfort came from Tertan's never-to-be-comforted mind.

3

In an academic community, even an efficient one, official matters move slowly. The term drew to a close with no action in the case of Tertan, and Joseph Howe had to confront a curious problem. How should he grade his strange student, Tertan?

Tertan's final examination had been no different from all his writing, and what did one "give" such a student? De Witt must have his A, that was clear. Johnson would get a B. With Casebeer it was a question of a B-minus or a C-plus, and Stettenhover, who had been crammed by the team tutor to fill half a blue-book with his thin feminine scrawl, would have his C-minus which he would accept with mingled indifference and resentment. But with Tertan it was not so easy.

The boy was still in the college process and his name could not be omitted from the grade sheet. Yet what should a mind under suspicion of madness be graded? Until the medical verdict was given, it was for Howe to continue as Tertan's teacher and to keep his judgment pedagogical. Impossible to give him an F: he had not failed. B was for Johnson's stolid mediocrity. He could not be put on the edge of passing with Stettenhover, for he exactly did not pass. In energy and richness of intellect he was perhaps even De Witt's superior, and Howe toyed grimly with the notion of giving him an A, but that would lower the value of the A De Witt had won with his beautiful and clear, if still somewhat arrogant, mind. There was a notation which the Registrar recognized—Inc., for Incomplete, and in the horrible comedy of the situation, Howe considered that. But really only a mark of M for Mad would serve.

In his perplexity, Howe sought the Dean, but the Dean was out of town. In the end, he decided to maintain the A-minus he had given Tertan at mid-term. After all, there had been no falling away from that quality. He entered it on the grade sheet with something like bravado.

Academic time moves quickly. A college year is not really a year, lacking as it does three months. And it is endlessly divided into units which, at their beginning, appear larger than they are—terms, half terms, months, weeks. And the ultimate unit, the hour, is not really an hour, lacking as it does ten minutes. And so the new term advanced rapidly, and one day the fields about the town were all brown, cleared of even the few thin patches of snow which had lingered so long.

Howe, as he lectured on the romantic poets, became conscious of Blackburn emanating wrath. Blackburn did it well, did it with enormous dignity. He did not stir in his seat, he kept his eyes fixed on Howe in perfect attention, but he abstained from using his notebook, there was no mistaking what he proposed to himself as an attitude. His elbow on the writing-wing of the chair, his chin on the curled fingers of his hand, he was the embodiment of intellectual indignation. He was thinking his own thoughts, would give no public offense, yet would claim his due, was not to be intimidated. Howe knew that he would present himself at the end of the hour.

Blackburn entered the office without invitation. He did not smile; there was no cajolery about him. Without invitation he sat down beside Howe's desk. He did not speak until he had taken the blue-book from his pocket. He said, "What does this mean, sir?"

It was a sound and conservative student tactic. Said in the usual way it meant, "How could you have so misunderstood me?" or "What does this mean for my future in the course?" But there were none of the humbler tones in Blackburn's way of saying it.

Howe made the established reply, "I think that's for you to tell me."

Blackburn continued icy. "I'm sure I can't, sir."

There was a silence between them. Both dropped their eyes to the blue-book on the desk. On its cover Howe had penciled: "F. This is very poor work."

Howe picked up the blue-book. There was always the possibility of injustice. The teacher may be bored by the mass of papers and not wholly attentive. A phrase, even the student's handwriting, may irritate him unreasonably. "Well," said Howe, "let's go through it."

He opened the first page. "Now here: you write, 'In *The Ancient Mariner,* Coleridge lives in and transports us to a honey-sweet world where all is rich and strange, a world of charm to which we can escape from the humdrum existence of our daily lives, the world of romance. Here, in this warm and honey-sweet land of charming dreams we can relax and enjoy ourselves.' "

Howe lowered the paper and waited with a neutral look for Blackburn to speak. Blackburn returned the look boldly, did not speak, sat stolid and lofty. At last Howe said, speaking gently, "Did you mean that, or were you just at a loss for something to say?"

"You imply that I was just 'bluffing'?" The quotation marks hung palpable in the air about the word.

"I'd like to know. I'd prefer believing that you were bluffing to believing that you really thought this."

Blackburn's eyebrows went up. From the height of a great and firm-based idea he looked at his teacher. He clasped the crags for a moment and then pounced, craftily, suavely. "Do you mean, Doctor Howe, that there aren't two opinions possible?"

It was superbly done in its air of putting all of Howe's intellectual life into the balance. Howe remained patient and simple. "Yes, many opinions are possible, but not that one. Whatever anyone believes of *The Ancient Mariner,* no one can in reason believe that it represents a—a honey-sweet world in which we can relax."

"But that is what I *feel,* sir."

This was well-done, too. Howe said, "Look, Mr. Blackburn. Do you really relax with hunger and thirst, the heat and the sea-serpents, the dead men with staring eyes, Life in Death and the skeletons? Come now, Mr. Blackburn."

Blackburn made no answer, and Howe pressed forward. "Now, you say of Wordsworth, 'Of peasant stock himself, he turned from the effete life of the salons and found in the peasant the hope of a flaming revolution which would sweep away all the old ideas. This is the subject of his best poems.' "

Beaming at his teacher with youthful eagerness, Blackburn said, "Yes, sir, a rebel, a bringer of light to suffering mankind. I see him as a kind of Prothemeus."

"A kind of what?"

"Prothemeus, sir."

"Think, Mr. Blackburn. We were talking about him only today and I mentioned his name a dozen times. You don't mean Prothemeus. You mean—" Howe waited, but there was no response.

"You mean Prometheus."

Blackburn gave no assent and Howe took the reins. "You've done a bad job here, Mr. Blackburn, about as bad as could be done." He saw Blackburn stiffen and his genial face harden again. "It shows either a lack of preparation or a complete lack of understanding." He saw Blackburn's face begin to go to pieces and he stopped.

"Oh, sir," Blackburn burst out, "I've never had a mark like this before, never anything below a B, never. A thing like this has never happened to me before."

It must be true, it was a statement too easily verified. Could it be that other instructors accepted such flaunting nonsense? Howe wanted to end the interview. "I'll set it down to lack of preparation," he said. "I know you're busy. That's not an excuse, but it's an explanation. Now suppose you really prepare, and then take another quiz in two weeks. We'll forget this one and count the other."

Blackburn squirmed with pleasure and gratitude. "Thank you, sir. You're really very kind, very kind."

Howe rose to conclude the visit. "All right, then—in two weeks."

It was that day that the Dean imparted to Howe the conclusion of the case of Tertan. It was simple and a little anti-climactic. A physician had been called in, and had said the word, given the name.

"A classic case, he called it," the Dean said. "Not a doubt in the world," he said. His eyes were full of miserable pity, and he clutched at a word. "A classic case, a classic case." To his aid and to Howe's there came the Parthenon and the form of the Greek drama, the Aristotelian logic, Racine and the Well-Tempered Clavichord, the blueness of the Aegean and its clear sky. Classic—that is to say, without a doubt, perfect in its way, a veritable model, and, as the Dean had been told, sure to take a perfectly predictable and inevitable course to a foreknown conclusion.

It was not only pity that stood in the Dean's eyes. For a moment there was fear too. "Terrible," he said, "it is simply terrible."

Then he went on briskly. "Naturally, we've told the boy nothing. And, naturally, we won't. His tuition's paid by his scholarship, and we'll continue him on the rolls until the end of the year. That will be kindest. After that the matter will be out of our control. We'll see, of course, that he gets into proper hands. I'm told there will be no change, he'll go on like this, be as good as this, for four to six months. And so we'll just go along as usual."

So Tertan continued to sit in Section 5 of English IA, to his classmates still a figure of curiously dignified fun, symbol to most of them of the respectable but absurd intellectual life. But to his teacher he was now very different. He had not changed—he was still the greyhound casting for the scent of ideas, and Howe could see that he was still the same Tertan, but he could not feel it. What he felt as he looked at the boy sitting in his accustomed place was the hard blank of a fact. The fact itself was formidable and depressing. But what Howe was chiefly aware of was that he had permitted the metamorphosis of Tertan from person to fact.

As much as possible he avoided seeing Tertan's upraised hand and eager eye. But the fact did not know of its mere factuality, it continued its existence as if it were Tertan, hand up and eye questioning, and one day it appeared in Howe's office with a document.

"Even the spirit who lives egregiously, above the herd, must have its relations with the fellowman," Tertan declared. He laid the document on Howe's desk. It was headed "Quill and Scroll Society of Dwight College. Application for membership."

"In most ways these are crass minds," Tertan said, touching the paper. "Yet as a whole, bound together in their common love of letters, they transcend their intellectual lacks since it is not a paradox that the whole is greater than the sum of its parts."

"When are the elections?" Howe asked.

"They take place tomorrow."

"I certainly hope you will be successful."

"Thank you. Would you wish to implement that hope?" A rather dirty finger pointed to the bottom of the sheet. "A faculty recommender is necessary," Tertan said stiffly and waited.

"And you wish me to recommend you?"

"It would be an honor."

"You may use my name."

Tertan's finger pointed again. "It must be a written sponsorship, signed by the sponsor." There was a large blank space on the form under the heading, "Opinion of Faculty Sponsor."

This was almost another thing and Howe hesitated. Yet there was nothing else to do and he took out his fountain pen. He wrote, "Mr. Ferdinand Tertan is marked by his intense devotion to letters and by his exceptional love of all things of the mind." To this he signed his name, which looked bold and assertive on the white page. It disturbed him, the strange affirming power of a name. With a businesslike air, Tertan whipped up the paper, folding it with decision, and put it in his pocket. He bowed and took his departure, leaving Howe with the sense of having done something oddly momentous.

And so much now seemed odd and momentous to Howe that should not have seemed so. It was odd and momentous, he felt, when he sat with Blackburn's second quiz before him, and wrote in an excessively firm hand the grade of C-minus. The paper was a clear and undisputable failure. He was carefully and consciously committing a cowardice. Blackburn had told the truth when he had pleaded his past record. Howe had consulted it in the Dean's office. It showed no grade lower than a B-minus. A canvass of some of Blackburn's previous instructors had brought vague attestations to the adequate powers of a student imperfectly remembered, and sometimes surprise that his abilities could be questioned at all.

As he wrote the grade, Howe told himself that his cowardice sprang from an unwillingness to have more dealings with a student he disliked. He knew it was simpler than that. He knew he feared Blackburn: that was the absurd truth. And cowardice did not solve the matter after all. Blackburn, flushed with the first success, attacked at once. The minimal passing grade had not assuaged his feelings and he sat at Howe's desk and again the blue-book lay between them. Blackburn said nothing. With an enormous impudence, he was waiting for Howe to speak and explain himself.

At last Howe said sharply and rudely, "Well?" His throat was tense and the blood was hammering in his head. His mouth was tight with anger at himself for his disturbance.

Blackburn's glance was almost baleful. "This is impossible, sir."

"But there it is," Howe answered.

"Sir?" Blackburn had not caught the meaning but his tone was still haughty.

Impatiently Howe said, "There it is, plain as day. Are you here to complain again?"

"Indeed I am, sir." There was surprise in Blackburn's voice that Howe should ask the question.

"I shouldn't complain if I were you. You did a thoroughly bad job on your first quiz. This one is a little, only a very little better." This was not true. If anything, it was worse.

"That might be a matter of opinion, sir."

"It is a matter of opinion. Of my opinion."

"Another opinion might be different, sir."

"You really believe that?" Howe said.

"Yes." The omission of the "sir" was monumental.

"Whose, for example?"

"The Dean's, for example." Then the fleshy jaw came forward a little. "Or a certain literary critic's, for example."

It was colossal and almost too much for Blackburn himself to handle. The solidity of his face almost crumpled under it. But he withstood his own audacity and went on. "And the Dean's opinion might be guided by the knowledge that the person who gave me this mark is the man whom a famous critic, the most eminent judge of literature in this country, called a drunken man. The Dean might think twice about whether such a man is fit to teach Dwight students."

Howe said in quiet admonition. "Blackburn, you're mad," meaning no more than to check the boy's extravagance.

But Blackburn paid no heed. He had another shot in the locker. "And the Dean might be guided by the information, of which I have evidence, documentary evidence,"—he slapped his breast pocket twice—"that this same person personally recommended to the college literary society, the oldest in the country, that he personally recommended a student who is crazy, who threw the meeting into an uproar—a psychiatric case. The Dean might take that into account."

Howe was never to learn the details of that "uproar." He had always to content himself with the dim but passionate picture which at that moment sprang into his mind, of Tertan standing on some abstract height and madly denouncing the multitude of Quill and Scroll who howled him down.

He sat quiet a moment and looked at Blackburn. The ferocity had entirely gone from the student's face. He sat regarding his teacher almost benevolently. He had played a good card and now, scarcely at all unfriendly, he was waiting to see the effect. Howe took up the blue-book and negligently sifted through it. He read a page, closed the book, struck out the C-minus and wrote an F.

"Now you may take the paper to the Dean," he said. "You may tell him that after reconsidering it, I lowered the grade."

The gasp was audible. "Oh, sir!" Blackburn cried. "Please!" His face was agonized. "It means my graduation, my livelihood, my future. Don't do this to me."

"It's done already."

Blackburn stood up. "I spoke rashly, sir, hastily. I had no intention, no real intention, of seeing the Dean. It rests with you—entirely, entirely. I *hope* you will restore the first mark."

"Take the matter to the Dean or not, just as you choose. The grade is what you deserve and it stands."

Blackburn's head dropped. "And will I be failed at mid-term, sir?"

"Of course."

From deep out of Blackburn's great chest rose a cry of anguish. "Oh, sir, if you want me to go down on my knees to you, I will, I will."

Howe looked at him in amazement.

"I will, I will. On my knees, sir. This mustn't, mustn't happen."

He spoke so literally, meaning so very truly that his knees and exactly his knees were involved and seeming to think that he was offering something of tangible value to his teacher, that Howe, whose head had become icy clear in the nonsensical drama, thought, "The boy is mad," and began to speculate fantastically whether something in himself attracted or developed aberration. He could see himself standing absurdly before the Dean and saying, "I've found another. This time it's the vice-president of the Council, the manager of the debating team and secretary of Quill and Scroll."

One more such discovery, he thought, and he himself would be discovered! And there, suddenly, Blackburn was on his knees with a thump, his huge thighs straining his trousers, his hand outstretched in a great gesture of supplication.

With a cry, Howe shoved back his swivel chair and it rolled away on its casters half across the little room. Blackburn knelt for a moment to nothing at all, then got to his feet.

Howe rose abruptly. He said, "Blackburn, you will stop acting like an idiot. Dust your knees off, take your paper and get out. You've behaved like a fool and a malicious person. You have half a term to do a decent job. Keep your silly mouth shut and try to do it. Now get out."

Blackburn's head was low. He raised it and there was a pious light in his eyes. "Will you shake hands, sir?" he said. He thrust out his hand.

"I will not," Howe said.

Head and hand sank together. Blackburn picked up his blue-book and walked to the door. He turned and said, "Thank you, sir." His back, as he departed, was heavy with tragedy and stateliness.

4

After years of bad luck with the weather, the College had a perfect day for Commencement. It was wonderfully bright, the air so transparent, the wind so brisk that no one could resist talking about it.

As Howe set out for the campus, he heard Hilda calling from the back yard. She called, "Professor, professor," and came running to him.

Howe said, "What's this 'professor' business?"

"Mother told me," Hilda said. "You've been promoted. And I want to take your picture."

"Next year," said Howe. "I won't be a professor until next year. And you know better than to call anybody 'professor.' "

"It was just in fun," Hilda said. She seemed disappointed.

"But you can take my picture if you want. I won't look much different next year." Still, it was frightening. It might mean that he was to stay in this town all his life.

Hilda brightened. "Can I take it in this?" she said, and touched the gown he carried over his arm.

Howe laughed. "Yes, you can take it in this."

"I'll get my things and meet you in front of Otis," Hilda said. "I have the background all picked out."

On the campus the Commencement crowd was already large. It stood about in eager, nervous little family groups. As he crossed, Howe was greeted by a student, capped and gowned, glad of the chance to make an event for his parents by introducing one of his teachers. It was while Howe stood there chatting that he saw Tertan.

He had never seen anyone quite so alone, as though a circle had been woven about him to separate him from the gay crowd on the campus. Not that Tertan was not gay, he was the gayest of all. Three weeks had passed since Howe had last seen him, the weeks of examination, the lazy week before Commencement, and this was now a different Tertan. On his head he wore a Panama hat, broad brimmed and fine, of the shape associated with South American planters. He wore a suit of raw silk, luxurious, but yellowed with age and much too tight, and he sported a whangee cane. He walked sedately, the hat tilted at a devastating angle, the stick coming up and down in time to his measured tread. He had, Howe guessed, outfitted himself to greet the day in the clothes of that ruined father whose existence was on record in the Dean's office. Gravely and arrogantly he surveyed the scene—in it, his whole bearing seemed to say, but not of it. With his haughty step, with his flashing eye, Tertan was coming nearer. Howe did not wish to be seen. He shifted his position slightly. When he looked again, Tertan was not in sight.

The chapel clock struck the quarter hour. Howe detached himself from his chat and hurried to Otis Hall at the far end of the campus. Hilda had not yet come. He went up into the high portico and, using the glass of the door for a mirror, put on his gown, adjusted the hood on his shoulders and set the mortar board on his head. When he came down the steps, Hilda had arrived.

Nothing could have told him more forcibly that a year had passed than the development of Hilda's photographic possessions from the box camera of the previous fall. By a strap about her neck was hung a leather case, so thick and strong, so carefully stitched and so molded to its contents that it could only hold a costly camera. The appearance was deceptive, Howe knew, for he had been present at the Aikens' pre-Christmas conference about its purchase. It was only a fairly good domestic camera. Still, it looked very impressive. Hilda carried another leather case from which she drew a collapsible tripod. Decisively she extended each of its gleaming legs and set it up on the path. She removed the camera from its case and fixed it to the tripod. In its compact efficiency the camera almost had a life of its own, but Hilda treated it with easy familiarity, looked into its eye, glanced casually at its guages. Then from a pocket she took still another leather case and drew from it a small instrument through which she looked first at Howe, who began to feel inanimate and lost, and then at the sky. She made some adjustment on the instrument, then some adjustment on the camera. She swept the scene with her eye, found a spot and pointed the camera in its direction. She walked to the spot, stood on it and beckoned to Howe. With each new leather case, with each new instrument, and with each new adjustment she had grown in ease and now she said, "Joe, will you stand here?"

Obediently Howe stood where he was bidden. She had yet another instrument. She took out a tape-measure on a mechanical spool. Kneeling down before Howe, she put the little metal ring of the tape under the tip of his shoe. At her request, Howe pressed it with his toe. When she had measured her distance, she nodded to Howe who released the tape. At a touch, it sprang back into the spool. "You have to be careful if you're going to get what you want," Hilda said. "I don't believe in all this snap-snap-snapping," she remarked loftily. Howe nodded in agreement, although he was beginning to think Hilda's care excessive.

Now at last the moment had come. Hilda squinted into the camera, moved the tripod slightly. She stood to the side, holding the plunger of the shutter-cable. "Ready," she said. "Will you relax, Joseph, please?" Howe realized that he was standing frozen, Hilda stood poised and precise as a setter, one hand holding the little cable, the other extended with curled dainty fingers like a dancer's, as if expressing to her subject the precarious delicacy of the moment. She pressed the plunger and there was a click. At once she stirred to action, got behind the camera, turned a new exposure. "Thank you," she said. "Would you stand under that tree and let me do a character study with light and shade?"

The childish absurdity of the remark restored Howe's ease. He went to the little tree. The pattern the leaves made on his gown was what Hilda was after. He had just taken a satisfactory position when he heard in the unmistakable voice, "Ah, Doctor! Having your picture taken?"

Howe gave up the pose and turned to Blackburn, who stood on the walk, his hands behind his back, a little too large for his bachelor's gown. Annoyed that Blackburn should see him posing for a character study in light and shade, Howe said irritably, "Yes, having my picture taken."

Blackburn beamed at Hilda. "And the little photographer?" he said. Hilda fixed her eyes on the ground and stood closer to her brilliant and aggressive camera. Blackburn, teetering on his heels, his hands behind his back, wholly prelatical and benignly patient, was not abashed at the silence. At last Howe said, "If you'll excuse us, Mr. Blackburn, we'll go on with the picture."

"Go right ahead, sir. I'm running along." But he only came closer. "Doctor Howe," he said fervently, "I want to tell you how glad I am that I was able to satisfy your standards at last."

Howe was surprised at the hard, insulting brightness of his own voice, and even Hilda looked up curiously as he said, "Nothing you have ever done has satisfied me, and nothing you could ever do would satisfy me, Blackburn."

With a glance at Hilda, Blackburn made a gesture as if to hush Howe—as though all his former bold malice had taken for granted a kind of understanding between himself and his teacher, a secret which must not be betrayed to a third person. "I only meant, sir," he said, "that I was able to pass your course after all."

Howe said, "You didn't pass my course. I passed you out of my course. I passed you without reading your paper. I wanted to be sure the college would be rid of you. And when all the grades were in and I did read your paper, I saw I was right not to have read it first."

Blackburn presented a stricken face. "It was very bad, sir?"

But Howe had turned away. The paper had been fantastic. The paper had been, if he wished to see it so, mad. It was at this moment that the Dean came up behind Howe and caught his arm. "Hello, Joseph," he said. "We'd better be getting along, it's almost late."

He was not a familiar man, but when he saw Blackburn, who approached to greet him, he took Blackburn's arm, too. "Hello, Theodore," he said. Leaning forward on Howe's arm and on Blackburn's, he said, "Hello, Hilda dear." Hilda replied quietly, "Hello, Uncle George."

Still clinging to their arms, still linking Howe and Blackburn, the Dean said, "Another year gone, Joe, and we've turned out another crop. After you've been here a few years, you'll find it reasonably upsetting—you wonder how there can be so many graduating classes while you stay the same. But of course you don't stay the same." Then he said, "Well," sharply, to dismiss the thought. He pulled Blackburn's arm and swung him around to Howe. "Have you heard about Teddy Blackburn?" he asked. "He has a job already, before graduation—the first man of his class to be placed." Expectant of congratulations, Blackburn beamed at Howe. Howe remained silent.

"Isn't that good?" the Dean said. Still Howe did not answer and the Dean, puzzled and put out, turned to Hilda. "That's a very fine-looking camera, Hilda." She touched it with affectionate pride.

"Instruments of precision," said a voice. "Instruments of precision." Of the three with joined arms, Howe was the nearest to Tertan, whose gaze took in all the scene except the smile and the nod which Howe gave him. The boy leaned on his cane. The broad-brimmed hat, canting jauntily over his eye, confused the image of his face that Howe had established, suppressed the rigid lines of the ascetic and brought out the baroque curves. It made an effect of perverse majesty.

"Instruments of precision," said Tertan for the last time, addressing no one, making a casual comment to the universe. And it occurred to Howe that Tertan might not be referring to Hilda's equipment. The sense of the thrice-woven circle of the boy's loneliness smote him fiercely. Tertan stood in majestic jauntiness, superior to all the scene, but his isolation made Howe ache with a pity of which Tertan was more the cause than the object, so general and indiscriminate was it.

Whether in his sorrow he made some unintended movement toward Tertan which the Dean checked, or whether the suddenly tightened grip on his arm was the Dean's own sorrow and fear, he did not know. Tertan watched them in the incurious way people watch a photograph being taken, and suddenly the thought that, to the boy, it must seem that the three were posing for a picture together made Howe detach himself almost rudely from the Dean's grasp.

"I promised Hilda another picture," he announced—needlessly, for Tertan was no longer there, he had vanished in the last sudden flux of visitors who, now that the band had struck up, were rushing nervously to find seats.

"You'd better hurry," the Dean said. "I'll go along, it's getting late for me." He departed and Blackburn walked sedately by his side.

Howe again took his position under the little tree which cast its shadow over his face and gown. "Just hurry, Hilda, won't you?" he said. Hilda held the cable at arm's length, her other arm crooked and her fingers crisped. She rose on her toes and said, "Ready," and pressed the release. "Thank you," she said gravely and began to dismantle her camera as he hurried to join the procession.

LIONEL TRILLING, who is presently Professor of English at Columbia University, was born in New York City in 1905. He has taught at the University of Wisconsin and Hunter College, and joined the Columbia faculty in 1931.

His first published work, *Matthew Arnold* (1943), was a critical biography that reflected a long interest in Arnold and provided many new insights into his life and work. It was followed by *E. M. Forster* (1943), several other distinguished critical works, and a novel, *The Middle of the Journey* (1947). His essays have appeared in *The Nation, The New Republic, The New York Times Book Review, Kenyon Review,* and *Partisan Review.*

Partisan Review first published two notable short stories by Lionel Trilling: "The Other Margaret" and the story included here. Considered one of the finest stories ever written about college life, "Of This Time, Of That Place" was included in Martha Foley's *Best American Short Stories of 1944.*